FRAMES PER
SECOND

ALSO BY BILL EIDSON FROM TOM DOHERTY ASSOCIATES

The Guardian
Adrenaline

FRAMES PER
SECOND

BILL EIDSON

A TOM DOHERTY ASSOCIATES BOOK

NEW YORK

FRAMES PER SECOND

Copyright © 1999 by Bill Eidson

Edited by David G. Hartwell

This book is printed on acid-free paper.

A Forge Book
Published by Tom Doherty Associates, LLC
175 Fifth Avenue
New York, NY 10010

Forge® is a registered trademark of Tom Doherty Associates, LLC.

ISBN: 0-312-86809-X

First Edition: October 1999

Printed in the United States of America

0   9   8   7   6   5   4   3   2   1

FOR MY FATHER, WILLIAM B. EIDSON

ACKNOWLEDGMENTS

I would like to thank Frank Robinson, Richard Parks, David Hartwell, Jim Minz, Chris Dao, Catherine Sinkys, Rick Berry, Kate Mattes, Nancy Childs, Sibylle Barrasso, and John Cole for their help with my career and this story. And a special thanks to Donna for everything.

FRAMES PER
SECOND

PROLOGUE

"COMPANY, THAD," LOUISE SAID. SHE STOOD LOOKING OUT THE barn door for a moment, and then came over to him with a cup of coffee.

"Somebody in a hurry," she said.

Thad Greene looked over his wife's shoulder. Over a mile away, he could see the plume of dust rising from the road. A car, coming along pretty fast. Greene felt a touch of irritation. He liked these mornings alone with his family; he had since he was a boy on the very same farm. Get everybody up, feed the animals.

"Early." Greene set the wheelbarrow down, and shoveled a scoop of grain into SnackPack's bucket. His daughter, Katy, was grooming the horse. "Probably just another lost tourist." It happened all the time—the main drag was a dirt road, and plenty of times people ignored the private property sign and simply took a wrong turn at the bend onto his road. Some apologized, some got out with their cameras and asked him to stand in front of his old red barn like a real farmer.

Katy said, "SnackPack says thanks, Dad."

"And she's welcome." Greene took the coffee from Louise, and put his arm around her shoulders. As always, she felt good under his arm. Together, they watched Katy groom her horse.

The chestnut mare stretched her neck out, inhaled deeply from the bucket, and then stepped forward to take in the first mouthful.

Greene said, "Must be a boyfriend for Katy here. Come to take her to school, I bet."

Katy rolled her eyes. "Right, Dad."

He grinned. Nine years old, she had had his number since birth. Behind him, his son, Thad Jr., tossed out a section of hay into the stall. He was twelve, but as big as a fifteen-year-old.

Thad Jr. leaned on the pitchfork. "Dad, he's *flying*."

Greene let go of Louise and went to look out the window himself. She followed him over.

"Thad . . ." she said.

But he had already felt the first jab of alarm himself.

"Cops," Thad Jr. said. "There's cops behind them."

The car in the lead, a Ford, must've been up near sixty or seventy on the dirt road leading to his house, his barn.

His family.

Behind the Ford was a Virginia State Police car with the lights swirling.

"Get in the back," Greene said. He waved at Katy. "All of you get behind the tractor."

He felt tired all of the sudden. Married late, ten years after he got out of the army. Damn near fifty now.

"I'll go with you," Thad Jr. said eagerly.

"You'll do what I tell you," Greene snapped. He hurried over to the open barn door, looked back at Louise who was frozen for just a second. Standing there in her quilted coat and jeans, coffee in hand.

He said, "Right now, honey."

She suddenly began to move. "You heard your father," she said to Katy. "Out of that stall."

Louise grasped Thad Jr. by the upper arm.

Greene saw the crowbar sitting there beside the doorjamb. It had been there for God knows how long, just sitting and rusting, waiting to be put away. He grabbed it, feeling as much foolish as anything, walking out there. Feeling that this could be nothing, this could be a speeder who got a little rambunctious, took the wrong turn, and went down a farmer's road.

But the siren on the Virginia State Police car was now wailing, and the car in front was floating up and down on the road, the engine roaring.

"Dad!" Katy said.

Greene turned. The three of them were standing there, scared. "Get them in the back, goddamn it," he said to Louise. He tried for frustration, but to his own ears, he sounded scared.

Louise did what he said. She hustled them away.

Greene turned back to the car. Wishing he could lock the barn behind him, but it'd take him fifteen minutes to find the padlock for the hasp on the sliding door.

"Get out of here," he yelled, as the Ford slewed into his barnyard. He kept the crowbar behind his leg. "Get the hell out of here!"

The cop car came right after it.

And the cops banged into the other car.

Greene's breath was rushing now. "Oh shit," he said, "Oh shit, and goddamn it."

Because it looked like the cops had rammed the car on purpose. Trying to shake up the two men inside.

But it was too late. The two men fell out of the open doors and scrambled to their feet. One of them bald. With a gun. Not just bald, a skinhead. With the leather.

The other was tall and handsome. Salt gray hair. Somehow familiar. "Get off my farm!" Greene yelled.

The skinhead fired his gun. Automatic weapon. Just a little thing, a big pistol. But the windshield of the cop car blew in, and then the two cops were out of their car and shooting from around the doors.

Then the man with the gray hair looked at Greene and then yelled to the skinhead. "The barn, Billy. Go for the barn!"

Greene began backing up. Looking to the cops.

Get them, he was thinking. *Put them down.*

And indeed the cops were shooting.

But Greene had done a tour in Vietnam. He knew how many shots it could take. Everyone running. Everyone scared. Harder to hit people than it looked in the movies.

The skinhead was out front, the familiar man was in back.

Greene backed up to the barn door. He kept the crowbar close, angled his left side toward them so they couldn't see it.

The skinhead saw him, just a glance, raised his gun, and there was flame. The barn door beside Greene splintered, and behind him, Greene could hear Louise scream out. He glanced back to see Thad Jr. rushing out to help him, and Louise took him by the arm again and pulled him back.

Greene shoved away from the wall and swung the crowbar.

It connected neatly, right on the guy's hand. The skinhead's. Must've broken the goddamn thing, the way he screamed, the way he dropped the gun and held his wrist.

The cops were shooting again.

And suddenly the skinhead staggered, and blood poured from his mouth.

Greene raised the bar and went for the familiar man. The guy who looked like he was supposed to be somebody.

But that guy lifted his revolver and shot Greene point-blank.

It was like the time Greene had been kicked by a horse. Big black stallion called Breaker that his dad kept for no more than a year. Broke Thad Greene's ribs badly, laid him up for almost six months.

Now Greene slid down the wall, suddenly weak and tired.

The cops were firing again, but the man wasn't hit. He slid open the barn door all the way, and Greene could hear the man grabbing Louise and maybe slapping Thad Jr. down.

"Stop," Greene said. He gasped, and coughed blood on himself. Praying even as he did that he wouldn't hear a gunshot inside the barn.

God, he felt so weak.

"I'll do it," the man screamed behind him. "So help me God, I'll do what I've got to do!"

Greene put his hands up to the cops. "Don't," he cried. His voice was barely a whisper, and his hands just fell to his lap. "Don't push him," he said. But his voice was barely audible even to himself.

The cops stopped anyway. Two tall, young cops. No older than thirty, either of them. They stood there, guns poised, uncertain. And then they backed away to the police car.

Greene looked up. He saw the man holding a gun to Louise's neck. That familiar man.

"Back off!" The man screamed. "Back off, and get me the media. Get me reporters, get me TV. I want cameras on this! You try to hurt me, these people die. Give me access to the people of America, or this family dies! You got that? I'll do what's got to be done!''

Greene coughed, and then there was more blood on his chin. Hell, on his shirt and lap, too. Just covered. And though he desperately tried to pay attention, tried to think of how he could get his family away from this terrible, familiar man, his ability to think seemed to be pouring out of him into the barnyard dirt.

The dirt of the farm where he was born, and, apparently, dying.

CHAPTER 1

AGENT PARKER'S RADIO CRACKLED. HE TURNED AWAY AND SPOKE into it and then came back to Ben. "OK, the two from NBC have agreed."

Ben said, "I'd be the only photographer?"

"That's right," Parker said. "You and two television guys from NBC that Johansen remembers from some interview before. He demanded a list of the media people covering him out here, and he picked you. He's got the politician's knack for remembering faces and names so we can't put one of my men in."

Ben looked over at the barn. Five days had passed since Jarrod Johansen had shot Thad Greene. Last night, the word had spread among the sandbags that Greene had been briefly conscious and was now expected to survive.

Now, the morning mist was just beginning to burn off the fields behind the barn, but the light inside would still be poor. Ben double-checked his camera to make sure he was shooting with his fastest film.

Parker said. "I take it that means I have you, too?"

"Wouldn't miss it." Ben knew that even if he didn't have a camera, he would have helped get those children out. Just as he hoped someone else would do the same for his ex-wife and kids.

But Ben also knew he simply wanted the shot.

"You talk to me first when you get out, OK?" Lucien said. He was the *Insider* reporter assigned to cover the story along with Ben. His black eyes were shining, his aftershave was coming on strong. "It's not like I have to actually *be* there. You know that Kurt is going to want us to tell our story first, not let everyone else have it. So even if Johansen starts shooting, kills somebody, don't talk in front of the TV cameras or anybody else. All right?"

"Jesus," Parker said. He was an enormous black man with skin so dark it was almost blue in some light. The black Kevlar bulletproof vest seemed to draw in even more light and somehow had the effect of making him appear larger.

Parker made Ben feel small, and Ben was six-two, two hundred pounds, himself.

Lucien pointed to the tripod-mounted camera with the six-hundred-millimeter lens and said, "I'll even cover you. Kurt'll like that."

"Who's Kurt?" Parker asked.

"Our editor," Lucien said.

Parker looked at Ben and the faintest of smiles crossed the agent's face. He swept his hand toward the barn door. "Then, by all means—cover him."

They wired Ben and strapped a bulletproof vest onto him. Parker waited with him just inside the command post, ready to begin the walk across.

Ben turned to watch the hostage negotiator, a guy by the name of Burnett, finish outfitting the two from NBC.

"How long?" Parker asked Burnett.

"Three minutes, we'll be all set."

Parker grunted. He looked over at Ben. "Tell me about this photo shoot you did of Johansen before."

Ben shrugged. "It was nothing special." Ben had photographed Johansen a year ago, back when he was making a surprisingly strong senate run from his home state of Alabama.

The day of the interview, Johansen had refused to allow any shots until he was ready—and that meant wearing jeans and an open-necked plaid shirt, one foot up on a bale of hay, the flag waving gently in the background. Strictly cornball.

"I hear you got yourself some prize for pictures of those prison kids in Rwanda," Johansen had said as Ben had settled in to take the shot. "I'm a great believer in the power of the press. So you help get me in the senate with this shot, and I'll send them nigras some food, tell them to stay home instead of coming here. Fair deal?"

"You meet Saunders?" Parker said.

"He looked familiar when I saw his picture later. He was there, but I guess he was keeping himself away from the camera."

"I'm sure he was," Parker said, dryly. "Something that under-cover agents learn early."

When Johansen had somehow discovered that Saunders was an FBI agent, he shot him himself. He did this even after the agent told him that he was wired, that surveillance cameras were tracking them right then. "I'm the America that you have forgotten," Johansen said.

That video appeared on the news every night for almost a week, making Johansen a hero to what a *New York Times* editorial called ". . . a depressingly large minority."

Parker sighed. "You see his 7-Eleven video?"

"Who could miss it?"

Johansen's name had faded from the media until three weeks ago, when he escaped from prison. A few days after his escape, he bolstered his hero status by politely introducing himself to a 7-Eleven convenience store clerk and making a statement into a handheld tape recorder saying that he was on the way to Washington, D.C., to "kill that draft dodger." The audio was mated to the security camera video and once again he made the nightly news.

"His little media campaign almost took a hit right here," Parker said, moving his chin toward the barnyard. "White farmer. Vietnam vet."

Ben looked over his shoulder at the top of the hill where picketers were holding up signs. From the distance, he could just make out some of the larger ones: "Not another WACO," "Free America— Free J. J." One with the old standby, "God Bless Jarrod Johansen."

Parker snorted quietly. "People."

"Think we'd be seeing those signs if Greene died?" Ben said.

"Count on it," Parker said. "You watch the news—lots of people went for Johansen's spin."

Ben nodded. Since the first news truck had arrived, Johansen had maintained that the cops had shot Greene, not him. All evidence to the contrary, it seemed many people still believed him.

"Just another government conspiracy," Ben had seen a woman in Alabama say. "Just like the Kennedy boys, only this time it's one of our own."

Parker looked at Ben. "The man knows his audience. And that you folks in the media are the way to them."

Ben rolled his shoulders, and exhaled, looking at that open barn door, the darkness inside. "Yeah, well here we are."

"They're all set," said Burnett. "Wired and vests."

Parker and Ben turned. Ben knew the reporter on sight as most people would. Chuck Heynes was rumored to be next in line for a national anchor slot at NBC if he could keep his visibility up. The videographer, Ben had never met before.

"Gentlemen," Parker's voice was a deep rumble. "Understand that we've only agreed to let you folks from the media in to appease this fool long enough to walk him out of the barn. You operate under our orders. You do *not* ask him questions that will incite him, do you understand me?"

"I know I speak for all of us, when I say we'll cooperate," Heynes said.

Ben turned back to look at the open door, scratching distractedly at his beard. He felt scruffy. Suddenly aware that in that small barn, he would be part of the news, too. On the other side of the lens. That had only happened once before in his career, and it had been a distinctly unpleasant experience. Ben had let his beard grow in long the past few years, and he wondered what he looked like underneath it now. He looked down at himself. His jeans were dirty from the past few days of lying on the ground peering through the camera at that barn door. His shirt was damp with sweat. He yawned, feeling that curious combination of sleepiness and excitement that he'd felt whenever he was waiting for something to start. Like high school football, back in Portland, Maine. Later, it was waiting with his camera in

hand, ready to jump out of an armored car with the marines in Sarajevo, or capturing images of young Zapatista rebels in Mexico.

Ben knew he usually did fine once things got started. But at the
moment, he couldn't help but wish he was back at the motel, taking
a shower, the exposed rolls of film tucked in his bag.

The two television guys were talking between themselves. The
same nervousness was apparent in their voices, but Heynes was trying
to hide it under bluster. "Just be damn sure that thing is on the whole
goddamn time," he was saying to the cameraman.

"Got it, got it, got it," said the cameraman.

Ben glanced back, smiling. Heynes was a big, good-looking guy
with just the right amount of gray at the temples. But he didn't have
a reputation for brains.

Heynes saw Ben's smile and he snapped, "Don't get in our way,
clear? We're capturing this live."

Ben laughed, shortly, and didn't answer the man. Instead, he
looked over at Parker. He thought of the *Newsweek* issue that had
just been distributed behind the sandbags that morning. Under the
headline, "Collision Course," the cover had depicted high school
photos of Johansen with a winning smile, Parker solemn and serious.

"Nervous?" Parker said.

"Hell, yes."

Both of them started slightly when the telephone on Burnett's belt
sounded. He flipped it open. "All right, Mr. Johansen. Give us a
second to secure everybody here."

He nodded to Parker, who spoke rapidly into his radio to the
SWAT team. "The girl's coming out. Everybody be *god*damn sure
you hold fire."

Katy was shoved into the doorway. Around Ben, he could feel
everyone relax slightly. This was the first they'd seen of her in the
whole stand, and although she seemed terrified, she looked all right
otherwise.

"I've got one her age at home," Parker said. He clapped Ben
lightly on the arm. "Swap with her."

Ben started across the grass. He lifted his camera slowly to his
eye and captured a shot of her standing in the doorway. Her lower
lip was trembling. "Hey," he said, as he got closer. "Hey, Katy."

Johansen spoke around the door. "Keep on coming. Once you're in, she goes."

Ben stepped into the gloom of the barn. In an instant, he took it all in: Johansen standing by the concrete wall, the gun on him; the mother and boy, bound and tied to a farm tractor. A shaft of light revealed the mother's face, looking imploringly between Johansen and her daughter. "Please now, can she go?"

"I don't want to," the girl said. "I want to stay with you, Mommy."

"Move it," Johansen snapped.

Ben did a mild double take when he looked at Johansen again. Somehow, the man had shaved and cleaned himself up. Ready for the cameras. "Can I?" Ben said, gesturing to the girl.

Johansen nodded abruptly.

Ben knelt down next to her. "Hey, I've got a girl your age." He pointed to Parker. "So does he." Ben looked back at the phalanx of men with guns and he understood her hesitation. He flapped his hand down to Parker and the agent got his point immediately and knelt down to child level. "Run to him, honey. He knows you're scared."

The girl looked at Ben closely, and then abruptly ran to Parker.

Without thinking, Ben raised the camera and captured two shots of the little girl with dirty blue coveralls and pigtails, running for the kneeling FBI agent.

"Never miss a shot, do you, Ben?" Johansen said. "Now come here, and take off that vest."

Ben hesitated, but Johansen simply raised his gun to Ben's right eye. "You'll miss *that,* in your business."

Ben took off the vest and Johansen had him kneel with his hands on his head while he put the vest onto himself. "Open your shirt and your pants and show me where the wires are—and then pull them."

After a moment's hesitation, Ben did.

"All right. You go against that wall and you can keep shooting. Just save a shot or two for me."

And that's what Ben did. He took shots of the twelve-year-old boy, looking back at his mother as Heynes and the cameraman walked toward him. After that, of Parker and Burnett filling the barn doorway, silhouetted by bright light. Johansen had all of them pull their wires. "You'll forgive me, I'm sure," he drawled. "I had a bad experience with these once."

Johansen's diatribe took a surprisingly short time to complete. "I make no apologies for my actions," he began, looking into the videocamera. "Although I was saddened that Thad Greene was pressed so violently into service in the war against the disintegration of America, I am delighted to hear the news that he'll recover . . ."

And so on.

A self-serving monologue that placed all of Johansen's acts of terrorism into "the larger context." This, with a gun jammed against Mrs. Greene's neck. Most of it had a singsong, practiced sound. Johansen kept his eyes on the videocamera, except when he would discuss the "institutions of entropy" that had "softened and weakened this great country in the name of equality."

Then he would look at Parker.

When he did that, Johansen's mouth turned ugly and his voice shook just slightly. Ben almost raised his camera to capture it, and then decided against it.

Johansen might read it as encouragement.

Finally, he was done.

Johansen bowed his head, and then waved the two television guys back.

"I've got some questions," Heynes said.

"No," Johansen said. "Just shut up and keep your camera rolling."

Parker and Burnett stared at the newscaster, and he backed off, but didn't look too happy about it.

Abruptly, Johansen shoved the woman away. "Thank you, Mrs. Greene. You may leave now. I'm sorry for the trouble." He waved the gun at Burnett. "Walk her out, see that your guys don't kill her."

She seemed stunned, and then her face flushed crimson. She looked as if she were going to say something, but then looked to the gun and the other men, and simply turned away.

"What's going on here?" Burnett asked.

"Do it," Parker growled.

Burnett hesitated.

"Move!" Parker said.

Burnett took the woman away.

"Now how about these guys?" Parker said. "It's time for them to walk."

Johansen shook his head. "The fourth estate stays. If I've learned anything, it's that leadership is all a matter of making the right symbols. Well, I'm going to make one right now."

Faster than Ben could have imagined, Johansen lashed out with the gun butt and cracked Parker on the head. The agent staggered, and Johansen did it again. Blood gushed from a scalp wound. "Get on your knees, nigger."

Ben started forward and Johansen swung the gun to him. "Time for your picture, you whore. Get over here!"

Ben's hands were shaking, but in a glance, he double-checked everything. He had already put the flash on a coil cord so he could hold it off the camera. The power light on the flash was glowing red. He zoomed the lens back to its widest setting.

"You about ready there, Ben?" Johansen smiled slightly as he placed the gun inches from Parker's head.

"Just about." Ben stepped closer.

"You got my flag waving in the background? I looked through a crack in the barn, so I know it's still flying out there."

"I've got it all." Ben's voice was shaking, too.

"Maybe you'll win some more awards here. The niggers have been good for you, haven't they?"

"You're fucking cold, Harris," the cameraman said, letting his videocamera down.

"Keep rolling," Heynes snapped.

The cameraman shrugged and lifted it up, the red light gleaming above the lens.

"Don't do this, Mr. Johansen," Heynes said, his voice conveying just the right sense of urgency and dismay. "I'm asking you—the *world* is asking you—not to do this."

The audio was, of course, rolling too.

Johansen struck a pose and, indeed, a part of Ben knew it was a hell of a shot: the powerful black man staring up at Johansen. Parker was bloodied and confused, but still defiant. Out of focus, the running SWAT team, clearly too late. Johansen held the big gun rigidly in his right arm, his entire body conveying self-righteous judgment.

"Look at me," Ben said, with the assurance of years.

Damned if Johansen didn't comply, the gun moving just slightly as he did so.

Ben reached over with the flash and jammed it mere inches away from Johansen's eyes.

And took the picture.

CHAPTER 2

"So it was Parker who got the gun away from Johansen?" Peter Gallagher said.

"That's right."

"And it was Parker who clubbed him to the ground?"

"Well, I smacked him on the head a few times with the camera, but Parker did the heavy work. Then I backed off and covered the SWAT team as they came storming into the barn."

Peter laughed and took a sip of his beer. They were sitting in a small bar on Boston's waterfront overlooking the harbor. From long habit as a reporter, Peter kept his voice low. "So all this hero shit I've been hearing is just Ben Harris giving yet another subject a bad case of red eye."

Ben nodded. "About sums it up. That distance from the flash, he'll probably have some permanent vision loss."

"Well, there's that."

"The picture was cool, though. Parker is this huge black force erupting from the floor; what you can see of Johansen's whited-out face has this funny little expression like he's just getting how much trouble he's in."

"I saw it. You might have a career in this business." Peter touched

Ben's mug with his own. "Congratulations. And when I write the article I'll make you a hero too."

"Get in line." Ben told him that after NBC released the footage, his answering machine at his studio in Fort Point Channel held over twenty offers for interviews. Kurt Tattinger, the new editor-in-chief, had fielded dozens more at the magazine. A literary agent who had unsuccessfully shopped around a book proposal of Ben's work about two years back had called to say, "Better strike while you're hot. Time/Life just returned my call, and they want to take a fresh look at you."

Peter lifted his eyebrows. "Enjoy your fifteen minutes. May work out to a half hour or more, given the TV coverage."

"Better than last time."

Peter nodded. "That thing with the priest? That was before I knew you, but I read the articles at the time. Thought you were a sleazeball paparazzi. Same kind that chased Princess Diana into that tunnel."

"You and several million people. This time, if I can land that book and guarantee some autonomy from Kurt it'll all be worthwhile."

"The book, maybe. Kurt, he's a fact of your life that's not going to go away as long as you work for *Insider*. Get used to it."

Peter Gallagher had joined *Insider* shortly after Ben, about three years ago. They had hit it off immediately. Gallagher was about twenty years out of Columbia's journalism school, and had traveled the world looking for stories ever since. He was tall, lanky, and prematurely gray. A recurring case of malaria he had contracted while covering a story in Papua New Guinea had cut into his health, contributed to his divorce, and forced him into the marginally more sedate pace of a weekly magazine rather than the adrenaline-pumping pace of his *Chicago Tribune* days.

At forty, he looked about fifty.

But none of that dampened the intelligence or curiosity in his steady gray eyes. Along with the publication's emphasis on photojournalism—one of the few remaining publications as dedicated—Gallagher's political and criminal investigative reports were the backbone of *Insider*'s growing reputation.

"So what have you got on?" Ben asked.

"Me? Nothing that would interest a man of your caliber."

"C'mon."

"Hell, I can't take you places. Robert DeNiro comes to town to promote his new movie, and I take you up to the Ritz to cover the interview, next thing he'll be asking you about your motivation, your love life, and all about those shutter speeds and f-stops. And you know I hate to hear about that shit."

"Like Kurt would send you in to interview someone who could cause him trouble."

Peter shook his head, marveling. "He's got a reputation for standing up for his people. That was his reputation at *Boston Magazine*."

"Uh-huh," Ben said, not wanting to pursue it. Because he knew Peter was right. Kurt was a solid guy, took his hits, seemed to be fair. Ben just didn't like him, and he had the best of reasons. "Tell me what you're working on now."

"Let's see, we've got a politician who can't keep his pants on, challenged me to prove different."

Ben made a face. "Leave it for the tabloids."

"The line gets blurry sometimes."

"Uh-huh." Ben sipped his beer.

Peter, ever observant, got the point and moved on. "Another round of women who killed their husbands looking to get out of prison early. Most of them deserve to. Maybe you can come out and improve upon their mug shots for me."

"I can do that. What else is local? I'd like to stay around long enough to see my kids before they start calling me 'Uncle Ben.' "

"When do you see them next?"

"Tomorrow. Weekend visitation."

"That sucks. Beats once a month, though."

"When are you down to New York?"

"Week after next." Peter told Ben about his last trip to see his daughter, and the afternoon they had spent at the Museum of Natural History. "That's all she wants to do. Third time in a row. Whole city of New York I'd give her if I could, and she just wants to go back and see those stuffed animals."

"She's four," Ben said, smiling. Thinking of his daughter, Lainnie, at that age. It struck him how he and Peter still talked freely about their children—Peter's one and Ben's two—but how they rarely talked about their ex-wives anymore.

Maybe a late-breaking sign of maturity, he thought.

He and Peter had a fair amount in common in regards to ex-wives. Both women were working journalists. Andi and Ben met when they were both in their early twenties back at the *Portland Press Herald* in Maine; Peter and his ex-wife, Sarah, had been a nationally recognized investigative team before their divorce. Her byline continued to turn up on major stories in the *New York Times*.

Ben was glad he and Peter had left off talking about Andi and Sarah. He never slept well afterwards. And Peter needed to be careful when it came to drinking. He swore that he never had more than their two beers here at the bar, and Ben never saw any evidence to the contrary.

"Hey, back to business," Peter said. "I've got a hood who's a real comer. Out of Southie, but he's more than a tough Irish kid. Been all the way to Stanford and back. Runs a commercial real estate consulting business supposedly, but the word is that he's not afraid to get his own hands dirty."

"Sounds promising."

"Oh, yeah, but he's a work in progress. You got some spare time, we could build a file on him."

"I'll have my agent call yours."

"Yeah, you do that." Peter lifted his glass. "Meanwhile, see if your wife's new boyfriend will cut you a break tomorrow. Tell him heroes sell magazines."

After Peter headed off in a taxi, Ben decided to walk to his studio. The city lights alone would clear his head and evoke a certain amount of magic. He stopped to look back when he was halfway across the bridge. When Boston was placed as a lighted backdrop to shifting water, and vaguely threatening black pilings, the effect was visually fascinating—both ominous and beautiful.

He counted the interesting view as one of the few—maybe the only—benefits of his new life. Because going home alone to the empty loft was just as dreary as it was cracked up to be.

As he slid the key into the lock, he placed his hand on the door, feeling the dead silence behind it. No sounds of Lainnie and Jake playing or arguing. No sound of a television or radio. No Andi telling the kids to calm down, that their father was home.

He swung the door open.

Everywhere he looked, he saw himself. On the white painted brick walls hung with his own work and that of other photojournalists and fine art photographers he admired: Robert Capa, Eugene Smith, Eddie Adams, Koresh, Steiglitz. Powerful images all, Capa's black and whites of children in wartime Paris, Ben's own shots taken throughout the U.S. and all over the world: Mexico, Bosnia, Rwanda, Liberia, Columbia. Mostly of people. People in war, people in trouble, people experiencing joy, people at work, caught mid-step in their daily lives.

Ben's answering machine was blinking, and when he played the messages back, he had three more offers for interviews and another call from his agent saying Time/Life had called again on the book idea and were moving "from a nibble to stretching their jaws for a fairly good bite."

Ben played all of the messages back from the beginning, ostensibly because he wanted to write them down, but truthfully, because he was hoping he had somehow missed a call from Andi.

He hadn't.

He consciously ignored his feelings about that and smiled again at the message from his agent. Ben moved to his light table and thumbed it on, feeling a bit like a midnight alchemist as the fluorescent light flickered. He began pulling out transparencies, fingers moving quickly through his files. He laid a sheaf of them across the table and colors and shapes began to spring to life in front of him, each a visual story that played before him when he bent to look through the loupe. He did the same with the black and whites, pulling out file after file of contact sheets. Soon, if the book possibility became a reality, he would need to organize his thoughts and images into a consistent theme. And truly, there were genuine patterns in his work, and nothing would delight him more than to pull it all together. But for the time being, he simply looked at his past.

And because it was all intertwined, and because it was late at night and he was lonely, he pulled out the file of family pictures. These were the better shots culled from more than a thousand rolls he had taken over the years: his and Andi's first apartment in New York, their dog, Burglar, long since gone. Jake's birth. Andi looking not much older than a teenager in the hospital gown. Exhausted. Wonderfully happy. At home, he and Andi holding their fat little baby in front of the old mirror with the cracked frame. It came back to him standing there over the light table, the exhilaration of those days: equal parts of fear and euphoria. *The baby is healthy, my wife is safe. How the hell am I going to feed them?*

And remembering that brought up the contrast, the difference between then and now.

I fed them, he thought. *I clothed them, I housed them, and I loved them. I still love them. And yet I'm alone.*

This book that his agent was calling about was something he and Andi had talked about for years. A project they could work on together: his images, her writing and editing.

Maybe now he would ask Peter if he was interested in writing it.

When Ben looked up at the clock, he was surprised to see it was almost two in the morning. "Oh, Christ." Ben didn't need much sleep, but he needed more than four hours. He filed the transparencies away and turned out the lights on the images surrounding him on the walls.

He was suddenly tired of his own thoughts and those who thought like him.

CHAPTER 3

ANDI MET KURT AT HER FRONT DOOR.

God, she was beautiful to him. Rich auburn hair, carelessly brushed. When she stepped out of the shadow of the doorway, the morning light brought out the gold in her green eyes, in her hair.

Like him, no longer a kid. Faint wrinkles at her eyes and mouth just added character. Her intelligence was there to read, right in those eyes. She smiled, which made him euphoric and more than a bit scared. There was no denying it, he was shaking inside.

What have you decided? he wanted to say.

Instead, he asked, ''Have you been watching the recap on the news this morning?'' His voice sounded perfectly calm. Sounded like him.

''As if I had a choice. Both of them hauled me in front of it every time they played that tape. Ben, the hero.''

He smiled. ''Come on, now. It was pretty impressive stuff.''

''I'm just glad you're here.'' She came down the steps and draped her arms around his neck. She kissed him so sweetly that he was convinced that they were all right.

''You thought about what I said?'' Kurt whispered.

''All night. And the answer is yes.''

He had to look away. He wanted to look at her so she could see his happiness, his outright exultation. But he felt so wide open he couldn't show it. Instead, he said lightly, "No worries?"

"I'm a little nervous," she said. "But I'm happy. So happy."

He held her tight, feeling in her heat against him the new life opening before him with her and the children. "I love you, Andi."

She pulled her head back so that she could look at him, her eyes welling with tears. "I love you too, Kurt. Let's go in and tell them the real news around here."

"Sure," he said, looking up at his new home. Ben's former home. An old colonial that Ben and Andi had carefully restored. Beautiful piece of property in Sudbury, up against conservation land.

Kurt wanted to take them away from it. As soon as possible. Andi, Lainnie, and Jake. He loved them all. More than he knew how to show them. He wanted to take them away and put them in a house he had built just for them. Start from scratch. He said, "Let's go in."

CHAPTER 4

Kurt let Ben in two hours later.

Even though Kurt had had plenty of time to figure out what to say beforehand, he was still at a momentary loss.

Apparently, so was Ben. Finally, he said, simply, "The kids ready?"

"Actually, we were hoping to talk to you a minute."

Andi joined him then. "Hey, Ben, home from the wars. Come on in." Her tone was sunny because that was her way when first greeting anyone. Kurt expected Ben knew she was furious with him.

Andi gave Ben a fierce hug before pulling back to give him a short, hard shot to the arm. "I'd like to have killed you."

"Jesus." Ben was half laughing, but hurting too. "You haven't lost a thing."

"You still have two children," she said.

"And where are they now?" Ben stepped around Kurt, his eyes eager for Lainnie and Jake.

"We asked them to stay upstairs while we talked," Andi said.

Ben glanced between Kurt and Andi. "About what?"

"Hey, Daddy."

It was Lainnie, standing at the head of the stairs.

"Ben, let's go into the library," Kurt said.

But Ben ignored him. He moved to the foot of the stairs. Lainnie's face was blotched, as if she had been crying. She said, "I saw you on TV."

"What's the matter, honey?"

Jake was behind her. Thirteen years old, everything was more complicated. He tugged at Lainnie. "Come on. Let them alone a minute."

"Hey, stranger," Ben said.

"Hi, Dad. You nailed that guy."

"Sort of."

Jake grinned and there was no equivocation there. "Not 'sort of.' I saw it on TV. So did every kid in my school."

"Well, that's got to be worth something."

"Kids, your dad will be right with you," Kurt said.

Ben glanced at him, but said to the children, easily enough, "I'll see you in a few minutes."

Jake nodded abruptly and began to pull Lainnie toward her room. "Come on. I'll play with you."

She was crying again.

Ben noticed the library had changed. Once he ran the business end of his freelance work out of this study, and Andi had done her writing. Now her desk was pushed over by the window and on his former desk there was a computer set-up complete with CD-ROM, scanner, and color printer.

"Somebody's finally gone digital around here?" Ben asked.

"It's mine," Kurt said. "It's an interest that Jake and I share."

Ben winced internally, but he kept it to himself. Strange stuff when your ex-wife is dating your boss.

Not for the first time, Ben thought, *So this is who she wants.*

Kurt was about the same age as Ben, somewhere in his early forties. But while Ben saw himself as all angles and bone, Kurt was fighting a gut and pale. Carefully combed brown hair, blue eyes. Not a bad-looking guy, Ben knew objectively. In spite of the slight pot-belly, Kurt looked as if he worked out, played handball, did something. He was just a little bland. Edges worn a bit too smooth by years of corporate life. A gloss of sophistication and respectability that probably showed better beside Andi at her various fund-raising functions and dinners than a weather-beaten photographer husband.

Ben abruptly forced himself to get rid of the dour look he could feel forming on his face, and say, "What's up?"

Kurt flashed him a quick smile to acknowledge the question had been asked, but he didn't answer. Something Ben had seen more than once at the office, but something he appreciated even less in his own former study.

Kurt poured coffee from a white carafe for all of them, and Andi laid out a plate of bagels and fruit. Ben sat back and watched. This was Kurt all the way. Andi was many wonderful things, but an organized hostess she was not. Kurt had a precision about him at the office that apparently extended into the weekend. Although he wore jeans and a simple cotton shirt, there was a crease in the jeans showing they had been ironed. His white leather running shoes didn't show a single grass stain.

"Will you be following up on the publicity possibilities for yourself on this thing?" Kurt asked politely. Andi settled in on the love seat beside him.

Ben's heart sank. He could feel what this was about and he found himself talking, not wanting to hear their words. "Not too much," he said. "I'm not that comfortable being on that side of the lens."

"You won't be in the public eye for long, take advantage of it." Kurt's voice was rich with assurance. The businessman telling the artist how to cash in on his talent and luck. "I know Peter will do a wonderful job with our coverage itself. And I'll assure you latitude as other opportunities come up."

"I appreciate that."

"Speaking of Peter, I know he wants to work with you on some of his projects coming up. Why don't the two of you get together and talk them through and come back to me with a plan."

Ben nodded. Kurt knew full well the way he and Peter worked and this was just his way of trying to regain some control. Ben told them about the book, as much to keep from discussing the real issue as anything else. "The offer is now firm. We're still negotiating money—it won't be huge, it never is for photo books. But I can take from my existing body of work and anything new I want to shoot. Develop my own themes."

Andi's hands flew to her mouth and Ben was gratified to see her pleasure was genuine. She said, "It's what we always wanted."

"You were going to write and edit it," he said. And then, because he suddenly realized it was so, he added, "You still can."

He saw her lower lip tremble ever so slightly and he knew what was coming. "Look," he said, gently. "Whatever's happening here, we still have those two upstairs to see through life. We might as well stay friends. We always had that."

She looked down, smoothing her skirt. When she looked up, she said, simply, "Kurt and I are getting married."

Hearing the words felt like getting punched in the stomach.

Ben paused. "I figured that."

He saw the light of victory in Kurt's eyes and the slightest smile touched his mouth before he forced it away.

Ben forced himself equally hard to keep his face calm. That, and to not stand up and kick the guy onto his ass.

Kurt said, "I expect this must be hard to hear."

"You expect right. When?"

"Tomorrow," Kurt said.

Ben looked between the two of them, not sure he'd heard right. "What?"

"Tomorrow," Kurt said. "The kids and us here at the house with the justice of the peace. We're anxious to begin our new life."

"When did you two decide this?"

"What difference does that makes?" Kurt asked.

"It didn't correspond to the news of me walking into that barn, did it?"

"Of all the ego . . ." Kurt said.

But Andi's face blanched.

"Jesus, Andi," Ben said.

She kept her voice low. "We need someone who'd think about us before taking a suicidal risk just to impress a piece of film. Kurt loves us in a way that doesn't leave room for disappearing for three months to capture a war on some other side of the globe."

There were a lot of things Ben could have said. Not the least of which was the "us" instead of "me." Or that her husband-to-be was the one who typically sent him off on those long shoots. Or that she was once a reporter herself so she should understand the goddamn obligations of the profession.

But these were old arguments.

Ben said, "Kurt, could you give us a minute alone?"

"I will not," he said.

Ben exhaled carefully, aware of the kids upstairs. "I would appreciate a moment of privacy to talk to my former wife. You think you can cut me that break?"

"Please, Kurt," Andi said, squeezing his arm.

His face flushed crimson suddenly and for a moment, Ben saw a side of him that he hadn't seen before. But then Kurt regained himself and said, "I'll be back in five minutes." He closed the door quietly on the way out.

"Sorry," she said, smiling quickly. "Kurt feels things more deeply than you might realize. And while I know this is bad for you, it's hard for him to accept the place you've already made in our lives."

"Kind of immature, wouldn't you think?" Ben snapped.

"I don't call being passionate about me—and therefore, a little jealous—as being immature. If it is, I can live with it."

"I was always passionate about you."

She smiled. "Of course you were. That's the way you do everything. But we were down the list."

"So you're telling me this idea of us getting back together is something I've been carrying around all by myself?"

She took his hands in hers and kissed the back of his wrist. "Neither of us tried to really make it happen, did we? I know that I've changed. I accept that. I accept that the things that worked for us in our twenties aren't working for us now. We've got two children who need a real father, and I need a real husband—not someone who's just blowing in for a few days between shoots."

"What would you say if I said I would change?"

"I'd say you're too late. I'd say I don't believe you."

"You love him?"

"I surely do."

Ben wanted to be big about it all.

But what he felt more than anything was angry. *How could you do this to us,* he thought. *This is me.*

What he said was, "This wasn't what I had in mind for us." His voice was hoarse.

"Who would?" She lifted her shoulders.

"Right." He nodded. Looked about the place, his old home, because he could no longer look at her directly. He wanted to get out of there. Upstairs, he could hear Lainnie and Jake moving around, the soft thud of their feet on the floorboards. Ben said, "We'll have to make it work between us until the kids are grown. Agreed?"

She put her hand out. "Agreed."

After they shook, she dabbed her eyes. "I'm going to call Kurt back in."

When he arrived, Ben surprised both of them by reaching over to cover their tightly clasped hands. "Congratulations, then. I wish you the best, wherever your lives take you."

Kurt looked surprised and Andi laughed suddenly, a sudden gust of relief. "We'll be here," she said.

Damn straight, Ben thought. Their child custody agreements precluded either of them from moving out of state without mutual consent.

"In the area, anyhow," Kurt said. "Sudbury is a good town and this is a nice enough house, but if some of my investments pay off the way I expect, we'll be building a new home."

"Good," Ben said, nodding. *Change every goddamn thing, why don't you.* "Good."

Andi said, "Maybe we'll even still work on that book together."

"Sure. The offer still stands."

"Well, let's talk about it." Kurt put his arm around Andi. The man of the house.

Ben paused. This was going to take more than a little getting used to. "I'd better get going."

They began to follow him and he waved them back. "Please. I'll let myself out."

He closed the library door behind himself and hesitated a moment in the hallway. He wiped his eyes with the back of his sleeve, and then walked to the stairwell and called up, "Let's go, Jake and Lainnie. We're going to have some fun now."

CHAPTER 5

JAKE FOUND HER ON THE SIDEWALK.

"I'm getting out of here," Lainnie said. "If you had any balls you'd come with me."

Jake grabbed the seatpost of her bike. He pulled her back, gently enough so that she didn't fall, hard enough to show her he meant it. "Got the balls to knock you onto the floor, mess up that pretty dress, Garbage Mouth."

"That'll work, too," she said. "They wouldn't do this stupid-ass wedding if I got a big grease spot all over me. Kurt couldn't stand it."

Jake liked that but he didn't have it in him to smile right then. "If I thought that'd work, I'd drop you in a tub of motor oil. But they'd do the wedding anyhow. You see the way Kurt looks at Mom?"

"Why isn't Daddy stopping this?"

Jake could see she was swallowing hard to keep from crying. He couldn't think of a thing to help her. He felt like crying himself, but, at thirteen, he was way too old.

Their dad had taken them out to Nahant the day before to go swimming at Forty Steps, where a lot of the scuba divers came in. Water so cold it made you scream when you first hit it. But lots of sun-heated rocks to climb on afterwards, great tidal pools to explore. When they were younger, their dad used to play hide and seek out there with them.

But Dad didn't act much like himself yesterday.

It was like he had turned gray. His dad tried to make it seem like everything was all right. He put his arms around them, told them he and Mom knew what was for the best and that they would all make it work. Told them that he thought Kurt was a good man.

And the funny thing was, Jake mostly agreed.

Kurt was a little stiff and tried too hard, but he was a nice guy. He listened to Jake when he talked and he seemed to really care about what he heard. He bought the computer as a bribe, Jake knew that. But Kurt would spend hours with Jake and the software manuals doing all sorts of things, from computer games to scanning in pictures and doing crazy things with PhotoShop.

Jake knew his dad loved him, but, until the divorce, he never spent the kind of time with them that he now did. Even now when he took them out, he sometimes wasn't really *with* them.

Jake knew that his dad was fun and creative and cool. His photographs took Jake's breath away. And the stuff on the television with that Johansen guy. . . . Jake always knew his dad was a hero but now all his friends knew it, too.

But when his dad picked up a camera, Jake could suddenly feel unimportant, not even there.

So Jake knew that Mom and Kurt might actually be right. Kurt talked a lot about moving to a new home and starting from the beginning. Jake could tell that Kurt wanted to be his father.

But Jake also knew that yesterday, his *real* dad had looked even more tired and beaten than when he had first moved out of the house.

"Everything's going to be fine," Jake said.

"No it's *not*." Lainnie burst into tears.

When Jake went to put his arms around her, he surprised himself as much as her by joining right in.

CHAPTER 6

PETER ARRIVED JUST AS BEN WAS FINISHING LOADING HIS JEEP. "What's this?"

"This is good-bye for a few days. Maybe a week."

Peter gestured toward Ben's face. "Barely recognized you."

Ben rubbed his bare chin. He'd shaved his beard off last night. "I'm in sort of a change mode these days. Besides, my face was getting a little too familiar with all this television coverage."

Peter looked in at the camping gear, the tent, the cooler. "You've got a shoot?"

Ben shook his head. "Going up to our place in Maine."

"Going to have to stop calling it 'ours.' It's yours alone, isn't it?"

Ben nodded. His father had left it to him. Not much more than a big rambling shack, but it was on a spectacular lake about two hours north of Portland. In his heart, it was home. Andi hadn't tried to gain any possession of it during the divorce and he had given her a lifelong promise to let her use it. Now he supposed that meant Kurt would be resting up in the Harris family cabin.

Suggesting improvements, no doubt.

Ben said, "Do you know about Kurt and Andi?"

"Yeah, he called me this morning. Romantic bastard, keeping up with his workload on his wedding day. The way I read it, he jumped so fast when Andi said yes that he forgot he's got an issue to get out this week. He said you might be in the market for some work yourself right now, join me on a little surveillance.''

Ben slung his duffel bag into the Jeep. ''I told him last night when I dropped the kids off that I'd be taking a week. Who the hell does he think he is?''

Peter looked at Ben like he was an idiot. ''He's your *editor*. Besides, what makes you think you're so special? With three out of five marriages ending in divorce, and a lot of them remarrying with kids in between, plenty of guys are locked in with some bastard.''

Ben closed the tailgate. ''Well, I'm going to try to forget that for a few days.''

''You're going to leave me to chase these nuts by myself?''

''God knows there are enough hungry kids out there who would be thrilled to work with the famous Peter Gallagher.''

Ben started to get into the Jeep when Peter grabbed his arm. ''None of them are my old drinking buddies. Look, the *work* is what keeps you going. And the work you and I've done together is the best of our careers, and you know it. You going to let this new situation ruin *everything*?''

''I'm coming back. Just need some time away.''

Peter shook his head. ''These stories won't wait.''

Ben laughed. ''Nothing I hate more than a goddamn pushy reporter. Listen, ask Kurt for another photographer. He'll assign one.''

Peter shook his head. ''You know I wouldn't trust anyone else this early in the story. Give me a camera, I'll do it myself.''

''You'd put your thumb in front of the lens.''

''C'mon,'' Peter said. ''Stay and shoot. Keep your mind on your work, the rest of this shit will fade away.''

Ben just looked at Peter, who kept his face sincere for a couple of beats before giving up and smiling sheepishly. ''Hell, that's what I tell myself, anyhow. Sometimes I'll go a whole hour or two without thinking about Sarah or Cindy.''

Ben smiled slowly and got out of the truck. ''Come here.'' He opened the tailgate and pulled out a camera bag. He mounted a four-hundred millimeter lens onto an autofocus camera body, switched on the camera, and made sure it was set to the simplest programmed exposure mode. ''This is where you turn it on. You press this button, and the lens will focus. You press it a little harder and it'll take the picture. There are thirty-six shots of fast film in there and there's plenty more in the bag. You know where I keep the key to the van." He pointed to his old Ford Econoline, painted a nondescript gray. "That'll give you room to shoot, a tripod, and a little urban camouflage. But stick to the horny senator, if you think you've got to do that story. Don't go after that gangland boy on your own. Some of them are pretty camera shy."

Ben switched the camera off and put it back into the bag. He draped the strap over Peter's shoulder.

"I think you're missing the point," Peter said.

"So are you. Whether or not I quit *Insider,* and how I'll learn to live with Kurt playing daddy to my kids are things that I need to think about long and hard—and on my own. I'd also like to do it without spying on someone through that hunk of metal, plastic, and glass. All right?"

Peter smiled ruefully. "Just took me so long to break you in, I don't want to have to start from scratch with some Jimmy Olson."

Ben shook Peter's hand. "I appreciate the concern."

He got in the Jeep and turned it around. Peter was bowed under the heavy weight of the bag. Ben rolled down the window. "All that said, don't leave that camera out in the rain. I'll need it when I get back."

"It'll all be here," Peter said. "Safe and sound."

Ben almost turned around several times on the five-hour drive north. It was one thing to pack and take off with the intention of being alone with your thoughts. It was quite another to actually be alone with them.

He stopped to pick up groceries and continued on to reach the lake just as the sun was falling behind the mountains. It was a marvelous sunset, the sky and water turning first scarlet, and then deep gold. A part of him ached for a camera to record it; a part of him felt relief that he had nothing to do but observe it.

He carried his supplies into the cabin quickly, feeling a bittersweet nostalgia for the place. The vacation excitement as a kid. Coming in and seeing his grandparents waiting. Swimming with his mother and father. His mother had thick black hair that would float against Ben's arm when his dad towed them side by side on their backs.

"Harris family train," his dad would say, his hand cupped under their chins.

Then as an adult, there were so many good memories embedded in the place with him and Andi. Even when they lived in San Francisco, they made it back to the cabin for vacations most years. Visit the old man, give the kids a sense of home. The kids on the braided rug in their bathing suits as Ben's father told them one of his hunting stories.

"Will you take us sometime?" Jake would ask. "I'd use my dad's gun."

"That old thing?" Ben's dad would jerk his thumb at the shotgun hanging over the mantelpiece. "It'd blow us all up."

Ben's father and grandfather had built the cabin themselves in the early fifties, several years before Ben was born. The image of his dad as a young veteran back from Europe felling trees alongside his own father had been alive in Ben ever since he was first old enough to hear the story.

The cabin was simple: a living area with the kitchen off to one side. Fireplace, to the left. Two small rooms in the back: one with a double bed, the other, bunks.

In the past few years, Ben felt the only thing he had managed to accomplish himself with the property was to keep up with the taxes and do minor repairs. Though his father had been dead for almost three years, and his grandfather twelve, Ben always felt as if the two of them were with him in the cabin.

And although neither had been judgmental men, now he felt ashamed in their presence.

Divorced man. Lost his children.

Ben's mother was killed by a drunk behind the wheel of a logging truck when Ben was eleven. She was just a few weeks past her thirtieth birthday. As an adult, Ben could look back and see that his dad must have gone through what was a clinical depression. He lost his asphalt paving business by failing to show up at jobs. For days at a time, he didn't leave the house. He just sat in front of the television. Face stubbled, gaunt. Smoking cigarette after cigarette.

Finally, Grandfather Harris came by late one night and said,

"C'mon, deer season opens tomorrow. Dog's in the truck."

"No," Ben's dad said.

"I didn't ask you. Just move your butt. You, too, Ben."

Ben's dad had been only an occasional hunter before his wife's death. However, on that trip, Ben could still remember the color beginning to come back into his dad's face. A sense of purpose, if not happiness, as he made his way through the woods with Grandfather Harris's old Remington shotgun broken over his arm, loaded with deer slugs. They found nothing that day, nor the next two. But on their last morning out, he led Ben and Grandfather Harris into the woods and shot a buck.

Although Ben was sickened by the blood and the deer's lolling head, the grim satisfaction on his father's face was better than the crushing hopelessness he had been seeing.

Ben asked his father to teach him to hunt like that.

"If you want," his dad said. "What else have we got to do?"

For the next two years, Ben hunted with his father and grandfather after whatever was in season. Duck, deer, coons, even bear. Ben's father built up an impressive array of racks and mounted trophies, including the head of a four-hundred-fifty-pound black bear.

He also got a job at the Bath Iron Works, and forced himself through the motions of taking care of Ben. At night, Ben's dad still spent hours in front of the television, smoking cigarettes. Not talking.

Ben learned to track, he learned how to control the dogs, he learned how to keep upwind of the animal he was stalking. He learned patience. The old Remington became his, and his father told him if he bagged a deer by his thirteenth birthday, he would give him a rifle.

But it wasn't until a few weeks before that birthday that Ben fully realized how completely he had conned himself for the sake of his father. They were waiting in a stand the first week of deer season. It was a crisp, cold day with the sun just beginning to lower. A buck emerged from a thicket to drink from the stream. The deer picked its way along a carpet of red maple leaves, sniffing the wind cautiously, before splaying its legs wide to put its muzzle into the water.

Ben's dad gestured for him to make the shot. Ben braced himself carefully, took aim . . . and realized that he had no desire to kill that deer.

To pull the trigger, yes.

To capture it, yes.

To somehow *own* what he was seeing before him, the liquid brown eyes, the arch of the deer's powerful neck.

But to kill it, no.

And he didn't want his dad to do it either.

Ben pointed the barrel off to the left and pulled the trigger. The deer wheeled away and was gone.

Anger flashed in his dad's eyes. "What the hell happened?"

Ben slid down from the stand and walked back to the cabin alone.

Three weeks later, Ben caught what he believed was the same deer on film. It was a wet, raw November morning. His dad was in another stand about a mile away, unwilling to be part of "this nonsense."

Truthfully, the shot was barely a success as a photo. Ben was using his mother's old Brownie and from the distance away with the relatively wide lens, the deer was just a thumbnail-sized shape on the first prints. He had a camera store in Portland blow the shot up, crop it. He hung it on the wall in his bedroom. The shot was so soft after all the enlargement that it was more symbolic of the deer than representative. Ben knew that most people would find the shot nothing special.

But he kept coming back to it. The breathless feeling was there for him. The tension in his legs from the long wait. The cold. The soft sunlight filtering through a heavy cloud cover. The pressure to simply *take the shot* competing against the desire to get the composition right, to wait until the deer turned his way, cocked that rack of antlers in silhouette against the mountain stream.

Throughout that winter, Ben's father moved from anger to confusion as Ben turned from hunting magazines to studying the work of Ansel Adams. That spring, the day before bear hunting season, his father told Ben that he would buy him the rifle even though Ben hadn't bagged the deer.

Ben told him what he really wanted.

His dad looked at him silently, then said, "We'll talk about it."

But the next morning, his father postponed the hunting trip until the camera store opened and they went in together to buy a used Nikon. His dad smiled in the background as Ben haggled over a telephoto lens.

As they drove away in his dad's old Plymouth, Ben looked at the camera on his lap, the jewel-like finish of the body, the heavy lens. Holding it gave him the same feeling as being out on a winding trail early in the morning. Breath making a white fog in the cold air. Not knowing what was around the next bend, but eager for it.

His dad said, "Just learn how to do it right."

"Thanks, Dad." Ben's voice was husky.

His father rested his hand on his shoulder. "I should've seen it sooner, what you were doing." His father paused. "I miss her, Ben. What I've really wanted to do since your mom was killed was to shoot that trucker. Not the guy that's in prison now. I hate him, but now it's too late. What I've wanted to do is hunt him down and shoot him *before* he got behind the rig, before he killed your mother. If I could, that's what I'd do."

His dad sighed. "But that can't happen. And stacking up racks and mounting heads won't make it happen. Neither is shoving you along to do something you don't want. It's time I sell my guns. Put your old Remington up on the wall for display. Maybe use it to bag a few ducks for dinner now and then." His father smiled crookedly. "I'd kill for my family, but it's too late. So I'm gonna stick close to the family I've still got."

His father's love had warmed Ben all his life. His dad had embraced Andi and the children completely. It was devastating for all of them when he died of a heart attack.

And yet, a year ago, Ben had been glad that his father wasn't around to see him separated, going through a divorce. Ben couldn't help wonder what his dad would think of him now. What would he think of Ben arriving at the cabin without his family? Of him leaving his wife and children to another man?

After flipping the circuit breaker to turn on the power, Ben loaded up the refrigerator. He felt the cans of beer. Still cold. He grabbed two, and then hurried out to drag the old aluminum rowboat down to the water. He shoved off into the lake. He rowed for a long time, until the light he'd left glowing in the cabin was just a faint pinprick. His hands and back ached.

He laid along the thwart with his legs bent, his head on a flotation cushion. Slowly, the last color from the sky disappeared, and the stars emerged.

He sipped at the beer, waiting for some epiphany, some better understanding. But even in doing that, he knew he was using the old steps for himself. Why should the stars reveal anything about Ben Harris? Without him being able to frame them through ground glass, without being able to compose them against a stand of trees, black and silver in the moonlight, he had no control over them.

And without that, he could find little meaning.

How could she do it to us?

That's what he really wanted to think about. A year ago, when she asked him to move out, he stumbled around for months, thinking, How could you do it? Have you forgotten who we are?

Fifteen years of marriage, gone.

His lover and best friend, gone.

Now this. *Married.*

The idea of Kurt dating Andi had been bad enough when Ben first heard through the kids that she was dating a senior editor at *Boston Magazine.* At the time, Ben knew Kurt only through his reputation, which was as an effective, if somewhat staid, editor. At that distance, the idea of Andi dating was barely palatable. The idea became hellish when Kurt won the hotly contested editor-in-chief position at the *Insider,* and became Ben's boss.

Ben had been tortured by the image of them in bed; physically repelled at the thought of Kurt's broad back moving over her. At times, it had taken all Ben had in him not to stand up in the office and knock Kurt out of his chair.

But the finality of this was worse. The idea of Kurt sitting at the breakfast table, pouring cereal for the kids, talking to them as if he were their father . . . and worse, the possibility, the *likelihood* that they would respond, that they would love this interloper.

Ben sat up, dipped his hand into the lake water and rubbed his face. Tried to wash some acceptance into himself. Told himself that times had changed; that Kurt was in and he was out. That he had to accept that he was joined at the hip with Kurt, a man he doubted he would've liked under any circumstances.

It was a nauseating pill, but Ben knew he had to swallow it somehow. For the sake of the kids. For some semblance of a friendship with Andi. As for the *Insider,* he'd give it a little more time. His work with Peter was the best of his career and he saw no reason to let Kurt take that away, too.

Ben shifted on the thwart, squirming to find some comfort on the hard wood, but he couldn't. He felt out of sorts with the world. Not for the first time, he thought, *How did I let this happen?*

Andi had been just twenty-one when they met. Good girl from an old Boston family who had long ago lost their money, but not their expectations.

"Help her out," said Jack Griswald, their editor from the *Portland Press Herald.* Ben, a veteran photojournalist of all of twenty-five himself, had taken her out on her first hard news assignment to cover an accident at a paper mill.

A workman had been killed, a horrific accident where his jacket had caught in a roller press and he had been pulled in. The accident itself was too gruesome for the paper. Ben limited himself to reaction shots from co-workers, and the spokesman for the mill. Then they went to the workman's home to talk to his widow. Absolute de rigueur in those days. Ben hated it himself, but when he looked over at the new reporter then, her face white, her fists clenched over her notebook, he thought he would have to conduct the interview himself.

But she did her job as well as anyone could have expected. She talked quietly with the widow and learned about the workman, Jeff Kirkland, and listened to the woman's grief, without ever asking that brutally cruel question so many reporters favored: "What are you feeling?"

And in the car on the way back to the paper, Andi cried quietly, making no objection when Ben rested his hand on her shoulder. However, upstairs in the newsroom, she went back to her business, and wrote an article that was factual, but sensitively conveyed the loss of Kirkland to his wife and son.

All very professional, and Ben respected that about her.

On the side, she continued to help Dorothy Kirkland, first by helping her find a job, then with a follow-up article months later that brought in enough cash to establish a college trust fund for the Kirkland boy. For this, Andi gained the nickname "PollyAndi" from her peers. Griswald admonished her, saying that although the Kirkland articles had worked out, if she was to be a reporter, her role was not advocacy or charity.

"For me, he's wrong," Andi said, looking over Ben's photos one night. They were friends at that point. He thought she was interested in him, but couldn't tell for sure. He, on the other hand, was hopelessly in love. He was feeling like a coward for not pursuing things further.

She touched his prints, shots of children, of criminals, of accident victims. Shots of loneliness, of happiness, of loss, of serenity and euphoria.

"You manage it, though," she said. "You show your indignation, your respect, your compassion. It's all here."

"I report first, though."

"It's still filtered through your head. Just like I choose what to write, you choose what to shoot. It's inevitable that we editorialize."

"That's the challenge," Ben agreed. "What I capture is not necessarily the whole reality, but the one I see. But I try to keep myself out of it."

"Mmmm. I want my words to do some good and I have to go about it the direct way." Her eyes met his. "As a matter of fact, I appreciate directness in most things. I like to know what people are feeling."

"Uh-huh," he said, feeling suddenly like he was about to jump out of a plane. "Seeing as you appreciate directness . . ."

"Which I do," she said, smiling.

He told her how he felt about her. Stumbling a bit, but getting the words out.

She took his hand and pulled it to her, kissing the back of his wrist, for the first time. He pulled her into his arms.

They didn't stop until the bedclothes were tangled and they were lying side by side, breathless.

Those first few years, they just drank each other in. They moved together, sometimes for his jobs, sometimes for hers. New York first, then San Francisco. Andi quickly moved away from daily news into more in-depth articles for magazines. Then she secured a column in the *San Francisco Chronicle* soon after she learned she was pregnant with Jake. "Andi's Attitude," based upon the concept of a one-year weekly observation of a woman stepping away from her career to have a baby. Woman in workforce issues were big in the media then and her timing couldn't have been better.

"Andi's Attitude" slowly began to build toward what it would eventually become—a nationally syndicated column that covered a wide variety of issues, from homelessness to race relations, all from her unabashedly opinionated viewpoint. But the way there was rocky. And, perhaps it was somewhere in there that her stated opinions made her rigid, made her unforgiving.

They had moved back to Boston to be close to her family when she was pregnant with Lainnie. It was a tough pregnancy, and right after Lainnie was born Andi was laid low with a bout of pneumonia and unable to write. She had to set aside the column for six months, and with it, her income.

Ben had been doing increasingly frequent shoots for *Newsweek* at that point; his career was essentially on the rise. But he ran into a dry spell just at the time they needed cash the most. As freelancers, neither he nor Andi had the best insurance coverage, and her medical bills had sapped their savings.

A photo editor from the *National Enquirer* called right about that time saying they had been admiring his surveillance photography and the *Enquirer* wanted to hire him for a shoot right in Boston. The editor positioned the piece as an exposé on the plight of street hustlers.

Ben didn't believe the shoot would be that straightforward, but after a moment's hesitation, he said yes. The rent was due.

The night of the shoot, the reporter on the job, Larry Hall, set him straight, "Get me shots of young, pretty hookers with older-looking business guys. We've got to titillate the shoppers in the grocery stores, get them to buy an issue to cluck over those skimpy outfits, and wonder if hubby is one of the guys screwing around on the side with teenage pros."

"I don't like this," Ben said.

"You don't need the work, just drive away," Larry said, looking through his binoculars.

Ben took the pictures.

Just around midnight Father Ray Caldwell showed up in the Combat Zone. He was wearing street clothes and even though Ben had covered him once—at a fund-raiser where both Caldwell and Andi were speaking—Ben didn't recognize him until he was loading his second roll of film.

Larry Hall recognized Caldwell at the same time and immediately pocketed the exposed roll. "Father *Ray?* The guy who's always standing up for children's rights? This is good shit. You keep shooting, follow him home while I get this in. If God's on our side tonight, he'll take her home and screw her brains out on film."

"Wait a second," Ben said. "You've got to talk to him. See what he says. Maybe there's another explanation, maybe he's trying to help her."

Larry laughed as he slid open the door of the van. "Maybe. That's not my job. I've got what I need right here."

Ben put his hand out. "Give me that and go talk to the girl after he leaves."

"*If* he leaves."

"Get the facts straight."

"We've got a deadline." Larry slammed the door and ran like hell. By the time Ben got out of the van, Larry was in his car and gone.

Ben got back into the van and refocused on Caldwell. He didn't release the shutter until it became apparent the priest was indeed going upstairs with the young girl. He came out about a half hour later. Ben got the shot.

Father Ray was on the cover of the next issue. Big XXXs behind him on a marquee reading "Girls, Girls, Girls." Holding the hand of a young prostitute who could have been asking his advice, or could have been soliciting him.

Either was possible.

The headline read: *"Got a Confession, Father?"*

Larry Hall's article nailed it home. Famous priest caught skulking around the Combat Zone "in disguise." The girl wasn't identified, but she clearly appeared underage.

Speculation crossed over into the "legitimate" media within the day. Father Caldwell held a press conference two days later, denying any involvement beyond his counseling. He refused to identify the girl, saying he had gone upstairs to talk with her and give her money to return home. He said she came to him originally in confession.

The camera flashes flickered across his face time and again, revealing the shine of sweat, the fear in his eyes.

He looked guilty.

With the number of priests who had been prosecuted in recent years for child molestation, Father Ray was openly doubted on the news night after night. "Man on the street interviews" judged him as guilty. "Smoke and fire," said one woman. "You know the way it works."

David Letterman worked Father Ray into his opening monologue.

At home Andi said to Ben. "But you don't know." She was sitting in the chair by their bed, giving Laurie a bottle. Andi was still weak from the pneumonia. Her cheekbones were more pronounced than usual and her eyes blazed with indignation. "You can't *know.*"

Ben was angry and trying to keep himself under control. "So that's it? You just going to distance yourself from me?"

"Don't tell me you did it for us! You didn't talk to me before you took this job."

Ben had put up his hand. "Look, I don't like any of this either. But given Father Ray's position, this is news. If he didn't do anything, he should identify her. And the girl should come forward if he's unwilling to give her name."

"What if he is telling the truth?"

"I don't know," Ben said, rubbing his forehead. "I don't know."

And he still didn't.

Because Father Caldwell killed himself after the fourth day of intense media scrutiny. Hung himself in the basement of the rectory. He left no note, and the girl was never found.

Public speculation swung evenly between this being the proof of his guilt to outrage over the impact of the media on a man of God. For the first time in his career, Ben found himself on the other side of the lens. And so was Andi.

Tabloids—particularly those that didn't carry her column—ran shrill headlines: *"What's Andi's Attitude about Paparazzi Husband?" "Andi—Did Hubby Drive Priest to Suicide?"*

One morning, Andi opened the morning edition of the *Boston Herald* to see a photo of herself and Father Ray standing together at their speaking engagement a year back. *"Andi & Father Ray's Story. Page 4."*

The media storm was over within a few weeks.

It took Ben not much longer than that to realize that the damage between him and Andi was permanent. She looked at him differently, as if his goal was to reveal the ugliness of the world. But by the very nature of who she was, dispensing advice about forgiveness and understanding to the public at large, she couldn't admit that and still be married to him.

Instead, she rehashed his time away, worrying it.

"We need you *here,*" Andi said. "Not on the other side of the world for a month at a time."

"You know I can't. Not in my business, you know I can't."

"The kids need more of you," she would say. "Do you see how tentative Jake is? Do you see how he's trying to force himself to be like you even though he's very different? And Lainnie is acting out— she swears like a trooper. It's not just the travel, it's your attention when you're here."

He was stabbed with guilt knowing what he would be saying next. "I'm going to Nepal tomorrow."

Or Burma or Moscow or Topeka.

"You make your own priorities," she would say. "You could build your own studio right here in Boston, or work with Leonard Penn and do advertising or corporate work. Do you still want to be living out of a suitcase when you're fifty? Peeping at people, catching them at their dirty tricks? Don't you want to be here while your kids grow up? You make your own priorities, Ben."

One of Andi's famous attitudes, published nationally. *You Make Your Own Priorities.*

That's convenient, Ben would think. Sometimes he would say it.

Ben sat up in the rowboat, and grabbed the oars. He spun the boat around and headed back toward the cabin, suddenly angry. Damned convenient of her.

Reinventing himself into a commercial photographer would involve far more than developing different skills—he simply had no passion for the work. And he couldn't see that killing his own ambitions for the sake of the children would serve them well.

Particularly since the real problem wasn't his time away. Or that sometimes his photos revealed things that were base and ugly about the world around them.

The real problem was brutally simple.

She didn't love him anymore.

CHAPTER 7

"HE'S HERE," LISA SAID.

Kurt didn't look up from his laptop. "Send him in, please."

A few minutes later, Ben stepped into his office. As always, Kurt had to steel himself from withdrawing a bit in his presence. Ben was an inch or two taller and more athletically built than Kurt.

"Have a seat," Kurt offered.

He asked Lisa for some coffee and she returned immediately with a carafe. Kurt and Ben didn't speak while she poured, both simply observing each other politely enough, waiting until the door would be shut. "Peter called this morning," she said to Ben. "He said he's got something for you."

"Good."

Kurt realized he had never seen Ben without the beard. His eyes were clear, his skin ruddied by the sun.

"Have you talked to Peter at all?" Kurt asked. "He's been busy."

"No, I drove in from Maine early this morning."

"You're looking well. Good vacation?"

"Great." His voice was flat. "Good honeymoon?"

Kurt smiled, but didn't answer the question. Instead, he said, "Obviously, this has every opportunity of being awkward for us."

Ben nodded and sipped his coffee.

"The solution to me seems to be that we maintain absolutely the same professional courtesy that we have already established. I've always respected your work and integrity and would hate to see you go elsewhere."

"Bullshit," Ben said, quietly. "You would love to see me leave. But you know Andi and everyone else would think you pressured me into it, and you don't want that."

Kurt shrugged. It was true, but he saw no sense in confirming it.

Ben continued. "And it may come to that. My first reaction was to quit. But, I like working for this magazine and I like the people I work with. I think I've made some remarkable images on behalf of *Insider*."

"Who could disagree?" Kurt pointed to one of Ben's framed shots on his wall.

"So, I'm staying for the time being. If it doesn't work out, I'll let you know. As for you and Andi, it's taken me a week of being alone to really work it into my system, but I've accepted that she made her choice."

"She has."

"But when it comes to the children, you've got to remember they're mine." Ben's eyes were hard now. "What I've also come to in the past week is how much I've let them down. And I know you've got a role with them, but I'm still their father."

"Well, if you're talking about increasing visitation rights, we'd need to talk that through with Andi."

"I realize that. And I will talk with Andi. But I'm talking about how you see yourself."

Kurt tried for a calming tone. "Look, Ben, as you know, my first wife and I were divorced so I have some sense of what you're going through."

Ben sat back. "I didn't know you were married before, no."

"Well, I was. Beyond the financial ramifications, which were bad enough, I remember the loneliness. Once she remarried, I found myself trying to reestablish some relationship—"

"That's not what this is about. I'm talking about the children."

"And I'm the children's new stepfather," Kurt said. "That means I will love them and try my damnedest to form a new family with the woman I married."

Ben's face flushed.

Kurt kept himself steady; kept his face calm and understanding until he saw Ben settle back.

"Fair enough." Ben rubbed his face. "What I've got to do is find a way to keep my relationship alive with them without screwing up yours. And that means some help from you in not sending me off to the far ends of the world, at least for a while."

"Your career will suffer if I can't send you where the stories are . . . and with your vacation, you've already blown off so many of those interviews that would've helped you secure outside projects." Kurt glanced at his notebook. "The fact is, I was planning on sending you off to Oregon. Seems that the clash between the timber companies and the environmental groups is coming to a head again. I wanted you to go out, spend some time with both groups, including some of the small logging operations. Show it's a two-sided issue, not just do a knee-jerk support on the side of the environmentalists. You handle that kind of duality well, and if I've got you pegged right, a little more time tramping through the woods wouldn't hurt you or your career. Maybe even capture some shots on our dime to help that book of yours along."

"Thanks, but no. I need to be here, and for once, I'm going to let my career come second. I'm talking about regaining something of my family before it's too late."

Kurt looked dubious. "I'm just trying to help you readjust to the new reality here."

Ben paused. "Losing myself in my work isn't the answer for any of us."

Kurt nodded, but he still didn't look convinced.

"Instead of cold professionalism, I think you and I will have to find a way to be friends," Ben said. "Even though it's not going to be a natural for either of us." He put out his hand.

Just as Kurt was reaching out, Lisa stuck her head in the door. "Excuse me, but Peter is on the line. He's on his car phone and said he's just pulling up and that I should, quote, 'Tell Ben to get his ass out front.' "

"Duty calls," Kurt said, withdrawing his hand.

"You heard it." Ben started for the door. He looked back. "We'll keep talking. And you should tell Andi I will be calling her about those visitation rights.''

"I'll tell her to expect it." Kurt smiled genially. "Thanks for coming in.''

Kurt straightened his desk and took the coffee cups out to the sink.

"I'll do that," Lisa said.

"Not a problem." Keeping his hands busy always helped calm him down and he needed it now. When he went back into his office, he looked out the window onto Clarendon Street. It was a beautiful, sunlit morning and he had a corner office that also gave him a fantastic view of Copley Square. He caught sight of Peter pulling up across the street in Ben's old van.

Kurt felt a sharp pang of jealousy.

Both Peter and Ben were doers. They got in, they got close, their talent was in capturing stories and ideas on the fly. Somehow, they weren't afraid of following and then challenging guys like Johansen, or now this young hood Peter had been following, Jimbo McGuire.

Kurt had his own talents measured to the inch and he knew he was an office man. A competent editor with a good visual sense. A fair administrator. Before Andi, no one saw more than that in him, no matter what he knew was inside. Even she used terms like "steady" or "loving" to describe him; words that didn't begin to convey the passion he felt for her.

Kurt could feel in his gut that Ben wanted to do the right thing by his children. And they would love him for it.

Some people are loved more easily than others, he told himself.

Through the passenger window, Kurt could see Peter grinning as Ben started to cross the street. Peter was holding up something gray.

And then that something exploded.

Kurt would remember it afterwards, the flash igniting right in Peter's arms. The police would say later that it pretty much vaporized him before bursting windows up and down the block and leaving the van engulfed in a fireball.

But that was later.

Then, Kurt stood behind his own cracked window, momentarily confused into total inaction. His eyes were focused on Ben, lying in the street, obviously bloodied, maybe dead.

CHAPTER 8

NO SOUND, AT FIRST.

Ringing, but no identifiable sounds.

Blurred vision.

Crazy corner view. The street. Lying in the street, smelling the oil in the asphalt.

Color off to one side, bright orange.

Heat.

Try to look. Can't see it clearly. Still blurred. Yellow, orange, and black. Moving.

God, not my eyes.

Ringing louder.

People suddenly there. Someone dragging him.

Faint voices. "Watch his neck, watch his neck!"

Try the eyes again. Seeing. Seeing someone over him.

Pain. Incredible white pain. Taking his breath away.

Looking again. Seeing Kurt above him now, pushing people away, yelling something. Not hearing a goddamn thing now except for the louder ringing.

Jesus! The fire. Fire burning his legs, the back of his hands, his head.

He sat up to look again, to see if the bright orange had moved onto him, if he was inflamed. Someone pushed him back down. He wondered mutely why they hadn't pulled him away far enough.

But the flames, the orange, was still in the blurred distance.

Close up, he could see red. Blood. He looked at his hands. Just dripping. He moved them and it hurt like hell, and he opened his mouth and he probably screamed something, but he couldn't hear anything.

Just that goddamn ringing.

He looked up, saw Kurt above him now, saw his face sharp and clear, saw that the guy was worried and saying something to him, and then faintly Ben heard the word, first heard "ittle," and then he listened closer, so damn happy that he could hear and see that he forgot that agonizing pain that was spreading hot along the backs of his legs and alongside his head. He heard Kurt say, ". . . hospital . . ."

It took the ambulance just about forever to arrive. By the time they had strapped Ben onto a stretcher, he had arrived safely into a semblance of the world he knew. By then, he could hear clearly enough past the ringing. And although his eyes still watered, he could see clearly when he wiped them.

"You'll be fine," Kurt told him.

"Yeah," Ben managed. "I'm fine."

Fine enough to see that he had dozens upon dozens of cuts from flying glass and that his clothes were soaked with blood. Fine enough to believe the EMT who was saying he'd be all right if they could keep the infection from setting in.

Fine enough to see inside that roiling mass of flames that had once been his van.

Andi was there when he awoke at the hospital.

"Hey, you," she said. "Are you going to keep scaring the hell out of me every two weeks from now on?"

He started to talk, but his voice was barely a croak.

"Here." She handed him a cup of water with a straw. "They said you'd be thirsty when you awoke. They've picked about fifty slivers of glass out of you. Mostly your left leg and a bit of your shoulder and scalp. Your windbreaker and camera bag stopped most of the glass, and your world-famous reflexes turned your face away in time.''

She bent over and kissed him on the cheek.

''I'm so sorry about Peter,'' she whispered.

He drew her head down to his chest, and closed his eyes. Seeing Peter standing there, bowed under that bag, worrying about him.

When Ben opened his eyes, Kurt was there. Ben saw his mouth tighten.

Andi sat up and saw him, and wiped her eyes. ''Caught us,'' she said, wanly. ''We're just feeling bad about Peter.''

Kurt nodded. ''All of us are.'' He looked at Ben. ''How's the patient?''

Andi interjected. ''Could you tell the nurse he's awake? And then bring the kids in?''

Kurt hesitated, and then turned away abruptly.

Ben flashed back to Kurt clearing people away, his worried face hovering over Ben.

Ben said, ''He came through for me.'' He told her about Kurt keeping people back, about calling for an ambulance.

Andi smiled. ''That's the kind of a guy he is.''

Ben sipped more water and then asked, ''Do the police know anything?''

''About who did it? No. In fact, they were here a while ago and then they said they'd come back to ask you some questions. But give the kids a few minutes first, they're beside themselves with worry.''

And indeed, when Kurt walked them in, Ben could see it in the paleness of their faces. Both moved toward his bed slowly, acting diffident. Perhaps steeling themselves for what they would see.

Ben took a look down at himself, the bandages covering his legs, arm, and side.

''You know how much glass they found in me?'' he said.

Both stopped and then Lainnie looked at her brother, a smile touching her lips, and said, ''How much?''

''Enough that some guy came around with a stencil to spray paint me, 'Glass—Handle with Care.' I told him to get lost.''

Lainnie giggled.

Jake said, ''Buh-dump-dump.''

Lainnie said. "That stinks."

"What do you want, a van blew up in my face. Now come here and find a spot to kiss that doesn't have these overgrown Band-Aids."

Lainnie climbed up onto the bed and leaned over Ben to give him a kiss. It was apparent Jake was feeling too old to kiss his dad, but he stood closer and put his hand on Ben's shoulder.

Lainnie said, "Is it true about Mister Pete?"

Mister Pete. Ben had forgotten that name.

Peter had been a guest in their home often before the divorce, and the kids loved him. "Call me Mister Pete," he'd growl with mock ferocity. "I'm too mean to be anybody's uncle."

"I'm sorry, honey." Ben stroked Lainnie's hair as he saw her eyes fill. Jake's mouth worked, and Ben could see him trying to pull himself together.

"Hey, I could use another hug down here," Ben said, and Lainnie flung herself on his chest. Jake took Ben's hand, and stood with his head down. Ben closed his eyes and held Lainnie tight. Breathing in her warmth, the scent of both of them. Well worth the pain to his left arm that the movement cost him.

"I miss you, Daddy," Lainnie said into his chest.

"I know," he said.

"I want you to come home!" she cried. "I don't care who Mommy married, I want you to come home!"

"Lainnie," Andi said, sharply.

"Sssssh." Ben ran his hand up and down her back. "That can't happen. But you're still my girl."

"I don't want him," she said.

"Sssssh."

She said no more. But her tears were hot, soaking through Ben's hospital gown. Jake tugged at Lainnie's shoulder and said, "Come on, Lainnie, cut it out." Ben looked past them to Kurt watching. A good man. Steady. Holding his hurt, if any, well in check.

How did I let this happen, Ben thought.

Soon after the doctor made his examination, he sent the police in. Both cops were big, but otherwise as different as possible. One was fat, with a big hard gut that stuck out aggressively past his blue blazer. He had a square face and brushed back white hair that Ben tended to identify as a politician's look.

The other was tall and gawky thin, with a bald head and sharp eyes in deep sunk sockets. He moved well despite the impression of awkwardness.

The guy with the gut showed Ben his detective shield and said, "I'm Calabro, he's Brace. I understand you had a lot of glass taken out of your hide this morning, but we'd appreciate a chance to ask you some questions so we can figure out what happened."

Ben nodded to the chairs, but both men remained standing.

"We just want to be sure—you're that guy we saw in the news, the Johansen thing, right?" Calabro asked.

"That's right."

"Tell us what happened this morning," Brace said.

Ben told them about the message Peter had given to Lisa, and then outlined everything from the moment he walked out of the building.

"We talked with the secretary." Calabro flipped through the pages of his notebook. "She told us he said to tell you to 'get your ass out front,' is that correct?"

Ben nodded.

"Apparently he also said something to the effect of, 'I've got something hot for him.' She said he sounded excited, but in control. Like a story was breaking." Calabro looked up directly at Ben. "What do you think that might be?"

"I don't know." Ben told them how he just driven in from Maine that morning.

Brace said, "Did you see the actual explosion? Any sense of where it went off in the van?"

Ben shook his head. "I was walking right toward him and then I glanced down. He yelled something and then, bam. I was on the ground."

"What did he yell?"

"Something like, 'told you it'd be safe.' I think he was talking about my camera. I'd loaned him a camera."

"As well as the van," Brace said.

"That's right."

"Tell me about what you *think* he was working on," Calabro asked.

Ben paused. The habit of keeping sources and story ideas in confidence was deeply ingrained.

"If it's a help, your editor already outlined the projects." Brace glanced at his notebook. "Some of them include these women in jail who killed their husbands, Senator Cheever supposedly caught with his zipper down, and Jimbo McGuire. We'll look into all of them, but naturally, we find that he was following around a local gangland boy particularly interesting."

"Those are the ones I knew about," Ben admitted. "But I really don't know much more than that. We talked about these ideas over a few beers about a week ago, and he asked me to help just before I took off on vacation. I told him I couldn't and that's when I loaned him the camera and van."

"Uh-huh. You find that significant?" Calabro asked.

"Like was it meant for me?" Ben shrugged. "I can't help but think about it, seeing as it was my van. But I haven't really been working on anything for the past two weeks, ever since I got back from this Johansen thing."

"What about that?"

Yeah, what about that, Ben thought.

"Sure, that's possible," he said. "Blowing up things is the sort of thing that Johansen's people do. And God knows I've made some enemies with that crowd."

"Hell, never mind the *crowd,*" Brace said. "Johansen himself is still alive in jail. These are strings he could pull."

Calabro said, "Or it just could be some sympathizer coming out of the woodwork."

Brace nodded. "Now about the van, is it yours or registered to the magazine?"

"The magazine," Ben said. "Officially, it's a company vehicle, but I'm the only one who uses it."

Brace nodded. "That's a break. Because no one else in the media has tipped to this being your van yet. It's news enough that you were near an explosion so soon after the thing with Johansen, but if it looks like the bomb was set for you, you'll get swamped. More important, it could excite the random nuts to try for another shot. You think you can keep this quiet, including your own magazine?''

"Sure," Ben said. "And I'll talk to Kurt. I expect I can get him to agree.''

Brace pulled a plastic bag from his pocket. Inside was a ripped piece of gray cloth backing a piece of leather. "Recognize this?''

Ben nodded. "That's the insignia on my camera bag, the one I loaned to Peter.''

"Uh-huh. Well, we just came from the lab. They say it's looking like the explosion came from this side.''

He tapped the cloth side.

Ben cocked his head. "That side?''

"Yeah," Brace said. "The bomb was inside your camera bag.''

CHAPTER 9

BEN WAS IN THE BACK OF THE VAN HE HAD BOUGHT THAT MORNING when Lucien found him. They were in the parking garage underneath the building where *Insider* was based. The van was a beat-to-hell Chevy with a strong engine, a good suspension and tires. Six thousand bucks, paid by the *Insider*'s financial officer with a sigh and shake of his head. Everything, from the beige color to the missing hubcaps, only encouraged the eye to slide right past it.

Lucien clambered in. "Here, let me help."

The smell of his aftershave filled the van immediately, and he hovered beside Ben. Lucien grabbed an end of the curtain rod and pulled it to the fitting Ben had just installed. "Like this, right?"

"Uh-huh." Ben was thinking how typical this was of the guy. Lucien was looking back at Ben not so much for approval, but to see if he was earning the points he intended.

Lucien said, "You think I've got a shot on the lead?"

"I really don't know."

Ben wanted to like Lucien, but from everything he had seen so far, Lucien's ambition outweighed his talent.

"There's talk that Kurt is looking for a replacement for Peter," Lucien said. "I don't think that makes sense, do you? I mean, I could hit the ground running with Peter's assignments."

"Huh," Ben said.

Lucien had been dogging him for answers for days, presumably because he thought Kurt's marriage to Andi gave Ben some sort of inside pipeline.

"So you haven't heard anything?"

Ben attached the rod on his side. The act of kneeling made him want to scream. He expected his bandages under his jeans were beginning to seep blood. "Not a thing."

"Ah." Lucien looked at his watch. "Well, let's go. Kurt's called an editorial meeting and you know how he hates it when people are late."

Ben bit back his immediate comment. Part of his new policy of giving his children's stepfather every chance.

Kurt sat waiting quietly while Lucien, Ed Liston, and Ben joined the group. Already Sid Barrett, Glenda Pierce, and Leslie Shea were seated. Sid handled business and finance reporting; Glenda, the society pages; and Leslie handled entertainment. Ben was somewhat surprised to see them all gathered at once: perhaps Kurt intended a staff meeting more than an editorial meeting. None of these three typically worked on the investigative projects and Kurt rarely brought people to a meeting without a reason.

Kurt looked up from his notebook. When he spoke, his voice was quiet. "As you're all well aware, we're dealing with the tragic loss of Peter. He was a friend and colleague to all of us. But before that, he was a husband and father. Some of you may know that Peter had been previously married to Sarah Taylor, when they were both on the *Chicago Tribune*. I expect all of you are familiar with her work when she was with the *New York Times*."

"Was?" Lucien said.

Kurt paused.

"Shortly after Peter's death was made public, I received a call from Sarah. This is a rather unusual move, but because of her talents I felt my instincts were on target . . . and when she said that she wanted to move to Boston to work for the *Insider*—so she could find out what happened to Peter . . . I offered her a position on the spot."

"But . . . she won't have any contacts here." Lucien's face was stricken. He shot a look at Ben. "Hell, most likely Peter got killed because he was driving Ben's van. I was in on the Johansen story. What good is an investigative reporter who doesn't know anyone?"

"I know you were on the story," Kurt said. "In fact, I seem to remember assigning it to you. The point is that Sarah's a highly talented investigator and writer and we're lucky to have her. Surely you read her piece on the Teamsters."

Lucien colored. Rumor had it that her piece missed a Pulitzer by degrees. In reputation and skill, she dwarfed Lucien, and everyone in the room knew it.

"So," Kurt said, "I'd like to start this meeting off with a welcome to Sarah Taylor." Kurt picked up the phone and asked his secretary to bring Sarah in.

A moment later, she entered, and Ben was struck that this was the first time he had ever met his best friend's wife. Ex-wife, anyhow.

Sarah was in her early to mid-thirties. She was relatively small, with fine features, dark blue eyes, and a light complexion. There was a faint dusting of freckles on her cheeks and nose. Short, curly black hair.

"Face like a Girl Scout," Peter had said. "A Girl Scout who can sell you a half dozen boxes of cookies and get you to confess every bad thing you ever did just because this nice girl is so damn *interested* in you."

Ben could see it, the openness of her face. But now, tension was also evident there, the tightness of her mouth and a hollowness about her eyes.

Kurt introduced her to the group.

"Thank you," she said. She looked around the group quietly before speaking. "I expect all of you are surprised that I'm here. I expect some of you aren't too happy about it either, feel that I might be upsetting the balance of order. To which I'll tell you that I'm sorry, but that it can't be helped. I have a consuming interest in finding out what happened to Peter. And I know it sounds arrogant, but I've found that when I'm truly interested in getting to the truth of the matter, I just about always do."

She looked around at each of them. Her eyes settled on Ben, locked briefly. She said, "I'd appreciate any help you can offer."

Lucien looked down, but everyone else spoke up, made sounds of welcome and condolences. She thanked them all, but her eyes kept coming back to Ben.

Kurt stood up and formally welcomed her aboard. He told Sid, Glenda, and Leslie that they were free to go back to work now that the staff portion of the meeting was over. They filed out, leaving the new investigative team of Ed, Ben, Sarah, and Lucien. Sarah opened a notebook computer while Kurt turned over the first page of a flip chart he had standing in the corner.

On it was a list:

1. Johansen
2. Battered Wives
3. Cheever
4. McGuire
5. ???

"Anything else?" Kurt pointed to the question marks. "Any other stories that Peter was working on that he may have mentioned to you and not me?"

Lucien and Ed looked to each other and smiled, wryly.

"Kurt," Ed said, "until you handed me that story about the battered women to follow up on, I knew nothing about it. Peter kept his stories to himself."

Lucien nodded to Ben. "Maybe a word or two to his buddy here, but otherwise, you'd know more than us."

"Fine," Kurt said. "So this will be our base of stories and I'll expect you to keep me informed if others appear." Kurt smiled faintly. "We've promised the police to keep quiet to any other media outlets about the projects Peter was working on. Naturally, this is something we'd want to hold on to anyhow, because I want Peter's story on the cover of *Insider* next week. Sarah and Lucien, this week I want you to work together on a lead-in starting from Ben's experience with Johansen to a quick and dramatic summary of the explosion that killed Peter. Sarah, I also see a sidebar on your own reaction when you heard of Peter's death and insight into the risks reporters take."

Ben winced.

She appeared to pause, but then she simply nodded. "Makes sense," she said.

Ben saw Lucien's shoulders slump.

Kurt continued. "Now, all the other media outlets think Peter was simply using a company van when this happened. Let's keep it that way for Ben's sake, keep the random nuts from thinking they should go after him, do it right."

"I'd appreciate it," Ben said.

Kurt continued. "In any case, from there we go on to some background on Peter himself, and then we go into the violence the press can run into in the course of doing our jobs. Ben, see if your new friend at the FBI can secure an interview for you and Sarah."

"Sure."

"Sarah, you're going to be the lead on any new investigation of both Jarrod Johansen and Jimbo McGuire. Ed, you've already started the prison ladies' story, and I've got another assignment for Lucien, which I'll get into."

Prison ladies, Ben thought. Peter's term, Peter's irreverence. It sounded forced coming from Kurt.

"So, first thing, go establish yourself with the cops," Kurt said to Sarah. "If they don't come through, we'll write it as a slice of one reporter's life and we'll leave open the door as to which story killed him . . . if it was any one of these. Obviously it's possible that it was something in his past. The police are leaning toward the possibility that it was someone after Ben because of Johansen."

Kurt shrugged and looked back at the list. "But this is what we've got for now. All right, how are you doing so far on the prison ladies, Ed?"

"I'm taking each woman's story a case at a time," Ed said. "Some of them should probably get out. Others, it's not so clear."

"The police forming any opinions about their husbands' families or friends in regards to Peter's death?"

Ed smiled. "The police don't tell me all their opinions. But my impression is that they're looking into it without a hell of a lot of interest. Most of the guys these ladies killed didn't sound smart enough to set an alarm clock, never mind a bomb. I think the cops are assuming the same of their friends and family."

"Well, keep on it. Ben, you coordinate with Ed when he's ready for you to go in. I'll be looking for group shots and individual portraits."

"All right."

"That assumes you're not too tied up on these other three angles. If so, let me know and I'll send someone else out to the prison." Kurt went back to the flip chart. "On Johansen, Lucien, I'd like you to share your notes with Sarah."

Lucien's face flushed, and Ben and the others looked away, embarrassed for him. Everyone had stories pulled away from them from time to time, but it was never easy to take.

"What about me?" Lucien said. "You said there was another assignment?" The plaintive tone in his voice was so clear Ben was again embarrassed for him. Ben looked at Kurt, as the others did, wondering if he was going to land on the young reporter with both boots.

But Kurt was smooth. "I've been looking for an opportunity for you to expand your political coverage. Therefore, I'm going to have you cover Senator Cheever."

Lucien sat a little straighter. "That's cool. What have we got?"

"Not much. I had met with Peter on Wednesday and he brought me up to speed then." Kurt slid out a sheaf of photos and Ben, Lucien, and the others swung around to his side of the table to look. Sarah stood well back from Lucien, clearly letting him take the lead. There were over thirty prints of what were essentially three scenes.

Kurt didn't try to hide his frustration. "Peter said he dinked around with your camera, Ben, and set the motordrive onto high speed and didn't know how to stop it. He essentially took about ten to twelve shots each of what should have been only three photos before blasting through a roll of film. By the time he figured out how to rewind and reload the camera, there was nothing worth taking."

Ben felt his stomach drop.

"You should've *insisted* Peter take another photographer," Kurt said. "I can't believe an operation like ours is being hobbled by ego like this. Peter was a great reporter, but too damn secretive for his own good. . . . In any case, this is what we've got through the window of Cheever's town house on Beacon Street. Him sipping wine with an attractive young woman up in his office in the daytime with her clothes on.''

Indeed, there were three sets of black and white shots taken through the window. One set of the senator smiling as he put down a tray of two wine glasses on a table. The second was of a young woman standing in the window. She was laughing, her head back, the line of her throat revealed. The last was of the woman looking pensively out the window, the afternoon light revealing her to be a beauty. Ben stacked the prints of the second set and fanned them against his thumb, making a small quick-time movie with the minor movements the woman had made while being photographed at eight frames per second.

Even in the jerkiness of the rudimentary film method, he could read her appeal, the way her chest and shoulders lifted slightly as she laughed, the sidelong look she directed back into the room, presumably at the senator.

''And who are Peter's sources on Cheever?'' Lucien asked.

''Damned if we know. From what the police told me, they've found nothing in his apartment, we've found nothing substantive in his computer here.''

Ed said, ''The police say there was a burned vinyl notebook inside the van. Totally unreadable, even for their labs.''

''You want me to walk those shots into Cheever and ask who she is?'' Lucien asked. ''Get his reaction?''

Kurt paused.

''All right,'' he said, slowly. ''Do that. But go easy with him. Just say you're following up on Peter's story, relate the situation. Ask him if he has any comments, if he could identify the girl for us. Somehow, I don't see the senator wiring bombs to hide screwing around on his wife. Not in the same state that voted for Teddy Kennedy year after year.''

''Cheever's still going to blow,'' Ed said.

''Probably,'' Kurt said. ''Wear your asbestos suit, Lucien. And Ben, go along when Lucien gets the appointment. See if you can get Cheever's reaction on film.''

Kurt turned back to Sarah. ''All right, Peter was also working on a young punk from Southie.'' He pulled out another manila envelope and laid out a sheaf of black and white prints. "Jimbo McGuire."

Ben looked at the prints and sighed. He'd told Peter to stay away from McGuire. And yet, the story was right there to see. Peter had gotten too close. With the four-hundred-millimeter lens that Ben had left him with, he was achieving full head and shoulder shots.

Far too close for a guy like McGuire.

McGuire was an exceedingly handsome young man, with dark hair, an open, chipper look to him. The first shot showed him leaving a warehouse not too far from Ben's studio down off the piers. Another of him going into Jimmy's Harborside Restaurant, looking back over his shoulder in front of the pebbled glass. A set taken most likely in Charlestown talking to a small balding man outside of a candy store. And the final was of him in a Mercedes with a young woman. His hand was on her thigh, and his head was turned directly toward the camera. Just her body was visible, wearing shorts and a halter top.

Lucien whistled. "Wished Peter got the full shot on her."

Ben glanced at Sarah, who smiled faintly. Kurt laid out the rest of the pictures. There was another shot of McGuire talking with the same shopkeeper outside a redbrick building. And finally one that looked like the North Shore. Ben could see beachfront property, the Boston skyline faintly in the background. A home in Nahant, perhaps.

In the last three shots, there were two of McGuire. One, looking back over his shoulder, a scowl forming. The other of him pointing directly into the camera.

The third shot was a quick, poorly framed photo of a thick-bodied man walking close to the camera, his shoulders forward, his head down. Out of focus.

"McGuire saw Peter and sent somebody over," Ben said.

"That's right," Kurt said. "Peter said he took off before the guy got hold of him."

"They say anything? Make any threat?"

"No. Peter said it was all there to see in this guy's face and the way McGuire was standing there, hands on his hips."

"Huh." Ben said. "Have the cops talked to them?"

"They're not sharing that with me. That's up to you and Sarah."

Ben said, "I sure don't see anything here that's worth killing about."

"I know." Kurt leaned over the shots, looking at them closely. "Neither did Peter."

Kurt asked Ben to stay a moment as the others were leaving the room. "I just outlined a lot of work for you here. Are you really up to it, physically?"

"I'm hurting a bit, but I'm all right," Ben said. Thanking God for the little vial of Darvon in his pocket to help keep the pain at bay.

"Have the police said anything to you about protection?"

"Yeah. They can't afford it. Besides, I can't have a couple of guys following me around while I'm trying to cover the very people who may have done it."

"I see." Kurt drummed his fingers lightly on the table. "That leads me to what I have to say now. I talked with Andi about our conversation about additional visitation rights."

"I left a message on your machine for her yesterday," Ben said.

"I know. But I'm relaying our thoughts to you. At this time, with what's going on, we don't think it's safe for the children to be around you more than they are already. If anything, we think you should stay away from the children for a while. Including canceling this coming weekend."

Ben stood up and walked to the front of the room. *Our thoughts . . . We can't see . . . We think . . .*

Ben exhaled carefully. "You know, Kurt, I truly admire your ability to manage a room full of people. I don't admire you using it for managing my family life."

"Our family life," Kurt said.

Ben had planned this weekend two months ago. He had bought tickets for an Eric Clapton concert at Great Woods, something he knew they all would enjoy.

He thought of Lainnie, crying on his chest at the hospital.

"I think you can understand my logic," Kurt said.

And, of course, Ben could. It *was* safer for the kids to stay away from him at least for a week or so.

He just needed to get past Kurt laying it out for him.

"All right," Ben said, shortly. "But Jake's birthday is the end of

next week. Nine days. Let's all meet someplace public . . . you and
Andi can bring the kids, take them home.''

　　Kurt said, ''Naturally, I can't commit until I talk with Andi.''

　　''Naturally,'' Ben said.

CHAPTER 10

SARAH KNOCKED ON THE OPEN DOOR OF BEN'S CUBICLE. "GOT A minute for me?"

"Of course." Ben took a box of transparency sleeves off a chair and she sat down. He had been thinking about this meeting all morning, knowing it would have to come soon.

"Well," he said.

"Yes . . ." she said. "I know you and Peter were friends. Close friends if I heard him right."

"We were."

"You probably know he took the shuttle down to visit me and Cindy every month."

Ben nodded.

"I was jealous of you, actually."

Ben raised his eyebrows. "We weren't *that* close."

She smiled wanly. "He'd show me the pieces the two of you did together. You know he and I started as a team first. I saw us as a girl/boy version of Woodward and Bernstein. Being lovers, wedding bells, and Cindy came afterwards. Ever so much more difficult." Her smile curved. "You two boys could keep it simple: work together, do amazing things on the street, and just stay buddies."

"Buddies who sat around bars whining about loneliness after all that 'amazing' work."

She hesitated, seemingly lost within herself, and then said, "Maybe we can have a drink sometime, talk this all over. In the meantime, what I wanted to say is that I'm going to have to lean on you as Peter's former partner."

"That's fine. But I've got to warn you that in recent months, Kurt's had me off on other things. Peter and I were just getting back to work together when this happened. I don't know anything more than what you heard in the editorial meeting."

"Understood. We're also going to have to look hard at this thing of yours with Johansen. It looks like a pretty promising lead, wouldn't you say?"

"Promising . . ." he grimaced.

She waited.

He said, "If promising means I lie awake nights wondering if I got Peter killed, then, yes, it's promising. It was my van, it was my camera bag. But there's also this kid, this Jimbo McGuire. We know Peter was found out, at least to the extent that he was chased off by McGuire's bodyguard."

"Tell me again why Peter was taking photographs himself?"

"Because he was stubborn," Ben said. "And more than a little paranoid. He wasn't willing to take someone else along and I needed a vacation."

"I see." She said it calmly enough, but he could see—or thought he could—the flash of resentment.

"Got to be tough, sitting here being civil when you're thinking, *It should've been you.*"

"I've got my own guilt to worry about," she said, with a slight edge to her voice. "I did my part destroying our marriage. He wouldn't even be working for *Insider* . . ."

She stopped and abruptly brushed away a tear before it even started. When her attention returned to him, her eyes somehow seemed darker. "Look, if it motivates you to feel guilty, then who am I to get in the way of it? Use it to help me find the bastards who did this. And yes, if McGuire looks like a possibility, by all means let's follow that up, too."

Ben put out his hand and she held it.

"Deal," he said.

She squeezed his hand briefly, with surprising strength. She flipped open her notebook to show him a phone number. "That's the FBI in D.C." she said. "How about you call in that favor with that agent you saved and get us an interview with Johansen?"

After only two rings, the number was picked up and Ben asked for Agent Parker.

A man identifying himself as Agent Blaine answered Parker's phone. "Who's calling?"

"Ben Harris. I'm the photographer who—"

"I know who you are." The man's voice was flat. "What can we do for you?"

"Is Parker there?"

"He's not."

Ben explained they were looking for an interview with Johansen.

"This in relation to the bombing up there in Boston or is this just some color for your celebrity issue?" Blaine asked.

"I'd kind of like to know if that bomb was meant for me."

"Well, you're a hell of a photographer, Mr. Harris. And we appreciate what you did for Agent Parker. But people as good at interrogation as you are at pushing a shutter button have been grilling Johansen about Boston and a whole lot of other activities. So far, his answer is 'no,' and we don't have any evidence to show otherwise. If we did, we would pass it along to . . ." Ben heard the rapid tap of a keyboard. ". . . Detective Brace on the Boston Police. Have you met with him?"

"I expect you know I have," Ben said. "Seeing as you know so much already."

"You're right," Blaine said, cheerfully. "I do. So I'm afraid I'm going to have to tell you what I tell all the reporters—no interviews."

"Parker made the offer of a favor, and I'm asking."

The agent paused. "He did, did he? Then you'll have to wait for him to call you back. But don't hold your breath. Agent Parker's extremely busy right now, and our policy right now is to keep the press away from Johansen. It builds his ego up and we're trying to wear him down."

"His ego also trips him up," Ben said. "I've seen it."

"That you have," the agent said, mildly. "And maybe Parker will see it your way. I'll tell him you called."

Ben found the next day at the prison in Framingham hard going. The grim consistency of the women's stories. Stories of men who were forgiven again and again even as they beat and abused women they had sworn to love. Of men who wouldn't stay away even when restraining orders were issued. Of women who had been pressed beyond their limits and had finally reacted with guns, with knives, with poison.

But, Ben heard nothing from any of the women that shed any light on Peter.

By the time Ben and Ed got to the last woman's cell, most of the day was gone. Her name was Maria and she had been convicted of walking into a bar and shooting her boyfriend. Her body had been covered with bruises and cigarette burns at the time; her two children from a previous relationship had been taken to the emergency room a half dozen times in as many months.

They were in a foster home now.

Ben started setting up his shot on autopilot, his hands and eyes knowing what to do. Simple instructions: Stand here, please. Look there, Maria. Thank you.

No thought added.

Some of his distance was due to the pain in his leg, and the floating feeling from the painkillers. But the women's stories evoked images within himself, images from his own world: of Parker blurring up from the floor as Ben fired the strobe into Johansen's eyes; of Andi and Kurt sitting across from him on the love seat telling him they were to be married; of rowing alone under the moonlight in Maine; the sound and heat as Peter disappeared right in front of him.

Of waking up in the hospital bed . . . Lainnie's tears, Jake's awkward distance . . . of Kurt saying after the meeting, ". . . we think you should stay away from the children for a while."

Ben came out of the reverie, his own anger alive in him, the taste of it bitter.

Maria was looking at him challengingly. "Uh-uh, honey, you

don't tell me where to sit. This is the picture I want." She stood in front of the prison bars, hip cocked, her well-muscled arms crossed just under her breasts. Anger swept off her, but, even so, she laughed harshly at herself. "I know I'm a bitch, but that's the way it's gonna be. I let a man come in my house and tell me *what* I do and *how* I do it and *who* I see and that's not gonna happen again for this girl."

"How did it happen?" Ben asked.

"Ain't you been listening?"

Ben raised the camera and repeated his question. Through the glass, he saw for a moment a desperate vulnerability replace the challenge in her eyes. He almost squeezed the shutter button to capture what was perhaps a truer portrait of her.

But he waited.

She said, "You know . . . a man puts it all together for you like that, turns all that attention on you . . . it feels like love."

Her face hardened. "But it ain't."

Ben released the shutter.

It was just after six when they left the prison. "Grim stuff," Ed said. "I think I'll head to a bar and see if a few beers can help convince me the male side of the human race isn't as despicable as I just heard. Want to join me?"

"No thanks," Ben said, stretching carefully. He itched all over. "Home and shower. Change some bandages."

"I didn't hear anything that helps us with Peter, did you?"

Ben shook his head. "Not a thing."

"Tomorrow, then."

Ben thought about home, the empty studio, the shower. He was exhausted, and the pain had sapped a lot out of him.

He took another pill, and headed the van back toward Boston. Thirty minutes later, he impulsively took a left at the Alewife MBTA station and continued toward the North Shore. Continued on to Jimbo McGuire's home in Nahant.

On the second day of following McGuire, Ben spotted an excellent vantage point to oversee McGuire's real estate office on Atlantic

Avenue in Boston. It was an air-conditioning unit on the roof of the brownstone across the street. Ben walked into the lobby and quickly found a small plate reading, "Walker Management Corp." Back in the van, Ben parked around the corner, and made a quick call to information, and then to Walker. When the receptionist answered, he said, "Good morning, I represent SteamKleen rug service, and I wanted to know who I should talk to about our maintenance programs—"

As quickly as possible, she told him to send whatever literature he wanted to Chuck Crenshaw, the head of maintenance services, but that no, he was not available to take a sales call at this time.

Ben put the phone down and knelt over his bag of tricks. That's the way he thought of the oversized suitcase filled with a jumble of clothes, hats, jewelry, and other assorted junk. He selected a blue workshirt with the name "Louis" sewn over the pocket, put a thick gold-plated chain about his neck, dark sunglasses, and a baseball cap turned backwards. He quickly filled out a photocopied "Work Order" and signed Crenshaw's name at the bottom with his left hand.

At the front door, he buzzed his way in by saying to the super that Crenshaw over at Walker had sent him to service the AC. The super came out wearing a bathrobe and a sour expression. He glanced at the work order and let Ben on the roof and told him to lock the door behind him on the way down.

Ben took the cover off the AC unit and spread some tools around, before taking his camera out of the toolbox and laying it on a bean bag to support the long lens.

The next day, the same ruse worked at the building two doors down.

McGuire, however, did absolutely nothing of interest.

CHAPTER 11

ON THE MORNING OF THE FOURTH DAY, BEN WAS BACK IN THE VAN. He figured it was safe to use for at least the next day, and after that, he would need to think of something else. Maybe just get a rental van.

The camera was poised at the window of McGuire's office as two men arrived in separate cabs in the space of five minutes. Neither of them turned his head so Ben could get a clear shot of his face.

"Damn it," Ben muttered. He started laying out his gear and was about to make his move when Sarah called him on the phone and asked if she could meet with him. Ben hesitated, and then said yes. He told her to find her way to a pizza restaurant about a half mile away from his stakeout. He got there before her, and went in and ordered a large pepperoni. While it was cooking, he went back to the van to wait for her.

When she arrived, Sarah got in and tucked one stockinged leg under the other. She was wearing a nicely cut dove gray business suit, managing to look both terrific and entirely professional. She took off her sunglasses and wrinkled her nose at the clutter in the van, the accumulated bags of take-out food and coffee cups. "You're making me feel right at home. I spent weeks in a box on wheels like this for my Teamsters piece."

Ben smiled. "And look at you now. Love the suit."

"I just came from the police station. Wanted to make a good first impression. What have you got for me?"

"Not that much." Ben showed Sarah the photos that Huey in the lab had developed and printed the night before. The shots were much the same as the previous days: McGuire getting in his car. McGuire, seen through a restaurant window, having lunch with the big bald guy who had chased Peter off. McGuire going to his office, which overlooked Boston Harbor. Beside the office door there was a discreet little sign reading, "By Appointment Only."

"What did the cops have to say?" Ben asked.

Sarah pulled out her file. "Brace and Calabro gave me more than I expected."

Inside the file there was a surveillance photo taken of McGuire during what must have been a black tie occasion. The picture was taken at a low angle and very grainy. Probably a video grab shot from an undercover cop posing as a waiter or another guest.

Sarah said, "This is from the FBI files."

"No mug shot?"

"I haven't got one. But he has been arrested a few times. Assault. He was under suspicion but never arrested on a home invasion, most likely trying to rip off cash stolen from an armored car. I pulled the files on that . . . but the only thing that stuck was when he was a juvenile, when he beat another kid with a baseball bat. Crippled him. Should've been enough to get McGuire at least reform school, but even though he was convicted, his lawyer got him off with probation."

"Somebody's got some weight."

"Calabro said his family packed him off to school after the home invasion thing . . . and then there was a nasty date-rape story at Stanford, but the girl backed off before it even made the paper."

"Who's cleaning up after him?"

"His uncle." Sarah showed him a picture of a hawk-faced older man.

"Patrick Clooney," Ben said.

"That's right. He took over the Irish mob after Whitey Bulger took off and now the cops say he keeps a tight rein on McGuire. They say McGuire talks up the reformed tough guy schtick and they assume he's still into something, but they haven't been able to find out what.''

"So why did the cops give you all this?''

She raised her eyebrows. "Combination. Grieving ex-wife and I'm wearing a nice suit.''

"So cynical.''

"Runs in the family,'' she said. "But, still. They were more generous with information on the first go-round than I'd expect. What do you think?''

"Did they tell you what McGuire said when they went to him about Peter's death?''

"They didn't.''

"Did you ask?''

She simply looked at him, her slate-blue eyes showing just a touch of frost.

"Sorry,'' he said. "What did they say?''

"Nothing. I mean, they haven't talked to him yet.''

"Why not?''

"They gave me your basic cop blah-blah. 'Our investigation hasn't taken us there yet.' ''

"Huh. I've been looking closely for other surveillance for three days now. Three days I've been following McGuire. I should've stumbled over someone else by now. Seen somebody else following in a van or car. Some cop or FBI agent should've come forward and told us to scram by now.''

"Meaning?''

"Meaning we're it, as far as I can see.''

"Why would that be?''

Ben shrugged. "Every good trap needs bait.''

"Tell me what Peter would've done, who he would've talked to,'' she said.

He caught a flash of Peter, his leg cocked up on the dashboard of the car, rooting through a fat file folder. It was during the article they did on Whitey Bulger. "Paper, paper,'' Peter was saying.

Something else around that time . . .

Ben couldn't remember, someone that Peter had talked to. The name flickered, and in his mind's eye, Ben could see a green door opening. A bar? A restaurant?

"What're you thinking?" Sarah asked.

Ben shook his head. "Trying to remember something."

"Let me know if it's something good." She met his eyes. "I'll catch up fast, but I need all the introductions I can get."

"Understood. In the meantime . . ." He went through the photos he had printed from the day before and pulled out the picture he had taken of the little sign in front of McGuire's office. Bayside Realty Corporation, Inc. Ben handed the picture to Sarah. "Let's find out what his company supposedly does. You could talk to Sid over in the Finance section. He could probably get you started."

"Sounds exciting," she said. "But probably right. Don't let that go to your head, shutterbug."

Ben looked over at the restaurant take-out window and saw the girl behind the counter wave. "My pizza's up."

Sarah looked at her watch, amused. "It's just past eleven. Hungry already?"

"No, actually," he said, looking at her consideringly. "Have you got a few minutes?"

They parked three blocks away from McGuire's office while Ben got ready. Ben opened his video case and attached a cable to a tiny videocamera, then attached the cable to what looked like the neck loop on a pair of thick black eyeglasses. Embedded in the middle of the eyeglass frame was a tiny video optic.

He took off his shirt and strapped the videocamera to his back, put the glasses on, and then pulled an ancient Grateful Dead T-shirt back on.

Sarah didn't look away as he dressed. "You going for some sort of geek hunk look?"

"Wait'll you see the hair." Ben rummaged through his suitcase, and took out a scraggly blond wig, tucking the hair behind his ears to help hide the wire. He topped it off with a Red Sox jacket and hat. He checked himself out in the mirror he kept in the back. He hadn't shaved that morning, and though the eyeglasses held only plate glass, they were thick enough to give him a goggly look.

He slid the pizza into a red vinyl warm-up case and cocked a slightly goofy grin at Sarah. "Your pizza, ma'am."

She nodded approvingly. "You'll pass. Just don't count on a big tip."

Ben's legs began shaking as he walked up the sidewalk to McGuire's office building. He'd played this part before and he told himself that would make it easier.

He pushed the door open and strode right in. Saw a pretty girl at a receptionist desk, looking at him in surprise. "Suzanne" on a nameplate on her desk.

"Got your pizza," Ben said, cheerfully. "Man, what a day outside, innit?"

"What pizza?" she said.

Ben turned his head from left to right, getting the layout of the place down. Big bay window out the back, throwing in a lot of light. He got his back to that fast so it wouldn't screw up the exposure and slid the pizza on the surprised girl's desk. "*Your* pizza," he said. "Ten ninety-five. Tip's extra, if you're interested."

He looked past her, saw through a glassed-in conference room that McGuire was sitting with his feet up on the table, his hands behind his head. He was talking to two men in business suits. One of the men was probably about forty, with jet-black hair and a goatee. He wore a beautifully tailored dark pinstripe suit, with a tightly knotted rep tie. Even though his clothing was conservative in style, the effect was of a high gloss, a man with an ego. The other man was slightly older and heavier. Reddish hair, sunburned. Strong and tough looking, with quick eyes. He glanced at Ben through the window and then turned his attention back to McGuire.

Ben smiled vaguely in their direction long enough to be sure he had taped them all, then turned back to the girl. Who was saying for the second time, "We didn't order any pizza."

Ben became aware of movement to his left and turned abruptly to find a big man beside him. The bald guy. The one who went after Peter. There was a side door open, must be where he'd come from.

"Hey," Ben said to the guy. "Maybe you called it in. She doesn't know nothing about it."

The guy got close to Ben, and without a word took the pizza box away.

Ben lifted his hands up to the girl as if to say, "See?"

"Did you order it?" she asked the man curiously.

"Shut up," he said.

With bored and impersonal assurance, he patted Ben's coat and opened it quickly, presumably looking for a gun. He reached around and patted Ben's waistband in the back, missing the videocamera by inches.

Ben didn't have to fake the fear and indignation. "Hey, what the *hell?*"

"You shut up, too." The bald guy opened the box, slid the pizza out, and opened it. He looked quickly through the case and then shoved the pizza back in. "Get out of here. We didn't order this."

Ben pulled a piece of paper from his front pants pocket. "Forty-six Atlantic Ave, I've got it right here!"

"This is sixty-four, you dipshit," the guy said. "Now get out of here."

Ben snatched the pizza box away and said as he walked away, "Still. No call for that, man. No call at all."

"*Dyslexic* dipshit," the girl said, laughing. "What a goof."

Back in the van, Sarah put the cell phone down as he got into the front seat and drove away. "Five minutes you were in there. I almost called the cops."

"I almost needed you to," he said, rolling his shoulders to let the tension go.

"You get what you wanted?"

"Uh-huh. But you were right."

"How's that?"

"Not even a lousy tip."

Late the next morning, as Ben was sitting behind the camera across from McGuire's office, the name came to him unbidden: Sean Deegan.

He was the guy Ben had been trying to think of. Peter had used him as a source when Whitey Bulger had hit the road.

Sean Deegan, an ex-cop who had been out on disability for years.

Ben called Sarah on the cell phone and got the message that her phone was turned off. He left a message at the office for her to call him, and then he started off toward South Boston. Ben had once tagged along with Peter to buy Deegan lunch, and, as Ben remembered it, Deegan had pretty much drunk his meal. If Ben was going to get anything useful, he knew he'd want to get to the man before too late in the afternoon.

Even though Ben had only a few miles to travel, the road construction from the Greater Harbor project slowed him down. Then, it took him forty-five minutes to find the bar. When he finally saw the dirty windows and faded green door under a flickering Budweiser sign, Ben was sure he'd found the place. "The Waterford Men's Tavern," the sign read.

Ben stepped into the gloom of the bar. There was old-world charm to the place: a beautiful wooden bar, high-backed wooden booths, a tile floor. But masking this was a layer of grime, the definite odor of urine, and the smell of old and unwashed men. There were half a dozen of them there already. "Help you?" the bartender said, managing to make it sound like a threat.

"I'm looking for Sean Deegan."

"Why?"

Ben smiled. "Because I owe him some money."

The bartender grinned, showing yellow teeth. "A comedian." He looked at the clock. "Buy yourself a beer while you wait. He'll sniff the stuff out within ten minutes, I guarantee it."

And, a little before one, he did arrive. He was a formerly big man, his chest now shrunken and his stomach a hard medicine ball thrust in front of him. Ben thought of the cop, Calabro. Deegan walked by Ben, glancing at him with no apparent recognition, and then said to the bartender, "I'll get started properly in a minute, Tommy. Just give me something to clear my head?"

Tommy handed a broom over the bar. "Clear the cigarette butts off the floor first, then we'll talk."

Deegan's face flushed, but he took the broom and began sweeping.

Tommy drifted over to Ben and winked. "Don't interrupt him, 'til he's done. He's damn useless after that first few drinks, and I've got to get some work out of him until his disability check arrives next week. Then he goes back to being a paying customer."

Ben laid a ten on the bar. "Two beers. Keep the change."

The bartender grinned, and bellowed down the bar. "Deegan! Put the goddamn broom down, the man wants to talk to you."

Ben took the beers down as Deegan turned around to look at him. The old man moved in a kind of shuffle, and Ben thought to himself that he had almost certainly just wasted ten dollars when Deegan said, quietly, "Fucking shame what happened to Gallagher."

Deegan took both beers from Ben and downed one quickly, and put the other on the table in front of himself. "You don't need this shit, son. It's bad for you. Now what do you want?"

"Some information."

"My name can't be used. Me and Gallagher were real clear on that. And keep your goddamn camera to yourself. I'm like a Boston version of Deep Throat. You got that?"

Ben said that he did.

Deegan leaned forward, his eyes sharp even though his face was filled with broken blood vessels. "You're smart to get me early. Past two o'clock, I don't make much sense to myself."

"What can you tell me about Jimbo McGuire?"

"One, to keep your goddamn voice to a whisper if you're gonna talk about that son-of-a-bitch. Two, don't call him Jimbo to his face. He thinks he's all grown up."

"You hear anything about him being behind killing Peter?"

"The first piece of advice was my only freebie," Deegan said. "Let's see some cash."

Ben put a twenty on the table, but kept his hand on it. "Tell me something I don't know and it's yours."

The old man began talking, speaking clearly enough, but so that he couldn't be heard more than a few feet away. He rattled off history: McGuire's juvenile record, his protection from Clooney, the rape case in Stanford. Ben held on to the money.

"What's McGuire up to now?" Ben asked.

"I'm just an old fart cop, I don't know high finance. But that's what I hear he's trying to do."

"Go straight?"

The old man laughed. "Not in his frigging genes to do that. Came back from Stanford all pumped up with these ideas about himself. I'd guess he wants to mix his talent for hurting people with bigger returns. Real estate, construction, all sorts of stuff.'' Deegan shook his head. ''That financial stuff always threw me, I was more the kind of cop that dealt with people busting each other's heads, or shooting each other.'' Deegan brightened, and looked at the money in Ben's hand. ''One thing I can tell you is to watch your ass if he knows it's you. He's a real good hater, comes to it naturally. He decides you're pissing in his soup, he'll come right after you.''

''Bad news, huh?''

''Oh, yeah. He's part of the new generation, all right. He never got picked up for it, but there were rumors around before his uncle hustled him off to college that he went in on one of those home invasion things. Sort of shit that the Jamaicans do, but Irish kids are supposed to know better. Blew into Derrick Coughlin's home, killed him, beat the wife, killed her, and then was moving on to the kids when one of them saw the sense of telling McGuire where Mommy and Daddy hid a big suitcase that they were never supposed to touch. It was the cash from an armored car heist.''

''He was never charged?''

''The two guys rumored to have gone in with him, Donny and John Gendron, they never got to testify,'' Deegan said. ''McGuire didn't even get arrested, far as I know. Right after, his uncle got him out to California. The story goes that Patrick Clooney used to have a full head of black hair until his nephew became a teenager. It's strange, I seen the two of them together myself: Clooney is kinda disgusted by some of the things his nephew does, but he still takes care of him.''

Ben cocked an eyebrow. ''Does that include buying off someone on the force?''

''You haven't got enough money in your bank account for me to talk about that.''

''Do you know Calabro or Brace? Are they clean?''

Deegan hesitated, then said, ''I know them and I think you heard me the first time. As for McGuire, all you've really got to take away from our little drink here is that if he loses his temper with you, get the hell out of town. Him and his uncle clean up good.'' He winked. ''Seems Donny and John's car blew up with them in it.''

Ben slid the twenty over.

CHAPTER 12

"THAT'S ALL YOU'VE GOT?" KURT SAID, LOOKING THROUGH THE prints. "So what?"

Ben laid his palms up. Inwardly, he seethed. "I know you'd like to see a few shots of him wiring up bombs. So would I. But he's not doing it."

Kurt rubbed his face, looking sour. He looked over at Sarah, whose face was unreadable. "And what's this I hear that Ben interviewed a source without you, Sarah?"

"We'll work it out," she said.

Ben sighed. "It was a matter of me doing it alone or wasting another day." He explained about Deegan's drinking.

Kurt shook his head. "Let's keep our strengths in front of us here. Ben, you're the photographer. Sarah's the reporter. We've already had one disaster with Peter trying to take on your work. Don't repeat his mistake now. And Sarah, check out a pager. Now tell us what you learned, Ben."

He went through it with them, and both of them sat forward when they heard about the Gendron brothers. "Blew up, huh?" Kurt said. "Let's see if we can get photos of those two and follow this up, Sarah." Kurt pursed his lips. "What was your read, Ben? Was Deegan suggesting that Boston Police were letting it slide with McGuire?''

''I couldn't get a straight answer.''

''That's what we pay Sarah for,'' Kurt said.

Ben glanced at her and he saw he had his work cut out there, too. *I don't need this shit,* he thought. He said, ''If we're done here, I'd just as soon get out and keep following McGuire.''

''We're done when I say we're done,'' Kurt said. He held his gaze on Ben for a moment, before shifting his attention to Sarah. ''I want you to be extremely careful with what you share with the cops. And, Ben, I want you to connect with Lucien. It looks like he might have that interview with Senator Cheever this afternoon. We're looking pretty thin for this issue and I'll have to lead with the prison ladies if you've got nothing else for me. You think you can contain yourself to taking pictures?''

''I'm getting pretty good at containing myself,'' Ben said.

Kurt smiled. ''Lucky for me. Then you and Sarah should work out your problems. Find out what McGuire wants, find out what he's doing, find out what Peter could have dug up that McGuire wanted to hide. Sarah, are you up for interviewing him?''

''We don't have anything solid on him. It would be a fishing expedition.''

''So go fish.'' Kurt said. ''Get me a story.'' He pressed the intercom and told Lisa he was ready for his next meeting.

''Guess it must have seemed pretty funny when I asked you to lend a hand,'' Sarah said, minutes later in the hallway.

Ben followed her into her office. ''Get over it. I called you, you didn't answer. Leave your cell phone on if you want me to involve you every time I have a brainstorm. Where were you anyway?''

''Personal business,'' she snapped.

Ben leaned onto her desk and said, ''Listen, Sarah. I know that you're hurting. But for me it's personal business that my best friend got killed. And it's personal business that I can't see my children until we figure out if I'm on someone's hit list for God knows what reason. Have you got that?''

"Have you got that I don't give a shit!" she snapped. "There wasn't enough left of him for me to even say good-bye, never mind show Cindy that her daddy was gone. She still doesn't believe it, and, frankly, neither do I."

"Then where were you yesterday, if you're so damn anxious?"

"Church," she said, shortly. She glanced at Ben and said, "Don't look at me so carefully, I'm not some sort of zealot. Cindy wanted some way, some formal way of going to talk to her dad. She didn't want to go to the cemetery, that scared her. So I turned off the phone and took her to church."

"Did it help?"

Sarah rubbed her eyes. "I think so. She cried, but she seemed happier later. I felt a little better, too. Afterwards, I interviewed a former teacher who can take care of Cindy in my apartment. Cindy seemed to like her and I needed to get it settled."

"Did you?"

"I did. So I'm fully in business. Call me with interview ideas. Call me with contacts." Sarah put her hand out. "Just call me."

Ben shook her hand. "Got it."

On the cab ride to the senator's town house, Ben noticed Lucien was wiping his mouth, but a faint sheen of sweat kept reappearing on his upper lip.

"Nervous?" Ben asked as they started up the stairs.

"Wouldn't you be?" Lucien looked at the beautiful redbrick building before them, and back at the lush beauty of the Boston Gardens. "This is old Boston, this is one of the most powerful guys in the country, and I've got to ask him what he thinks about our pictures of him playing with some chickie. I get something out of him, then I've got a story that'll make my career. I screw it up, I get an enemy who can shut me down."

Lucien stopped at the top of the stairs and looked at Ben, apparently looking for a different perspective. A way to make everything OK.

Ben thought of Father Caldwell, standing at that press conference with the flashes popping repeatedly, freezing the sweat on his brow for posterity. Ben said, "Cheever has more to fear from you than you do from him."

Lucien raked his fingers through his hair as Ben pushed the door-bell to Cheever's town house. "Yeah? Does he know that?"

A receptionist let them in and walked them up through the town house to a small waiting area on the second floor. She offered them coffee and after they declined, she went back to work on her computer. Cheever kept them waiting for about fifteen minutes, and then came out saying, "Gentlemen, thank you for your patience. Come on in."

The senator chatted briskly with Lucien as he escorted them into his office. "It's lucky you caught me in town," he said. "Just keeping *track* of my schedule is a huge task in and of itself."

Ben automatically checked out the window, seeing where Peter must have parked the van on Beacon Street to have gotten the angle. The senator's office was dominated by a huge mahogany desk, photos and paintings of Boston scenes from the turn of the century, and a beautiful globe on a floor pedestal. Cheever's military (Marines) and school (Harvard) affiliations were subtle, but evident. Photos of his family, two handsome boys and a rather imperious looking wife, flanked him on each side as he sat behind his desk.

Cheever said, "I was devastated to read about Peter Gallagher. He certainly kept me hopping over the years, but I always liked the man personally and respected his professionalism."

Suddenly, the senator fell silent and Ben looked up to see him staring directly at him. "What's your name again?"

Ben told him.

The senator stood. "My god, I didn't recognize you without the beard." He reached out to shake Ben's hand. "I didn't realize *Insider* would be sending over such a famous photographer. I want to thank you personally for what you did to stop that lunatic Johansen. Bad enough that it got as far as it did, at least we conservatives don't have his success hanging over us." The senator shook his head. "Believe me, it's tough enough being a Republican senator for Massachusetts without nuts like Johansen around to pull the public's impression of the right even further off center."

"That's how you see yourself, Senator?" Lucien began. "Just about center?"

"Little further right than that," the senator chuckled, and they began a traditional political interview. Ben wandered about the room as they did so, capturing shots of the senator. Cheever was an easy subject. Too easy, actually. Long familiar with having the camera lens pointed at him, Cheever posed constantly. He took off his coat and rolled up his sleeves; he made his points using his hands for emphasis; he even positioned himself so the photos of him with Ronald Reagan and George Bush were evident, if slightly out of focus.

Ben could see the pictures in his head. Although he knew the senator would have been pleased, the shots were too staged. Everything in place, including the looks and moves of a former athlete blessed with intelligence and drive: black hair going gray, friendly blue eyes that Ben saw he could change at will to convey anger, sadness, indignation, commitment, and resolve. Lots of resolve.

After fifteen minutes of a steady delivery of views and statistics, the senator looked at his watch. "Well, I appreciate you two coming in."

Lucien took the manila envelope from his briefcase and Ben lined up the shot. "Senator," Lucien said. "There's one more thing that we'd like to discuss with you. As you may remember, Peter brought up the rumors about infidelity. Given the Clinton scandal and the weight the character issue played in your own election campaign . . ."

"I'll tell you what I told Gallagher," the senator began, his voice suddenly hard.

But then he stopped.

Lucien pulled out the three photographs and the senator said, "What's this?" The senator looked through the photos, his face suddenly unreadable.

"This is your evidence?" the senator asked. Ben noticed a slight relaxation of the man's shoulders. Relief, possibly. Cheever glanced up at Ben. "I would have thought you were above this kind of thing."

The senator turned his attention back to Lucien and spoke in a slow, patronizing voice. "Yes, I sometimes have meetings up in these offices just as we are now. I sometimes serve wine, just as we are now drinking coffee. And, yes, sometimes the people who come to see me on state or federal business are women—and sometimes those women are young and attractive.''

"I understand that, sir," Lucien began. "Perhaps you can comment on why she . . .''

"No." The senator shook his head sternly. "I will not comment. I will not allow you to speculate and put my comments in print about goddamn *nothing*. There's not an iota of evidence of me doing a damn thing wrong here, but if you run these photos the public will jump to damaging conclusions.''

"Sir, we're not trying to hurt your career, it's just that we're following up on all of the stories that Peter was working on as an all-encompassing article that reporters run risks . . .''

Ben lifted his camera and caught a couple of frames of the senator pushing himself back from the desk, as if to better comprehend this new angle.

"Stop with that damn camera," the senator said sharply to Ben. When he returned his attention to Lucien, his voice was quiet, well-measured, and shaking ever so slightly.

Ben couldn't tell if the outrage was feigned or genuine.

Cheever said, "Let me understand you. You intend to run these photos in the context of the things that Gallagher was investigating that got him killed? Excuse me, but are you so damned irresponsible that you'd tar me with the suspicion of being involved in a reporter's *death?* I'm a U.S. senator. Do you know what that would do to my career with all the nuts out there who have nothing to do but entertain conspiracy theories?''

"No, senator, no," Lucien stood. "Look, let me talk with my editor. I don't want you getting the wrong idea here. . . .''

"Who is she?" Ben said.

"What?" The senator looked at Ben, confused. "Did you take these?''

"Who's the woman?''

The senator shook his head, and then shrugged. "Go ahead, call her. Her name is Teri Wheeler. Heads up the New England Software Foundation, NESF.''

"A political action committee?" Lucien said.

"They don't refer to themselves as a PAC group, but that's what they are," the senator said.

"So you're saying you have no romantic relationship with her," Lucien asked, his pen poised.

"Emphatically." The senator opened his drawer and flipped through some cards before finding hers. He tossed it to Lucien. "I'm also saying go ahead, talk to her. Clear your own minds. But you print something as damaging as what we discussed, with so little grounds, and I'll come after you. Public figure or not, I've got some rights. Now get out of here."

CHAPTER 13

"WHAT'RE YOU DOING?" JAKE ASKED, LETTING HIMSELF INTO THE library.

"Dumping off some old files," Kurt said. "I'll be done in a minute if you want to use the computer."

"Yeah, OK." Jake sat on the love seat, quietly watching his stepfather work for a few minutes. "My dad hates computers."

"I know," Kurt said. "He's competent with them, but it's a challenge to get him to do his expenses or log his shots. But his other talents overshadow that, don't you think?"

"Sure." Jake looked up at the prints of his father's still up on the wall. "He's incredible."

Kurt caught the envy in Jake's voice along with the admiration. Not for the first time, Kurt thought that those pictures should come down. For the kids' sake, as well as his own. But he knew it would raise holy hell if he broached the subject. Better to wait until the new house.

"You think my dad will ever use a digital camera?"

Kurt smiled. "Miracles can happen. I tried to foist the new digital Nikon on him. He could still use his own old lenses, I thought that'd appeal to him. We'd cut out the processing, streamline production. He gave me half a dozen pretty good reasons why not, with the top three being, 'I don't want to.' Your dad is a talented, creative guy, but he goes his own way. I expect that's kind of tough on you and Lainnie, isn't it?''

Jake shifted uneasily, wary now. "Maybe sometimes."

It saddened Kurt to see how much Jake wanted to be like his father—and how different he was. The two of them didn't even look alike: Jake had his mother's light skin and dark hair, while Lainnie had her father's coloring.

And Jake's manner was entirely different. More hesitant. More cautious. Kurt wished Jake were his own. He just knew the kid would shine with the right kind of attention.

Kurt said, "If ever I can be of any help, talking, just listening, that's one of the things I'm here for."

"Yeah, well. . . . Do you know where my dad is now? It's been like a week."

"You know he's very busy trying to find out what happened with Peter."

"I know, but still."

"I understand." Kurt looked at his watch. "He's in Washington, D.C."

"What's he doing there?"

Kurt thought about it, and decided there was no harm. He told him how Ben was going to see Johansen.

"Cool," Jake said, his eyes lighting up briefly. "You think he'll be on TV?"

"Better not be," Kurt said, smiling. "This is part of a feature we're doing for *Insider.*"

Kurt saw the boy's enthusiasm fade. Kurt felt he could decipher the look: *My dad is cool, but there's no time left for me.*

"My own dad was a captain in the navy. Commanded a destroyer," Kurt said. "I was proud as hell of him, but I sure didn't see much of him. And even when I did, it sometimes felt like I didn't . . ." He paused. ". . . it felt like I didn't exactly *register.* You know what I mean?"

"Yeah," the boy said. "I know what you mean."

Kurt ejected the disk and exchanged it in his briefcase for packaged software that was still in the store bag. "OK. We've got some room on this drive again. I just picked up a copy of SimCity. You want to help me load it and start rebuilding Boston to our own liking?''

Jake straightened and reached for the software package. His eyes met Kurt's directly for the first time since he came into the room. "Hey, thanks." Those eyes were bright, and alive, and, for the moment, Kurt felt as if Jake was truly his own son.

"You knew I wanted this, didn't you?" Jake said.

Kurt smiled. "That's one of the other things I'm around here for."

CHAPTER 14

THE TRIP TO LORTON STATE PRISON TO SEE JOHANSEN WAS A BUST. Worst than a bust.

While Parker watched through one-way glass, Ben and Sarah sat down across the table from Johansen. His hands were manacled to a belt around his stomach. Johansen's face looked puffier than before, but there was a malicious excitement in his eyes. On an impulse, Ben asked him flat out if he had arranged for the bomb.

Johansen shook his head dismissively. "I expect someone took a swat at you for what you've done to me, and to the country. But I wouldn't waste my resources to deal with people on your level."

"Then why did you agree to see us?" Ben said.

"For entirely personal reasons," Johansen said.

And then he spit in Ben's face.

He moved so fast that Ben had barely reacted before Johansen's face was in his own.

The door behind Ben opened immediately, and the guard came in and grasped Ben by the arm. Parker came in moments later. Together, they pulled Ben and Sarah out of the room as Johansen said quietly, "Think twice before you open a package. Sweat it out before turning the key in your car. The free people of America will decide whether or not you live or die. The free people of America will no longer tolerate the collusion of the media and government—''

''Ah, shut up,'' Parker said, and slammed the door shut. He looked at Ben with bemused sympathy. ''Tell me—what are you feeling right now?''

Within fifteen minutes they were in Parker's car on the way back to the airport.

''OK, what have we got?'' Parker said. ''I wouldn't be surprised if Johansen was actually telling the truth on this. We've been responding to all sorts of shit. Guy out in Seattle killed a state cop who stopped him for speeding. Said it was his revenge for Johansen. Federal buildings are all back on full alert for bombs. Couple of white supremacist enlisted men in Norfolk kidnapped, raped, and murdered a young black woman supposedly as a 'political statement.' Admitted the rape part was a little something for themselves. And burning black churches is back in fashion, only with a new twist. You know about that church down in Alabama last month? Preacher opened his bible that somebody had hooked up to a motion detector detonator. Pulpit had enough plastique to take out him and eight people in the front pew.''

Parker looked in the rearview mirror, back at Ben sitting there with his gear. ''Got to say that your friend Gallagher is the first one in the media to take it, though, if that's what it was. Most of these nuts seem to like the attention of the press just fine.''

''What do you know about Jimbo McGuire?''

Parker shrugged his massive shoulders. ''I'd look at him hard.''

''Have you?''

''Not directly, not on this. I understand the Bureau's Organized Crime unit in Boston has been looking at him for some time. I know an Agent Ludlow has a file on him but there's nothing conclusive. Again, as far as the death of Peter Gallagher, it's Boston Police's show.''

When they reached the airport, Parker walked around to open Sarah's door. He shook Ben's hand. ''I'll keep in touch. Anything that I think you can use, I'll call.''

Parker touched Ben on the shoulder. ''Watch yourself.''

Ben took another few minutes in the men's room to wash his face again before they boarded the plane. He could still feel the spittle on his cheek even though he had scrubbed the skin raw.

When he came out, Sarah was sitting at the gate. Her face was pale.

"How are you doing?" he asked.

She simply nodded. She was silent the whole time they were boarding the plane. A single, angry tear slipped down her face as the plane took off, and she looked out her window in the direction of the prison. It was too far away to see, but still she looked. "The bastard," she said. "The bastard still doesn't even know who I am."

That night, as Ben walked down the hallway to his studio, he was thinking of his kids, thinking about tucking them in when they were younger. Thinking how often he'd missed it because he wasn't home or he had begged off to Andi, "I've got processing to do."

Thinking about Sarah, too, on her way home to her little girl.

He slipped the key into the lock and opened the door. He smelled gasoline.

It was faint, but it was there. Ben instinctively began to back away, but the man inside made his move before Ben realized he was there.

He grabbed Ben by the upper arm and spun him around. The door slammed behind him, throwing the room into darkness. Ben cried out as the man sunk two hard punches into Ben's stomach.

The man worked in terrifying silence.

Ben tried to cover his stomach. There was a whistling sound and a crashing blow alongside his head. Ben staggered, and then fell to his knees. The whistling sound came again. Ben ducked and the blow glanced off his head and landed on his shoulder. He fell onto the floor, his right arm numb.

"That'll do you," the man said. Ben could hear him breathing hard now.

The man felt down and rapped Ben hard on the head with his knuckles.

Ben lay still, certain that reacting would only put the guy back to work.

After a moment, the guy shuffled away.

There was a faint glow of light, and Ben opened his eyes to see the man standing by the file cabinets. He had a small flashlight in his hand, and the beam hit his face for moment. Ben captured the image in his head with the clarity of a photograph. It was the security guy from McGuire's office. The one who had come after Peter.

The man slid open one of Ben's file cabinet drawers of negatives. He swore, and opened several more. "Jesus Christ, how many you got here?"

The man quickly opened all of the drawers on Ben's six cabinets before bending down to lift up a big metal can, which he rested on top of the cabinet. He unscrewed the cap.

The smell of raw gasoline filled the room, and that galvanized Ben.

He's going to burn them, Ben thought.

His life's work.

Ben squeezed his eyes shut, thinking of the layout of his loft.

Ben saw the place in his head, the door leading to the kitchen area.

Knives. They were all in drawers, he would never get to them fast enough.

What else?

And then, probably because fire was imminent, he saw it in his head and even saw it when he opened his eyes. The fire extinguisher. In the bracket outside of the kitchen area. At his angle on the floor, he could see it outlined against the light from the window. When he was on his feet, it would be in shadow. He'd have to get his bearings on the countertop, and then reach straight down.

The flashlight beam turned his way for a moment, and Ben kept himself still as the light washed over him. Then the man turned it back to the files.

Ben came up from the floor.

The room spun as Ben charged forward. The man grunted in surprise. Ben bumped his hip into the counter, then caught hold of the extinguisher and tugged it away. The man dropped the flashlight, the beam playing over his face as it fell. He was pulling a blackjack out of his pocket as Ben crashed into him.

Ben was too unsteady to make it a solid hit, but it was enough to spin the man around. Ben fell to his knees but then came, up and swung the heavy extinguisher around, hitting the guy with a hollow clunking sound on the elbow.

The man cried out, and that was damn good to hear.

Ben swung the extinguisher and connected again, but the man remained on his feet. Ben hit him again, a blow to the head that made the guy stagger back against the file cabinet.

The man saw the gas can beside him and flung it, covering Ben with a sheet of gasoline.

"You're gonna burn, you nosy bastard," the guy said, sweeping a manila folder into a puddle of gas and coming up with a lighter.

Ben slipped and fell, and with the drugged slowness of nightmares, he saw the man step up to the edge of the glimmering pool of liquid.

Ben pulled the pin on the extinguisher and squeezed the handle.

The blast caught the guy full in the face.

He staggered back and Ben came after him.

Ben shoved his elbow in his face, and landed two punches in the guy's stomach. It was like punching a bag of wet cement. The guy spun the wheel on the lighter. Sparks flew but the gasoline didn't ignite.

Ben jumped back, terrified of those sparks. And then he did what came naturally when the guy again started to put the lighter to the gasoline-soaked folder—Ben kicked him in the balls.

The guy made some noise then.

He also bent double to protect himself.

Ben took him in a headlock and rolled him over his hip into the puddle of gasoline. "You'll go too, you'll burn too."

As suddenly as the attack started, it was over. The guy got to his feet and bulled past Ben.

It took Ben a split second to get it. He stood, slipping and sliding in the acrid gasoline, waiting for the next attack, when the light from the hallway spilled into the room as the man opened the door and ran.

Brace and Calabro arrived immediately after the fire department.

"This is an improvement," Brace said. "You don't even need a trip to the hospital. Next time, how about you just wrap things up for us?''

Ben looked up from his file cabinets. After putting on dry clothes, he had checked through the files repeatedly, and had finally assured himself that none of the negatives were ruined. The firemen had spread foam in the room and all the windows were open. Ben said, "Keep talking, I'll let you know when you get funny.''

Brace smiled. "It's just when I hear about the exciting boy photographer investigations with Johansen in D.C. and surveillance on McGuire that I get jealous we don't have your skills at work for us on the Boston Police.''

"Makes him testy as hell,'' Calabro said. "Jealous that he's stuck with a fat-assed old cop like me as a partner.'' Calabro breathed deep, taking in the gasoline fumes. "Jesus, I love what you've done with the place.''

"So who did it?'' Brace asked, opening his notebook. "Guy with eyes as sharp as yours must have a pretty good description for us. Didn't manage to snap off a shot, did you?''

"Afraid not.'' Ben waved them out the balcony. "Let's get some air.'' As they walked out, Ben thought fast, thinking about what Deegan had—possibly—hinted about Brace and Calabro.

Ben said, "Sarah Taylor tells me that you haven't been out to see McGuire yet. How come?''

"Was that who you saw?''

"You didn't answer my question.''

"That's because you're confused,'' Calabro said. "You media types get to ask us cops questions, but we don't have to answer. On the other hand, when we cop types ask you questions, you *do* have to answer.''

"Not unless you're arresting me for spilling gasoline in my own home,'' Ben said. "Now how about it?''

Brace shrugged. "We told Ms. Taylor the truth. Sure, McGuire is a suspect, he and your Mr. Johansen are at the top of our list. But we had nothing on him, and why get his guard up any more than it'll already be? If you've got something for us on him, I'll roust him out of bed tonight.''

Ben told them about the fight, gave him what description he could of his assailant.

"This him? Rod Dawson?" Brace said. He pulled out a copy of the photo that Peter had taken, and then, a mug shot with head-on and profile shots. Ben studied them, carefully.

"That's him. The guy was bald. And the size is right, six-one, two hundred pounds. Hard as a rock, when I hit him."

"Could you pick him out of a lineup?"

Ben closed his eyes. Saw the brief flash of light playing on his face: the blue of his eyes, the wide nose, the coarse skin, the harsh slash of his mouth. "I can pick him out. Besides, right about now he's probably taking care of a cut on the back of his head. I hit him with the fire extinguisher."

"Good move." Calabro looked at Brace. "He'll be scrubbing that gas and the foam off himself somewhere right now."

"Might as well start with his home address," Brace said. "Sometimes we get lucky." He took out a cellular phone and began making calls for backup for an address in South Boston.

"Take me along." Ben stepped into his apartment to grab his camera bag.

Calabro looked at Brace.

"All right," Brace said, grudgingly. "Got some more questions for you on the way, anyhow."

"So what was he after?" Brace said. "What have you got that he wants?" The cop spoke easily even though he was making the big Ford fly down the Southeast Expressway, heading down toward South Boston.

"The obvious, I'd guess. A photo. Negatives."

"Of what? What have you got?"

"I don't know," Ben said. "I've been shooting, but I can't think of a goddamn thing that I've captured that's worth this."

"Maybe you wouldn't recognize it. Maybe it's of him talking to somebody he shouldn't be talking to," Calabro said. "A competitive family, maybe. Making alliances that'll get him burned, maybe going around Uncle Clooney."

"The sort of thing we officers of the law might recognize that a paparazzi might miss," Brace said.

"I'll share," Ben said. "I'll talk to my editor, I expect he'll go along. But that's the thing. All that film I shot of McGuire was processed and printed at the *Insider*. This stuff at home is my personal freelance."

"Oof," Calabro said. "Imagine that?" he said to Brace, with a grin. "These goons burn down his studio, all his work, probably take out the building and they don't even get the shots they want."

"Him, too," Brace said, jerking his head at Ben. "They were going to burn him to a crisp, too. Always said these guys were mean. Never said they were smart."

The radio crackled just before they reached Dawson's apartment building.

Ben could barely decipher the fast squawk of words coming from the speaker, but Calabro and Brace looked at each other, and listened carefully.

"Shit," Brace said, as they turned the corner.

A police cruiser was parked in front of the building, and two cops were leaning against the porch rail, coughing. A small crowd of people stood around them, many of them dressed in pajamas. Flames poured out of a third-story window. Brace floored the car and brought it up behind the crowd and then jumped out. He and Calabro pushed their way through to the two uniformed cops with Ben right behind. Sirens wailed in the distance.

"Everybody out?" Brace asked.

"Think so," one of the cops said, the younger one. His face was smoke streaked, but he was regaining his breath faster than the older cop who was wracked with coughs. "We hit all the doors. Heard somebody running down the back stairwell, but didn't see him. We couldn't go for him though, we had to get everyone out."

"What about Dawson?" Calabro asked.

The young cop looked at his partner. "I don't know what Dawson looks like, but Lenny does. Was that Dawson, Lenny? The one up in his apartment? He was still alive when we saw him. He can't be now."

The older cop nodded. He wiped his mouth and broke into a fresh spasm of coughing. Then he jerked his head at the flames that were now roaring out the third-floor window and rushing up the side of the building. He said in a rasping voice, "Yeah, that was him. Couldn't be a nicer end to an asshole like that. Somebody lit him up like a goddamn torch."

CHAPTER 15

JIMBO MCGUIRE TURNED THE SHOWER ON HOT, AND SOAPED UP. HE felt the tension drain from his shoulders, and went through his mental checklist.

Suzanne was drowsing in his bed, and she knew her job.

His lawyer was on alert, a call from a phone booth. The gun tossed off the General Edwards Bridge in Lynn. Unregistered, anyhow.

McGuire's clothes were wrapped around a brick in the bottom of the Charles River. The spare set of clothes in the trunk paid off. He knew he would need to talk to Uncle Patrick, but tomorrow would be soon enough.

McGuire was pleased with himself, pleased that the old moves were still alive and well. Pleased that his time and growth at Stanford hadn't dulled his ability to think fast, to get his hands dirty.

Replacing Dawson would be an annoyance, true. The guy had been pretty good at his work, even if he did have the attitude that he was just on loan from Uncle Pat. Like he was indulging little Jimbo. Tonight he looked like a goddamn clown, standing there, soaked in gasoline, face still white with the extinguisher foam. "He saw me," Dawson said. "I've gotta get out of town. Gimme some cash, will-ya?"

"Why didn't you shoot him?"

Dawson had gestured to himself. "Look at me! He soaked me with this shit. I couldn't take a chance on the flash."

"You should've," McGuire had said, tossing a match. "Odds would've been better."

Dawson had screamed like a baby. McGuire had put two rounds into him just to help things along.

That goddamn photographer. Who could've figured?

McGuire stepped out of the shower and toweled off. He admired himself in the full mirror: deep chest, the proverbial washboard stomach, well-defined arms. He had swum competitively as a kid and still kept up with it, doing two miles at the pool every other day. He did weights at least three times a week. Curly black hair, blue eyes. Winning smile.

Let the fags at the holding cell give him a try, he'd snap bones and dislocate a shoulder or two before they even got close. Assuming they even tried once he passed the word he was Patrick Clooney's nephew.

Most everybody knew to back off at that name, but there was always some amateur who didn't get the news. That was fine with McGuire. He didn't mind an opportunity to show off his years of martial arts training. To show that he wasn't just some punk living off Uncle Patrick's name.

He dried his hair quickly, and then padded into the bedroom and laid out jeans, his favorite oxford shirt, and Nikes. Might as well be comfortable.

He had kept quiet, not wanting to wake Suzanne. She wasn't the smartest girl. So he preferred to keep the talk to a minimum. But Suzanne was ready for him, after all, when he slipped under the covers. She went right down on him, making him gasp aloud. "Jesus," he said. He reached down to touch her. Such heat below him.

The image of Dawson flashed in front of him, screaming. The flames rushing up his shirt, first licking, then covering his face. Dawson beating his hands all over himself, until they too were inflamed.

The image only made McGuire harder. Some guys were meant to lose; some to win. It was that simple. He reached down and touched her. She was soft and firm at the same time. All rounded hip, smooth muscle. Full breasts. He gave her the time off every other day for her aerobics class and it was paying off right here . . . big Barbie Doll hot and alive at the touch of his telephone keypad.

He groaned. "Goddamn," he said. "Goddamn."

She knew what to do to perk up a man who was about to spend the night with the cops.

She took him out of her mouth and moved up his body. "Put it in," she whispered in his ear. "Put it in me, and do me fast and hard. Before they get here."

As it was, he finished just as they arrived.

"Officer," she cried as they were hustling McGuire to the car, tousled and bemused. "He was with me! All night, he was with me!"

CHAPTER 16

Kreiger, the attorney, dropped him off at his uncle's house early the next morning.

"Jesus, when's the guy going to buy the kind of place he can afford," McGuire said, sitting in the lawyer's Mercedes. The house was a pretty enough Victorian with a great view of Boston Harbor.

But it was in South Boston.

Kreiger started to say something, thought better of it, and simply shrugged.

"Good thinking," McGuire said, looking at the guy. Kreiger was a smart bastard. He had been around since Uncle Pat hired him to make that piddling settlement for Ricky Deardron, back when McGuire broke both his knees with a baseball bat for whistling at his girlfriend. They were both thirteen at the time. Goddamn Ricky long since spent the money. Last McGuire saw, he was tending bar at his dad's pub. Drinking the profits; wearing his hair in a pony tail like he was some kind of Vietnam vet. Pissing in his wheelchair, people said.

McGuire strolled up to the front door. It opened by the time he reached the porch and Warren Reynolds stepped out. Reynolds was huge. Late thirties, black wavy hair already going gray. He was wearing one of his hundreds of Hawaiian shirts, glasses sticking out of the front pocket. Those shirts were all the guy wore ever since his one and only vacation to Hawaii. Winter, he'd put a coat over them. All of them were just a little short for his gut. Powerful arms, though. Massive things, as thick as McGuire's legs. Covered with a mat of black fur.

"He's in the kitchen," Reynolds said, his eyes locking with McGuire's for just a moment.

Reynolds and Dawson had gone way back. Together they had broken a lot of bones, repelled four attempts on Uncle Pat's life. McGuire knew of at least three trips they'd made to the airport parking garage to leave a car with a body in the trunk. Things like that bound some guys together.

McGuire knew Reynolds thought he was a punk.

It made McGuire want to take him on. But he knew how it would look, wrestling around on the porch with the hired help. And there was no getting away from the fact that Reynolds was too smart and capable to be just written off as muscle. Before McGuire was old enough to do much, Reynolds had planned and executed two bank jobs that had brought in over a million dollars.

McGuire said, "I bet you were right up there beside Dawson's mama, the last thing he saw as his life flashed by."

Reynolds stared at him, half smiling. His eyes conveying murder. He said, "Your uncle's waiting for you."

Jimbo brushed passed him and went down the hallway. He opened the kitchen door quietly.

Uncle Pat was there at the table, his reading glasses on, the paper open. He looked up and grimaced.

"Long night," McGuire said. "Mind if I make myself some breakfast?"

His uncle stared at him over his half glasses.

McGuire waited. His uncle continuing to give him that look. Finally McGuire snapped, "Am I going to just stand here and starve or what?"

Uncle Pat jerked his head toward the refrigerator and looked back down at the paper.

McGuire whistled tunelessly as he found bacon and eggs in the refrigerator. He put about a third of the bacon in the pan and scrambled three eggs on top of them, and put a couple of pieces of bread in the toaster. "Jesus, I'm hungry."

His uncle said nothing the entire time McGuire's breakfast sizzled in the pan.

Ah, well, McGuire thought. He sat down and began to eat. Looking at his uncle from time to time.

Big old guy with a bald head, still pretty trim for an old man. Massive shoulders. Dockworker, once upon a time.

"You through?" Uncle Pat asked, softly. He folded his paper and set it aside.

"All set."

Uncle Pat swung his right hand hard, smacking McGuire across the face. Those big, dockworker hands. The palm worn smooth and hard as a piece of polished oak.

"Whoa," McGuire said, feeling his jaw. Trying not to let it show how much it hurt. He spit blood into his napkin. "You must still be working out on the weights, Uncle Pat."

"Shut up," his uncle said and hit him again. "You're too smart for your own good."

McGuire considered killing him. The knife was right there. He could probably do it before Reynolds got in.

McGuire let the moment pass. He'd be giving up far too much to do it right now. Besides, the old guy had pretty much raised him, and McGuire came as close to loving him as it was possible for him to feel.

"Now tell me what happened," his uncle said.

So McGuire told him, using another napkin to dab at the blood welling up where his uncle's ring had cut him. He told him right up until the point where Kreiger got him out of the police station. "So don't worry. They've got nothing on me. On Dawson, they had plenty. On me, nothing. I was with Suzanne."

"She'll stick?"

"Oh, yeah. She's not that bright, but she knows what's good for her. Now, if they had *Dawson,* then we'd have something to worry about, but he's . . ." McGuire held up a crust of his bread. ". . . he's toast."

"You think this is funny, you little bastard?"

McGuire locked eyes with his uncle, and the older man threw up his hands slightly and looked away, which was as close to an apology as he would come.

Because, in truth, ''bastard'' was accurate. Though McGuire took his father's name, the man had never actually married his mother. Seems Uncle Pat had killed the original Jimbo McGuire with his own hands in a fit of passion when it came out that he'd knocked up Patrick's lovely younger sister Anna. This was years before she became a drunken embarrassment who had to be institutionalized.

That had taken a good ten years to unfold.

But the night Uncle Pat had killed McGuire's father, he had started trying to recoup from his mistake immediately. He arranged the ''car accident'' for the body, and a wedding certificate for his sister. He sat across from her and made her repeat her story until she had it right: as a young bride of only two hours, she lost her husband when he went out for cigarettes right after they consummated their marriage.

Just about everyone knew the truth, but Uncle Pat made sure everyone assumed the fiction as reality while young Jimbo was growing up. It had, in fact, been Dawson, drunk one night when Jimbo was eighteen, who had spilled it.

The bald fuck had thought it was pretty funny.

Uncle Pat continued. ''What do you think killing your own men buys you?''

''You've seen what we've been able to buy.'' McGuire locked eyes with his uncle.

''Yeah, well, I've seen things go wrong. Lotta people got hurt.''

''Not us. Not you and me.''

''I don't feel good about that bridge thing. There were kids.''

''That could've been anything,'' McGuire said.

His uncle shook his head and McGuire could tell it really weighed on him. This was only about the tenth time he'd brought it up. ''Three kids. I don't like that.''

''We got no proof that was our involvement, caused that to happen,'' McGuire said, somewhat bewildered. Kids, adults, he really didn't see the difference. ''No one has even *accused* us.''

''We know.''

McGuire shrugged. ''If you say so.''

"The whole thing, I'm not comfortable."

"C'mon, I've brought us national, that's all. You *know* it's already paying off."

His uncle made a pushing-away gesture. "I know we're out of control, that I know. And then this with Dawson? He was one of ours."

"You've been telling me since I was a kid the things you've done to people you thought would talk. How's this different?"

"I had permission. That's the difference." His uncle lifted his eyebrows, but his lips twitched close to a smile. "It does make the rest of them pay attention, I'll say that. But you've got to try to keep their loyalty, too."

"I've got a loyal bunch. Paulie would put his head through a brick wall if I told him. Dawson was always too much old school."

"Oh, now you're getting tough on the old school, huh?" Uncle Pat raised his hand, mockingly now. "Next you'll be trying me." He tapped McGuire's chin, lightly. "You know, I'd do you too, if I had to. Make me sad, but I'd do it."

"It goes both ways, Uncle Pat." McGuire looked at him calmly. Let him see that he wasn't kidding.

"Jimbo," his uncle said softly. "I know you've got balls of your own. But you talk to me like that—especially in front of someone else—you're not going to leave me any choice, you got that?"

McGuire gestured to the empty kitchen. "Hey, we're alone."

"You spent your whole life proving how tough you are, far as I can tell. Now use your brains."

"My brains are making us richer than we've ever been."

Uncle Pat lifted his eyebrows. "*Your* brains," he said. "I'm putting Reynolds on your team. He's steady and smart. You could learn from him."

"I don't need Reynolds."

"Tough shit. You've got him." Uncle Pat picked up his paper. "Now get out of here and don't fuck up anymore." He pushed the glasses down on his nose so he could level those cold blues at him directly. "Listen good now—I'm not gonna clean up after you again. Do you get that?"

McGuire didn't move. "You know that I can't just sit on my hands. We've got to nail this last contract."

His uncle didn't look away. "I know that. I just said don't fuck up."

CHAPTER 17

LUCIEN SAID, "SO I HEAR YOU HAD A HOUSE GUEST EARLIER THIS week. Made a hell of a mess."

"Humor," Ben said. "And so early yet." He sipped his coffee.

Lucien was at the wheel, driving fast in his Saab Turbo. They were on their way to Lexington to see Teri Wheeler at the New England Software Foundation. "She got it across that she was an early riser and expected us to be, too. Also got across that she thinks of us as only a step up from the *National Enquirer.*"

"Does she know I'm coming?"

Lucien shook his head. "You might be wasting your time."

"Long as she doesn't spit on me."

Lucien shuddered. "Don't know how I would have handled that." He switched topics. "So how's it going with McGuire? The cops hauled him in, right?"

Ben nodded. He told him how he and Sarah had gone to the station again yesterday and Calabro told them that McGuire had an alibi for the time Dawson was being burned alive. There was no physical evidence to prove otherwise, and though the police canvassed the neighborhood, no one saw McGuire or his car near Dawson's apartment building that night.

Lucien glanced over, his eyebrows raised. "So they just kicked him free?"

"No evidence to keep him. I followed him from the police station, watched him go visit his Uncle Patrick."

"They must recognize your van by now."

"I got Kurt to OK the use of rentals. I'll be changing them on a daily basis now."

"The fact that Dawson was McGuire's boy didn't matter?"

"They say they can't prove Dawson was acting under his orders."

"Jesus." Lucien drove in silence. "So you think McGuire will try again?"

"Could be."

Lucien shifted in his seat. "Hell, next time take your own car."

Ben smiled, sourly. "That's the way everyone feels." Jake's birthday dinner was that night. It would be a "full family" affair as Kurt called it. Meaning all of them would meet at The Top of the Hub, the restaurant on top of the Prudential Building in Boston.

"So what have you learned about Teri Wheeler?" Ben asked.

"Well respected up and comer. Sort of a poster child for the Young Republicans. Twenty-nine, went to Columbia Business School, was a rising star in marketing with Goodhue Software Corporation before stepping away to run the NESF. Now she influences just about any legislation regarding computer software on a national level."

They pulled off Route 2, and made a few quick turns before pulling into a circular driveway in front of an elegant redbrick home with a slate roof. The lawn was a deep rich green. The sprinkler system threw up a fine mist of water, making the grass and shrubs sparkle. Even the air tasted good. Only when they got of the car and were closer to the door did they see the plaque with the name of the organization.

"Not what I envisioned," Ben said. "I figured we were heading toward a little office park."

Lucien said, "This was Alexander Goodhue's family home. He's got a more palatial estate up in Hamilton now, keeps his horses. This, he donated to the foundation."

"How nice of him." Ben judged the value of the property into the millions. The Goodhue family had been a force in Massachusetts for almost a century. Textiles and shoe manufacturing first, then plastics. Computer software in the eighties and nineties. A reputation for conservative politics. "So is this organization just a front for Goodhue?"

"And people who agree with him," Lucien said. "NESF also has a branch in D.C. Apparently, Teri splits her time here and there most weeks. But Goodhue's campaign contributions through the foundation are within limits."

Immediately after they rang the bell a young woman opened the door. She had dark brown eyes, wore a dark blue blazer and white pants. She was probably in her early twenties. "Welcome," she said, after they identified themselves. "Teri is expecting you. Wait here just a moment, please."

Ben and Lucien stood in the hallway.

"Coffee?" a receptionist asked.

"No thanks," Ben said, and stepped further into the hallway. To the right, a large sliding door revealed an office area that was nicely integrated into the architecture of the small mansion. The secretary's computer monitor was tucked deep within a rolltop desk; the lamp appeared to be solid brass.

A young woman came out of the back office, and extended her hand to Lucien. "Teri Wheeler," she said.

Ben recognized her from the photos immediately. She was tall, with an athletic grace, dark green eyes, honey blond hair. When he shook her hand, he was surprised by the warmth of her touch.

"Pretty impressive lot, aren't they?" she said, looking in the direction of the two women on her staff. Both smiled back at him sweetly.

Ben smiled back without answering. They were a little too perfect for his taste. As was Teri herself, on first impression. Striking profile, flawless skin. Her dark blue business suit was nicely cut, accentuating her long legs.

But there was a vitality to her, a secret amusement behind those green eyes, as if she saw what he saw and it tickled her too. She said, "Let me give you the nickel tour."

With what appeared to be practiced ease, she gave them a quick history while walking through the building. She revealed a large dining room with an enormous cherry table with seating for twenty. A beautiful chandelier hung overhead. "We frequently host dinners that bring the right people together." She led them on to a well-appointed library, complete with leather chairs, an enormous hearth, and access to a stone patio through leaded glass doors.

She said, "The NESF is not simply a business organization. In addition to our agenda supporting initiatives within our industry—such as legislation affecting Internet standards and software copyright—we also place an emphasis on supporting leaders who represent strong family values and a traditional moral structure. This is somewhat contrary to the viewpoint of our counterparts in Cupertino and San Jose, which is why we felt a New England–based foundation was necessary. Our tools are communication, education, and we're supportive of legislation that furthers the values we esteem." Over the hearth, she showed them a black and white portrait photo of a slightly priggish-looking man who appeared to be in his sixties. His head was cocked back, perhaps to thrust his otherwise weak chin out further. "Alexander Goodhue, our founder."

Ben stepped forward, inspecting the photo closely. He thought he recognized the style, and indeed, there was the small signature of the photographer. Leonard Penn, one of the top corporate photographers on the East Coast. Ben had forgotten Goodhue Corporation was one of Leonard's major accounts.

"Terrible picture," a voice said from behind them.

"Oh, Alex." Teri Wheeler's smile was a wonder: teasing, radiant, and yet demure at the same time.

Goodhue looked at Ben and winked. "No offense to your profession, of course."

Goodhue was over six feet tall and more physically imposing than the photograph would have suggested. He wore a well-cut sport jacket and wool slacks. His eyes were a bright blue and a bristling gray beard took care of the weak chin.

Teri Wheeler said, "Gentlemen, I'd like to introduce the two of you to Alexander Goodhue. When I explained to him your concerns, he asked to join us for this interview."

Goodhue focused his attention on Lucien. With the easy shift of a man long accustomed to authority, his features hardened. "We all have our jobs to do in life, and I realize you have yours. Nevertheless, what I understand you're about now is a damaging, unnecessary, and entirely erroneous little mission. And I'd like to talk with you about it before it goes any further. Your office, Teri?''

"Please," she said, gesturing him forward.

As she lead them past her receptionist to her office, Lucien wiped his mouth nervously. Ben remembered him doing that before the meeting with Cheever, and he sighed internally. If intimidation was what Teri Wheeler had in mind by pulling Goodhue out of a hat, it was working.

She gestured for both of them to sit on the couch, and sat in the chair across from them. "Mr. Harris, I must admit I didn't know that you would be joining us today. You're welcome, of course, but I ask that you don't take any pictures."

"Certainly not," Goodhue said. He pulled up a chair and leaned forward. "And, in fact, I must take exception to Teri's earlier reference to this as an 'interview.' ''

She dipped her head slightly in acknowledgment.

He continued. "What I'd like to have here is a *conservation*. Off the record.''

Lucien appeared troubled, but after a moment's hesitation, he said, "That's fine.''

Ben looked at him. "Really?''

Lucien's face flushed. "That's what I said. Off the record.''

Goodhue smiled, benevolently. "I see we'll be taking questions from both quarters. That's fine. I'm here for two reasons. One, to protect the interests of an employee who I trust and admire. And . . .''

Here he smiled apologetically at Teri Wheeler. ''. . . perhaps more importantly, our affiliation with Senator Cheever. Ms. Wheeler is our link with him, and she's done a tremendous job. She came to me because she was concerned about the damage a scandal could do to both us and him—and, perhaps it sounds grandiose—and to the country at large if his position is weakened.''

Teri said, "It would be one thing if there was any truth to your supposition. But there simply is not. May I see the photographs you showed the senator? He and I have of course talked about this . . . situation.''

Although she chose her words carefully, Ben didn't get the feeling she was particularly nervous.

Lucien pulled out his manila envelope and laid out the shots. Goodhue looked over them as well.

He said, "What's the harm here?"

Lucien said to Teri, "Can you could tell us about your relationship with the senator?"

"I'll be delighted," she said, glancing quickly at Goodhue. She held her palm out to reveal her office, a big, conservatively decorated room with a beautiful wooden desk and windows that looked out onto a small rose garden. "This is my relationship with him. The NESF."

"You have no other feelings for him?"

"Actually, I do." Her smile was brilliant. "I think the senator is a wonderful man, a committed statesman, and a force for Massachusetts. He broke the Democratic stranglehold on Massachusetts against Senator Kennedy . . ."

"And you know how hard that was to achieve," Goodhue said.

Teri continued. "The senator did that based upon keeping his word. The public is crying out for someone they can trust, and he is that man. I believe that if he continues on track, he could well be the next GOP candidate for president."

Lucien nodded.

Ben said, "Ms. Wheeler, what can you tell us about your personal relationship?"

She turned her attention to him. "I believe I answered that. However, I will say that I'm pleased to call him my friend. A *married* friend. That means something to him and it means something to me." She looked at Lucien and then Ben. "And it means what you are chasing here can ruin the ambitions of one man who is doing his life's work, embarrass and hurt his family, and damage my career as well. For what? Me doing my job." She gestured to the pictures. "There's no evidence of a romantic liaison here for a simple reason—we're not having one."

Lucien made a feeble comeback. That she and Cheever were alone together in the town house, that they were drinking . . .

She was too polite to laugh at him, but Goodhue wasn't.

"For God's sake, gentlemen. So what if she was alone with him in his town house? I've been his visitor, too, am I suspected of having an affair with him?" He laughed at his own comment and then said,

"Isn't she being accused of impropriety simply because she is an attractive young woman?"

Lucien glanced at Ben and gave a slight shrug. He shifted, getting ready to leave. "I really don't have any more questions."

Ben asked her, "How much does NESF provide to Senator Cheever's campaigns?"

"The legal limit," she said. "It's a matter of public record."

"All from Goodhue Industries?"

"Not at all," she said. "We also raise funds from individuals and corporations."

"And influence others to make contributions independent of you?"

She smiled, as if to a child. "I am guilty of participating in politics in America, yes."

"Some of those others going through you . . . do any of them include Johansen's Free America organization?"

"They do not," Goodhue snapped. "While we are a more conservative organization than is perhaps typical for the software industry overall, we avoid extremist organizations. They would only be damaging to us."

"And what do you ask the senator for in return for these contributions?"

"What anyone in our position asks," Teri said. "That he be true to the vision for which he was elected. That he understand the issues in our industry and make well-informed decisions."

"You feel he keeps his promises?"

"He makes no promises to us," Teri said. "However, I share the public's enthusiasm for the man. He's committed to his ideals. Go read his speeches—and then look at his voting record, Mr. Harris."

"I have," Ben said. Which was true. He had suspected Lucien wouldn't come prepared and so Ben had waded through *Insider*'s fat clippings folder on Cheever while keeping up his surveillance on McGuire. Ben had also tried, unsuccessfully, to chase down who might have tipped off Peter to the senator's supposed infidelity in the first place.

The file showed that Cheever voted a straight right-wing ticket pretty much down the line. Anti-abortion, anti–gay rights, active welfare reform agenda. He was a strong campaigner for federal funding for Massachusetts as well as recruiting new businesses to the state. The only step out of line was that he voted for a ban on assault rifles and a waiting period for handguns—a stand that had drawn considerable heat from his own party, faint praise from the Democrats, and the widespread public impression that he was a man who was truthful to his ideals. By and large Ben shared that opinion, even if he disagreed with many of Cheever's political views.

"Guys," Teri said, "You really have nothing here. Don't damage us without cause."

Goodhue turned back to Ben and Lucien. He said, "Understand something. Maybe the rest of the country has turned to the media and Hollywood for their values. But people like Senator Cheever, and like me, and Miss Wheeler here, care deeply about how we are presented to the outside world. Can I assume this business is settled or do we need to take a more formal route?"

Lucien cleared his throat. "Well, I've got to talk to my editor again. But I think from my earlier conversations with him and from what you said today, this is probably the end of it. Unless some other evidence comes to light."

Teri Wheeler sat back. "Good. There's nothing else to come to light, so there's no story."

Goodhue looked at Teri. "I believe you're all set here?"

Ben watched the two of them carefully. Wondering what there was between them exactly.

"Thank you for your support, Alex," she said.

Goodhue stood and put out his hand to Lucien. "It's been a pleasure talking with you, Lucien. And Ben." Goodhue put his hand on Lucien's shoulder. "Now, will you call the senator and tell him just what you told us? I'm sure it'll be a relief."

Lucien was smiling now, apparently looking forward to a friendly conversation with the senator. "I'll be happy to."

CHAPTER 18

BOTH BEN AND LUCIEN WERE QUIET ON THE DRIVE BACK TO THE magazine. They pulled into the parking garage, and headed up the stairway to the office.

"So that's what you're going to tell Kurt?" Ben asked.

Lucien shrugged. "We've got shit."

"You don't think it was interesting that a CEO was acting like some sort of corporate legal counsel?"

"I think it means Goodhue is boffing her himself and wanted to see what the pictures showed."

"There was something between them, but I didn't necessarily catch that," Ben said. "Why would she say anything to him at all until she saw the photos herself?"

"Don't know. Still means we've got shit as far as Cheever's concerned." Lucien continued to jog up the stairs. Ben shook his head. Lucien, the tough guy—now that he wasn't face to face with somebody who might hurt his career.

As they walked into the office, Lucien said, "I'll brief with Kurt myself." He hurried away, not waiting for an answer.

Ben was considering following him in anyhow, when Sarah came out of her office. "Turn yourself around, partner." She slipped the strap of her bag over her shoulder. "We're headed out."

"What's up?" Ben asked.

"An interview with McGuire," Sarah said. "Interested?"

The receptionist, Suzanne, let them into the office waiting room. McGuire was on the phone inside his office, and he looked at them, but didn't acknowledge them.

Suzanne looked at Ben curiously. "Do I know you?"

He smiled. "Don't think so."

She looked at his hands. "No ring. Maybe I've seen you at the clubs."

"That must be it."

"Come say hi next time." She looked in at McGuire. "He's gonna be a minute. And you gotta get checked out by Warren anyhow."

A thick-bodied man wearing a Hawaiian shirt came out of the inside door. He asked them for ID and to open their bags.

"What's your name?" Sarah asked.

"Warren Reynolds." His inflection was flat. A faint smile touched his lips. "Head of security."

"And what does that entail beyond checking ID?"

"Have a seat, Miss," he said, and returned to the back room. Ben saw there was a mirror on the wall that he presumed was one-way glass.

He and Sarah sat watching Jimbo McGuire talk on the phone for almost twenty minutes. He made no effort to hide his conversation, a booming dialogue with someone named Gary about the number and size of the fish he had caught and his best bets in the stock market. He did this with his feet up on the desk, fingering his silk tie. Gucci loafers, tailored linen pants, a dazzling white shirt.

Ben had the feeling that somewhere in McGuire's home there was a stack of *GQ* back issues.

Finally, McGuire put the phone down and gave them a wave to come into his office.

Ben had taken enough distant portraits to know McGuire was handsome, but the shots didn't begin to convey his cockiness. As Ben and Sarah walked in, McGuire stood behind his desk, undoing his shirt cuffs to display rippling forearm muscles. "I'll give you five minutes," he said, waving them to the chairs. Ben held Sarah's chair out for her, and then stepped back against the wall to give himself some shooting room.

McGuire said, "I'd like to put this nonsense to rest. I don't even read your rag, but I've got the cops pestering me with questions about you people. First off, tell me who this Peter Gallagher is."

"You're saying you have no idea?" Sarah's voice remained neutral.

"Never met the man." Suddenly McGuire called out to the receptionist. "Suzanne, did I ever have an appointment with a Peter Gallagher?"

"No," she said, immediately. "Never did."

McGuire put his hands out, palms up. "There you go."

"I didn't ask if he interviewed you. I asked if you knew of him."

"Not until I read about his car troubles in the *Globe*. But that's got nothing to do with me."

"Car troubles," Sarah said. "That's your idea of a joke?"

McGuire leaned into her, turning on the aggression as if with a switch. "Don't piss me off, lady."

"Or what?" Sarah observed him calmly, pen poised over her pad.

Ben released the shutter, taking a fast set of shots of McGuire's handsome face turning hard. It was clear to Ben as he looked through the viewfinder that McGuire was still a kid. A dangerous kid, perhaps, but a kid nonetheless.

"Put that goddamn camera down," McGuire snapped.

"How about me?" Ben said. "When Dawson tried to kill me in my apartment—was that one of your little jokes, too?"

McGuire pulled back, smiling coolly. "I barely caught your name, much less have reason or the ability to send people to your house to murder you."

"I believe the police may have shown you the photos that Peter took." Sarah laid the prints on the table. She didn't include any of the recent shots Ben had taken.

"No," McGuire said, shuffling through them carelessly. "This is the first I've seen of them. . . . Crappy shot of Suzanne, but she leads with her body, so I guess that's not so bad . . ." He shuffled through the other shots. "OK, you see what a nut Dawson was. Started chasing your guy soon as he saw him. I had to call him off."

McGuire's face colored slightly when they came to the shot of him with the old man outside the candy store. "Big shit, you've got me talking to Red Donnelly. He may've been a wild guy in his time, but he's an old man, runs a candy store now."

McGuire tossed the sheaf of photos back to Sarah.

He said to Ben, "You people are lucky I don't go after you for invasion of privacy. Maybe I would if this Gallagher were still alive. As for Dawson, he was an unstable guy. I let him go earlier this week myself. Maybe he was distraught, turned to burglary. I believe he may have had drug problems."

"That's your story?" Sarah asked.

McGuire's smile widened. "No, that's just my attempt to guess at what could've been motivating a troubled former employee. I've got no *real* clue as to what happened. But seeing as you've come to me, I've tried to help you as best I can."

Sarah said, "I'll be frank. We know that Peter was looking at you as an up and coming crime figure on the Boston scene—"

"It's flattering to be seen as up and coming in any field, but . . ."

"And we know the police are looking at you hard as the individual behind Dawson," she continued.

Ben spoke before McGuire could continue his banter. "Just what were you looking for in my studio? Peter took those shots, not me."

McGuire put his palms out. "Sorry, I don't know anything about this. I'm just a young guy trying to do something new here." He seemed calmer now, less hostile than earlier. As if he were enjoying himself.

"And what is that?" Sarah asked.

"I'm a consultant."

"Consulting who? About what?"

"Real estate development," he said. "As for my clients, that's confidential. But the point is that my family has been attacked like this for years, and it breaks my uncle's heart the things people say about him. And because they say it about him, they say it about me."

Here McGuire's voice dropped a notch and he leaned forward slightly. "And that's the tough thing about families." He pointed to Sarah and then to Ben, his voice growing softer. "*You* do something, or *you* do something . . . and somebody's blaming your families next.

Not just you. It's a shame, it's not fair—but there it is. We're all connected to the people we love, and they take the heat right along with us.''

"You get that?" Ben said to Sarah. "He just threatened our families."

"Got it," she said.

McGuire sat back, shaking his head. "That's why I rarely talk to the press. You say one thing, they twist it to mean another."

Behind them, the door opened.

A tall, older man with a shock of white hair strode into the office.

"What's up?" McGuire said.

Ben was interested to see that McGuire's ease of a moment before vanished. He looked like a kid caught outside peeing in the flower bushes.

McGuire said, "I'll be done in a second, Uncle Pat. These folks were on their way out."

Ben saw Warren Reynolds step into the waiting room behind them.

An ugly flush crept up McGuire's neck. "You made a call, Warren?"

"I was driving by, thought I'd stop in," his uncle said.

Sarah and Ben stood, and she put her hand out to Clooney and introduced herself and Ben. She said, "Mr. Clooney, your nephew just finished threatening our families. Do you have any comment on that?"

McGuire laughed.

But the look his uncle gave him showed no trace of humor. "That's nonsense," Clooney said, looking with cold eyes first to Sarah, and then to Ben. "Absolute nonsense." The older man looked at McGuire. He turned his attention back to Sarah and Ben. "This interview is over."

"Uncle Pat, I've got this handled," McGuire said.

"Shut up," Clooney said. He reached into his pocket and drew out a business card and put it in Sarah's hand. "In the future, you got a question that involves my family, you talk to me."

"And how about my family?" she said, flatly. "I already lost Peter Gallagher, my ex-husband."

"Gallagher was your ex?" McGuire said. "You didn't say that."

Sarah continued talking to Clooney. "Do I have to worry about my daughter now? And his kids?'' She nodded to Ben.

"Lady, I don't even know who they are." Clooney looked first to Sarah, and then to Ben. And though his eyes were far from kind, they were steady. "If I got a complaint with you, I'll take it up directly with you. Not your children."

"How about him?" Ben said, jerking his head at McGuire. "Have you got a tight enough leash for him?"

"You asshole," McGuire said, coming around the desk. "You got nothing, you *are* nothing. Now just get the fuck out of my office."

His uncle put his hand flat on McGuire's chest. Clooney looked at Ben and said, softly, "You're looking for trouble?"

"I'm looking for your assurance that you can keep this boy away from our families. That's what I'm looking for."

A smile touched Clooney's lips. "You got it," he said. He put his hand out to shake.

Ben took his hand and said, "Why did you try to have me killed?"

"I didn't." Clooney's hand was smooth and dry, like leather stretched over steel.

"Did you have Peter Gallagher killed? Or is your boy here just out of control?"

"I'm never out of control," Clooney said, as he drew Ben off balance with his right hand, and shoved him from behind.

The move from the old man surprised Ben. Before he knew it, Reynolds had grabbed him and Sarah by their upper arms and was hauling them through the waiting room fast, never giving them the time to get their feet under themselves. Suzanne was waiting with the door open and Reynolds shoved them outside.

"Bye-bye." Suzanne slammed the door behind them.

They stood blinking in the sudden bright sunshine.

"Jesus *Christ,*" Sarah said, straightening her clothes.

Ben rolled his shoulders, both angry and daunted by Reynold's strength. "Yeah," he said. He could still feel the imprint of the guy's fingers on his triceps, and the pressure the old man had left on his hand. "Yeah."

CHAPTER 19

THE FIRST THING BEN NOTICED WHEN HE ARRIVED AT THE RESTAU-
rant that night was that Jake was wearing a blue blazer. Like the girl
at the NESF. Like the one Kurt was wearing as well.

"Hey, Dad," Jake said, standing up to shake his hand.

"Jake." Ben fought back the urge to hug his son tight and muss
his hair. Jake clearly felt he was too grown up for that.

Lainnie, however, jumped off her chair into his arms.

"Lainnie!" Andi said.

Ben laughed as he staggered back. He set Jake's present on the
table so he could support her full weight. Jake sat down.

After Lainnie returned to her chair, Ben placed his hands on Jake's
shoulders and squeezed. "I command you to stop growing so fast.
You'll be in college by the time I blink."

Jake smiled shyly.

Kurt said, "How was your surveillance today?"

"Nothing that can't wait," Ben said. Damned if he was going to
spend his son's birthday talking about this.

"The kids have missed you," Andi said.

"I certainly hope so. I missed them." Ben sat down and looked
out the window. The view of Boston, with the Charles River silver
in the moonlight, was truly phenomenal.

Lainnie said, "I heard Kurt and Mom talking about a fire in your building."

Ben looked at Andi, and she said, "They know there was an accident at your building and your pictures were almost burned."

"But everything's all right," he said. "Including my pictures of you two kids."

"Especially mine," Lainnie said.

"Especially yours."

But Jake didn't look satisfied. He looked at his mother and at Kurt, and then back to Lainnie. He didn't press for any more information. Ben tried to catch his eye, but the boy looked away. Not just being cautious. Resentful, maybe. Perhaps at being lumped along with Lainnie as too young for the truth.

The waiter came and they took turns ordering. Lainnie still directed her attention to Ben without hesitation, but Jake maintained the formal distance of Andi and Kurt. That saddened Ben, but he kept it from his face.

"Lucien says we should drop our investigation of Cheever," Kurt said. "What do you think?"

"There's probably nothing there," Ben said. "But let's talk about this later, all right? I want to hear what's been happening with these two."

Kurt smiled diplomatically, and Andi surprised Ben by touching his forearm. "And I know they'd like to tell you. Lainnie, how about you start?"

She grinned and looked at Jake. "Even though it's your birthday, ha!"

Ben winked at Jake, but he didn't smile back.

Lainnie said, "Molly Rindge threw a party and you know how she's been kind've mean to me? Well, she invited me anyhow and I found out she's not so bad. In fact, her mom and dad are getting divorced like you and Mom, only it's just starting now. So it really sucks, and—"

"Lainnie!" Ben, Andi, and Kurt said in perfect unison. Their combined voices were enough to make people at the surrounding tables look over.

Lainnie was embarrassed. She blinked for a moment, teetering between being upset and seeing the humor in it. Ben and Andi let her see their smiles behind their disapproval. Kurt remained stern. Lainnie came down on the side of giggling.

"Sorry," she said. She finished her story with a lot of "and then . . ." transitions, and Ben settled back, enjoying the rhythm as much as the content of his daughter's stories.

"Now how about you?" he asked Jake.

His son shrugged. "Nothing. Finished up school this week, now I'm off."

"What have you got going this summer?"

He shook his head. "Nothing." He looked down, then shrugged again, and said, his voice barely audible, "Maybe you need an assistant."

Kurt looked at him sharply, and Andi turned to Ben. Their eyes conveyed their concern.

"There's nothing I'd love more," Ben said.

Jake stared at his plate stonily. "But I can't."

"It's just not the right time," Ben said. "I'm all over the place . . . and . . . well, it's just not something we can do right now, not until this business is settled."

"Why?" Jake asked. "Are you still in trouble with whoever hurt Mister Pete?"

Lainnie sat up, her eyes round. "Was the fire about that? Did someone *set* the fire on purpose?"

Kurt put his hand on Jake's shoulder and looked at Lainnie. "Listen, kids, none of us knows exactly what's going on. But the police and your dad and I are trying to find out. But for now, this is a birthday party, and let's just concentrate on things like presents and cake and stuff like that."

"Great idea," Ben said.

"I think the part about presents was a particularly good one," Andi said. "How about we jump ahead of the cake? You go first, Ben."

"Sure." He handed Jake his gift.

Jake took it slowly, still not meeting his eyes. But once he started unwrapping the package, his interest quickened. "Cool!" he said. "A digital camera."

"Which is?" Andi asked.

"I can take the shot and it captures the image digitally, not on film." Jake said. "I can put it directly into the computer, send it onto the net, do whatever I want with it." He turned to Ben directly, his eyes questioning. "I thought you hated these things. Thought you said it was wrong to manipulate images, that people wouldn't be able to trust their eyes after a while, or trust pictures."

"Ah, sometimes I get on a soap box. I do still believe that's true for photojournalism. But for family photos or fine art . . . Who knows? I figured you and I could do some shooting together and after you've done your magic in the computer we can compare results. See if you can pull me kicking and screaming into the digital age."

"You won't have a chance! Hey, maybe we could go to the cabin. We can do sunsets. You'll be stuck with whatever happens that day, but I'll be able to make the sky any color I want. No more missed shots."

"Stuck with whatever happens . . ." Ben growled. "Is that what you kids call reality these days?"

"Reality bites," Lainnie said, pealing with laughter even though all three parents cast a stern eye to her once again.

Jake laughed along with her, his face flushed.

Ben was delighted to see some ego surface in Jake.

"Speaking of creating your own world . . ." Kurt said, pulling a present from under the table.

"I'm as curious as you," Andi said to Jake. "Kurt insisted upon getting your gift from us this year."

Jake hesitated, looking from the camera, to his father, to Kurt. Clearly torn between conflicting loyalties and his interest in the suitcase-sized present Kurt was holding out.

"Go ahead," Ben said. "Open it."

Jake tore into the present.

When the paper was halfway off, he stopped, apparently stunned. *"Whoa."*

He ripped off the rest of the paper to reveal a cardboard box that was indeed shaped like a suitcase, right down to the carrying handle on the top. On the side of the box was a picture of a notebook computer.

"Top of the line," Kurt said, with satisfaction. "Same one I've got. Color monitor and a modem. And I had them upgrade it to the maximum RAM and storage." He picked up the digital camera.

"Take it along on vacation along with this thing here, and you'll be able to make an electronic postcard and send it to all your friends via the net. Fix those sunsets right after you take the shot."

"This is incredible." Jake's eyes were shining.

Ben felt a touch breathless, and hated to feel it. Hated the small-ness of it in himself, hated to think he was competing on this level. But there it was. The computer probably cost about five times as much as the camera. At least several thousand dollars.

"Kurt," Andi said, her hand to her neck, her smile now uncertain. "How much . . ."

She stopped herself.

The table went silent.

Then Jake said, "Are you saying I can't keep it?"

"It's just that we're saving for the new house," Andi said. "I just had no idea . . ."

"We don't have to go through this now." Kurt glanced at Ben. "Jake deserves only the best."

The table went silent again.

Andi looked at the table, and then settled back in her chair.

It was Lainnie who put it into words. She said to the two men solemnly, "Are you two fighting?"

Jake said, "Sssh."

Andi said, "Of course not, honey."

Lainnie said, "They are so. Who won?"

CHAPTER 20

ON THE ELEVATOR ON THE WAY DOWN FROM THE RESTAURANT, Lainnie said, "I want Daddy to put me to bed."

This into the stony silence of the elevator. Andi was looking straight ahead, as were the others.

Ben put his hand on Lainnie's head.

"You're too old for that," Jake said.

"I don't care," she said.

She took Ben's hand and squeezed it hard. "I want you to come home and just do that tonight. Can't you?"

God, not those words again, Ben thought. *I'd love to, honey . . . but . . .*

"You can if you like," Andi said.

"I'm not sure that's wise," Kurt said. "Given Ben's situation."

"I do," she said. "Given that ridiculous situation we just went through in the restaurant." Two bright spots formed on Andi's cheeks, and Ben could feel the anger emanating off of her. "Both of you need to make room for the other."

Kurt's face froze but he didn't argue.

"Can you?" Lainnie said, looking up at Ben. He thought of Patrick Clooney's assurance, cold though it was. *"If I got a complaint*

with you, I'll take it up directly with you. Not your children.''
He smiled at her. "I'd love to, honey."

Ben stayed with her until she fell asleep.

She had talked for a long time, too excited by having him there to fall asleep right away. It was an indulgence for them both; he knew she would probably be upset tomorrow night when he wasn't there.

Hell, so would he.

He smoothed her hair as her breathing evened out. Her hair was sandy like his and his father's. It was easy for Ben to see himself in her. She clutched her fist near her face, reminiscent of the days when she sucked her thumb. They'd had a hell of a time breaking her of the habit. Her room showed her to be teetering between childhood and her teenage years: rock posters—mostly of girl bands—alongside childish illustrations of her own. Dolls leaning up against a stack of CDs.

He ached dully inside, seeing how fast she was growing; seeing how much he was missing.

He kissed her on the cheek and left the room.

The light was on under Jake's door. Ben knocked and Jake said, quietly, "Come in."

Jake looked up briefly, and then turned back to his new computer. "I just backed up the software." He gestured to his owner's manual. "They really want you to do that."

Ben saw the digital camera sitting on the dresser still in its package. Right beside the Buck knife Ben had given Jake the year before. Jake wanted the knife for when the two of them went camping. Something that Ben had somehow never found the time to do with Jake in the past year.

"I need to get this set up first," Jake said, apologetically. "Then I can store the images I get with the camera."

Ben sighed. "It's all right, Jake, it really is." Ben sat on the edge of the bed. "Listen, I'm sorry it got weird at dinner. But you don't need to apologize to me. You've done nothing wrong."

"Uh-huh." Jake went back to the keyboard, apparently methodically reviewing each of the installed programs. His fingers flew lightly over the board, making windows open and close on the screen. "You say that."

He didn't look at Ben. But when he continued, his voice was cool and remote, as if his concentration were truly upon the computer. Ben was certain it wasn't. Jake said, "But what you really mean is you wish I was like you. I'm not. I like doing this, using computers. Kurt knows that, and that's what he got me. He and Mom want me to be me, but you don't."

Ben said, "Since when?"

"Since always."

Ben was silent for a moment. Wondering if it was true. He thought of his own father talking with him in the Plymouth. Ben said, "OK, let's talk about that."

Jake shook his head. "Forget it."

Ben leaned forward. "Look, Jake. The divorce was between me and your mother, not you and Lainnie."

"Yeah . . . bullshit." Jake's face turned red as he wheeled away from the computer and faced Ben. "Bullshit. You divorced us, too."

Your mother divorced me, Ben thought. But he didn't say it. Wasn't kosher to point fingers.

Jake said, "You moved out, right? Now you go put Lainnie to bed, she's gonna be crying most of the day tomorrow and I'll be telling her it's OK, but it's not."

"Jake . . ." Ben reached out but his son dropped his shoulder.

"Kurt would never do this to us," Jake yelled.

"Ah, Jake." Ben waited for him. Feeling bad, but wanting all of it out in the open. Jake had been a soldier about the divorce for far too long. Ben said, "What else?"

Jake's lower lip trembled.

"Come on," Ben said, gently. "Tell me."

At that point, the door swung open.

Kurt.

"I told you this was a mistake." He put himself between the two of them.

"Kurt, not now," Ben said.

"Let's go. You're upsetting our whole household."

Ben's temper flared but he kept his voice steady. "Jake and I need to finish this conversation in private. We'll keep it down." Ben remained seated on the bed.

Jake turned away, wiping his cheek. "Just forget it."

"I won't. Tell me what you need to tell me."

Kurt grabbed Ben's arm and pulled. "C'mon."

It all came together. Peter's death. The man waiting in Ben's apartment. Johansen spitting in his face.

Kurt trying to control every goddamn element of Ben's life. Ben stood up and yanked his arm away. "Let go of me."

Kurt grabbed at Ben's arm again. "We don't want you here."

Ben didn't hit Kurt, but he did push him. Just trying to clear him away, get him out of his face. Ben would think about that later. He did push the man in his own home.

And then Kurt hit him. It was a looping, ineffective punch. Something that probably surprised Kurt as much as it did Ben.

But the blow jarred Ben and before he knew it, he responded with his fists. Two fast hooks to Kurt's stomach, one to his mouth.

Kurt's legs buckled. He grabbed at the open door for balance, but it moved and he fell against the doorjamb and hit his head. He slid down onto his butt.

"Oh, Jesus," Ben said.

Jake rushed over to help his stepfather.

Blood streaked down Kurt's face from his forehead.

"I'm sorry." Ben bent down to help him.

"My God!" Andi stood in the doorway in her nightgown, her hand to her mouth. "What's the matter with you?" She pushed Ben's hands away.

"I'm sorry," Ben said, again. He was genuinely stunned.

Lainnie was in the hallway, her eyes round.

Jake was close to tears and breathing hard to regain control.

"Get out," Andi said, her voice cold and remote from Ben in a way that he had never heard through fifteen years of marriage and a divorce. "Just get the hell out of our house."

CHAPTER 21

BEN LAY IN BED, THE DIGITAL CLOCK SLOWLY CHANGING NUMBERS: two-fifty, three-twenty, four-eighteen. Five-ten was the last one he saw before the alarm sounded at six-thirty and he awoke to grainy eyes and the weight of depression pressing down onto his chest.

Replaying the whole God-awful mess in his head.

Jesus.

He got up and stood in the shower, his body swaying with exhaustion. He shaved quickly, looking in the mirror at the dark thumbprints underneath his red-rimmed eyes.

Ready to interpret the world through them.

Ready to go to work, deal with the boss.

But Kurt wasn't there.

"You look terrible," Sarah said as she stopped by Ben's office on her way to the lab. She peered closer, concerned. "Actually, you look like shit. I mean that in the nice way."

"You can leave now. And I mean that in the nice way, too."

"What's the trouble?"

He smiled. "I'll see you later."

She touched his shoulder and then left.

He bent over the table going through the contact sheets of the prison ladies shoot. They wouldn't have been his first choice for review that morning, but Ed Liston needed some selections for a meeting he was to have later that day with Kurt.

Huey, the darkroom lab attendant, brought the last set of prints over. He gestured toward Kurt's office. "Not like the boss to come in late. Didn't snuff him out, did you, Ben?"

Ben didn't bother to answer him and Huey didn't wait. Irritating people was a hobby for him.

Ben went back to the starkness of the prison photos. With what had happened last night, he felt strangely apart from these women.

He felt that he had changed sides, as if he was no longer a photojournalist hoping to reveal their plight, but an abuser himself.

On the wrong side of domestic violence himself.

It was a hard image to hold; hard to see himself in that light.

I pushed the man in his own house.

True, Kurt's poker-up-the-ass righteous attitude was a factor. True, the pompous bastard had bulldozed into Jake's room as if he needed protection from his own father. And true, Kurt did take the first swing.

But still Ben couldn't excuse himself. *Pushed him. Hit him. Scared the kids. Made both of them cry.*

Andi. "Get out of our house."

Ben bent down and looked carefully at the shot of Maria, the last woman he had photographed that day. Her tough, hurt, scared face. *". . . it feels like love. But it ain't."*

Lisa buzzed Ben through the intercom to tell him the FBI was on the phone. It was Parker. "I hear you had a welcoming committee the night you flew back from D.C."

"What else are you hearing?"

"Can't tell you exactly. But it may be time to go directly to your local police force, see if they can."

"Give me a hint. Knowledge is power and all that."

Parker chuckled. "So I've heard. You remember that bombing down at a black church in Alabama I told you about? Well, we got an informant who says the guy who set it took off for Boston . . . and he would've been there in time for the Gallagher thing. The way the bomb was detonated is pretty damn close to this guy's MO."

Ben sat up. "I thought they didn't know how it was detonated."

"They just didn't tell you. A piece of it was found imbedded in the wall across from your van. A mercury-filled-type motion device."

"So that'd most likely be a connection through Johansen?"

"Possibly. Brace and Calabro are looking at your boy McGuire for a previous car bombing . . ."

"That'd be the one that took out the Gendron brothers?"

"Yeah, that's what they were hoping to match it against. But it was entirely different. Detonator on that was hardwired to the ignition; dynamite instead of plastique."

"Is this guy a member of the Free America movement?"

"I don't know, but he's definitely in the vicinity. Everything I read about him says he's a mean piece of white trash with a talent for blowing things up. Former Special Forces grunt in Vietnam."

"What's his name and address?"

"Ah, now that's going a little too far," Parker said. "Can't have you spoiling Boston Police's surprise. Agent Ludlow from our Boston office is going to lead the questioning about the Alabama charges. He's here in D.C. now. I'll get word out to him to head home, and maybe he can run some interference for you later today. But if you head over to see Calabro and Brace yourself—right now—they might let you come along for the ride."

Ben no longer felt tired at all. "What ride's that?"

"They're going to pick up Mr. White Trash this afternoon."

Ben and Sarah got to the new police headquarters in Roxbury just as Brace, Calabro, and a SWAT team of half a dozen men were leaving the building.

"Let's wait," Sarah said. "Better to beg forgiveness. Let's just follow them."

The two cops led the way in their unmarked Ford with the SWAT team following in an equally nondescript van. Ben kept as far back as he could without losing them. They wound through the city and headed down Commonwealth Avenue past Boston University into Brighton. They turned up a side street and parked. Ben banged a U-turn at the next light and parked the van on the other side of the wide avenue.

"Let's go." He slung a camera bag over his shoulder. He and Sarah walked across the busy street, and then waited for one of the Green Line electric trolley cars to pass before crossing the access road.

Ben took her hand as a car rushed by them on the access road. "Just an old married couple, out for a walk."

She looked startled, and then smiled. "Is this really for the cops, or are you just an opportunist?"

"Both," he said, pleased that she didn't take her hand away. "We'll identify ourselves once we get closer. We don't want to surprise any cops once they start running around with guns."

They continued up the block. Already several of the SWAT members were fanning around the back of a small apartment building. The remaining police were waiting at the front door with a pale-looking man who was standing in his bathrobe, holding a key. Presumably the landlord. The cops held a small battering ram with handles on each side.

Calabro and Brace were crouched before their car, putting blue and white Boston Police windbreakers over bulletproof vests. Calabro saw Ben and Sarah first and said, "Ah, for Christsakes. The two of you, get out of here."

Ben said, "We'll stay out of your way."

"What's the suspect's name?" Sarah asked.

Calabro shook his head, exasperated.

Brace said to his partner, "Let's stop screwing around and do it." To Ben and Sarah, he said, "You two stay behind our car. You might get lucky, get some shots of him coming out with a coat over his head. That's it for now, got me? No more questions."

He picked up his walkie-talkie and he and Calabro ran to the door.

It took a few minutes before things heated up. Ben and Sarah waited behind the police car, watching the cops have a quiet conference on the walkie-talkies.

"Making sure everyone's in place," Ben said to Sarah.

"Golly, you think so?"

"Sorry." Ben mounted a long-range zoom lens onto his camera and panned it across the windows at the front of the building, and then those that he could see in the alley.

He almost missed it at first, but then there was a bright flash of light, and he pulled back and focused carefully.

Midway up the building someone was holding a small hand mirror out the window. Ben could see the mirror was first angled to one side of the alley, and then the man switched hands and angled the mirror to the other side, and upward to the roofline. The lens brought Ben in close enough to see the man's hands. There was a small tattoo across the back of his right hand that Ben couldn't quite identify.

"See him?" Ben asked quietly.

Sarah pressed beside him, looking at where the lens was angled. "Somebody's scoping out the alley," she said. "And I don't think that cop's seeing it."

Ben saw a cop below, looking down momentarily, apparently not seeing the mirror.

The window slid down quietly.

"Not good," Ben said, starting off to tell Brace.

Just then, the landlord opened the door and the cops flew in, the pounding of their feet up the stairs audible even out on the curb.

Ben jumped back behind the car, focusing his lens up at the window. Ready for the suspect to make for the fire escape.

But the window remained closed.

He could hear the cops using the battering ram and a moment later, the window did open.

A cop stuck his head out, black smoke pouring out behind him. The cop coughed, and then yelled out to the officer in the alley. "He come out this way?"

"Clear here," the cop yelled back. "You want me to call a truck in?"

"Naw, it was just set in the garbage can. We got it out."

"That's not right," Ben said.

"He's still in there?" Sarah said. "You think he's hiding in the apartment?"

There was a flat cracking sound, and then another.

Gunshots.

Then they saw him. On the roof. The head peering down into the alley. Bright, short hair. The man jerked back when the cop on the ground looked up.

"Oh, Christ," Ben said. "They're missing him."

The guy jumped.

They saw him for just a second. Just a shape in black jumping to the next building. Then he was out of their view.

"He didn't see him," Sarah said, pointing to the cop in the alley. "He missed it."

Ben said, "Go over to him slowly. Don't surprise him."

Ben ran down the street, parallel to the buildings, back toward Commonwealth Avenue. He reached the next alley just in time to see the guy make it across the third building.

Ben kept up the pace.

Buildings four, five, and six, Ben saw him. The guy made it to the last building, the one along Commonwealth Avenue. He peered out over the edge. Ben raised his Nikon and banged away, the lens bringing the suspect close enough for solid identification.

The way Ben saw it, the guy was trapped.

By now, the cops were probably after him on the rooftops. The guy's best choice would probably be to find his way down through the building—but most likely the roof door was locked from the inside. And if he went for the fire escape in the back of the building, the cops would almost certainly be waiting. Possibly the guy could take a left and continue hopping from building to building parallel to Commonwealth, but that would only give the cops more time to position themselves.

Ben took a few more shots.

Then he saw the guy leaning far out over the edge of the building, his sharp-edged features tense as he craned his neck. He seemed to be looking for something. Ben heard it before he saw it. Another one of the Green Line trolley cars was coming toward him about a block away. Bumping along at about twenty miles an hour, swinging from side to side.

The guy was looking at it.

"Dream on," Ben said. The man was five stories up. Between him and the trolley line there was a sidewalk and the narrow access road lined with cars and trucks on each side. Nevertheless, Ben stopped shooting and checked his film count. A half dozen shots left before he had to reload.

The guy made his move.

He pulled off his belt, and swung over the edge of the building to step out onto a small roof overlooking the top apartment's narrow deck. Laying on his belly, he leaned out over the gutter, looped his belt around one of the pillars supporting the deck roof—and without hesitation, slid off the roof.

Ben's stomach dropped.

At first, the man swung wildly, but he quickly got his legs around the pillar, and slid down.

He did pretty much the same thing to get to the third floor, moving with the efficiency of a soldier.

Special Forces, Parker had said.

Ben got three shots of it, the guy sliding, almost falling, but catching himself.

On the roof of the third-floor deck, he stood balanced on the edge, poised as if to dive.

What the hell are you doing? Ben thought.

Then he saw it. There was a big flagpole angled out from the building alongside the roof. And underneath the pole, there was a UPS truck parked in front of the building. A panel truck with a big flat roof.

Ben could hear the cops coming up the side street now, the tramp of many feet.

The man stood on the edge of the little roof and jumped. Ben released the shutter and caught the power of his dive. The guy made it to the end of the flagpole, and swung through the air to land on the top of the truck with a hollow boom.

He pulled a revolver from his shoulder harness, slid down the front windshield of the truck, and was running on the ground alongside the trolley within seconds.

It began to slow for the next intersection.

Ben took another frame, capturing the man running alongside the approaching train.

Ben turned.

The cops were just rounding the corner. Brace and then Calabro. The SWAT guys not there yet.

Ben saw how it was going to happen. The trolley was half full of people. The guy shoving his way in and taking it over. Maybe shooting the driver, pulling him out of the way and going on for a few blocks. Surrounding himself with more than a dozen hostages.

By the time the cops got back to their cars and around the block to follow the trolley, the guy would be three blocks away.

From there, he could hijack a car just the way he was going to hijack the trolley car.

Ben took the camera from his eye.

He looked at the people inside the trolley.

College students. Near the front, an Asian woman looked out the window tiredly. Behind her was a young mother with two preschool kids who were slapping their hands on the window.

The driver. A middle-aged white man with a tough, square face. The sort of guy who might fight back.

Ben saw the running man cock the gun; saw it with the sort of eye for detail that was truly Ben's talent. Everything else fell away. Ben saw the little tattoo on the back of the man's hand as he thumbed back the hammer on the revolver. Ben felt he actually could hear the click of metal on metal, although that was impossible over the racket of the trolley.

The man's eyes slid over Ben but then came back to the camera. His eyes widened as if in recognition, and then the gun was on Ben himself.

Someone shouted, maybe Brace, and the gunman looked over at them and fired a shot. He didn't miss a step, he kept running alongside the trolley, just about to pass Ben on the way to the door near the driver. Ben saw the door was loose already, partially open. Nothing that would hold up against a good shove.

The guy was less than twenty feet from Ben now.

Calabro and Brace were yelling, but the first of the SWAT team was just rounding the corner.

Ben dropped his shoulder and charged the man.

It surprised the guy and he bounced off the moving train, saying, ''Huh!'' He spun and tripped.

Ben went for the gun, but the guy was too quick. He yanked it away and cracked Ben across the face and then turned to face the cops, the train still running behind him, his back inches away from that moving green wall.

The guy fired three fast rounds at the cops and they dropped to the ground. Ben expect a fusillade in return, but the cops held off, probably because of the people in the train.

Maybe because of him.

The guy turned as soon as the train went by, starting across the tracks. He fired immediately at an approaching car that was already slowing for the intersection ahead. The bullet starred the windshield and the car veered hard to the left and collided with the one beside it.

Ben leapt out and grabbed the man by the legs, taking him down.

A dumb move because the guy still had the gun. He rolled onto his back, and sat up with the pistol steady in his right hand.

Ben shoved himself back, and then there was an explosion of noise, a metallic screaming sound that couldn't have come from him, but somehow felt as if it did.

Ben told Sarah minutes later that he was damn lucky. He told Brace, and then Calabro. For a couple of minutes there, Ben was telling anyone who would listen.

They all agreed with him, looking down at the bloody wreckage of the man that none of them would ever get to question.

Because neither Ben nor the gunman had figured on the oncoming train.

CHAPTER 22

"WE'VE GOT A TERM IN THE POLICE BUSINESS FOR THAT STUNT YOU pulled," Calabro said to Ben. "We call it 'Fucking up.' "

Ben and Sarah were back at the new police headquarters, sitting in an interrogation room. The smell of new carpets and fresh linen-white paint competed with the sweat stink from the previous confrontation.

Detective Brace had disappeared to make a phone call.

A tall man wearing an impeccable gray suit entered the room without knocking. Calabro seemed to know him but didn't like him.

"Agent Ludlow, FBI," he said to Sarah and Ben. Ludlow was clean shaven, with an otherwise handsome face pitted by ancient acne scars. Right now, his face looked thunderous. He said to Calabro, "That was a goddamn important arrest for us. You assured us you had the team that could bring him in and we let you have him."

"Screw your important arrest," Calabro snapped. "I got two SWAT team members in surgery right now. I got to deal with this reporter's interference, who *you* Feebies tipped off."

Ludlow said, "The way I hear it you guys were losing him and Harris here kept him from making a train full of juicy hostages. The way I hear it your two SWAT guys got taken down on the roof by one man with a handgun."

"Yeah, well, you hear shit," Calabro said.

Ludlow snorted. "That's a cogent argument."

"Fuck your cogent argument," Calabro said. "This interfering bastard—"

"Find another scapegoat," Ben said. He had calmed down considerably on the drive back. "You were caught flat-footed and you know it."

Calabro leaned forward, his cigarette breath badly masked by wintergreen mint. "Don't count on your press pass to stop me from kicking your butt."

"Boys, boys," Sarah said. "This isn't getting us anywhere."

Just then Brace slipped back into the room. He put his hand on his partner's shoulder. "Calm down, Tony." Brace looked at Ben, his black eyes shining with animosity. "I just gave your editor a call, tell him the effect one of his employees had on an arrest. It sounds like you've been screwing up on a coupla fronts. Tells me you hit him, right in front of the kids, huh? I gave him a name on the Sudbury police department. He's looking into getting a restraining order, keep you away from him and the family. I think he's got a shot."

"Jesus Christ," Ben said. He sat back in his chair, stunned.

Sarah looked at him sharply. When he looked back at her, she seemed to withdraw slightly, her face closing down.

There was a brief silence, with both cops smiling with grim satisfaction.

It was Ludlow who broke it. "I don't see what that has got to do with anything," he said. "Let's get back on track. There's the physical evidence in the suspect's room. Let's work together here and make some sense of it."

Calabro rolled his eyes. "Is that what they teach in 'media relations' at the academy these days?"

Ludlow said, mildly, "Seeing as the bomb may well have been meant for Mr. Harris here, that he has already been assaulted once, and that Lee Sands drew a bead on him right in front of you, our feeling at the FBI is Mr. Harris should be regarded as the target—not our adversary."

Sarah jotted down Sands's name. She said, "What about that physical evidence? Does it point to Johansen or McGuire?"

Brace and Calabro looked at each other and Calabro grinned.

"Keep your eyes peeled for the evening news. Or maybe we'll do an exclusive with the *Boston Globe*. Either way, your interview is over."

Kurt's secretary, Lisa, smiled wanly at Ben when he and Sarah got back to the office. "Kurt wants to see you," Lisa said. "He's in the conference room."

Huey appeared. "Kurt told me to process this last roll right away."

When Ben gave it to him, he practically scuttled off. He looked over his shoulder, grinning.

Ben looked around the newsroom. He could see it in the studied casualness of the others: the way Ed Liston gave a smile that was more of a grimace before turning; the way Lucien talked on the phone with his eyes following Ben.

Sarah caught it all. "You want me to come and back you up?"

Ben shook his head. "The agenda's longer than what happened to Sands."

As he started away, she caught him by the elbow. "Listen, I'm having a hard time seeing you as someone on the wrong side of a restraining order."

"You and me both."

Ben looked through the window of the conference room. Kurt stared back at him impassively, a notebook and a blue personnel folder on the table in front of him. Ben said, "But I've given some reason, I'm afraid."

Sarah took out her business card, and jotted an address on the back. "Tell me about it. That's my home address. Dinner at seven." She squeezed his hand. "Good luck in there."

Ben sat down opposite Kurt.

Both waited in silence momentarily, simply looking at each other. There was a noticeable bruise on Kurt's cheekbone, his lip was swollen, and there was a small bandage on his forehead.

"What's this about a restraining order?" Ben said.

Kurt didn't answer the question. Instead, he said, "Maybe this thing with Johansen has made you feel that you *are* the news. The police tell me that your showboating resulted in the death of a suspect and put innocent lives in danger.''

Showboating. Ben felt his face flush. When he spoke, his voice shook slightly. ''You haven't even asked what happened and you accuse me of that.''

Kurt's lips curled slightly. ''What's clear here is that we've got personal as well as professional issues that aren't going away.''

Kurt paused. ''So I'll put it to you bluntly. Take the assignment I offered you before. Go out and do the logging story in Oregon.''

Ben shook his head. ''I can't do that, Kurt. I've got to follow this up.''

''I'm not asking you, I'm telling you.''

''You're telling me because you want me out of your life.''

Kurt released a sigh. ''You're not leaving me any choice. Your next option is to resign now, and stay away from the family at least until this business with Johansen is settled. Otherwise, I'll go after you through the court system. For your assault on me, my attorney tells me we have an excellent chance of securing a restraining order.''

Ben said quietly, ''You know damn well what happened last night wasn't just a one-way street. You threw the first punch.''

''My word against yours.''

''Jake knows what happened.''

''And Jake wants you to go away.''

''Bullshit. Are you that insecure? For Christsakes, you and Andi are already married.''

A dull red flush moved up Kurt's neck to his face. ''We're not here to talk about me. It's your career that's the issue. I'm prepared to offer you a two-month severance package if you resign now. Time to work on that book of yours.''

From the folder, he gave Ben a signed release giving him permission to use those photographs Ben had done on work-for-hire basis for the magazine. ''As you can see, we're prepared to be generous.''

He held the severance package agreement, and then put it back in the file. Basically waving it in Ben's face. ''However, if you fight us, you get nothing. You're not union, you'll have no recourse.''

''Nonsense. There are plenty of attorneys that'll take on a wrongful termination.''

Kurt shrugged. ''You might get back on staff—but you'll never get the prime projects again, I can assure you. I suggest you accept that we'll all be better for it if you just move on.''

"You must have been doing some serious lying to Reed and Andi to get them to go along with this.'' Even as he said this, Ben knew he could expect no help from Reed. As publisher, he was far more concerned with advertising pages than he was with editorial. He would leave any such staffing decisions entirely to Kurt.

"Reed doesn't like reporters getting killed,'' Kurt said.

"Since when did either of you hesitate to send me where it's hot? You remember Biafra or Sarajevo? Or that it was you who assigned me to Johansen? This is all part of my job and if I'm not complaining there's no reason why you should.''

Kurt shook his head stubbornly. "You seem intent on putting yourself and others in harm's way. Sarah could've been killed out there today. You think her daughter should lose both her parents for you?''

Ben spread out his hands on the table. It was a little hard to breathe. "Watch yourself, Kurt.''

"You threatening me again?''

Ben said, tightly, "It's not clear yet who killed Peter or why.''

"It is to the police.''

"What'd they tell you? They said there was physical evidence.''

Kurt shook his head. "We're not here to discuss that.''

Ben slapped his palm on the table. "Don't play games with me on this, Kurt! You had Huey waiting by the door to make sure you have my shots for your story, the least you can do is tell me what you heard.''

"Of course *Insider* will cover it,'' Kurt said. "And those photos were shot for a story you were following up in our behalf. There's no question they fall under our work-for-hire arrangement.''

"What about McGuire sending Dawson to my place?''

"I don't know,'' Kurt said. "That's for you to take up with the police.'' Abruptly, he shifted topics, adopting a frank, confidential tone. "Look, it's true that Andi would rather we don't go for the restraining order if you'll agree to stay away. But she'll go along if you don't.''

"That I'd need to hear from her directly.''

"Not at this moment. You've got a decision in front of you right now, before you leave this room."

"I'm not leaving town and I'm not resigning," Ben said.

"All right." Kurt sat back. "That's your choice." He opened the blue folder to pull out another typewritten letter. He signed it and tossed it across the table to Ben. "In which case, you're fired. I'll have Security walk you to the door."

CHAPTER 23

THE FBI TOOK UP FIVE FLOORS AT ONE CENTER PLAZA IN GOVERN-ment Center. Ben waited in the lobby for about ten minutes before a woman of about forty with dark hair and great cheekbones came down to escort him to Ludlow's office. She put her hand out to Ben. "I'm Cynthia," she said. "I want to thank you for what you did for Agent Parker. We like him around here."

Ludlow was pouring himself coffee when Ben walked in. The agent said to the woman, "Didn't I tell you we'd probably be seeing the intrepid Ben Harris sometime soon?"

"The trained investigator knows all," she said, before going back to her desk.

"So what can I do for you?" Ludlow sipped his coffee. His handsome/ugly face was friendly enough, but he didn't wave Ben back to his office. Cynthia looked at him and waited.

Ben said, "Seems that I'll be following up on this story on a freelance basis."

"Fired your ass, huh?"

"That's right."

Ludlow made a sympathetic noise, but there was faint amusement in his eyes. He said, "We'll think of you when we need surveillance photography."

"I was thinking of something a little more immediate."

"Oh, I bet you were. But I have to agree with the Boston Police that investigations are best handled by law enforcement. Give me your card, and if something breaks where there may be some sort of photo opportunity I'll be sure to call you." He winked. "Maybe you can scoop your former employer."

"I understand there was enough evidence in Sands's room that the cops are saying he set the bomb that killed Peter. What can you tell me?"

He looked faintly annoyed. "Weren't you listening?"

Ben held up his portfolio case. "Let's trade. I've been following McGuire for more than a week now and I've got prints of everything. I've gotten through to one informant of Peter's who gave me some background . . . and you said it yourself. I seem to be the target, or at least *a* target for some reason."

Ludlow lifted his eyebrows. "Well, I'm sure Parker told you that this is Boston Police's show and they're pretty satisfied that the bombing was a result of Sands seeking vengeance for what you did to Johansen."

"Tell me why you're so certain. Everyone's just dropping the fact that McGuire sent Dawson to my studio."

Ludlow sighed. "Come on back and show me some pictures."

Inside the office, Ben pulled out a half dozen shots of McGuire going through his day: McGuire in and out of his car; McGuire going into his office. The video grab shots inside McGuire's office, including the two other men around the conference room table. Shots of McGuire with Dawson. McGuire coming out of the police station with his attorney, and then coming and going from his uncle Clooney's house.

"Nicely focused and composed," Ludlow said. "But I don't see anything here." Nevertheless, he looked carefully at all the shots. "These two guys in his office. I don't recognize them from Adam, but I'll run their photos, see if we come up with something."

"Has McGuire's phone been tapped?"

"Not by us. His uncle, yes. But I led a small investigation into McGuire myself soon after he came back from college and we never found any evidence to support racketeering charges."

"Isn't the Dawson killing enough to get a tap?"

"Boston Police tried. Judge said the likelihood of him talking about that on the phone was so little that it amounted to a fishing expedition on our part. And that just won't cut it these days." Ludlow shrugged his shoulders. "Let me see what Gallagher took."

"You haven't seen them?"

"No, and I've asked. Boston Police have used us where they've wanted us. Haven't parted the kimono on those."

Ben laid out the photos Peter had taken. Ludlow shuffled through the pictures fast. He stopped at the one of the man outside the candy store; he said, "So he was with Red Donnelly. Now that might have embarrassed him. Red's a tough old shit. He's one of the boys that gave Charlestown the rep for home-grown armed bank robbers. Supposedly retired to run a little candy store, but he's definitely into loansharking, numbers, that shit . . . and he and Uncle Pat are not the best of friends. Maybe some turf problems going on here."

Ben told him about the meeting at the NESF with Teri Wheeler.

"We ran her name at the Boston Police's request," Ludlow said. "She's there, simply because she's a political consultant. No criminal record."

"Is she part of the Free America group?"

The agent shook his head. "No evidence of that. More to the center. In fact, the D.C. field office tells me there was a move afoot by the GOP to start grooming her as a candidate herself—start her off as a state rep, maybe. Smart, attractive young woman. Makes sense these days. She said no. Wanted to keep focused on the business at hand. She's on just about any national board you want to name that could affect Internet legislation or software standards. Word is she's got informal links that are as strong as steel with other lobbyists from transportation to the NRA. Now Alexander Goodhue himself's got a rep as a right-winger, but not in the Free America league, not that extreme."

"OK," Ben said, waving to the table covered with prints. Showing that he'd done his part. "What can you tell me about Sands?"

"Who was that informant you mentioned?" Ludlow idly picked up a pen.

Ben smiled. "Tell me about Sands."

Ludlow smiled back. "Pretty good for a shutterbug. OK, Lee Sands. Special Forces, made it to the last years of Vietnam, apparently loved it. Forty-five years old, kept himself pumped up like he was an athletic thirty. Has shown up in all sorts of nasty situations, and has spent more than twelve years on two different convictions behind bars. Wasn't the brightest bulb on the planet, but he seemed to have a real talent for destruction. Clever with his hands. That bomb that took out Gallagher definitely used the same type of detonator that took out that preacher in the black church in Alabama earlier this year. He was questioned right after, but he had a couple of buddies provide an alibi and we had to let him go. Now one of those buddies is in trouble himself and is singing a different song.''

"Was Sands part of the Free America group?''

"If he was, he never admitted it. Mind you, I've never talked to him myself. But from what I've read of the report, we considered him more of a rightist zealot than your basic mercenary. Grew up on a hardscrabble farm in Alabama, Bible-thumping father. Vietnam and Special Forces simply gave him some new skills.''

"Alabama,'' Ben said. "Johansen's home state. You think he's working for Johansen?''

"Certainly possible. Again, whether directly or simply taking his own initiative, it's not clear.'' Ludlow slid open his drawer and took out a file folder. "Now you can look at *my* photos. See if you recognize anything. I took these this morning in Sands's apartment.''

Ben opened the folder and found several acetate sleeves holding Polaroid shots of an austere apartment. There was a wide shot of a series of burned photographs laid out on a bedsheet, and then close shots of each. Most of them were burned beyond recognition, but others were just singed.

"These were in the fire?''

"These *were* the fire,'' Ludlow said. "In the garbage can. Apparently, he set it just before running up to the rooftop. Squirted some lighter fluid on them, tossed a match.''

In several of the photographs, there was enough remaining, an edge here and there, which made Ben uneasy at first and then hit him with a jolt. "That's the parking lot behind my building . . . that's my old van . . . that's the hall outside my studio . . .''

He flipped the sleeve and fell silent. These shots were virtually unscathed by the fire.

The inside of his studio. His kitchen. Bedroom.

Ben felt ill.

There were more shots. Close-ups of the van. The undercarriage of the van.

The camera bag.

"Like I said, not the brightest bulb, keeping these photos in his sock drawer," Ludlow reiterated. "Looks like he used them for a reference. Scope out your place, go home, make up the bomb and triggering device to fit right in. Definitely a talent in his own right. Maybe putting the bomb in the bag was his best way of ensuring it was you who got killed. He was wrong, but the logic was there. Or maybe it was his idea of poetic justice. You being killed while trying to take a picture. A preacher being killed just as he was about to preach. See? I tend to lean toward that angle."

"The sort of thing Johansen might order."

"Or Sands might do as his own act of vengeance for what you did to Johansen," Ludlow said. His voice was sympathetic.

Ben felt lightheaded suddenly and had to look away from the agent. It was one thing to suspect. It was quite another to know.

The agent's words crashed over him.

"Either way, the evidence is fairly conclusive that Lee Sands set the bomb—and that he was trying for you when your friend bought it."

CHAPTER 24

"SO," SARAH SAID, WHEN SHE OPENED THE DOOR FOR BEN. "I SUP-
pose you'll need the leftovers to tide you through until unemployment
starts?"

Ben forced a smile. "Sounds like Kurt made an announcement."

Sarah took Ben by the hand, and pulled him in. She quoted,
" 'We're all members of a team, and no matter how talented any one
individual is, the team, comes first.' " She slipped her arm through
his, walking him down the hall. "He said this through a fat lip.
You?"

"Long story."

"Reporters love long stories."

Ben shook his head.

Sarah was wearing black jeans, a slate-blue sweater that brought
out the color of her eyes, and small silver earrings. The effect with
her rich black hair and fine cheekbones was simple, casual, and absolutely stunning.

As it was, he could barely look at her with what he had just
learned.

She said, "I'm glad you came."

He turned from her to take in the apartment. It was a high-
ceilinged Back Bay apartment, with walls painted antique white, dark

wood trim and wainscoting. From the hallway, he could see a view of the Charles River through a bay window in the living room. On the Beacon Street side of the apartment, there were two bedrooms; a kitchen and small dining room were right before him. She led him toward the living room.

Ben's stomach tightened even further as Peter's four-year-old daughter, Cindy, looked up at him from a picture book. Ben had only seen her in photos before, and even those were at least six months out of date.

Unlike her mother's blue eyes, Cindy's were gray. Her fine hair was honey-colored and there was a smattering of freckles across her nose and cheeks.

She's her father's girl, Ben thought.

Ben could feel Peter's presence even though he had never lived in the apartment. There was a picture of him holding Cindy as an infant, his arm around Sarah. The shot was taken in winter, snow-flakes were falling. Ben looked closely. He could see a stiffness to Peter's pose, a bit of withdrawal from Sarah.

"Not the best picture," Sarah said. "Just the last that has us to-gether."

Cindy looked at Ben quietly over the edge of her book.

"Cindy, say hello to Mr. Harris. He was a friend of Daddy's."

The girl continued to observe him, but said nothing. Her lower lip trembled slightly but she didn't take her eyes away from him. Finally, she said, "My daddy's dead."

"I know that, honey," Ben said. Seeing his van explode.

"Why are you here?" Cindy said.

"I'm a friend of your mom's, too."

"We don't want any friends," the little girl said.

"Cindy," Sarah said, a faint warning in her tone.

"It's OK." Ben squeezed Sarah's arm slightly. "I know good manners are important, and I'm sure Cindy has them."

He took his folding loupe from his pocket and knelt down beside her.

"I see you're looking at your book. When my daughter was about your age, she liked to play with this. It makes the letters and pictures really big."

"You've got a girl?"

"And a boy."

"Why aren't you at their house now? Are you divorced?" At four, she had no trouble pronouncing even the last word.

"Yes."

She looked at him somberly.

After a moment, he ran the loupe over the page, magnifying letters and bits of the picture.

"Like it?" He tried to give her the loupe, but she folded her hands in her lap.

He set it on the table beside her. "It's here if you want it."

Sarah told her daughter to say thank you, which the girl did, in a small voice. Her eyes no longer met Ben's.

"Cindy's already eaten," Sarah said. He followed her into the dining room. "We're having Cornish game hens and wild rice."

"Sarah . . . please sit with me." Ben pulled up a chair at the end of the table so they could talk quietly. He told her what Ludlow had showed him.

Sarah's face turned pale as she listened. She sat back, and sipped her wine.

Ben waited.

Finally, she said, "It does seem different, actually knowing. But it's what I suspected since we saw Sands this morning. It was certainly the way the police were headed. Kurt told me some of this as well, from conversations he had with the police this afternoon. Not in this detail, but enough."

"Maybe I should leave."

She looked at him evenly. "Go if you want to. I could've called you if I didn't want you to come. I didn't because I know you did the right thing back in that barn. And if that's what ended up killing Peter then it is certainly someone's fault, but it's not yours. Sands is dead. Maybe they'll put Johansen to death for it someday. If so, I'll go cover the story if they let me. But *you* didn't do this to Peter and I'm not holding you accountable."

"She would," Ben said, inclining his head toward Cindy.

"Probably. But that's not a conversation I'll be having with her for many years." Sarah put her arms around Ben and whispered in his ear. "You did nothing wrong."

*   *   *

Ben poured the wine while Sarah served the dinner. They ate in silence, both concentrating on the food. Ben found he was famished, even though he was swaying from exhaustion. He realized he hadn't eaten all day.

"I'm sorry about Cindy's reception," Sarah said, quietly.

"Don't be. Has she reacted this way to other men before?"

Sarah shrugged. "I've had a few dates, here and there, but I always just met them someplace. One four-month disaster with a *Washington Post* reporter that I broke off."

Sarah kept her eyes on Ben for a half second before she returned to her meal. "I suppose Peter told you about how he and I broke up."

"Some," Ben agreed.

Sarah waited.

"The way he tells the story, he blew it."

"We both did." Sarah kept her voice low so that Cindy couldn't hear. "The fact is, we got married for the wrong reasons. I wish I could blame it on youth, but I wasn't *that* young. I was so enamored with what we were together as a team that I just thought it'd extend right to our wedding bed. I respected Peter so much, and just *liked* him so . . . but in that first year, not long after Cindy was conceived, I knew that I'd made a mistake. Before Cindy, our life was like a roller-coaster anyhow, the kind of stories we were chasing. Sometimes after finishing something big, he would get drunk for a day, say he was just chilling out. After that, he'd pull himself right up, barely touch a drop. I didn't worry about it.

"But not long after Cindy was born, he took on a story in Papua New Guinea. I couldn't go, because Cindy was too young. The U.S. has spent over a billion dollars in the past twenty years trying to eradicate malaria and it's come back stronger than ever, defeating the drugs. Classic case of a reporter thinking he was invulnerable to everything around him. The mosquito didn't care about Peter's press pass. He came back with malaria. And I saw a side I had never seen of him before. He was so depressed because he couldn't keep up the pace . . . and he just gave up for a while. He and I were always competitive, but because we were so well matched, workwise, it was fun.

Both of us could hold our own. Once he couldn't, he turned to drinking . . .

"Finally, it looked like he was on the road back. I had given him an ultimatum not long after Cindy reached her first birthday. Us or the bottle. And he took me seriously. He quit drinking, his health was far better. He began to take on more assignments, and we were given a couple to work on together again . . ."

Sarah shook her head.

"Then I picked up Cindy at day care one night, came straight home, and found him with this girl, Pamela Bartlett, this cute little summer intern from Columbia J School. Kid who you knew would be a rising star. Hell, he was in his mid-thirties, I wasn't even thirty yet, and I came home to find him in bed with this *kid.* And he was drunk. Both of them were. Pamela got dressed in seconds flat, just said, 'Sorry, Sarah,' like, 'God, isn't this *embarrassing?*' She scooted out of there while he just lay there, waiting."

"Sounds like he burned his bridges on purpose."

"That's right," Sarah said. "He got up, started packing. Weaving around the room looking for a suitcase. I let him. I let him go out and get a hotel that night, and we were even cordial two days later when he showed up and apologized and said he would be looking for a job out of town. I remember thinking that it would either kill him or cure him."

"He was never much of a drinker here," Ben said. "He was careful about it."

"I certainly thought of picking up the phone about a hundred times. We were both lonely, these past three years. When I got the job at the *Times* we saw more of him. He'd come down to the city, take Cindy out. That made it harder in some ways, because I could see he wasn't drinking, he seemed to have his head on straight."

She looked down at her glass. "He asked for another chance, but I said no. I loved him, but not the way I needed to."

"So why this?" Ben asked. "Why did you quit your job, come to *Insider,* and invest so much in finding out what happened to him?"

Sarah looked up from her glass. "When it seems as if I don't care? That's what the cops think, that I'm just here for the story."

"That's not what I think."

There was a glint in her eyes that she quickly brushed away. "The one thing Peter and I had besides Cindy and a really good friendship that we screwed up . . . was that we were both good at digging up the truth. Even when this time the truth meant we didn't love each other well enough to go through the hard stuff together. So I figured for him, for me, and for Cindy someday, I should come here and at least find out the truth about what happened to him."

Sarah poured more wine for them both. "And since we're on the subject of the truth, tell me why Kurt is walking around with a fat lip."

Ben looked at her carefully. He believed he saw—and *wanted* to see—more than simple curiosity.

"C'mon," she said, kicking him lightly under the table. "If you're a thug, I want to know it before I fall for you completely."

"Is that what you're doing?"

Her gaze was steady. "You're telling me I'm alone in it?"

"No. You're not. It's just that everything is so . . . complex."

"Tell me about it," she said, looking over at Cindy sitting in her chair. "And tell me what happened with Kurt."

Ben told her about the dinner, the argument with Jake. About hitting Kurt. She listened well, her eyes intent upon him. He felt no sense of judgment from her, which he sincerely hoped was not simply a reporter's trick.

When he was done, he felt relieved. Somewhat ashamed, left wide open . . . but relieved. "So," he said. "That's *my* baggage. Want to skip dessert?"

She looked at him carefully. "Is this a one shot deal? Or has this happened to you before?" She smiled faintly. "Don't lie now, I'm a trained reporter. I can find out."

"Check all you want," he said. "My one and only brush with this kind of thing."

"And Kurt hit you first?"

Ben nodded.

She considered him carefully, and then said, "OK. Let's say that's the end of it and take it from there."

She turned and opened a cardboard bakery box to reveal two raspberry tarts and a selection of cookies. "Ta-dah. I bought them myself." She asked Cindy if she wanted to join them for dessert.

Ben turned and was pleased to see that Cindy had picked up the loupe and was curiously looking through it at the pages of her book.

He smiled. As he did, he thought abruptly of Kurt handing that expensive present to Jake. Buying his way in. As Ben had reflexively just done himself.

Cindy saw Ben looking.

Abruptly she drew back her arm and threw the loupe at the fireplace, shattering the glass.

"You're not my daddy!" she cried. "You're never going to be my daddy!"

Cindy began crying. Big, shivering sobs that Ben knew were for real.

Sarah left the table and picked her up. "Sssshh, ssssh. You're all right, honey. You're all right."

"I know that I won't, Cindy," Ben said, quietly. "Believe me, I know."

CHAPTER 25

"SHE'S ASLEEP," SARAH WHISPERED AS SHE JOINED BEN IN THE living room a half hour later. He had swept up the broken glass and was sitting on the couch looking at the empty fireplace.

"I made us some coffee," Ben said. "I hope you don't mind."

"Not at all." She sat beside him, tucking her leg under herself as she had that day in the van. "As long as you're not turning too serious on me."

"Might have to."

"Uh-oh," she said. "Cindy's scene scared you off?"

Ben smiled. "No. Gave me some insight, but she certainly didn't scare me away."

"So what is it?"

He took her hand. "It's those complexities."

"How about I list them? Let's see if I've got them all: the bomb that killed Peter was probably meant for you? You were his best friend and best friends don't date the other guy's girls? You already have two children and troubles of your own?"

"Add in that I don't know if I'm still a target. Johansen has more than a few nuts he can send my way. And I still don't know why Dawson was in my studio. I'm keeping my distance from my own family, why should yours be different?"

"All valid points," she said. "Tell me what you *want*."

He hesitated, just looking at her.

Then he reached over and touched her face, running his hand down the line of her jaw. She closed her eyes, and let him. "I want this." His voice grew hoarse. "I've wanted to do this since I met you."

She opened her eyes. "And I've wanted you to." She grinned, suddenly. "Ever since you went into McGuire's wearing that ridiculous pizza-man outfit, anyhow . . . I know you're a good man, Ben. I simply know it. Everything else is truly complex. But you didn't kill Peter. And I've already shoved my face in front of McGuire and Johansen, and so those risks are mine just as much as they are yours. The damage is done. What're we going to do about it?"

He leaned forward and kissed her cheek. She closed her eyes and he kissed them, feeling her lashes against his lips. When she turned her mouth up to his, he felt as if he were drinking from her. He pulled her close so the swell of her breasts pressed against his chest. And though he was as excited as a schoolboy, he didn't feel particularly nervous. There was a sense of calm underneath it all, as if they had done this before, or at least knew it was coming.

She took his hand and led him to the little office off the living room and closed the door.

Ben quickly opened a small pullout couch while Sarah lit a candle near the window. They turned to each other, awkward for only a moment before she began unbuttoning his shirt. The top of her head came just under his chin.

She said, "I want to see you."

Once his shirt was off, Ben said, "My turn," and pulled off her sweater. He stepped behind her to help her draw off her jeans. Ben felt his throat constrict and his breathing began to rush as he explored the surprising voluptuousness of her body. She turned around and tugged at his belt. Moments later, he arched forward to receive her touch, shivering with pleasure.

Although there was urgency, they didn't hurry.

"Where were you hurt?" she asked, and kissed his scars along his back and touched his leg lightly, her hand warm. She had him turn around and worked her way up, until her mouth was on him. She took her time, teasing, and licking. Looking up at him in the candlelight.

With that, the urgency overwhelmed the essential calmness of their lovemaking. Ben drew her up. For that first time, they never made it to the little bed. She wrapped her arms around his neck as he slid into her and they kissed as he stumbled against a chair, her desk, and finally against the wall.

They made some noise, to be sure. But even when they climaxed together minutes later, they kept their cries between themselves, between their tightly pressed lips.

All passion aside, they didn't want to wake Cindy.

He awakened as she was pulling another blanket over them. He looked blearily over at the digital clock on her desk. Just before three-thirty in the morning. She was silhouetted against the windows, naked in the moonlight. It was cold in the room and he welcomed the blanket.

"Get in here," he said.

She scooted in beside him and he rubbed his hands over her quickly, warming her. He said, "Goose bumps."

"Mmmm," she said. "I just made the rounds, put another blanket on Cindy, too. I thought Boston was hot in the summer."

"It's whatever it wants to be." He hugged her tight, reveling in the newness of it all. He said, "I guess I must've crashed right after."

"Like a big tree. No time for chitchat and snuggling." She rubbed her face against his chest, her nose still cold. "You're a terrible bum."

"We can talk now," he whispered.

"Uh-uh," she said, grasping hold of him. "Save it for later."

Afterwards, she turned her hip into him and he spooned around her.

She said, "You must think I'm such a slut."

He kissed her hair. "That's just what I've been thinking."

"It's been almost a year for me."

"That *Washington Post* reporter? I'm jealous already."

"Don't be. It was a disappointing four months." She turned to look at him in the faint moonlight. "Thanks for reintroducing me to how good it can feel."

"The pleasure's all mine."

"Not true," she said. "But was it just the horniness? From both of us?"

He thought about it. "Not from me. Maybe for you? Was I just some sort of substitute for Peter? A way for you to say good-bye?"

He felt tears against his chest. "No. Not a substitute. But maybe good-bye."

"Hey," he said, running his hands down her back. "You're missing him?"

She nodded. "Already you and I have something that Peter and I never really had. I can feel it. He's dead and gone, and he's never going to have the chance to get it right."

CHAPTER 26

BEN KISSED SARAH GOOD-BYE AT THE DOOR AND STOPPED ONE flight down to put his shoes on. He got behind the wheel just before six and headed back toward his apartment. Instead of getting onto the faster Storrow Drive, Ben circled around to head up Commonwealth Avenue and enjoy the view of redbrick town houses, the green of the park, brilliant with early morning dew.

The morning air was still brisk so he cranked up the heat and rolled the window down to take in the fresh breeze as he drove through Boston on the way back to his apartment.

He was thinking about the difference of a day.

About the drugs his body must be releasing into him to make him feel this way. He had still hit Kurt in front of Jake; he was still out of a job; the police had pretty much confirmed that the bomb that had killed Peter had been meant for him. There would probably be articles about it in the morning editions of the *Globe* and *Herald*.

Sleeping with Sarah should've only compounded his problems. Probably *did* compound them.

But he didn't feel that way.

He probed himself lightly, looking to see if the euphoria was going to fade. He hadn't had all that many relationships since his divorce— two, exactly—and he knew this morning-after felt entirely different.

In both cases, he had driven away from those first nights together with regret seeping into his system.

The first was with a woman he met at a bar in Boston. They parted amicably at the end of a month.

The other was with Janine Gold, a longtime photographer friend at the *Boston Globe*. She had left Ben at the end of three months, with tears and recrimination.

Ben still mourned their ruined friendship.

But what had happened between him and Sarah felt good, felt right. In fact, Ben was feeling at the moment that he could deal with whatever came his way: Johansen, McGuire, and any of their minions. Even Andi and Kurt.

And so it was in this mood that he swung into his parking lot, just as the sun began to rise. He was only faintly aware that there was an unfamiliar car parked next to his space, and that the windows were fogged from the inside.

He was three steps away from his van, heading toward his apartment building when the implications of that clicked. By the time he'd turned around, a big man had climbed out of the black Ford sedan.

"I came for it," the man said. "Give it to me, you spying son-of-a-bitch."

Ben didn't even recognize him at first.

Instead, Ben took in that the man was wearing an expensive blue suit, and clearly quite drunk. That even though the man was striding forward with a heavy belligerence, he held no weapons—other than his balled fists.

Ben started to say something, but thought better of it. Then he said it anyhow. "Senator Cheever, what the hell are you doing?"

Cheever stepped forward. Staggered forward.

"Shut up. Fucking snoop." The senator's voice was thick. Ben could smell the bourbon on his breath.

"Came to get it," the senator said. "Then sat here the whole goddamn night, waiting while you're out spying on some other poor son-of-a-bitch. I figured I'd save somebody else the shit I've been going through." He stepped closer to Ben. He was equal in height and probably weighed another twenty pounds. Some of it was soft, but the way the blood was pumping in the senator's face, Ben knew it wouldn't be easy to stop him once he got started. "Maybe I'll shove your face in," the senator said. He put his hand on Ben's chest and pushed.

Ben stepped back easily. The senator almost fell. He regained himself, looking around the parking lot in some surprise. Carefully, he refocused on Ben. "After I go to work on your career, you'll be lucky to cover weddings."

Ben said. "Senator, I don't know what you think I have. But come on up and we'll talk about it."

"Don't bullshit me! You're trying to ruin me with that fucking camera. What the hell did I ever do to you?"

Then the senator waved away that last bit, apparently disgusted with himself. "Stupid-ass question. I can take my battles in public . . . but doing it like this. I don't get it. You didn't seem like that kind of guy. Then I checked up on you, found you were the guy who took down Father Caldwell."

Abruptly, the senator staggered over to Ben's van and braced himself against it heavily. He squinted at the morning sunlight and said, "I'm so fucked up."

"Come on." Ben took him by the arm. "I'll make you some coffee."

The senator leaned against the back of the elevator as they rose to Ben's floor. His lower jaw was slack, and he rubbed his face often.

Once inside the studio, Ben waved the senator toward the easy chair near the balcony.

The senator sat down heavily. He was still wearing his suit coat and looked uncomfortable. He picked at his jacket for a moment, then apparently realized he'd have to stand to take it off, and gave up on it.

"Just curious." Ben slid open the balcony door to get some fresh air. "You just didn't strike me as the drinking type." Ben put a cup of instant coffee in the microwave to heat.

"I'm not supposed to be," Cheever said. "I'm supposed to be a fucking paragon of virtue. Usually don't even swear. I say that profanity shows not only a weak vocabulary but a weak mind. Fucking pompous ass that I am.''

''Uh-huh,'' Ben said, coming to sit across from him. ''The coffee will be ready in a minute.''

The senator continued. ''My dad was a drinker. It looks like I got his genes there. That's why I don't usually have more than a glass of wine at fund-raisers, maybe one at dinner or with friends. I get drunk, I get just like he'd get. Like this. My mom held us together, brought me up right.''

''So you've done this sort of thing before?''

Cheever snorted, caught somewhere between amusement and dismay underneath his drunkenness. He raised his right arm and pointed, as if responding to a question at a press conference. ''Ah, I'd have to say to the reporter in the front, this is my first and only time I accosted a journalist at his home. And I will certainly reprimand my driver for leaving a pint of bourbon in the glove compartment— although I, of course, take full responsibility for my own actions, regrettable though they may be.''

The senator burped. ''How's that? If you've got your quote, maybe you'll give me that fucking picture and the negative and call me a cab so I don't kill anybody on the way home.''

Ben saw the coffee was ready and he put the mug into the senator's hands. ''Drink this.''

Cheever took a couple of sips and carefully set the coffee on the end table. ''You know, I'm not a rich man. My dad went through what we had. He left me the town house and that's it. Beyond the campaign funds, it's Mariel's family that had the money, the connections that primed the pump to get me where I am.''

''And so, upsetting Mariel would play hell with your career.''

The senator looked at Ben sharply. ''I love my wife. My kids. Maybe you think that's some sort of joke, that a politician is just a robot that says platitudes . . . and sometimes that's true. But with me it's not. Not when it comes to Mariel and the boys . . .'' He rubbed his face again. ''I don't know how it happened, exactly. Teri and I were working together so closely . . . young woman, so attractive, so smart. She's a power in her own right, yet she admired me. I lost my head.''

"Sure." Ben believed Cheever meant what he was saying. At least for the moment. The senator's expression was turned inward and Ben could imagine the surge of maudlin feelings: the powerful rush of self-pity, twisted affection, and remorse.

Soon, Ben would be crying right along with the guy.

Ben said, "So exactly what pictures do you think I have? Lucien and I showed you everything."

Cheever shook his head and then raised his right hand angrily, and then put it down again on his knee. Apparently trying to control his temper. "Look," he said, "let's just cut the shit here, OK? I can't figure you out, mister, I really can't. You don't seem like a bad guy. That thing with Johansen . . . I meant it when I said I admired you. But then I found out you were also the one who screwed Father Ray. Hounded him until he killed himself."

"Let's stick to the present," Ben said. "What do you think I have?"

"You *know* what I'm talking about."

Ben shifted gears. "Did you send somebody after Peter?"

"I don't know a damn thing about your precious Peter Gallagher."

"Well, then both you and I are confused," Ben said. "So why don't I call the cops and the FBI and maybe they can come help sort this out for us."

Fear flashed into Cheever's eyes, but his chin lifted slightly. "We can do that," he said. "I guess I ruined my career. I'll take the hit. But you're going down with me, too. Frigging hero photojournalist is really a frigging blackmailer." Suddenly he swept the cup of coffee at Ben, but his aim was so bad that most of the coffee sloshed on his own leg and the cup missed Ben and smashed on the floor.

Ben sighed. "Let's try this again. The photo. It's of what?"

Cheever looked at the smashed cup in some surprise, then started to wind himself up into indignation again. As he started to get on his feet, Ben stood up and put his hand on Cheever's shoulder and shoved. "Sit down, Senator."

The senator tried once more, and Ben shoved him down again. The third time, Ben simply leaned hard on Cheever and got his face up close and said, "I don't want to dance with you anymore, Senator. Tell me what photo you're talking about. Now."

Cheever looked confused. He shoved Ben's hand away and this time Ben let him. The senator felt inside his right pocket and pulled out an envelope. He handed it to Ben.

Ben took out a folded five-by-seven black and white photo. Ben flipped it over. It was on standard black-and-white photographic paper, dog-eared from being folded and smoothed many a time. Ben had a sudden image of Cheever studying this shot in private, anguished by the implications.

It was from the same scene as those that Peter had shot—through the window of Cheever's town house. Only in this frame, Cheever was behind Teri Wheeler, his hands pulling her hips back against him. He was kissing her neck, as she arched her head back, laughing. Though it wasn't the clearest shot, there was no doubt it was the two of them. And while they were both fully clothed, there was also no doubt that this was an intimate moment between them, nothing that could ever be construed as that of a casual kiss between friends.

Ben reached back in the envelope. There was a white sheet of paper with a stark laser-printed message:

You have to ask yourself three questions:
1) What will Mariel and the kids think?
2) What will divorce and scandal do to your career?
3) Isn't avoiding questions one and two worth a one-time $200,000 investment?
Get the cash together, Senator.
We'll let you know when and where.

"I see," Ben said.

"Yeah, you see," the senator said. "Fuck you and your two hundred thousand dollars."

"Senator," Ben said, quietly. "Look at me."

When he was sure he had Cheever's attention, Ben said, "I didn't take this picture. I'm not blackmailing you."

Cheever held his gaze for a moment and Ben saw doubt flicker across the senator's face. And then he rolled his eyes away. "Ah, cut the crap. You and that little shit reporter walked into my office with all those other shots you took, and it's obvious they were taken at the same time. I should've known better than kissing her like that in front of the window, but she was right there and I'd had a couple of glasses of wine and I just did it.''

Ben looked at the picture again. "It does look like it was shot from the same angle," he said. "But I didn't take it. I didn't take the others, either. I was on vacation in Maine when these were taken. Lucien and I let you think I took them when we came in on the interview to add a little pressure. But the truth is, Peter took the shots we showed you himself. And this one wasn't in it."

"You're lying." The senator's voice was harsh, but Ben could read the uncertainty in the man's eyes.

"I'm not," Ben said, mildly. Not that he felt that way inside. The shot *did* look like it came from Peter's series.

"When did you get this?" Ben asked. "And how?"

The senator's stared at him, clearly debating whether or not answering would be participating in a charade. "In my mailbox at the town house. Marked 'Personal.' After I got the call."

"What call?"

"*Your* call. Or your buddy's. Whoever 'we' is."

"What'd he say?"

"That I'd been indiscreet and he had a picture to prove it."

"How'd he get through to you?"

"Told my secretary he was Senator Atkins from Missouri. So naturally, I took the call. Said that I should go downstairs and open my own mail to find out what he meant."

"Was this before or after Lucien and I interviewed you?"

"After."

"How long after?"

"Three days," Cheever said. "What'd you want to do, look me in the face first? See if I'd fold? Well, I won't."

Ben took his calendar from the wall and tossed it onto the senator's lap. "Show me."

Cheever sniffed, and then studied the calendar. "Right here," he said.

Ben looked over his shoulder. The senator's forefinger was resting on the date two days *after* Dawson had been waiting for Ben in his apartment.

"You're sure?" Ben said.

"Positive." Cheever fumbled inside his jacket pocket and pulled out a leather day timer. "See, right here. I had two speaking engagements the day before. I was in the office this day, and that's when he called."

Ben leaned forward. "There was a man waiting in my apartment who tried to kill me—and then tried to burn every photograph in those file cabinets, Senator. What do you know about that?"

Ben had been reading people's faces through the lens for years. Reading fear, anger, happiness—and reading the truth and lies. There were all sorts of ways to lie. The bad ones shifted their eyes away and made deprecating gestures with their hands, their bodies denying the truth of their words. Or they took on an overly casual tone and delivered pat, well-thought-out answers with honeyed sincerity to every question.

The good ones could look you straight in the eye and with a catch in their voice tell you a whopper that was full of the details and inconsistencies that were often representative of the truth.

Because Cheever was a politician, Ben expected him to be good.

But when he saw the senator's reaction, Ben decided abruptly that he might be actually hearing the truth. There was a sudden sallowness behind Cheever's ruddy skin, something that was probably impossible to fake. A blank look crossed his face, and he said, "Oh shit, this can't be getting worse. Somebody tried to *kill* you?"

"And burn all my pictures," Ben said. "So who'd you tell that you had a little indiscretion problem?"

"No one! Besides, you said this happened two days *before*—I didn't even *know* I had a problem then."

Ben looked at him skeptically. "Even so, you're telling me that you don't have anyone assigned to your security that you could turn to with something like this?"

"I do. Brad Cole. But I wasn't going to get into that with him. Then *he'd* own me. Anyone you tell owns you." The senator's eyes flashed. "You may think it's a joke, but I'm an honest man. As honest as I can be and still get the job done. Either you or I worked it out between us, or I was going to tell you to screw."

Ben considered the senator. He was sobering up fast.

Cheever winced when he looked out at the sunlit balcony. "Jesus, my head hurts." He looked over at Ben ruefully. "You really didn't take that photo, did you?"

Ben shook his head.

Cheever laughed, shortly. Without mirth. "God, I've just dug myself a deeper hole here, haven't I?"

Ben ignored that. "Tell me something. Did you ever hear from Peter on any of the photos? Not just this one, but the others, the ones Lucien and I showed you."

Cheever shook his head. "I told you, I thought you had taken them. First I saw of them was when your reporter laid them out on my table. When Gallagher came to me, he just had rumors. No pictures."

"Did he say where the rumors came from?"

The senator made a snorting sound. "Of course not."

Ben looked at the shot again and then got up and went to his bag and pulled out his file folder of photos. He ran through the ones Peter had taken and the senator lumbered to his feet and looked over Ben's shoulder while he laid them out.

Ben went through the shots of McGuire. "Do you know this guy? How about these two people with him at the table?"

The senator studied them carefully. He was still swaying on his feet slightly, but his concentration appeared good. "No," he said, finally.

"You're sure?" Ben thought there was something there.

"I don't know any of these people."

Ben looked at him closely. "The name Jimbo McGuire mean anything to you?"

"No."

"Because he's most likely the one who sent a man by the name of Dawson to find a photo in my files and kill me. And when Dawson didn't succeed, McGuire either killed him or had him killed."

The color was gone from Cheever's face now. "You think he's the one who's blackmailing me?"

"I don't know," Ben said. "It seems like a hell of a coincidence. Do you know Patrick Clooney?"

"Of course I know *of* him," Cheever snapped. "But I don't see him here. Don't tell me you're setting me up with him now."

"I'm not setting you up for anything."

"Oh, you're a paragon of virtue."

"Listen, Senator, if I'd been on the shoot with Peter and I'd captured this shot of you and Teri, then Peter and I would've been on your doorstep the next morning asking for a quote right before the shot ran. You're a public figure and got elected largely on the character issue—so that makes your infidelity news. That's one of the things you signed up for when you ran for office."

"Don't you think I know that?" Cheever said. "That's why I'm here now. Either publish the shot or don't. But I won't stand for blackmail."

Ben considered it all while looking at the blackmail picture. "Let's take this one step at a time," he said, finally. "I want to look at the negatives for the roll that Peter took. See if this shot is on there and ask a few questions."

"And then what?"

Ben shrugged. "And then we'll see. You'll be happy to know that I lost my job at *Insider*. So I'd have to go out and find a paper to peddle any of my shots right about now."

"So you'll keep my secret?" the senator said, incredulously. "You're not going to publish it?"

"It's not mine to sell," Ben said. "Besides, I'm more interested in finding out if this had anything to do with Peter's death than spilling your little affair."

"Come on," the senator said, putting his hand out defensively. "I told you before, I've got nothing to do with that. He was killed weeks before I even heard from the blackmailer."

"That's a good point," Ben said. "And everything I've seen heads in another direction, anyhow. But if it turns out you do . . . well, then I'll be standing at the prison gates with my camera loaded and ready to immortalize Senator Cheever's first day in hell."

CHAPTER 27

BEN WAITED IN THE VAN FOR HUEY, THE PHOTO LAB TECH. IT DIDN'T take long: Huey was consistent about his tuna on rye with cheese and bacon. At twelve-thirty, he left the building and started down Boylston Street.

Huey marched along quickly, his shoulders hunched, but his head swiveling from side to side. At lunch hour there were a lot of young women passing by—secretaries, executives. Many of them good-looking, stylish.

Few of them escaped Huey's scrutiny.

Ben sped a half block ahead and double-parked. He met Huey at the door to a sub shop.

Huey almost bumped into him, so engrossed was he in trying to look down the blouse of a young woman who was bent over tying her black Labrador's leash to a parking meter.

"Careful, Huey," Ben said, quietly. "The dog knows what you're doing."

The girl looked at the two of them and Huey's face flushed. He tried to step around Ben, but Ben simply backed up. Huey said, "Frigging snoop. Where the hell did you come from?"

"Just drove up. Thought I'd buy my old buddy lunch."

Suspicion darkened Huey's face. "Why? You want kiss up to

somebody, go pucker up to your ex-wife. Maybe she'll get you your job back.''

"That's valuable career advice, Huey. But I had something a little more specific in mind.''

Suspicion turned to full-blown worry on Huey's face. Late one night, Ben had stopped back at the office to find Huey rolling a hand truck stacked with boxes of chemicals and photographic paper to his car. Huey had actually shed tears pleading for Ben to keep it quiet, telling a sad tale about how a hooker had cleaned him out and he needed the money to make rent that month.

Ben had finally relented by overseeing the return of the stolen goods and had driven Huey out to a photo supply house in Belmont to observe him buy a month's worth of photographic consumables out of his own pocket. At the time, Huey had complained bitterly that he was spending far more than he'd ever taken. And he had clearly resented the spot checks Ben had taken on him from time to time.

Yet they both knew that Kurt would've fired Huey if he'd ever known.

"I haven't got time for this shit,'' Huey said, trying to push past Ben into the sub shop.

"You will if I have to call Kurt.'' Ben eased himself in front of the shorter man. "Then you'll have lots of time to sit around with me and swap job leads.''

Huey gave a little shrug. "So talk. What do you want?''

Ben smiled at him. "Let me buy you that sub first.'' He held the door open and told Huey he could order anything he wanted, as long as it didn't come to more than five bucks.

They drove down to the waterfront in Ben's van and parked facing the bay. Huey ate quickly, looking at Ben with his suspicion no less assuaged. But when he finished his sub, he looked calmer. He said, "I gotta get back soon or my ass'll be fried.''

Ben took Huey's paper bag, stuffed it into his own, and tossed the ball into a trash can near the window. "Two points," he said, and then turned his attention fully on Huey. "Tell me about the frame none of us ever saw.''

Huey's eyes narrowed. "What?"

"Of Peter's shots. There was one frame missing." Ben was disappointed to see Huey look relieved.

"I don't know what the fuck you're talking about."

Ben stared at him.

"Really, I don't." Huey looked damned near happy. "Shit, I thought you were going to hold me up because of that other thing . . . you know, hold me up for some of my paycheck or something."

Abruptly, Huey looked worried. Apparently afraid he might have given Ben a bad idea.

"Did you do the printing and processing of both of Peter's rolls yourself?" Ben asked.

Huey snorted. "The police have been through this, man. I didn't touch your bag."

"I didn't ask about the bag, I asked about processing the film."

"Yeah, but I thought you were interested in the bag. Because when Peter came in, he didn't even know how to get the film out of the camera. This is after the Cheever shoot. He did McGuire the next day."

"Did he say anything about seeing any other photographers on either McGuire or Cheever?"

Huey shook his head. "We didn't have long chats, me and Gallagher. I guess I wasn't his favorite guy. You two Girl Scouts must've whispered about my money problems."

"No," Ben said. "That was between me and you. He probably just didn't like you because of your personality."

Huey worked his teeth with his tongue, apparently trying to dislodge some of the sub. "Whatever," he said, finally. "Peter was just pissed with himself and said he didn't know why he went through so many pictures so fast. I reset the motordrive onto single frame for him and started to show him how it worked, but he just took the camera and walked away. High and mighty prick."

Ben could imagine it. Huey wouldn't have been able to "just show" Peter anything. Huey would've been cackling over such a mistake.

"So you processed the roll right then?"

"No, he had me wait until the next day when he came in with the shots of McGuire and had me print all of them up at the same time as five by sevens instead of contact sheets.''

"So it was just the two rolls?"

"That's right."

"And you did all the shots on each? All thirty-six?"

"All thirty-six," Huey said.

"Sure you didn't miss any? No last frame squeezed on, no thirty-seventh shot?"

Huey looked affronted. "Hey, I know my job. Every frigging frame got a print. That's what the man asked for, and that's what he got."

"After that, who got prints?"

"Everybody who asked." Huey sighed. "Pain in the ass. Everybody came one at a time, goddamn inconsiderate of my time."

"So who?"

Huey tugged at his lip. "First Peter, who gave his set to Kurt. Then you, Lucien, and your girlfriend, Sarah. She wanted two sets, one for the cops."

Ben raised his eyebrows. "My girlfriend?"

Huey made a pumping gesture with his right arm. "I'm not sure how far you've gotten, but I've seen the looks between you two."

"Who would've known you were so observant."

"Oh, yeah. I keep my eyes open. Let's head back, all right? I told you everything I can."

Ben started the van and drove slowly back. Thinking about those sets. Kurt, Lucien, him, and Sarah. Kurt showed his set at the meeting, and Ben remembered Sarah asking him not long afterwards how she could get her own. He had sent her off in Huey's direction.

Ben said, "When did Lucien ask for his prints?"

The little man grunted. He had come up with a toothpick from somewhere and Ben waited impatiently until he was ready to talk. Finally, Huey said, "You know, I don't know why you're so frigging curious about this film. But it's got to be worth more than a lousy sub."

"Just a phone call to Kurt," Ben reminded him. "That's all you've got to know."

"Ah, I've been thinking about that. You're not that type of guy.

I am, but you're not.'' He snapped his fingers. ''Come on, twenty bucks. I'll put it on the dogs, see if I can make it grow.''

Ben couldn't help but smile. He picked up his wallet from the dashboard and gave Huey a twenty.

The little man said, ''You know that shit, Lucien. Acts like a friendly puppy dog, but he's just like anybody else, always looking to get an edge. He asked for a set of everything Peter had going the day *before* the editorial meeting.''

''And you just gave it all to him?''

Huey looked at Ben as if he were stupid. ''You thinking selling chemicals and paper is the only way to make an extra buck?''

CHAPTER 28

BEN CALLED SARAH FROM HIS CELL PHONE.

When she answered, he said, "Hey, it's me."

"Hello, me." She lowered her voice. "Calling to say it was all a big mistake but we can still be friends?"

"Nah. Friends don't get to have that kind of fun. Look, I just had lunch with Huey."

"I'll try not to feel shattered," she said. But he could hear the change in her tone. She recognized business when she heard it. "What's up?"

"He's been paid—don't let him tell you otherwise—to hand you two developed film strips. Peter's shots of Cheever and McGuire. Go meet Huey at the stairway and follow him into the lab and see that he gives it to you without trying to cut any of it."

"Cheever is Lucien's show. Should I get him in on this?"

"Absolutely not."

She hesitated and then said, "All right. I better go."

"I'll meet you across the street," he said. "And try to find out where Lucien is right now."

"Got it." She hung up.

*   *   *

She slid into the passenger seat about fifteen minutes later, looking fantastic in a simple black skirt, black stockings, and a tailored white blouse.

He grinned. "Get over here, you."

She kissed him swiftly. "I've been thinking about doing that all morning," she said, flushing. "You're getting in the way of my work." She held out a manila envelope. "Nasty little man, that Huey. What's this about?"

"Hold on a second." He took the envelope from her and pulled out the dozen negative strips and matched the numbers of each frame against the contact sheet Huey had enclosed. He did the same with the roll of McGuire's set just to be sure. They all matched. There were no unaccounted shots within each roll of thirty-six shots, and none of them showed the senator embracing Teri Wheeler. And there was sufficient blank leader and ending film still attached for Ben to feel confident an extra shot hadn't been squeezed on and then clipped away later.

"Huh." He sat back.

"Huh, what? Is this about Peter?"

"I don't know."

"Tell me what you do."

Ben hesitated. He needed her, he was falling for her . . . and she was a reporter.

He said, "I promised somebody I'd look into something."

She stared at him, before nodding toward the negatives. "Whoever you're working for, the subject is Cheever, right?" she said. "You looked most closely at his roll. You were matching the sheet up with the negs. Is there a shot missing?"

He shook his head. "It looks like there's not. But there should be. Or else there was another photographer taking shots the same time Peter was. Either way . . ."

He hesitated.

"What?"

"There may be a problem at *Insider*."

"What do you mean?"

"I mean there may be a blackmail problem."

She hesitated. "And that's why you want to know where Lucien is?"

"That's right."

They stared at each other.

"So what do you want from me?" Her voice was remote.

"Work with me," he said. "Let's find out what this whole story is about, not just the piece I know about Cheever. Let's take it all the way."

"And?"

"And let me be the arbiter of what goes to Kurt and everyone else."

"Oh, that's all. You're not asking for much." She closed her eyes briefly and then looked at him directly. "Meaning it's possible you might ask me to bury something I'd otherwise run with."

"Entirely possible," he said.

"If it has to do with Peter, I won't," she said. "I want to be with you, but I won't bury anything that had to do with him getting killed."

"I'd never ask you to."

She looked at him carefully. The same somber gaze as her daughter's the night before. Finally, she said, "All right."

Ben told her about Senator Cheever.

He showed her the photograph of the senator and Teri Wheeler.

"Mmmm," Sarah said. "So either Peter got this shot on another roll and didn't tell anyone—or else someone was nearby taking pictures at the same time. Couldn't it have been taken another time altogether?"

"It's possible, but unlikely. Cheever and Wheeler are wearing the same clothes, the lighting is the same."

"So someone must've followed Peter." She looked at the picture carefully. "It's fairly clean by today's scandal standards. But devastating to the wife who trusts him." She looked at Ben. "And Cheever convinced you that's his primary concern?"

"That and the damage to his political career."

"You remind him we've elected and reelected presidents with a more checkered past?"

"He seems to know his own political realities. But this seriously impedes on his self-image, and I think that's important to him."

"But not enough to come clean."

Ben shrugged. "He'll get away with it if he can. But he's balking at blackmail."

She shook her head. "I guess that's what passes for morality in a politician these days. So what's next?"

Ben told her about Lucien paying Huey for an early set of all of Peter's photographs. "Huey says Lucien's puppy-dog bit is just an act."

She raised her eyebrows. "Lucien is ambitious. I got that loud and clear in the first ten minutes. Dresses really well, drives a new Saab Turbo . . . but he's not a very good writer. Sloppy with his facts, weak research. I haven't been around him long enough to see how well he handles himself in interviews . . ."

"Not very well," Ben said, thinking of the interviews with Goodhue and with Cheever. "Lucien folds too easily."

"So—ambitious, incompetent, and money to burn."

"And assigned to Cheever's case."

"But if he got prints of just this roll, then he has no more than the rest of us."

"True. But he was always hounding Peter for leads. And it sounded like Peter was onto something new when he was coming to pick me up. So maybe Lucien followed him the night of the Cheever surveillance and got this shot." Ben thought back to the "covering" pictures Lucien had taken when Ben had walked into the barn during Johansen's standoff. They were well-framed and focused. Lucien clearly had some photography experience.

"I'll take him on." Sarah tossed her hair back with mocking seductiveness that still managed to make Ben feel a bit short of breath. "Maybe he'll take pity on a new hire and share some of his wisdom. We can start prying from there."

"That'd work on me," Ben said.

She leaned over to kiss him again. "I know."

CHAPTER 29

AFTER SARAH WENT BACK UP TO THE OFFICE, BEN CHECKED HIS watch. Just after two.

He sighed, knowing what he should do, but wishing he had an excuse, an out. There were plenty of other things he should be doing. Not the least of which was getting back onto Jimbo McGuire.

But he made the call to Andi anyhow.

She answered on the third ring and when she recognized his voice she fell silent.

"Andi?"

"You and Kurt have discussed everything we need to discuss," she said.

"For God's sake, Andi, you know me. You think everything that happened that night came entirely from my side of the court?"

"You were standing over him and he was bleeding. Are you suggesting that's not what I saw?"

"I'm suggesting it's not that simple. And I'd like to sit down and talk with you about it."

"No. Kurt and I have made our decision. We're not pressing charges, but we want you away from us. We want a chance for our new family."

"Andi," he said. "I'm not just going to fade away. You know

me. You know you're in no danger from me. You know the kids aren't either.''

"So it's just my husband who'll get hurt?''

"Assuming he doesn't punch me anymore, I'll be sure not to return the favor.''

"You're saying *he* hit you. Kurt?'' Ben could read uncertainty behind her skepticism. Or at least he felt he could.

Ben sat back in his van seat. "He never acknowledged that?''

She hesitated.

"How about Jake?''

She sighed. "He's keeping a lot to himself these days. Bottled up worse than ever.''

Ben waited. He avoided the temptation to fill the silence with words.

"All right,'' she said, finally. "Both the kids are out with friends this afternoon. Come over now, let's see if we can hammer out some semblance of sanity between us.''

She opened the door, and turned around and quickly walked back to the kitchen.

He blinked when he followed her in.

The kitchen had been painted. "Looks nice,'' he said.

And it did. Light gray walls. Ben's photos were gone, and replaced with framed prints from the Museum of Fine Arts. A little traditional for Ben's taste, but nice.

"Kurt,'' she said, smiling briefly. "Did it himself. Even though we probably won't be here that much longer, he wanted to make the change.''

She gestured to a stool and they sat across from each other at the kitchen island. She shook the carafe of coffee. "He's getting me organized, too. I even thought to make coffee.''

"Still planning to build that new house?'' Ben asked.

She nodded. "Marblehead.''

"Good for you,'' Ben said. Marblehead. One of the more expensive suburbs on the North Shore of Massachusetts. It would add another half hour to his visiting time under ideal conditions. Double that during rush hour.

But he wasn't here to argue.

"How are you doing on a new job?" she asked. "Your child support check is due this week."

Ben stiffened. "Have I ever missed one before?"

She shrugged. "No. But things are different." She kept her eyes averted from him.

Ben leaned forward. "Wouldn't you say a tad bit of that difference is because your new husband is still jealous even though he's got you and the kids? To the point of firing me in the hope I'd just go away? Even so, I will make my child support payment. I may choose to go back and sue him and *Insider* for wrongful termination, but I will certainly live up to my responsibilities."

"This is your idea of an apology?" she flared.

"Is the crap Kurt has been pulling your idea of working together for the sake of the kids?"

"He's taking care of us while you're off playing cops and robbers. You think I want to take the kids to your funeral? You think I want that myself?"

"For Christsakes, Andi, Kurt *assigned* me to chase this story. It's my job, or it was until he fired me. Besides, you think I should just let go what happened to Peter? He was your friend, too."

A tear slipped down Andi's cheek, surprising Ben.

It pulled him up short.

She said, "Kurt told me what the police said. He told me that man, Lee Sands, would've shot you if it wasn't for that train."

Ben put his hand on her shoulder and she slapped it away.

She rubbed the tears from her face angrily, and said, in a shaky voice, "Three times somebody's tried to kill you in the past month. And for what? So you can show the world how ugly it is? Catch people at their worst? I can't have you around if you're just going to get yourself killed. Can't you do something else? Go work on that book of yours. Get another job."

They heard the front door open.

Andi stood and turned away quickly, rubbed her eyes, and blew her nose. By the time Jake came through the door, she was able to turn and give him a small smile.

When he saw Ben there, he looked to his mother. "You've been crying, Mom?" He looked at Ben accusingly. "What did you do?"

"Oh, stop," Andi said. "He didn't do anything. We were just talking and I got upset."

Jake looked between the two of them uncertainly.

"Listen to me, Jake," Ben said. "You don't have to worry about what happened with me and Kurt ever happening again."

Jake looked between him and Andi.

She nodded. "I'm sure that's true."

"Yeah?" Jake looked at Ben. "I wouldn't want it to."

Ben put his hand out and made his second deal of the day.

Jake asked Ben if he'd like to go downstairs to see some of the shots he'd taken with the digital camera.

"Sure."

Andi looked at Ben warningly. "Not too long, OK? Kurt is going to be home for an early supper. He's taking us all to the movies tonight."

"I understand."

Ben and Jake went down to the family room. Jake handed Ben some photos, with an indifferent shrug. "Anyhow, these are what we've been doing."

Ben smiled. "Let's see what you've got."

He took them to the light.

"Hey, nice," he said, feeling relieved. He didn't have to fake his enthusiasm.

Some of them were just simple grab shots from around the house, of Lainnie being surprised awake; of Andi waving from the kitchen island as she poured dressing onto the salad. Kurt smiling over his newspaper. Looking fatherly.

But the digital manipulations were the most fun. Lainnie and Jake, side by side—but upside down from each other. Jake standing on the surface of a lake—apparently walking on water.

"My miracle boy," Ben said.

Jake laughed and stepped closer, his face flushed with pleasure. "You like them?"

"I do. Clever and creative. The picture quality's not bad either." Ben could still see the digital pattern fairly easily, but still it was a substantial improvement over what the earlier digital cameras could do.

"Yeah, but look at what I figured out," Jake said. "I used your old camera stand and reshot this one on film and had it printed."

He showed Ben a portrait he had taken of Andi. It was a soft focus shot, but the warmth of her expression made Ben's chest feel slightly tight. The love that was there for her son, the family of which Ben was no longer a part. He pulled out a loupe and looked at the print.

"See?" Jake said. "A little soft focus, and I'll bet you can't find the digital dot pattern now."

Ben straightened slowly.

"You see it?" Jake asked, the enthusiasm beginning to fade as he looked at his father. "You can't, can you?"

"No," said Ben. "No, I can't."

CHAPTER 30

It wasn't cold, but Ben felt numb.

He positioned himself beside the air-conditioning unit across from McGuire's office all afternoon. There was no sign of movement. Around six, Ben packed up and left to grab a sandwich. It had no taste.

He left his equipment in the van, and just before seven he walked up the street and crossed through Fanueil Hall. The evening light was painting the city in a warm, golden light and Ben took in the smell of sausage, pizza, pesto, coffee, cotton candy. A man flew mechanical birds in a winding loop outside his novelty store; a woman in a black beret called out that free face painting was available for anyone making a ten-dollar purchase or more at her poster shop. Ben took in the hustle in the Marketplace as people made their way to dinner together, couples, groups of friends. People talking and laughing.

He felt alone in all of it.

He suddenly wished that Sarah were with him now. That they could forget all of this, go to the raw bar at the Union Oyster House. Drink cold beers, tell each other stories.

Instead, he continued past City Hall, took a left onto Tremont, and then waited in the alley across the street from the restaurant on Bromfield Street where he had suggested Sarah take Lucien.

They showed up in a taxi about fifteen minutes later. She was good, she didn't even look Ben's way. He stood in the doorway of a closed jewelry store, doing what he always seemed to be doing. Watching and waiting.

A bit after eight, Ben entered the restaurant.

Sarah and Lucien were toward the rear of the restaurant, sitting in a high-backed wooden booth.

Ben saw her first. She had positioned herself so she could see the front door. Her smile widened ever so slightly and she brushed her hair back. He continued on, the bit with the hair being their signal that Lucien was ready.

Ben slid in beside Sarah.

Lucien was indeed ready. There was a champagne stand with an empty bottle turned upside down. A half-empty bottle of wine stood between them on the table. And Lucien's face was florid, his tie loose. Ben's entrance had caught him in mid-sentence. From his expression, he had just been about to say something he felt was truly clever. He sat back, blinked, and said in a voice that was just a little too loud. "Ben . . . it's good to see you, man."

Ben said it was good to see him, too.

And then Sarah kissed Ben on the cheek.

Lucien shook his head slightly as if to clear it. "What's this?"

Sarah said, brightly, "Lucien's been a great help showing me the ropes around *Insider*. The hidden ropes."

"Hey . . ." Lucien began.

Ben said. "Maybe if I knew those I wouldn't be out on the street right now."

"Well, you already knew about how Lucien could buy an early look at any reporter's photos," she said. "Gives you a great head's up if you're trying to steal a story from one of your co-workers."

"Sure," Ben said. "Heard that directly from my buddy, Huey."

She leaned back in the booth and sipped her wine, observing Lucien with cold amusement. She cocked her head at Ben. "Let me try this out on you. Lucien was telling me how good looking I am and that being a bit of a looker himself, he manages to learn things just being sweet to the right women around the office. I think he was leading up to a trade of information after he jumped me himself, but that may just be the champagne talking. But I specifically heard Lisa mentioned.''

Lisa. Kurt's secretary.

Ben said, ''She certainly knows a lot. She also has everyone's voice-mail code typed up in front of her phone.''

Lucien started.

Sarah leaned over and slapped Ben's palm. ''Bingo. Guilty conscience.'' She settled back in the booth and smiled at Lucien. ''Fess up, boy.''

Ben realized that she too was at least slightly drunk.

''That right, Lucien?'' Ben said. ''You listening in on voice-mail messages?''

''Screw you,'' Lucien snapped.

Sarah laughed. ''The puppy dog has teeth.''

This made Lucien's face flush even darker. ''You two are spinning this shit yourself. I never said that.''

Ben turned back to Sarah. ''You get to his clothes? His Turbo Saab? All that on a junior reporter's salary?''

''We were just on it.''

''What'd he say?''

''Vague,'' she said. ''Very vague.''

''What kind of computer do you have at home?'' Ben asked, abruptly. He watched Lucien carefully.

''Huh?'' Lucien seemed genuinely confused. ''What'd you ask me? My computer?''

''That's right.''

Lucien held up the notebook computer–sized case that was resting on the bench beside him. ''This is all I use. What of it?''

''Can I see it?''

If Sarah was as confused with this turn as Lucien, she kept it to herself. ''Go ahead, Lucien. What've you got to lose?''

Lucien handed it over to him.

Ben opened the case and found a low-end system. Black-and-white display. He turned it over and found a pressure stick label with the *Insider* insignia on it. Company issue. Peter had the same kind.

''Yeah, so what?'' Lucien asked, gathering a little anger together. ''I'm not a computer geek, never have been. So what?''

"You ever listen to Peter's messages? Find out who his original sources were on any of his stories? Cheever, McGuire, the prison ladies?"

"What's your point with this shit?"

Ben leaned forward, putting his face in Lucien's. Letting him see the rage that was right there on tap. "Answer my goddamn question."

Lucien put up his hands. "Hey, calm down." He looked away from Ben and then gave a little embarrassed shrug. "Peter was careful. Changed his voice-mail code on a regular basis. I didn't get anything from him."

Ben sat back. That sounded plausible. "Tell me what you said to Kurt after you and I went to see Cheever." Ben added a lie. "Kurt said you influenced his decision to give me the boot."

Lucien's eyes narrowed. He sat straighter. "Is this what you two are all about here?" Lucien seemed to reassess his position and find it not as damaging as he thought. "You're paranoid, Harris. I didn't say a goddamn thing about you. I just laid out what Cheever said and Kurt told me to call the senator back and tell him we were off the story."

"And you did that?"

"Yeah, I made the call. The senator said he understood we had our job to do and all that bull. Glad we were out of his hair."

"You're telling me that's all you or Kurt said? Nothing about me?"

Lucien's lips curled derisively. "Man, and I once thought you were a heavyweight." Lucien drained his wineglass, and then said, "OK, so you think you've got something on me? Going to Kurt about me and Huey won't get your job back, no matter what you think. If this is something you're trying to get out of me, I'll toss you a few hundred bucks to forget about it, but that's as far as it goes. Maybe as much as a thousand. After that, I'll just take my chances. Kurt has too much on his mind, far as I can tell. You, he fired just because he hates your guts for screwing his wife for the past fifteen years or so. Screwed his wife and gave her a couple of kids."

This last bit struck Lucien as funny, and he laughed until he had to wipe tears away. "Look at the two of you. Sitting there thinking you've figured something out."

"Where do you get your money?" Sarah asked. "Where do you get a thousand dollars to 'toss' us?"

Lucien shrugged. "It's clean and simple, and you can check it if you want. I've got a trust. My grandfather."

He took out his business card and wrote a name and phone number on it and tossed it to Sarah. "Go ahead, Ms. Hot Shit Reporter, call Bates and Cleese, my family's attorneys. I'll tell them to expect your call and give you the details. I don't need this job for the money. But I'm going to succeed at it and move on to bigger and better things. Ten years from now I'll be anchoring a national news desk while you'll still be clicking your pictures, Harris. And Sarah, you'll still be hoping your cute smile and hot little body will still make dopes like me talk too much. It'll be harder to pull off when you're on the wrong side of forty."

Lucien slid out of the booth. He was unsteady on his feet.

"Kurt's not going to stand for what you've been doing," Ben said.

Lucien snorted. "Like I said, Kurt's got too much on his mind than to worry about this shit. He's broke."

Ben laughed, making it sound rueful. "You don't know what you're talking about. He's going to build a new house in Marblehead, he must be doing all right."

Lucien lifted an imaginary phone to his ear and played back an imaginary message. A message he had apparently snagged from Kurt's voice-mail. "Mr. Tattinger, this is Bob Franklin at Paine Webber again. I'm sorry to say that the market has gone against your silver futures. For the fifth day in a row, it's opened down the limit. We need cash or market securities to cover your account—and we need them now. It's urgent that you return this call to me and settle this account immediately."

Lucien dropped his hand. "I used to talk investments with Kurt, kissing up. He figured because I came from money I might spill a good tip. He bought big in silver commodities—and if you follow the market at all, you'd know he's in big trouble. So me and my voice-mail messages aren't exactly major issues in his life right now."

Lucien put on his coat and grabbed his laptop and briefcase. He smiled pleasantly. "Call me if you're desperate for that thousand bucks. Otherwise, go fuck yourself."

CHAPTER 31

"WELL, AT LEAST HE THINKS I HAVE A HOT BODY AND A CUTE smile," Sarah said. "We got that out of the evening." She looked sidelong at Ben. "I'm a little looped."

"I noticed," he said. "You did a good job."

He put his arm around her and she leaned her head against his shoulder. She smelled of perfume and champagne, and with her warmth against him, he wished he had no other obligation that night except to take her home.

"You think so?" she said. "What exactly did we learn? *Insider* is a screwed-up place, full of screwed-up people. Most places are, you look too close." She looked up at him. "How come you're so sad?"

He held her tighter. Knowing what he had to do next.

"Ben?"

"It's like you said," he answered. "When you look too close."

The lights were off when he got back.

He waited in the van, thinking that maybe the best thing for everyone involved was to drive off.

But he knew that wouldn't work.

It was just that every instinct was urging him away. Telling him to hurry to Sarah's apartment, get there just after the cab dropped her off. Apologize for hustling her off.

"Shit," Ben said, and pulled around the corner so the van wouldn't be parked right out front.

"Shit," he said again, after he'd walked back and found the key in the flower pot, right where she always left it.

"Ah, shit and damn it to hell," he said, as he broke into Andi and Kurt's home.

He started in the office. While the computer was booting up, he went through all the drawers in his former desk, even the little hiding places in the desk, the two ornamental sliding slots that were actually small vertical drawers.

In one, he found what looked like love letters from Andi to Kurt. Ben put them away.

He felt sick to his stomach.

When the computer was ready, he wasted a good ten minutes finding his way through the system until he found two Photoshop folders, one labeled "Jake's Jokes," the other, "Kurt's Works."

Ben opened Kurt's folder and as quickly as the system would allow, he opened and closed a dozen files. Hobby-type stuff, showing manipulation of scenics and home shots like what Jake had shown.

Ben looked at his watch. Over forty minutes had passed.

On the desk was a SyQuest drive, and beside it, a file box of disks. Ben looked inside. There were a half dozen disks. Luckily, only two of them were identified as Kurt's.

Ben opened the two of them and ran through the files.

Nothing important there. But another twenty minutes wasted. He rolled his chair back, frustrated. And hit something soft. Kurt's briefcase.

Ben put it on the desk and flipped the locks. They snapped open loudly in the dark room. Using the glow of the computer screen, Ben found a half dozen file folders, including one with the black and white prints of Cheever and of McGuire. Nothing that Kurt hadn't displayed at their editorial meeting weeks ago.

Ben drummed his fingers on the desk, knowing his next logical step, and hating it.

He went upstairs to their bedroom.

There was the faint smell of Kurt's aftershave lotion mingled with Andi's perfume. "Oh, Jesus," Ben said. *Hating* what he was doing.

He swung open an old framed print of a Winslow Homer scene to reveal the safe. Courtesy of the previous owner of the house. Not something Ben or Andi would have ever gone to the trouble to install, but he knew she used it to store her jewelry, as well as certificates for the few stocks they owned.

Ben took out his wallet, and sifted through it until he found his Social Security card. The combination was scratched down on the back.

It didn't work.

Kurt must have changed the combination.

Ben was almost relieved.

If he couldn't find out, he couldn't find out.

But he knew Andi and her habits. And he knew there was still a chance he could move forward. He went back down to the office, and went to Andi's desk and found her diary. He opened it to the front page and saw the old combination scratched out, and the new one listed below.

He jotted the number down, and hurried back upstairs.

It worked.

Inside, he found more jewelry. More pieces that Kurt had apparently given her in the six months of dating than Ben had given her in all their time together. There was also a small bar of silver with a commemorative insignia. There were several flat envelopes with the Paine Webber label, and then a thick manila envelope.

Ben took that one out.

It was sealed. Something hard-edged bulged in the middle.

Ben hesitated.

Everything else, he could clean up. He could go downstairs, shut off the computer, neaten up.

And be done with it.

He closed his eyes, and then slid his finger inside the envelope and ripped it open. He dropped the contents onto the bed and turned on the bedside lamp.

There was a prospectus on the silver futures.

There were a series of letters from the Paine Webber broker confirming that Kurt had leveraged the growth in his silver contracts into
more contracts . . . that he simply kept reextending himself as the
price increased.

There was a SyQuest disk.

And another five-by-seven print of Senator Cheever and Teri
Wheeler embracing.

It took Ben just a moment to open the files on the computer.

There were almost a dozen separate files showing the stages of
individual elements of what were most likely scanned black-and-
white prints. Maybe Kurt had gotten hold of the negatives, but Huey
probably would have said so. And there was a scanner right beside
Kurt's computer.

There were what looked like the original shots of the senator holding the tray and then of Teri Wheeler laughing, her head arched back.
Then the same shots, only this time the senator's hands were empty
of the tray. And the background around Teri had been stripped away.
And then of the senator's image, rotated and placed so that his hands
were now around Teri's waist. The angle of his neck and head taken
from another shot and replaced on his shoulders in another . . . giving
the impression that he was kissing her or at least nuzzling her neck.

And then the individual pieces were overlaid onto each other, including the return of the background image, and the foreground frame
of the window.

Another version with what looked to be fine tuning of the shadows
and light on their faces.

And finally, there was the finished scene. The shot that Peter apparently saw, but missed.

The shot Kurt had constructed.

How handy, Ben thought. Thinking of what Jake had said at his
birthday dinner a million years ago. "No more missed shots."

CHAPTER 32

BEN WAITED IN THE VAN UNTIL THE BEDROOM LIGHTS WENT OUT. First Lainnie's around nine-thirty, and then Jake's about an hour later. Ben sat there for another half hour, hoping his son was drifting off deeply.

Ben had cleaned up any sign of his break-in before he had left. He had put everything back as he had found it. Everything but the packet containing the disk.

With that in hand, he took a deep breath, walked up to the front door, and rang the doorbell.

Andi opened the door a crack and peered out. She whispered, "Are you drunk?"

"We've got to talk."

"Not *now* we don't."

"Somebody at the door, honey?" Ben heard Kurt say.

And then the door swung open.

Kurt stood there in his bathrobe. Pajamas and slippers. His querulous look changing quickly to anger. "What the hell are you doing here?"

Ben held out the photo of the senator and Teri Wheeler. "I'm here to talk about this—and this.'' He held up the big Paine Webber envelope with the SyQuest disk in front of it.

Kurt's face blanched. He looked up the stairs behind him swiftly and then back at Ben. Clearly wondering how the worst had happened.

Ben almost felt sorry for him.

''What is that?'' Andi asked.

Kurt tried to close the door. ''Call me at the office.''

But Ben put his foot in the way. ''No. This concerns all of us.''

Andi said, ''What is it?'' She pulled at the door and at first Kurt wouldn't let her open it. ''Kurt!''

He relented and the door swung wide.

She said, ''What're you talking about?''

Ben looked at Kurt. The man had turned gray. He leaned back against the door. His breathing was shaky. ''How did you . . .''

''I broke in,'' Ben said. ''While you were at the movies.''

''Broke in *here*?'' Andi said.

''Let's go in the library and talk about it,'' Ben said. ''And keep your voice down so the kids don't have to listen to this.''

''They'll listen to you getting arrested if you don't get out of here,'' she began in a harsh whisper.

But Kurt put his hand on her shoulder. He shook his head ever so slightly. ''No, we'll listen.''

She went silent. She touched her husband's face, suddenly scared. ''What is it, Kurt?''

He took her hand. ''He's right. We need to go where the kids won't hear us.''

''I'll explain,'' Kurt said when they reached the library. His voice was hoarse.

After Ben closed the door Kurt held out his hand for the file and the disk. After a moment's hesitation, Ben let him have them.

Kurt waved him and Andi to the love seat and sat across from them with the coffee table in between.

Kurt stared at the photograph for a time, and then cleared his throat. His hands were shaking.

He looked up. ''I've always tried to do the right thing. Kept to my responsibilities. It's the way I was brought up, it's most likely my nature. Kind of dull, but that's who I am.''

He focused his attention on Andi. ''You're the best thing that's ever happened to me. You and the kids. I just wanted to keep it. Keep this life together.''

She looked confused. ''You have it. We're right here.''

''I know. I know you say that.'' He touched his chest. ''But inside I feel every day like I might lose it all. That disastrous marriage to Kathleen.''

He looked at Ben. ''And you. Having you around on the edges all of the time. Wanting back in.''

''Wanting a life with my kids,'' Ben said. ''I was clear about that.''

Kurt nodded. ''I know what you said. Maybe I even believed you. But it's not what I felt inside. You understand the difference?''

Ben didn't answer, and Kurt didn't wait. It seemed like he wanted to explain himself.

''So I took a risk,'' Kurt said. ''I wanted to move us away from this house. This damn house that feels in every board like you're still a part of the place. I wanted to make us our own home and move away from you and have a fresh start.''

''You wanted me discredited and ruined, the way it looks to me.''

Kurt shook his head. ''I didn't consciously go about that. I got myself into a jam, and I saw a way out.''

''What happened?'' Andi asked, quietly.

''Those investments I've been telling you about. You trusted me so completely. And they were good for a time, but they've gone south.''

Her face paled. ''How far south?''

He looked her in the eye. ''I've lost all my own capital. And most of what you gave me months ago to invest. And then I panicked and tried to recoup it all by buying silver futures. The market went against me. I was desperate.''

Her hand flew to her mouth.

Kurt continued, his voice heavy. ''There is no new house. We might lose this one. The market kept opening down the limit every day . . . I couldn't move the silver . . . with what I owe, I don't see how we can keep up the mortgage.''

He put the picture down in front of her. "And so I did this."

"What do you mean you *did* this?"

"I fabricated this photo." He jerked his head toward the computer. "Using Photoshop. Scanned in the prints."

He looked toward Ben. "When Peter was telling me what happened, how he blew it using your camera, he told me there was a shot like this. Right after he ran through the roll, he saw the senator come up and hug Miss Wheeler and kiss her. They were there for just a split second, and Peter was berating himself—and I was berating him—for missing the shot."

"Why didn't you mention this before?"

"It was useless without the picture. I . . . I didn't want to go up against the senator with just my word about what Peter saw."

"Sure," Ben said. "And you saw a way out of your money troubles."

Kurt shook his head. "Not right then. At that point, I wasn't in so much trouble. No, this has all happened very quickly. I'd been playing with Jake on a bunch of images, and I scanned in the photos myself at first just to see if I could do it. Sort of teased myself along—you know, could I *make* the shot that Peter missed. I kept at it. Telling myself it was just a hobby, a distraction. Get my mind off my money worries. I didn't take it seriously because I knew the dot pattern would show up and I had to print out on electronic imaging paper. But the picture I made turned out so well. So convincing. And then Jake showed me how he had used your old camera stand downstairs to photograph a digital print and then had it printed on conventional paper. And I suddenly realized that if I just softened the focus a little I'd be able to do it all."

Ben said, "And by then I had already gone in and presented the photos to the senator and you figured if it all went wrong, I'd be held up as the bad guy."

Kurt wet his lips. "Maybe. I didn't think of it so directly. I certainly figured you could talk yourself out of any problems. After all, you were in Maine when the shot was taken."

"So I would've said. Of course, I couldn't prove it."

"I didn't think it would get to that. I thought he'd pay up. I thought he was in a jam, and I was in a jam. The kind of campaign funds he has, access to people like Goodhue who want to see him president someday, I thought I could at least wipe out this problem with the margin and restore some of Andi's money to her. It wouldn't begin to cover the hit on my own money."

Andi had bent forward, covering her face. Kurt reached out to touch her and she pushed his hand away.

"I'm sorry, Andi," he said.

He looked at Ben. "And I apologize to you, too. I wanted you to take that damn logging assignment to get you out of town, make you unavailable in case the senator sent someone around. At the very least, I needed to get you off the staff."

"Bullshit. You wanted to get me away from you. You wanted to give me an apparent motive. 'Out of work photographer turns to blackmail.' "

Kurt considered this. "Maybe. I've been less than honest with myself. That's possible."

Ben shook his head, marveling. "Is that your version of 'I do not recall?' "

"I suppose it is." Kurt paused. "Who did the senator send around?"

"Himself." Ben told them about the meeting.

Andi took her hands from her face. She reached out and touched Ben's hand. "Oh my God. I've been listening to this, devastated about what it means in our life. Not thinking what could've happened to you." She laughed, shortly, on the verge of tears. "And here I was castigating you today for putting yourself at risk."

"What's the bottom line with the senator?" Kurt asked.

"He's not going to pay. He says he'll pull me down with him. Nail me for blackmail."

"Clearly, my blackmail of the senator ends here," Kurt said. "The question is, what are you going to do to me?"

"I'm not sure," Ben said.

The three of them sat in silence for a moment, at an impasse.

Ben cleared his throat, and the two of them looked at him expectantly. "Where did you have the shot processed and printed?"

"I did it myself. Used Huey's lab one night. I'd taken Photo 101 back in college, I just had to read up on it."

"Tell me exactly when all this happened."

Kurt went over to his desk and came around to Ben's side of the coffee table with a calendar. With a pen, he circled the date three days after Ben and Lucien's meeting with Cheever. "There. That's when Cheever would've gotten the photo. I mailed it outside the Kenmore Square post office. I figured it would arrive the next day. So I waited until the next day and called him from a pay phone. Said I was Senator Atkins, got right through."

That coincided with what the senator had said, Ben thought. The call came two days after Dawson attacked Ben in his studio and tried to burn all his photos.

"Have you contacted the senator again about picking up the money?"

"No."

"When were you going to do that?"

"I figured I'd give him a week. And then there was this thing with you and Sands. I gave it a couple more days. It's turned into almost two weeks since I called him."

"You think they're related? You blackmailing the senator and Sands wiring the bomb that killed Peter?"

"It couldn't be," Kurt said. "Peter was killed weeks before I sent that photo to the senator. Before I even had the *idea* of blackmailing him, never mind constructing the photo. And Dawson attacked you a good couple of days before I sent the photo, so it comes to the same thing. And we know he was McGuire's man."

"But nevertheless, it made you pause."

Kurt made a helpless gesture with his hands. "Everything about this has given me pause. I wasn't sure I was going to go through with it. Collecting the money. I'm honestly not sure."

"But if you did?"

"If I did, most likely what I would've done is called him again this week."

"And done what?"

Kurt made a disgusted face. "I've seen as many movies as anybody. I'd have sent him around to a half dozen phone booths and watched him at three of them to see if he had police or anyone else following. Had him leave the money someplace and then I'd mail the negative of the copy-stand photo."

"You would, huh?" Ben looked at him skeptically.

"Yes, I would." Kurt seemed somewhat surprised. "This has been chewing me up inside, doing this. I would've returned it, and been done with the whole mess. I would've told Andi that I'd taken a bath on my investments but that at least her money and the house were safe."

He looked to Andi. "I'm telling you the truth. Both of you."

Neither of them said anything.

"So . . ." Kurt waited. "So what are you going to do?"

Andi put her hand on Ben's arm. Stopping him from answering. "Walk with me please," she said.

Kurt began to shake his head. "Don't do it this way. Don't walk out with him."

"Can I trust you to just stay here and wait?" she asked, sharply. "The kids are asleep upstairs. Can I trust you?"

He jerked, as if she had just slapped him. When he answered, his voice was hoarse. "You can trust me," he said. "Give me time, I'll prove it to you."

Ben and Andi started up the winding trail behind the house. They climbed silently for about five minutes, a walk they had made hundreds, maybe thousands of times before. He let her go ahead into the moonlit woods up toward a rocky ledge. She moved fast and both of them were breathing raggedly by time she reached the outcropping.

She sat down, and put her head in her hands. He sat beside her, looking back at their former home, saying nothing. Sweat trickled down his back.

Finally, she sat up and brushed at her eyes with the palm of her hand "Enough," she said, her voice shaking slightly. "It's not as if I didn't know something was up. He hasn't been sleeping. The way he was reacting to you. I told myself it was all just adjusting to the new situation. Pretty stressful for anybody, to move into a family like this."

"Blackmail is pretty stressful too," Ben said. "If you're not used to it, that is."

"Please don't," she said. "You've certainly got the right, but please don't do that now."

He nodded.

"Thank you." She held his hand for a moment, and then let go. She was trembling.

"Is it true what he said?" Ben asked. "You gave him everything to invest?"

"I gave him a lot. But not all of it. I loved him—and I probably still do—but, no, the blue chips that I inherited from Uncle Gus are still in my name and I never made them available to him. Certainly the house and the equity in it are in my name. So if it's a matter of just keeping up the mortgage payments, I might be able to swing it on my own for a while."

"That's assuming your assets aren't seized. You're his wife and he's run up substantial debts—you're in trouble here."

She nodded. "Oh, we're in trouble, I don't think there's any doubt about that." She looked at him. "Ben, right now I'm so angry and disappointed with Kurt I'd like to stand up and scream and throw rocks and generally just have a good tantrum. But the fact is you and I have to make some decisions right now. So I'm going to try to keep it together and tell you some things. Because what you do is going to have a big impact on all of us—including the kids—for a long time to come."

"I'm listening."

"I know Kurt. Even though I'm shocked with what he's done, I believe what he's told us now is the whole truth. It's just that he's so insecure . . . his parents were a disaster. His dad was disappointed with everything Kurt did from day one. Dismissive, bitter mother who left them early on. And then Kurt's first wife left him because he couldn't give her children. He has a low sperm count. She filed for divorce the week they found out. Told him kids were important to her and she wanted her own from her own husband—and she left. . . . Well, the fact is children were pretty damn important to him too."

"Andi, how many rough life stories have you heard in your career? Somebody defending some heinous thing they did because their mommy wasn't nice to them? And what would we do? Take the picture, write up the story."

"That's what *you'd* do," she flashed. "Not me. Not my whole career, you know that."

Which was true enough. PollyAndi.

She said, "Kurt's love for me and the kids is genuine. I know it is. I've seen his face. I've seen his delight in the kids even when he didn't know that I was watching. He's felt like an outsider all his life."

"You certainly have become forgiving," Ben said. He immediately regretted the sarcasm.

"I'm working at it," she said, steadily. "I know I didn't stand behind you the way I should've and look where we are now." She gestured to the woods around them, their house down the hillside. "I didn't ask you up here to discuss whether or not I made a mistake marrying Kurt. He and I have to work that out."

"So what do you want from me?"

She leaned forward, and spoke softly. "Ben, at this moment, most of the damage is repairable. We can tell the senator it's over and give him the negative, erase the files. Kurt can rehire you."

"Do you think everything that's happened—Peter, Dawson, Sands—are all unrelated to this?"

"It sounds like Peter stirred up something with this McGuire guy and you with Johansen. And from what Kurt said earlier, the police are confident Peter was killed by Sands, right?"

Ben nodded.

"Besides," she said. "The timing's all wrong for what Kurt did to have caused anything else."

Ben rubbed his forehead. He agreed with her on the last point. "Are you asking me to just sweep this all under the rug? Me go back to my investigative reporting with Kurt leading the charge— while we both know he's a blackmailer? Doesn't that sound just a tad hypocritical to you?"

"I don't give a damn about hypocrisy at this moment, Ben! This is our family, and whether you like it or not, Kurt is a part of it now. And at this point, all he's done is send a photo and a letter. At this point, the senator can walk away relieved. At this point, we can get an accountant in and see what it'll take to straighten this mess out. Maybe we'll be living in a low rent apartment next month. Maybe we'll be bankrupt. That's better than having the kids watching you put Kurt in jail. And exposing him will mean exposing the senator.

I can tell you without even meeting the man what *his* choice would be.''

She held Ben's arm tight. ''Please. For me, for the kids, for everyone—let it end right here.''

CHAPTER 33

IT WAS ANOTHER LONG NIGHT. LITTLE SLEEP. FEELING AS IF HE HAD bit into something sickening and the result lay in his belly. And the healing cuts from the flying glass were still itching like crazy.

Ben circled the problem as the damn digital clock did its thing, spinning through the numbers.

At five-thirty, he got up and made some coffee. Took his binoculars and went up onto the roof and watched the sun come up.

Fantastic sunrise. One sailboat tacking out of the harbor against a fresh morning breeze. Not far past it, a huge cargo ship made its way out of the harbor with the help of three tugs. From that distance, it was beautiful in a form-follows-function sort of way. High bow pointing proudly at the horizon. Under the tighter focus of the binoculars, Ben could see rust at the waterline; the black soot on the stacks. He knew from a photo essay he had once done on the Merchant Marines that if he had been standing on deck, the juxtaposition of order and disorder would have been even more dramatic. Of rust eating away at the edges of painted deck equipment. Of the constant, daily business of repair and replacement.

And he thought of the constant squabbles among the men. The big and small dishonesties of the day. The pilfered food, the smuggled contraband, the brutality under the decks.

Still the ship would get there.

Most of the time.

Most of the time, the ship would get to its destination with all crew alive and well; the cargo delivered; the ship itself safe.

The tugs turned away and returned to harbor. He watched the ship steam away under its own power, until it was far enough away so that its imperfections were no longer recognizable even under the magnification of Ben's binoculars. And then Ben went down to his studio, grabbed his bag, and headed off to the senator's town house.

He made a call from a phone booth down the street. It was just past seven-thirty.

"Senator Cheever's office," a woman said, crisply.

"Please tell him that Ben Harris is calling."

"The senator doesn't take calls until nine. Would you like to leave a message?"

"But he's in?"

The woman paused. "Would you like to leave a message, sir?" Her tone was still polite, but ice was forming.

"Tell him I'll be there in five minutes."

"Sir—"

Ben hung up.

The senator met him at the door.

This time, the senator was sober, freshly shaved, and with the whiff of morning coffee about him. He called out Ben's name with a hearty boom, put his hand out. "Glad to see you."

All this presumably for whoever else was in the house.

"Do you want to go for a walk?" Ben gestured to the Boston Common across the street.

The senator looked out, clearly torn. Glancing up the stairs and then out at the golden light of the Common. He stepped outside onto the steps. His eyes narrowed. "You got somebody waiting out there for me? Another camera, maybe one of those long distance microphones?" He said this as if he were joking, but Ben could see that underneath his bonhomie he was still frightened.

Ben felt choked with sudden frustration. These scared, guilty men. And now he was out behaving like one himself. "Here," he said, abruptly. He shoved the packet containing the negative and Kurt's copy of the five by seven print into the senator's hands. Ben had destroyed the SyQuest disk himself before leaving Kurt and Andi's house.

The senator quickly put the packet into his inside jacket pocket.

"It's over," Ben said to Cheever. "That's the negative and the last picture. I suggest you burn them and consider yourself lucky. You won't hear from the person who sent you the letter again, I guarantee it."

"Who was it?"

"You don't get that." Ben started to leave.

Cheever put his hand on Ben's shoulder. "You can't just leave it at that. I've got to know."

"No, you don't, Senator." Ben knocked Cheever's hand off his arm. The man flinched.

"Was it you?"

Ben just looked at him.

The senator's gaze faltered. "I apologize."

"Look, consider that a one-time 'Get out of Jail Free Card.' If I run across you with your pants down next time, I'll take the shot. And you'll wind up in the news."

"No risk of that," Cheever said, quietly. Looking back up the stairs again. "I told Teri it was over." He shook his head. "She took it harder than I expected."

Ben nodded, his patience at an end. "Good-bye, Senator."

Kurt's secretary, Lisa, was waiting for Ben when he reached *Insider*.

"Welcome back," she said, sunnily. "He'd like to see you now."

Kurt smiled with his most statesmanlike smile as Ben came into his office. "Lisa, hold my calls, please."

Kurt closed the door behind her as she left. The blinds were already drawn.

"How'd it go?" He said it like Ben had been out at any other interview, but his face still had that gray pallor from the night before. Dark bags under his eyes.

Good, thought Ben. He should be losing sleep, too.

Ben said, "He was relieved."

"Did he ask who sent it?"

"Sure."

"But?"

Ben sighed. "You're just going to have to trust me on this."

"I do. I appreciate it, I really do."

"I didn't do this for your appreciation."

"I understand. Nevertheless, I do. And I want you to know I called Reed this morning and said the two of us have come to an agreement. He said it was up to me if I wanted to hire you back, so that's a done deal. I've already notified personnel. And at the staff meeting this morning, I'll welcome you back in a more informal manner. I'll just say that we've settled our differences."

"Fine. There's a couple of things you've got to watch out for yourself around here." He told Kurt about Lucien and Huey. Ben kept Sarah's knowledge to himself.

Kurt's face flushed. "He's been listening in on my messages? And you asked Huey about the Cheever negatives? Jesus." Kurt stood up, nervously.

Ben shrugged. "Hey, I was chasing a lead. I didn't know it was going to come down to you."

"But do they have enough to put it together?"

"I don't think so. I never suggested to either of them that Cheever was being blackmailed. That would have violated my confidence with him. Most likely Lucien and Huey will be more concerned with what you have on them, small as it is."

"That's right," Kurt said, slowly. "Besides, there's no evidence. They can guess all they want, but there's no evidence."

"Volunteer nothing," Ben said. "And we'll go back about our business. For me, I want to get back onto McGuire. I'll see if Sarah can join me. Have you got a problem with that?"

"No. No, of course not." Ben supposed it would be that way from now on with his assignments. Probably the same with Lucien and Huey. *Whatever you want.*

Useless as an editor.

Ben sighed. "You remember how I was in here before the explosion? The two of us offering our hands in friendship for the sake of the family and all that?"

Kurt nodded. Looking wary now.

"I realize you're in no position to be without a job right now," Ben said. "But I think it's time you found yourself another one— away from me. Somewhere in Boston, at the same or better salary. You won't be able to find a job like that overnight, but I think it's time you started looking."

Kurt sat back. "Or?"

"Or nothing. I won't expose you, regardless."

Kurt nodded slowly.

Ben saw him look out the window. Most likely saying good-bye to the corner office, the prestigious career path, the national view that he commanded at the helm of the *Insider*. Kurt might find the same money editing a trade publication, but there were only a handful of news publications in Boston with the clout of the *Insider,* and the editor-in-chief positions were well defended.

"God," Kurt said, quietly. "I wish I could take it all back."

Ben said, "This is as close as you're going to get."

"The staff meeting from hell," Sarah said as they got into the van. "All those wary looks and false smiles."

"*Insider* is just one happy family." Ben pulled out of the parking garage and took a left onto Boylston Street. It was a brilliant day and they both rolled down the windows.

"So . . ." She took off her sunglasses. "Kurt did it, didn't he? He was doing the blackmail."

Ben was silent.

She continued. "After two aspirins and about a half dozen glasses of ice water this morning, I thought about everything we'd learned and everything you'd told me. About him needing money. And here you are this morning back at your job." She stared at him. "Tell me why I shouldn't go to the police right now."

Ben laid out what Kurt had told him, including the timing of his constructing and sending the photo. "Kurt didn't even conceive of the idea until weeks after Peter was killed."

"And you believe him?"

"It corresponds with what the senator told me. And Dawson had already attacked me."

She was silent, then nodded. "All right. So this comes under the heading of 'incidental' as far as Peter is concerned."

"That's the way I see it. So I'm asking you to let it go. Bury it. Just what I told you might happen."

She stared at him. "Why'd he do it?"

He hesitated. "This has turned into a ... a family situation, Sarah."

Hating it. Hating the words, the situation.

She said, "You don't trust me."

"It's not a matter of trust. These aren't my confidences to give away."

"Since when does a reporter worry about that?"

"Since his own kids will get screwed because their new stepfather is an idiot," Ben flared. "That's when."

"Ah," she said, looking out the window. "Extenuating circumstances."

"That's right. Extenuating circumstances."

"Sure you're not just covering up for him so you could get your job back?"

Ben looked at her. "What do you think?"

She continued to watch him. He felt the weight of her intelligence and kept himself from saying anything else.

"No," she said, finally. "That's not what I think. But I do think this sucks. How can I work for this guy? I don't have the slightest respect for him."

Ben told her of his and Kurt's agreement.

"So he'll be gone." She looked straight at him. "This is the end of it. Right?"

"I've quit making promises."

That brought a smile. Faint, but there.

She said, "Good for you."

CHAPTER 34

LAINNIE ROLLED OVER INTO SOMETHING AS ANDI WALKED INTO THE room. Andi looked more closely. A file folder was visible just past her daughter's hip.

"What's that?" Andi made a point to smile. Her nerves were jagged from the night before and she was trying not to take it out on the kids.

"Just some pictures." Lainnie said it with such elaborate indifference that Andi went into high alert.

How could she know?

In two strides, Andi was across the room. She tugged the folder away.

"Mom!"

Lainnie grabbed at it, and the black-and-white glossies fell over the bed and floor.

In a glance, Andi saw it wasn't the picture of the senator and Teri Wheeler.

There were dozens of prints of women wearing some kind of uniform . . .

Then Andi recognized the shots. The women in prison at Framingham. Photos that Ben had shot for the upcoming issue. Kurt had asked Andi to read the piece Ed Liston had written. Something Kurt frequently did, asked her opinion.

Except about blackmail, she thought. Keeps that to himself.

"What're you doing with these?" Andi said.

Lainnie stuck out her lower lip. "I just saw Daddy's handwriting, and I wanted to see what he was doing. Was he here last night?"

"What makes you think that?" Andi looked at her carefully.

Lainnie shrugged. "I guess I dreamed I heard his voice."

Andi glanced on the outside of the manila folder. Indeed there was a brief note from Ben to Ed Liston:

Ed—the selections we discussed.

Ben

Andi said, "Where did you get these?"

"On the desk downstairs. It was just lying there. Did Daddy bring these over?"

"No. Kurt brought them home earlier this week. You took them off of Kurt's desk?"

Lainnie nodded. In a small voice, she said, "Sorry."

"You know better. Come on now, I'll help you pick them up." Together they began putting the pictures back in the folder. Andi looked at the photos as they went.

"You can tell Daddy is sorry for these women, can't you," Lainnie said. "I don't know how he does that."

"Yes, you can." Andi stopped to look at a group shot of the women crossed by the shadows of prison bars. Before long, Andi and Lainnie had spread out the prints on the bed.

"I miss Daddy," Lainnie said. "Don't you?"

"Sometimes, sweetie." Andi thought about Kurt sitting up after she had left him, looking at these shots. That's what he must have done. Gone up to the office and sat there at his desk, poring over these shots. She wondered what he was thinking. The possibility of prison? Or maybe he was looking at these women and thinking about his manipulation? His failure to his family?

If she knew him like she thought she did, it would be all those things.

But then again, what do I know?

After Ben had left, she and Kurt had gone down to the family room. "What have you done to us?" she had said.

A tear had slipped down his face abruptly, which he wiped away. "I'm sorry. God, I'm sorry."

She had sat there on the couch, just about choking on everything she was feeling. She was furious. Hot, bursting anger that forced tears into her eyes and made her dig her fingernails into her palm.

She felt some pity for him, but not a hell of a lot.

And, as always, there was that observer in her. The one who wrote the column. The one who was always aware of her audience. She hated that they had a place in this room, but they did.

Even so, the observer in her couldn't keep the hysteria away. In fact, Andi had found herself giggling abruptly. She said, "I've got the headline for this week's column. *What to Do When Your Husband Admits to Blackmail.*"

"Please," he said. His face was gray in that light.

She continued, the words spilling out. "Subheads clarifying that it was the blackmail of a senator. And that you tried to frame my ex-husband. I'll handle your motivation and our financial ruin in the body copy, what do you say? I think I'll be able to handle it more sensitively there." Her voice rose and she couldn't stop herself. "But I'll have to interview you. I'll have to ask you again, *What the hell were you thinking?*"

When Kurt looked at her without saying anything, she said, "Damn it, Kurt. We had everything here. I loved you. The children were trying their best."

"Did you love me?" Kurt's voice was a harsh whisper. "Or were you just reacting to him? Moving on from him to someone you thought would be safer?"

"I thought I loved you. But it's not a good time to ask."

Internally, she tried the rubrics she had handed down over the years: *People Make Mistakes. Forgiveness Is an Essential Component of Every Relationship.* But then there was also *Abusive Relationships Only Get Better When You Get Out.*

Andi didn't pass any of those pearls on to Kurt.

She didn't have the heart to do that.

Nor the biggie, of course: *Did I Make a Terrible Mistake Divorcing My First Husband?*

She had never been able to forgive Ben for what he had done to Father Caldwell. More accurately, she could never forgive Ben for showing the world that she was partner to the invasive, grasping press. She hated that about herself, that for all her advice, published and otherwise, she had never found it in herself to forgive Ben for making her look bad.

She was determined not to make the same mistake again.

Kurt tried to put his arm around her. "You'll see," he said.

She shrank away. "I don't know what to say to you."

Part of her did. Most of her wanted to scream it. Use the words that flickered through her head: Blackmailer. Liar. *Coward.*

Most of her wanted to send him away, never see him again.

"Is this it?" he said. She saw the desperation in his face, the raw fear of being left behind.

She saw the opening. The bright release. Nod, and tell him to go. End this mess now. Best for her and the kids. Do what she'd done with Ben, walk away when things got too tough.

She took a deep breath, and said. "Time. That's all I can give you. No promises other than that."

"How much?"

"I don't know," she said, sharply. "Don't ask me anything else."

In spite of everything, she believed his intentions were rooted in insecurity. That everything he'd done was to hold on to them. Hold on to her and the kids.

"I'll sleep here tonight." His voice was hoarse.

She nodded. Thinking, tomorrow . . . tomorrow they'd make up the guest room. Tomorrow they'd figure something out . . .

She was so tired.

She left him alone without another word.

And it must have been sometime after that he had gone up to the office to consider the photos of the imprisoned women. Thinking God knows what. She certainly didn't know.

Looking up from the pictures, Lainnie tried a more direct approach. "Don't you wish Daddy still lived with us?"

"No, sweetie." Andi looked her daughter in the eye and said, as steadily as she could, "I'm married to Kurt now."

CHAPTER 35

BEN AND SARAH WAITED IN THE VAN DIAGONALLY ACROSS THE street from McGuire's office throughout the morning. Either he was inside or he had not yet arrived.

Sarah had been quiet for much of the morning. She was sitting beside Ben on the foam exercise pad he kept on the van floor to ease the pressure on his knees. Her fingers made staccato bursts on her computer keyboard, revealing her mood.

Ben let her be.

Outside, the temperature rose and it became stifling in the van. But running the engine to use the air conditioner was a bit too obvious for surveillance work. He turned on a small exhaust fan that at least moved the air around a bit.

Sarah's collar was open. A tendril of hair clung to her neck, damp with perspiration.

"Another thing," she said, even though more than an hour had passed since she last spoke to him. "Give me a call the night before we do a stakeout will you? So I can dress a little more appropriately."

Despite the heat, despite that she was justifiably angry at him, Ben wanted to kiss her in the worst way. All morning, he had been wiping the sweat that formed around the eyepiece, looking over at her, then turning back to the camera. Taking the stony silence as his due.

With this, however, he reached over and undid the second button on her blouse. She looked down at his hand, then up at his eyes. He did another, watching her eyes the whole time.

There was a dangerous gleam there, something that might lead to a slap, but she didn't stop him.

Another button.

"You think we're going to do this in the back of your smelly old van?"

Another button.

"In the middle of the day, on a busy street? When I'm angry at you?"

"Curtains." His voice was husky. "We've got curtains."

Her blouse fell open.

He grazed her breasts with the back of his hand. The material of her brassiere was sheer and her nipples stiffened. He pushed the blouse from her shoulders.

"And my being angry?"

"Let's use it."

"Mmmm," she said. And then she reached behind her and the brassiere fell away.

Afterwards, she said, "Style. You've really got a lot of style. Taking me in the back of your van."

"I'm not proud of it," he said, kissing her lightly on the cheek. "Excited, maybe, but not proud."

"Least you can do is buy me lunch."

"We've got to keep a lookout for our boy here. Lunch would be subs and coffee in the back of the same old van."

"Uh-uh," she said. "Despite the, ah . . . *romance* of this van, I'm truly ready for a change. And my thinking's a little better after our interlude. So let's try the obvious." She took out her cell phone and punched in a number.

"Who're you calling?"

"McGuire," she said.

Ben sat back. When her call was answered, she adopted a sweet, obtuse, and slightly insistent tone. "Hello, my name is Danielle Keating and I was calling for the owner. . . . Well, I'll be happy to discuss that with *him*. Is he in? Uh-huh. Excuse me, but I think that's my business. Who'd you say the owner was? Uh-huh. Well, I'm a customer. . . . OK, I should have said a *potential* customer. In *any* case, I'm calling because me and Bunny are in a position to make a purchase soon. . . . Well, when will Mr. McGuire be in? We're free late this afternoon, about five? Uh-huh. Uh-huh. Well, it says right here in the white pages *Bayside Realty* Corporation and Bunny and I are looking for a condo right overlooking the water so if that doesn't represent what your business does, somebody ought to look twice at your name. Tonight we're—''

She stopped, lifting her eyebrows with amusement.

Then she continued, her voice hushed with outrage. ''There's no reason to behave like this, Miss. And I can assure you if I ever run across Mr. McGuire I will let him know of your—''

Sarah looked at Ben with shocked wonder. ''The little bitch. Hung up on a potential customer.''

''Bunny?'' Ben asked.

''Sort of name I thought would push her buttons. And it did.''

''I didn't know you had that kind of voice in you.''

''Well, *sure*.'' She smiled brightly and batted her lashes before continuing in her own voice. ''Suzanne not only told me Mr. McGuire wasn't in and that he wouldn't be interested in any piddlyshit condo deals . . .''

''She said 'piddlyshit?' ''

Sarah held up her right hand. ''I quote, 'He's not interested, lady. Tonight, he'll be on his boat, swinging deals a hundred times worth your piddlyshit condo deal.' ''

Ben grinned. ''Scares me how well you do that . . .''

''Yeah, yeah.''

''. . . but it's a nice piece of information. If we knew where he kept his boat we'd have a next step.''

Sarah smiled and reached into her file. ''I found it through boat registration. Right on the island. Nahant Yacht Club. A forty-foot sportsfisherman. *Speed Dreams*.''

''Hey . . .'' Ben said, pulling at her file.

She snatched it away.

He said, "You've been holding out on me."

"This from the guy who just seduced me in the back of his van," she said.

"What else have you got?"

"Stuff. Buy me lunch first."

He spread his arms wide. "You name it."

"That charming little place in South Boston where you met your friend. Sean Deegan, was it?"

"It's a dive." He checked his watch as he started the engine.

"We have time." She looked at her watch. "It'll be another hour before he's sloshed."

They waited out front of the Waterford Men's Tavern until they saw Deegan heading toward the door. Ben and Sarah got out. Deegan shook his head slightly at the two of them, but then continued past the door of the bar. Ben took Sarah by the elbow, and crossed the street.

They walked along the opposite side, slightly behind Deegan until he took his second right. They crossed the street and followed along-side, again on the opposite side. They continued on three more streets like this until they had in effect circled behind the bar. Deegan stopped in front of a liquor store, and looked back at Ben before continuing on slowly.

"Looks like we've got a stop to make," Ben said.

When they came out, Deegan was just turning the corner at the end of the block. Halfway down the next, he stopped and opened the right-hand door of a sagging two-family house.

Minutes later, when Ben turned the handle on the same door, he found it was unlocked.

Deegan was waiting at the top of the stairs. He pointed at Sarah. "Who's she?"

Ben introduced her as they climbed up to the landing.

"Huh. I barely know who the hell *you* are and you're bringing broads around already."

" 'Broad,' " Sarah said, grinning. "I haven't heard that in a while."

Ben said, "She's Peter's replacement."

"Send somebody that good-looking, somebody should've bombed Gallagher years ago."

Ben looked at Sarah, but she apparently decided to keep it to herself that she was Peter's ex-wife.

"What've you got for me?" Deegan asked.

Ben opened the bag to reveal a bottle of scotch and a six-pack of Budweiser long-neck bottles.

Deegan waved Ben and Sarah into his apartment. As he closed the door behind them, he said, "Next time, buy the imported shit, willya? I may be a broken-down old Southie cop, but I've still got some taste."

The room was surprisingly neat. It smelled of an unwashed old man, the very same sitting in front of them. But the bed in the corner was made, the dishes in the sink were clean. Deegan opened a porch door that looked out onto the aluminum siding of the building beside them. The smell of salt air mingled with those of the street below: car exhaust, a faint whiff of garbage. And crap. Lots of dog crap on the sidewalks, Ben remembered.

The room was crowded with furniture that was too big for the room. An old dining room table, low hutch, big plaid sofa. Pictures along the top of the hutch of a family: two kids and wife, and a younger, healthier looking Deegan.

Sarah's eyes lingered on the pictures for a moment, and Deegan saw her looking. "This ain't a museum," he snapped.

"I'm sorry," she said.

He looked mollified, and perhaps a little embarrassed. "Excuse my manners," he said, opening the bag. "I run sort of a double life here. Get up and puke in the morning. Spend a couple hours getting myself in shape. Clean the place up a little, maybe make myself a sandwich or something. Get out, shoot the shit with some buddies. Sometimes learn things that way. Mostly learn things by hanging out in places acting just a whore's heart more drunk than I really am. So I don't like people like you looking at my old life." He took a flat church key from his front pocket and opened one of the beers. He put the rest in the refrigerator, and came back and opened the seal from the pint of scotch, and placed a small, clean shot glass beside it and filled it to the top.

"OK," he said, knocking the shot back, and then chasing it with a long swallow of beer. He shook his head, as if clearing it, and then said with rueful satisfaction, "Jesus, it's a shame this stuff is killing me. It sure is sweet when you need it. Now what do you want to know and how much money have you got?"

"Names," she said, sliding out the video grab picture that Ben had taken inside McGuire's office. "Do you know either of these guys?"

Deegan stared at the photo. Ben watched his eyes widen slightly and then he sat back, relaxed, and took another long swallow of beer. "So what about the money?"

She said, "I know who this is." She pointed to the red-haired man.

Ben looked at her and raised his eyebrows.

"Like you've been sharing a hundred percent," she said.

She returned her attention to Deegan and pointed to the man next to McGuire. "But if you can identify this guy, I'll even top what Mister Moneybags here spent on you last time. Fifty."

"Oh, I like this girl," Deegan said, chuckling. "That's how to treat an informant." He jerked his thumb over at Ben. "This camera geek didn't know what was right. I was too under the weather to argue last time."

"He tries hard," she said. She pulled out a fifty and put it on the table, her hand on top.

"Simple fifty," Deegan said. "Know of him, don't know him personally. Bill Taves. Worked for Pratt Construction. You know who Pratt was?"

Ben said. "A scandal, right?"

"Uh-huh. Bobby Pratt I knew since we were kids. He was a local success story. Construction sites all over Boston first, then all over the country."

"He was legit?" Ben asked.

"Who can tell? He always looked that way. Good kid, one of those altar boys that guys like me used to torture in high school. Him, he was a little too tough for that, though. He had a rep for being fair with his workers, a rep for trying to steer clear of Bulger, and after him, Pat Clooney. But in the past couple of years, Billy Taves went to work for him.'' Deegan touched the back of Sarah's hand as if they were old friends. She failed to let go of the money.

Deegan grimaced. ''OK, I'd say the one job Pratt was most famous for people think he was a crook. The one where that bridge in New York collapsed. The one that dropped a half dozen cars into the drink, what? Last February? Not one of the people made it out alive. Fifteen people killed in all, men, women, and three kids.''

Ben remembered the name then. He had been in Bosnia when it broke, but he remembered the tail end of it. Big story. Big scandal. Repair work on the bridge had been done so shoddily as to weaken it further. Materials that were purchased were never actually delivered or installed. Inspectors paid off.

And Pratt, facing criminal charges, disappeared. His car was found at the airport, his suitcases were gone. But his wife and kids were left crying that he would never have abandoned them. The newspapers speculated openly that he might be dead.

''Wasn't Taves hurt on this?'' Ben asked.

''You kidding? He was a 'consultant' who managed to come up with all sorts of memos and witnesses where he had stated his concerns about the project and was able to cast himself as the expert that Pratt brushed aside while stuffing his pockets.''

''And here Taves is now, sitting down with McGuire.''

Sarah nodded. ''And with Teddy Stockard, one of the biggest wannabe contractors on the Greater Harbor project.''

''Huh. Jimbo's playing with high stakes. That traffic jam out on the expressway you went through to get here is part of the Greater Harbor project. Ripping up the whole damn highway, replacing it with wider roads, new tunnel, the works. Burning up money by the truckload.''

''And here is McGuire acting as host to Stockard,'' Ben said.

Deegan looked at the picture more closely and shook his head. ''Nah. Not host. See the way he's sitting there? See the way these guys are looking at him?'' Deegan held up the pint bottle. ''I'll bet you a fifth of this that he's the boss. He's finally turning out just the way his uncle wanted him to turn out . . . and not a minute too soon.''

''Meaning?'' Ben asked.

"Meaning I opened my ears about any rumors about Jimbo since the last time you came around. There's whispers about one of their soldiers, guy by the name of Dawson. He was killed. Burned alive. You hear about that?"

"Sounds familiar," Ben said.

"Well, rumor is Jimbo had something to do with it, and that it was the last straw with Uncle Pat. Everybody's looking at Jimbo now, see if he's going to grow up or disappoint the old man one more time. And looking at Uncle Pat to see if he'll keep his word or just keep bailing out little Jimbo."

"What do you think?" Ben asked.

"That's something I wouldn't even risk a beer on," Deegan said. "Too close to tell."

Sarah and Ben looked at each other, and then she pushed over the fifty.

"One other thing," Ben said, taking a twenty out of his wallet.

"Aw, haven't you learned anything?" Deegan said.

"Just a simple introduction to save us some time. Should be nothing for a guy like you who's been here on the water all your life."

"What's that?"

"A boat," Ben said. "We're going to need a boat."

CHAPTER 36

SARAH LOOKED AT HER WATCH AS SHE AND BEN LEFT DEEGAN'S apartment. "We've got time. What do you say we chase some paper?"

"Exactly what paper would we be chasing?"

She shaded her eyes and looked at him. "Sounds like Jimbo has moved into the big leagues. Greater Harbor contracts aren't that easy to come by at the level he seems to be working, right?"

Ben nodded.

"My experience," she said, "is that deals like that are almost always made on a political level."

"Ah," he said.

"We'll see."

Even though Ben drove them to the Old Courthouse building in Government Center, Sarah immediately assumed the lead when they reached the fifth floor. The Registry of Deeds. The ceilings were high, painted a light blue. Maybe thirty or forty people milled about the big room, talking freely as they pulled bound copies of computer printouts off the shelves. In the center a half dozen clerks stood behind a waist-high desk, dealing with questions. An enormous American flag hung over the desk.

"Same the world over," Sarah said. "Let's see if we get lucky." She quickly stepped in behind a woman who was tapping rapidly into one of the few computers on the side of the central desk. After a few minutes, she left, and Sarah stepped up. "Let's see if we get a hit on Cheever's name."

"I'm confused."

"Sure you are. Paper is not your thing."

"Why are we tracking real estate? How will this link us into Greater Harbor contracts?"

"Oh, naive one. First off, these are public records, so we might as well take a look. And real estate is McGuire's area of expertise, right?"

"Supposedly."

"And . . . there's a long tradition of bumping up politicians' war chests with real estate purchases . . . buy the place for a million more than it's worth, and you've given your guy a lump of cash he can put into the bank. Don't you remember the story about Kennedy selling his Virginia property to the Japanese that way?"

"Vaguely."

Sarah looked over her shoulder at Ben, and wrinkled her nose. "Liar. If there's no visual interest you don't pay attention."

Her fingers moved rapidly over the keys and records flashed up. "OK, we search Cheever's name for the past year."

Ben gave her the address on Beacon Street.

"Hah," she said. "There we go. He sold it. Three point three million."

She quickly did a comparison of similar-sized buildings within four blocks. "Hmm. . . . It's hard to say for sure whether his building was simply in better shape than the others—but he clearly did the best of any of them, by a seven-hundred-thousand-dollar margin."

"But he still lives there."

"So, maybe he made an arrangement. Leased it back or something. Let's search this buyer, Conant Holding Group. See what else they bought."

She jotted down reference numbers for three purchases that Conant

Holding had made in the past year within the Boston area in addition to Cheever's town house. "Here, you find two, I'll find two." She went through the stacks and selected two bound photocopies of deeds. It took him a few minutes longer to find his copies; by then she had already looked through the deeds on her desk.

"OK, let's see what you've got here." She flipped quickly to the deeds, tracing through each of them with her forefinger.

"What are you looking for?" Ben asked.

"Not sure. But . . ."

Ben looked over her shoulder. Mostly it was legal gobbledygook to him. On the surface, anyhow, the three purchases seemed to be commercial properties; Cheever's was the only residential. In each case, the mortgage was held by the same bank.

She stood straight. "Here we go. See on this one how they qualified 'Conant Holding Group, right here? 'G.H. Corp.' ''

"Uh-huh."

Sarah hurried back to the computer. She typed in "G.H. Corporation," and waited as two more records became available. On the second one, she inhaled sharply.

G.H. Corporation stood for "Goodhue Holding Corporation."

She grinned triumphantly, "We've made contact, Houston. It looks like Goodhue purchased Cheever's town house with corporate funds."

"Can we find the broker on this?" Ben touched the monitor.

"Not here," she said. "But I can get that from the mortgage company with a little luck. And with a little more, I bet we'll find that after a few twists and turns, it'll lead back to Jimbo McGuire, real estate consultant, Atlantic Avenue, Boston."

"I guess this is as good a time as any to grovel for a favor," Sarah said, as they were leaving the building. "Do some more of the research Lucien should've done on Cheever."

"From who?"

"My *Washington Post* reporter friend. Ex-friend. Chas Greer. You remember that one relationship I told you I had? Four wasted months for the both of us?"

"I still hate him."

"Well then, walk around the block." She took out her phone and said, "Wish me luck."

"I'll stay here."

He stood at the top of the escalator of the big semicircular Center Plaza, and watched her make the call.

It took a few minutes, but she got through to him. Her body was tense even though her voice was friendly. "Chas . . . it's Sarah . . ."

Ben took the escalator down. Suddenly he didn't want to see her do her act with an ex-lover.

After a few minutes, she came riding down after him.

Her shoulders were relaxed now, and she was smiling. "Good news. Chas is engaged and has forgiven me for dumping him."

Ben smiled. "That is good news."

"And, he was just the guy to talk to about your friend Senator Cheever and the New England Software Foundation."

Ben waited.

"He said that if *he* were Teri Wheeler at the NESF, he would be very unhappy with the senator's performance—on software related issues. The man has made virtually no significant legislation or concessions in that area."

"No?" Ben cocked his head. "Let me guess." He pointed at the expressway behind them, the stalled traffic on the elevated highway.

"That's right," she said. "Cheever heads the Greater Harbor committee. He's the man you have to convince if you want a big, lucrative contract."

On the way to the boat, Ben pulled a sudden left toward the Design Center.

"What's this?" Sarah said.

"Old warehouse that's been converted into individual studios. Artists, ad agencies, few photographers that I know."

"That's fascinating, Ben. Why are we here now?"

"You're not the only one with old friends. I want to see a photographer. Leonard Penn. One who learned how to make serious money."

"And?"

"And one who's taken Goodhue's portrait more than a few times. One who knows him better than me."

"OK, so he's taken the man's picture. What will he be able to tell us?"

"Don't know," Ben said. "But some of these photographers are pretty insightful guys, you know."

She looked at her watch. "Long as he can be that way in no more than ten minutes."

Leonard was in the middle of a shoot.

There were motorcycles all over his studio. High performance bikes, classic hogs, and mopeds. Bright lights flooded a small stage where two male models in business suits each sat on a motorcycle. One bike was a powerful BMW racer with clip-on handlebars and an integrated fairing. The other was a hopelessly dated-looking Triumph tricked out with a long extension fork, lots of chrome, swastika mirrors. An assistant was working with the first model to attach a monofilament line to his tie to pull it back as if it were flying in the breeze. A makeup woman in tight jeans worked with the second biker's helmet to make it look as if it had been blown askew by the windstream of the first bike. The model on the second bike kept working on his own expression, apparently striving for indignant confusion.

Leonard turned when Ben and Sarah walked in. He was over six foot three, with a completely bald head. He wore jeans, sneakers, and a doctor's green hospital shirt.

"Ben Harris," he said. "Come for some photo tips?"

"Just to watch the master at work."

Leonard turned to look at his models. He put his hand on his chin. "Don't *think* they're going to do anything newsworthy, but I'll call if they do."

"Got a minute for some questions?"

"I won't tell you how much I'm making here."

"Who's the motorcycle client?"

Penn laughed. "You're too literal for this side of the business. The image is *Performance*. Motorcycles represent performance, get it? Corporate account."

"Goodhue?"

Penn shook his head. "Haven't done anything for them for a few months. Fuckers pulled their ad campaign, want a different look. I'm out."

"How about portrait work? Goodhue himself."

Penn looked at him sharply. "What's that supposed to mean?"

"Can we talk privately, Mr. Penn?" Sarah said.

"Who're you?"

Leon's back was to the models now. His body was still, and his eyes went quickly between Ben and Sarah.

"Leon," Ben said. "Calm down. Can we talk in your office?"

Penn looked back at the shoot, and then said, irritably, "Two minutes."

He led them back to a tiny glassed-in office area where he could see the studio. "All right, what's this about?"

Ben looked around the office and out at the studio. At the ads up on the walls. Almost a whole wall devoted to the work Leon had done for Goodhue Corporation. The same stuff that had been up the last time Ben had visited Leon at his studio, more than a year back.

Ben looked back at the shoot. It was a good-sized effort by most standards. But Ben remembered when Leon would have had more than a half dozen assistants, plus agency types and a client or two eating and drinking on the sidelines while he held court.

"How's business?" Ben said.

"Peachy," Leon said. "Thanks for asking."

Both Ben and Sarah were silent.

Leon picked at some invisible lint on his jeans, and then rolled his shoulders. "So what's up?"

"We're looking at Senator Cheever," Ben said. "And possible links between him and Goodhue Corporation."

"So, I've taken Goodhue's picture. We talk about sailing when he poses, not politicians he's bribed."

"OK," Ben said. He waited. Leon seemed like he wanted to say something. Sarah waited as well.

Leon looked up at the walls, at the ads, back through the glass at the shoot. "Look, if I tell you something, can you keep it to yourself? At least that it was me that told it to you?"

"Sure," Ben said.

"Absolutely," Sarah added.

Leon sighed. "My business took a major hit when I lost Goodhue. You know how it is. All this . . ." He made a vague gesture to the studio. "It's like the entertainment business. Hell, it *is* the entertainment business. You're hot, and then you're not."

Ben waited, and Sarah did the same.

Leon said, "The way I hear it was that Goodhue himself suddenly didn't like my work. Told the agency the concepts, photography, everything, had to change. And suddenly Doug Stillwell has the great new look."

Ben looked askance. "Doug Stillwell? Dougie Stillwell, your photo assistant?"

"You knew he had ambitions."

"Who doesn't? But I never saw the talent. Former model, right?"

Leon shrugged his shoulders. "Look, I'm not one to knock anyone's lifestyle. I'm gay, everybody knows it. Who cares? Same with Doug. But Goodhue? Circles he moves in, that's bad news."

"You think Doug was involved with Goodhue?"

Leon nodded. "That was my impression. Nothing obvious, but at first Doug made a few jokes, that the guy was eyeing him. Then Doug suddenly stopped smirking and shut up about it. I got the impression there were dinners afterwards, some things going on. Hell, I didn't care. It was very discreet, the guy's a hawk, a captain of industry. But I think there was something there."

"You think he just handed off the business because of that?"

Leon made a face. "No, actually I don't. I've always had the impression Goodhue was a straight shooter business-wise. But I know Dougie can be a mean, manipulative piece of shit when he wants to be. And one day he's living on what I pay him . . . and then he doesn't show up to work. Next thing I hear, he's invested almost twenty-five grand in Hasselblad equipment and he's setting up his own studio. Took a while, after that, and I hear the work I'd been doing for the past three years isn't 'good enough for Goodhue' anymore. And once one agency shut me down, the others fell off. I'm not making half of what I once was."

"Let me ask you something," Sarah said. "Do you know Teri Wheeler?"

Leon looked at her. "You know all this already?"

"No."

"Because, yeah. I know Teri Wheeler. She was here during a couple of shoots we did for the Foundation. Including one with Good-hue himself. She was the one who introduced Doug to Goodhue."

He gestured to the walls, the ads that were already beginning to yellow inside their frames. "Yeah, I know Teri Wheeler."

CHAPTER 37

TERI FLIPPED THE CURTAINS BACK AND LOOKED OUT ONTO THE dock. She said, "I think this is a bad idea, Jimbo."

They were in the cabin of his sportfisherman. He patted the cushion beside him. "Let's stop thinking altogether."

She gave him that look. Icy, impatient, but a touch of humor under it all. Made him want to slap her, made him want to screw her. So far he'd done the latter a half dozen times, but never the former, so he had to give her credit there. She knew a thing or two about controlling men.

"You could ruin everything I've set up," Teri said. "He's just one guy."

"He's *my* guy," Jimbo snapped. "And it's time he knows it."

The fact was it pissed Jimbo off that Teri very likely saw Jimbo himself as *her* guy. She was discreet about it, but across the country she had other men like himself in place.

Teri had a couple years on him, maybe three or four. He liked that. Woman looking as good as she did, but just that bit of an age difference, that experience level. He figured in a few years he could move in the circles she did, work on a national level.

"Come on," he said, smiling at her. "Let's pass the time." She was wearing the cutoffs and halter top that she left on the boat from last time. So different from her usual look, and he liked to think she was being herself when she was with him.

She walked over and put a knee onto the cushion beside him. Her voice softened. Trying to work him. "Listen, why don't you just let me do this myself, all right? You stay up at the helm and be the hired captain. He's the type to find religion. Better that I break down, tell him I've got a confession. That I took some liberties helping him out with the town-house deal, that there were more strings attached than I let on before. That he's got to save me by playing ball. Stockard'll get this last contract and you'll stay hidden."

"Hmmmm," he said, letting her think he was considering it. As if she called the shots in his town.

She straddled him. God, the *heat* that came off her for such a cool-looking piece. She whispered, "You'll see, I know what I'm doing."

She kept sliding back and forth on him, kissing him, making him lose himself in the scent of her hair. Then she pulled back like some sort of high school tease. "Hey, you take care of that photographer?"

This too pissed off Jimbo. She thought she was riding him so tight she could set the pace.

"Better than you," he said, keeping the huskiness out of his voice. "Got the guys sweeping up and down in front of the club, looking for that scabby old van. Besides, the guy doesn't know shit."

"I guess." She shrugged. "Sounds like we overreacted before."

He caressed her hair, and then took a handful of it and twisted. That had to hurt some, but he saw no fear in her eyes. Just impatience. He said, "What do you mean, *we?*"

"Tough guy," she said. "A gentleman would let me forget."

"Who said I'm a gentleman?"

"Not me. Never." She smiled a little now as he released her hair and smoothed it along her shoulders. He unfastened her halter top.

"I don't care if he walks in on us," McGuire said, hoarsely. "Hell, it might even be a real good way of letting him know."

She leaned forward to give him a taste, and for a time, McGuire was truly lost. Recalcitrant senators, stalled construction contracts, and even the question of who was running who slipped out of his mind with the hardening of her small pink nipples.

But then she pulled away. A sound on the dock, footsteps. When Jimbo looked past her, through the slit in the curtains, he saw the guy walking down the ramp from the pier to the dock, wearing dark glasses and a baseball cap down low over his eyes. Windbreaker with the collar turned up even though it was almost eighty goddamn degrees out there. Should've been wearing a sign that said, "I'm wearing a disguise."

Jimbo sighed. "He's here." He reached down and handed Teri her halter top.

She stood, looking down at him. "You're sure you want to play it this way?"

"Positive," he said.

She straightened herself out, and tossed her hair back. "All right. It might be for the best. Not having to dance around him so much." She lifted her eyebrows. "Been a while since I just cut the bullshit and snapped on the leash. Used to be fun."

Jimbo grinned. He remembered the first time she dropped her mask on him. This cool little number who had come to Stanford to teach a graduate-level workshop on the use of foundations as marketing tools. He thought he'd been seducing the teacher only to find she'd been setting up the student. She had hinted about it then, but it wasn't until months later that he worked the entire truth out of her—that for all her Nordic good looks and sophistication, her roots were as twisted and vulgar as his own.

That first time together with Jimbo, she had simply suggested there was a story to be told. "I think we're in a unique position to help each other," she said, lying beside him in bed. "Between your contacts and mine, we can make a fortune." She smiled that quirky little smile she kept for only her closest friends.

She gave him that smile now, and bent swiftly to give him a kiss, before turning for the door, ready to let the fool in.

"OK, Ms. Wheeler," Jimbo drawled. "Go out there and get Cheever on the boat before he trips over his dick. I'll be listening up on the flybridge while you open him up for me. You know how."

"Yes, I do." She smiled, wryly. "Don't get jealous on me now. I'll be thinking about you the whole time."

Jimbo laughed. "Sure, I believe that."

Piss him off, she did. But he couldn't help but like her. He said, "Listen, figure about a half hour, forty minutes. I'll be down to tell him the facts of life."

CHAPTER 38

"YOU'RE GOOD AT THIS," BEN SAID.

"I'm good at a lot of things," Sarah said, pushing the throttles forward. The bow lifted on the little cruiser. The two of them had already charted the simple course to Nahant.

He brushed her hair back from her face and she smiled up at him. They had stopped off at an Army/Navy store before picking up the boat and she was wearing a pair of faded jeans, a pink tank top, and sneakers.

He said, "So it was true what you told him? About your dad?"

"Sure. He had a boat not too different from this on Lake Michigan. Wooden though, and slower. My dad would've loved this."

They were in a twenty-six-foot twin-engine cabin cruiser. It was far from new, but well maintained. The owner, a hard-eyed man named Palmer, had taken them out on a brief checkout run and luckily had also been impressed with Sarah's skill. The boat was perfect from Ben's standpoint: it was reasonably fast, nondescript, and had large portholes that were shaded by an inflatable dinghy lashed down to the deck.

They reached Nahant in about a half hour. Ben went below as they entered the yacht club harbor. It was a small, laid-back-looking club with a long single pier with just a few floating docks off that. Ben looked at the docked boats through his binoculars. "There it is," he said, quietly. *"Speed Dreams."*

Sarah deftly spun the boat around, went up on deck, and dropped anchor. She came back and went into the routine they had planned before, where she stayed out in the open, wearing a straw hat and sunglasses. She read from a paperback she found in the cabin.

Ben peered out at McGuire's boat through his binoculars. It was a powerful-looking sportfisherman, not as flashy as he would have expected. The curtains were drawn so that he couldn't see inside. Occasionally the curtains moved, he believed by a woman's hand. But he couldn't see much more than that.

He hoped something would happen soon. It had taken Deegan several hours of calls to line up the boat, and now the light was falling from the sky fast. Ben would soon be hard pressed to get an in-focus shot. Even with his fastest black-and-white film, a steady tripod, and a beanbag fitted into the porthole, he would need a fairly fast shutter speed to counteract the slight movement of the boat in the water.

"Come on," he said, to himself, to McGuire. "Show me something."

When, about fifteen minutes later, that something came along in the form of a poorly disguised Senator Cheever—being met by Teri Wheeler—Ben didn't hesitate. True, he found himself swearing a lot. Saying damn it, damn it, *damn it*. As always, it was one thing to suspect. Quite another to put it on film.

But he thumbed the motordrive onto high speed and nailed the shots. Including one of a clearly nervous Cheever pulling his sunglasses away, his face angry looking. As if he were demanding an explanation. Her face remained calm, somewhat cajoling.

Cheever turned away abruptly and fumbled with the sunglasses when McGuire came out of the cabin. Ben swung the lens over, and got a tightly compressed shot of all three.

McGuire grinned over his shoulder as he began casting off lines, and then he hurried up to the flybridge and put the boat in gear. When Teri turned away to lead Cheever down into the cabin, Ben captured a little smile on her face that he would never want to see a woman direct at him.

Sarah came down and picked up his binoculars and looked out the other porthole.

"Oh my God," she said.

Once Cheever was inside the cabin, Sarah looked over at Ben. He was rubbing his forehead.

"You know what else?" Sarah said.

"What?"

"That cute little halter and shorts she's wearing?"

"Yeah?"

"That's what the girl in the first set of shots was wearing—the ones Peter took. The girl sitting in the car with McGuire whose face we couldn't see."

"Same girl," Ben said. Feeling stupid.

"Yep." Sarah raised the binoculars again. "Same girl."

CHAPTER 39

As the sun set over the horizon, McGuire turned the intercom up just enough to know they were going at it, and then he turned it down. It had taken Teri all of a half hour to get past the senator's objections, past all his ''We can't ever see each other again'' shit.

Things moved along much more easily once she started pouring the booze.

It made Jimbo irritable, knowing the two of them were down there screwing. Even though it was what he told her to do. Jimbo couldn't figure out exactly what he felt for Teri. There was the sex, sure. But he also liked the twisting, turning way her brain worked. He liked that they saw the world the same way. He liked knowing her secrets.

She also brought a sophistication that allowed him to move in circles his uncle had never moved in before. That made him look good in front of the old man, which was important to McGuire.

Problem was, he and Teri had to keep their distance from each other, at least in Massachusetts. That damn reporter got too close with his camera the one time they'd been together and Teri had ''overreacted,'' as she called it. Brought in one of her right-wing mercenaries to blow the guy up.

She had the ability to make men do what she wanted. Jimbo would give her that. By any description, she was a pretty enough piece, but that didn't explain it. Didn't explain what she could do in bed. Didn't explain how she could figure out what you *wanted,* and put herself in the position of being able to give it to you—at a price. Hell, he had to admit he jumped through some hoops himself by sending Dawson in looking for the same damn shot.

Before she had legally changed her name while at college, she was known as Lynn Whalen. Her mother was a failed actress who turned to hooking. Lynn had grown up as a piece of white trash just outside of Newark and had been turned out by her mother's boyfriend, Daddy Bob, by her fifteenth birthday.

But as Teri had whispered in Jimbo's ear the very first time, she "always knew how to take care of myself."

By her seventeenth birthday, she convinced a private detective named Louis that they could form a profitable partnership. Her first task for him was to smash Daddy Bob's jaw with a tire iron and kneel on his throat so she could kick her "stepfather" in the balls. She told Jimbo that she kicked him so long and hard that her mother later complained that she was left with nothing but a mean gelding.

And then Lynn went into business. Simple stuff—she posed as the smart, elegant beauty that she knew was within her and put herself in the position to meet wealthy married men . . . and Louis did the rest. Sometimes he burst in with a camera, sometimes he just set up a hidden video.

The men always paid.

The problem was that those scams were terminally small-time. Five or ten thousand, usually. Once she brought in twenty thousand dollars off one guy. Even wealthy men couldn't spend the kinds of sums she truly wanted without attracting attention—and that would defeat her hold on them. It was a conundrum, not that she knew that word back then.

But she made enough to put herself, as Teri Wheeler, through Columbia. She told Jimbo that it was there that she developed her long-term plan.

And then she put eight or nine years into making it a reality.

*   *   *

McGuire put the boat on autopilot and went to the cooler to fill a beer mug with melting ice cubes and water. He found himself grinning as he climbed down and eased the cabinway door open. There they were on the center settee. The senator pumping away. Teri on her back, seeing McGuire now, that little smile of hers that she shared only with him.

McGuire poured half the ice water down Cheever's back.

Christ, but McGuire couldn't help but laugh. You'd think he'd branded the guy with a white-hot poker, the way he screamed and rolled over, trying to protect himself.

McGuire said, "Time for your wake-up call."

Then he poured most of what remained in Cheever's face. The final half inch he tossed off at Teri, making her squeal with laughter, "Don't, Jimbo, don't!"

And *that* was like dumping a tub of ice water onto the senator.

That little laugh. Made his head jerk around. Made his bellowing outrage die in his throat.

McGuire reached over to the bridge that was inside the cabin and pulled the throttles back so the engines were at a near idle. So he could hear himself think.

"Teri?" the senator was saying. "Teri, what the hell is going on?"

"It's time to shut up and listen," she said, still smiling. ". . . Senator."

McGuire gave Cheever his name.

The guy's face froze for a moment. And then he got to his feet, reaching for some clothes. "I've heard of you," he said. "I know who you are."

"Well, that's good," McGuire said. "Seeing as you've been working for me for damn near a year now."

Two hours later, McGuire said, "I'm losing my patience."

Christ, that was an understatement.

It was all he could do not to take his nine millimeter out from under his jacket and knock a few of the guy's teeth out of his head. The senator just didn't seem to get it.

Oh, he got that he was in trouble again. Swore up and down at

Teri at first. Came up with words he probably never used in a campaign election. Including, "Conniving . . . *cunt.*"

Sounded funny earlier in the evening when McGuire still had his sense of humor. But now it was old. Now Cheever was looking at McGuire as if he were some sort of punk.

McGuire had them all up on the flybridge now and they were puttering into Boston's inner harbor, the skyline of the city sparkling beside them. He continued under the Tobin Bridge, and headed to one of his construction sites.

The guy was talking nonsense.

"You can destroy my career, but you can't destroy *me.* Goddamn it, I'll tell you what I told that guy Harris—I'll take you down with me. I won't be blackmailed."

"Get off it," McGuire said. "Just do what you're told and all goes on like before. We'll even take care of this Harris guy if he's holding you up."

That seemed to confuse the senator. "You mean you didn't send him?"

McGuire shook his head. "Shit, no. He's been a pain in the ass for us, too."

Cheever rubbed his temple "Look, I've settled with him. And I'm not going to do what you ask."

"You've *been* doing what we asked for a goddamn year!" McGuire shouted for the first time that evening. Using his elbow, he suddenly cracked the guy behind his ear. He grabbed Cheever's shoulder before his face crashed into the GPS monitor. The guy was too public a figure to be showing up with facial bruises without people asking questions. It was like threatening a Ming vase. McGuire was tired of wearing kid gloves. And *very* tired of being treated like a kid himself.

"You hit me." Cheever touched the back of his head and then looked at his hand to see if he was bleeding.

"Listen, you idiot," McGuire hissed. "You've known you were in *somebody's* pocket. Maybe you didn't know it was such a sleazy pocket. Maybe you thought that money coming from Goodhue and the frigging NESF was business as usual from people who thought like you did so that made it OK. But let me make it clear. When that 'conniving cunt' over there stopped talking about software standards and whispered her thoughts on the different construction contractors for the Greater Harbor project, you *knew* she was repping somebody. You knew this wasn't her day job. Well, that somebody was me. Whenever she told you the good news about a flood of campaign contributions that just seemed to keep rolling in, that was *me* talking in your goddamn ear, and that was *me* filling your campaign chest, and that was *me* telling her to suck your dick. Christ, I'm even your goddamn landlord.''

Cheever looked at him as if he'd just eaten something awful. ''The town house?''

McGuire laughed. ''You think Teri swung that sweet lease-back deal by herself? Big hunk of cash for your campaign chest, plus low rent? You knew she was up to something, you're not that dumb. Now you've been a good boy so far, done pretty much everything she *influenced* you to do, but you've been a pain in the ass this last major assignment. So I'm going to put it to you real plain. Stockard is in. Stockard gets the bid. You see to it the others on the committee buy off on him, and you make sure that you squash any objections to Bill Taves on the project.''

''Bill Taves?'' the senator looked up. Bewildered. Still not believing that someone had actually smacked him. Goddamn U.S. senator. ''Stockard's paying you to do this?''

''No, Stockard's not paying me. I'm paying *him*. I own him, and I own you. Before him, I owned Pratt.''

The senator looked at him like he was lying. ''That's not possible, you're just a *kid*.''

McGuire smacked him with his elbow again. He spoke in the senator's ear. ''OK, my *family* owned him. That make you feel better?''

The senator was shaking his head again. Surprising McGuire. Coming up with stuff that McGuire never figured a politician would have. ''You can hit me all you want, you little shit.''

''Stop it, both of you,'' Teri said, sharply.

McGuire stared at her, and she gave it right back. He took a deep breath and waited to see what she had in mind.

She spoke to the senator in a more soothing voice. ''Bob, listen to me. I objected to bracing you like this at first, but then I decided you had to know. All we've shown you so far is the worst. Now let me tell you about the best.''

"This punk bastard hits me and you're going to sell me something?'' Cheever said.

"Bob, I've taken you as far as I can go with you still in the dark.''

"Taken me?'' The senator shook his head. "You little bitch, I did my first campaign when you were in junior high.''

"And look what's happened since I've been on the scene,'' she said, steadily. "Campaign chest better than you've ever had before. Major committee recommendations. I even saw to it that that ridiculous anti–assault weapon bill of yours got through   believe me, that only happened one way—we let you. We've got plans for you.''

"You . . .'' Cheever sat back suddenly. His face, if possible, turned more sallow.

She continued quickly, focusing upon him entirely. "You *know* I've made everything easier for you. I didn't do that on a winning smile and a cute ass.'' She gestured at McGuire. "I've got people like him set up all over the country. And I've got people running men like you. Senators, congressmen . . . both parties, Bob. Trust me, you're in good company. And we can move you forward.'' She leaned forward. "Consider it. I'm not saying it's a done deal, but you know you're one of the logical choices for the GOP next election. For president, maybe; vice-president almost certainly. It takes people like me behind you. And it takes money. When I tell someone like Goodhue to pay up, he says, "How much?'' And then I figure out how to make it look legal. For you, it was the town-house deal. We put you in the right position, you've got money, you've Congress and the Senate voting your way . . . voting *our* way . . . things can happen.''

"Who do you mean, 'our'?'' the senator said, sullenly.

She waved her hand dismissively. "They come and go.''

"Johansen?'' Cheever said.

She made a face. "I'm still well connected with the people behind him—they're not quite as nuts as he is—but you're closer to what the voters want.'' She put both hands on his left arm. "It'll be better than ever, Bob. I can take you further if you know the truth.''

He hit her across the face.

The senator had moved faster than McGuire had expected. He grabbed the man by the shoulder, spun him around, and sunk two solid punches to the man's gut.

The senator knelt there, winded.

McGuire said, "You OK?" to Teri.

She wiped a trace of blood from her mouth with the back of her hand. "I'm just fine," she said, coldly. She bent down swiftly and raked her nails down Cheever's ear to his jaw. He cried out, and tried to get to his feet, but McGuire shoved him down.

"You . . ." the senator said, able to breathe now. His hand on his face. "You two punks. People died in that thing with Pratt. Children. That bridge. You were in there mucking things up, cutting the corners, laundering money with work never done." He sneered. "Talking to me about the presidency. You're just a couple of punks out of your league."

"Couple of punks who *own* you," McGuire said.

"I won't do it," Cheever said. "Any of it. I'm going public with this."

McGuire said, slowly, " 'Going public'? Like a press conference?"

Cheever said. "I won't let this continue."

McGuire raised his hands as if to say, *Oh well.* He said to Teri, "Don't say it. You told me so."

"What a goddamn waste," Teri said.

They were just at the construction site dock. McGuire had planned on spinning the boat around and heading back by now. Instead, he bent down, opened a small cabinet to the right of the wheel, and took out a bottle of scotch and a shot glass. He handed both to the senator. "Here. Take what you want and pour one for Teri. We'll talk this through."

"Nothing to talk about," Cheever said. But after a moment's hesitation, he poured the shot.

McGuire said, "Take the wheel, Teri. I'm going to put out the fenders and then we'll show the senator some of the work we've already done together. We're a more solid team than he thinks."

"What?" Cheever had downed the first shot and was already pouring himself another. His hands were shaking.

As McGuire headed down the ladder, he heard Cheever say, "Jesus, Teri, you cut me. I'm bleeding."

She said, quietly, "Shut up, Bobby."

Alone in the cabin, McGuire took out his cellular phone and made a call.

CHAPTER 40

BEN AND SARAH SAW THEM DOCKING THE BOAT.

"What's this?" Ben said. He raised his night vision binoculars and watched them. The view was greenish and well defined enough so he could recognize the different figures by their relative sizes.

McGuire was walking in front of Cheever. It looked as if he was pointing out different parts of the bridge construction: his body language was cheerful, as if he were giving a tour. Teri came up alongside Cheever and she apparently tried to link her arm in his, but he shook her off.

"Is McGuire holding a gun on him?" Sarah asked.

"No."

"Can you get us in there?" Ben asked.

"Maybe." Sarah had kept the running lights off all the time she was following McGuire, and now she brought the engines down to idle speed as they passed the dock where McGuire's boat had landed. They came upon a barge a few minutes later—a huge, black hulk. Sarah brought the cabin cruiser before the bow of the barge and Ben hopped off and cleated a line to the dock. She backed the boat down, landing it gently. After she shut off the engines they both waited, becoming accustomed to the silence.

"You'd think there would be a security guard here by now asking us what the hell we were doing," she whispered.

"Let's move before that happens." Ben hurried down into the cabin to grab his tripod and camera. He mounted a shorter, faster lens.

"Let's go," he whispered. They made their way along the shore back toward McGuire's sportfisherman, picking their way carefully through the construction debris. The moon was bright enough for them to see the construction equipment, piles of sand and dirt, stacks of corrugated metal, and bundles of rebar. Ben paused alongside a crane, looking up at the light playing over the metal lattice of the big boom. The shadow of the bridge threw half of it into virtually total darkness. The latter portion again became visible past the shadow of the bridge.

From above, the sound of traffic made it difficult to hear anything else.

Ben and Sarah kept moving forward until, closer than they expected, they heard the rattle of rocks, and the faint sound of voices ahead.

They found them underneath one of the massive bridge supports. Sarah and Ben hid alongside a bulldozer. Sarah looked through the night vision binoculars. "It looks like they're still talking. They're just standing there, can you see them?"

Ben finished setting up the tripod and peered through the camera. The three of them were under the shadow of the bridge, silhouetted against the Charlestown skyline. Unless they moved forward or back, virtually no details could be made out in the shadows. Not for the first time, he wished he owned a starlight scope that he could mount on his camera. Amplify the light some 85,000 times and make night look like day. But he didn't, so he'd have to do it the old-fashioned way. He threaded a cable to the shutter release so he could keep the camera shake to a minimum and snapped off a few fast frames of their silhouettes. Then he waited. The silhouettes would prove useful only if he captured identifying shots to go along with them.

Ben's mouth was sour from tasting all those lies he'd been fed in the past few days.

He had believed the senator.

"Come on, you bastard," Ben muttered. "Just step a little forward."

Because just in front of them was all the light Ben would need. If they stepped out of the shadow, he would have the three of them together in the construction site. The moonlight was enough with the 3200 ISO film he was shooting.

But they didn't move out of the shadow.

Ben decided to take another shot. This time with enough depth of field to capture the skyline in focus as well as their silhouettes. So he stopped down the aperture and set the shutter to open two seconds. He stood straight and had just put the binoculars to his eyes when McGuire raised his right arm.

"Damn," Ben said.

And a gun went off.

A part of Ben kept cold.

Even though his heart was pounding. Even though he knew the senator had just been killed.

The gun flash would make the exposure, he knew. The gun flash would provide the detail, give light to the faces of all three: the astonished Senator Cheever, his hands barely up to his chest as he tried to ward off the bullet; Teri Wheeler, falling back on one leg, distancing herself. The grim satisfaction evident on McGuire's face as he held his arm out straight. As he shot the senator in the face.

Sarah cried out. She caught herself immediately. Hand to her mouth.

Ben heard the faint clack as the camera's mirror fell into place; the motordrive advanced another frame.

He knelt to the camera and peered through at once. Cheever had fallen out of the shadow. A dark spot on his forehead was running black in the moonlight. Ben saw no movement, nothing to suggest the man was still alive.

Ben immediately refocused and set a faster shutter speed as Teri and McGuire stepped into the moonlight. Ben pressed the cable release and captured the three of them: Teri kneeling over Cheever's body, McGuire standing above her.

The young man was peering in the darkness in the direction of Ben and Sarah. The gun glinted in his hand.

"What a mess," Teri said. "We better start doing something right, or we're as dead as he is."

"They never found Pratt, they'll never find him."

Teri said, "This is a U.S. senator, Jimbo—"

"Shut up. I heard something."

"Come on!" Sarah whispered in Ben's ear.

Ben scooped the camera and tripod in his arms and then they were moving.

"Hey!" he heard McGuire call from behind them, and then the gun cracked again and there was a whine as the bullet ricocheted off the bulldozer.

Ben did the calculations as they ran. Not only did they have to outrun McGuire to the boat, but they had to get the dock lines off. Get the engines started. Spin the boat around.

There was no way.

No way they were going to make it out on that boat as close as McGuire was on them.

Ben thought of Cindy. Little girl sitting by herself in the living room. Picture of her dead father on the mantelpiece.

Then Ben stumbled, and cried out at the blazing pain in his left ankle. Tearing pain. Goddamn pile of rebar.

"Come on!" Sarah said, grabbing at him. "Let's go."

He shoved the tripod and camera into her arms. "Get those lines off and get the boat going. If I'm not there in time to jump on, go to the police—no, to the FBI. Call Ludlow, then Parker."

"No!"

"Move!" He rasped in a harsh whisper.

"Ben?"

He pushed her. "Do it. Please do it."

She hesitated, looking past him. "You come running," she said. "I'm not leaving without you." She took off for the boat.

Ben could hear McGuire and Teri. "This way," McGuire was saying. "There's another dock down this way."

Ben eased a steel rod out from the stack. A good ten or twelve feet long, about an inch thick. Heavy. Ben had a hard time handling

it while kneeling. He laid it out across the path they had been following, and wedged the end furthest from him inside a cinder block.
He felt along the ground for something else, some other kind of
weapon. First he found a brick. Then another piece of rod, separate
from the stack . . . and only four feet long or so.

He hefted the weight of it.

Impressive, but not too much to handle. Not likely he was going
to do much better.

He threw the brick in the direction that Sarah had run, making a
soft clatter among the rocks and weeds. Ben could see her now, in
the faint light of the dock, untying the lines.

And then McGuire was upon him, moving faster than Ben had
expected. Ben grasped for the long bar, came up with dirt, and then
found it as McGuire came around the stack of metal. Ben lifted the
bar and caught McGuire in mid-stride, caught him on the back leg.

It was enough.

McGuire went down, but he tucked and rolled and was on his feet
almost immediately, the gun extended.

Ben swung the short bar, making it whistle.

He connected solidly with McGuire's forearm. The guy swore as
the gun flickered in the light and fell into the weeds.

Ben wheeled around fast, raising the bar to Teri.

And then spun back around to face McGuire. She had no weapon.

"You," McGuire said, his voice raising in amazement. "The
fucking *photographer?*" He stood up, holding his right arm.

"God, was he taking pictures?" Teri said. "Did this son-of-a-bitch
see you shoot him?"

"How about it, sport?"

"Shut up," Ben said. "Toss me that phone on your belt."

"Fuck, no."

Ben drew the bar back. "Now."

McGuire shook his head. Grinning. The guy really didn't look
scared. Which was troublesome, because Ben couldn't see leading
him all the way to the cops with just a length of steel.

"Take another swing." McGuire shook his right hand. "Go
ahead—shit, I guess I've got to give you one hand behind my back."

In the distance, Ben could hear the engines on the cabin cruiser
come to life.

McGuire used that distraction and moved faster than Ben could have imagined. Glided up and snapped a kick that Ben was able to block from his face only at the last second. The kick threw him off balance. McGuire feinted at doing it again, and laughed when Ben shuffled away. "C'mon, take your shot."

McGuire's eyes were sparkling in the moonlight. "You chicken-shit photographer, *do* something instead of spying from the bushes."

Ben noticed McGuire had raised his voice. He was also glancing to Ben's left. Ben told himself that it could be a fake, but his gut told him to look. The fact that no night watchmen had shown up yet still lacked an explanation.

So Ben risked a glance over his shoulder.

And saw two men coming up behind the woman. Both with guns in their hands, both moving along quietly.

Ben turned and heaved the bar at them with all his strength. All three of them ducked, Teri and the two men.

Ben was already running when he heard the satisfying sound of one of the men crying out.

McGuire tried to get in his way, and probably would've taken him down if he had both hands. But Ben swung his elbow into the younger man's face and put him back onto the ground. From behind, gunshots rang out, the rounds whisking through the tall weeds at his side. Ben saw the boat ahead. Sarah had turned it around so it was stern on. He risked a glance back, saw one of the men kneeling to draw a bead, and he threw himself to the ground as a shot rang out again. Then he was on his feet, making for the dock, cutting hard to the left and right, trying to throw them off. He hit the wooden dock fairly flying, his shoulders blades itching for the bullets he expected.

The rear-facing cabin porthole shattered as he dove over the transom. "Go, go, go!" he called to Sarah and she hit both throttles.

The engines roared. As the bow rose, Ben rolled down to the transom and ducked as bullets pocked the cockpit floor. Then the gunmen apparently aimed at Sarah, trying to stop the boat before she got them around the barge.

Ben lay on his back watching her spin the wheel around. She laid the boat over on its side and remained at the wheel even as the plexiglass windscreen on the flybridge cracked and splintered with two gunshots.

She swung them around the barge.

She looked back at him. "You all right?"

He gave her the thumbs-up and she grinned.

Ben laid back, regaining his breath. His camera lay in the cockpit where she dropped it. He pulled it over. Rewound the film. Put the roll in his pocket. He disengaged the tripod and put the camera strap around his neck before climbing the ladder to the flybridge.

She had been watching him. "You get the shots?"

"Sure did." He patted his pocket. "We've got them."

CHAPTER 41

SARAH KEPT THE RUNNING LIGHTS OFF AND THEY LOOPED PAST THE bridge and ran parallel to the shoreline of Boston. *Speed Dreams* was gaining in the distance, a dark shape against the lights of Charlestown.

The wind whipped Sarah's hair about her face as she looked over her shoulder. She pushed the throttles, but there was nothing left to give. "We're not going to last long on the water."

Ben swept the shoreline with the binoculars. "Right there, then. There's an open dock at the Charthouse."

She put the wheel over. "This is going to be rough."

She headed straight in and spun the wheel at the last minute, banging the boat hard against the dock. The two of them slid down the flybridge ladder and were jumping off the boat just as *Speed Dreams* roared up behind them, huge in the glow of dock lights. Ben looked back to see a tall, bony-looking man bracing a pistol on the rail.

He fired and the bow of the motor sailer beside Ben suddenly grew a hole about the size of a dime.

Ben pushed Sarah's head down and they ran hunched over.

There were people on the dock, and although some turned at the sound of the gunshot, no one seemed to recognize it for what it was.

"Please slow down, sir," a dock boy said as Ben and Sarah ran around him to the ramp.

Ben risked a look back to see McGuire wheeling the big boat around, momentarily flummoxed by the drifting cabin cruiser.

Sarah grabbed Ben's hand. "Come on."

They hurried to the taxi circle in front of the Marriott Long Wharf and slid into the backseat of the first cab. "Let's go, let's go," Sarah said.

The driver looked at the camera still clutched in Ben's hand and then turned to slip the cab into gear. "Tourists," he said.

The two of them leaned back a moment after the cab pulled into traffic. No one was following them so far. Ben gave the cabby the address of *Insider*.

Ben saw Sarah still had her cell phone clipped to her belt. "Good going."

She handed it to him.

Ben stared at the phone for a few seconds, thinking. It was certainly time to bring the cops in, but he still didn't trust Brace or Randall. Parker, he trusted. And Ludlow was Parker's man.

After sliding the plexiglass window shut between them and the cabby, he found Ludlow's card in his wallet and dialed the number.

Ben looked at his watch as the phone rang. Almost nine.

He gave Ludlow's extension. After the phone rang four times, he was about to hang up when Ludlow himself answered.

Ben gave his name and said, "Sit down and get a pen and paper. You're going to want this." And he told Ludlow what they had seen.

"Jesus Christ," Ludlow said. "*Senator Cheever?* Are you sure?"

"Positive. And I've got it on film. We're heading to *Insider* to print the shots right now. You coordinate with the cops, all right? I've heard stuff about Brace and Randall, but I don't know if it's true."

"I've heard shit, too," Ludlow said. "After they blew the thing with Lee Sands, I started asking around. What I hear is incompetence more than corruption. But I'll get my own team on this, and we'll coordinate with them later."

"Better get them going right now. I'd guess that McGuire is on his way back there on his boat to collect the body, dump it at sea."

"Tell me again where to find Cheever's body."

Ben gave Ludlow detailed directions. He could hear the scratch of pencil on paper over the phone.

"What's the name of McGuire's boat?"

Ben told him, and gave him a description. "Of course, the guys that showed up to help out McGuire could've taken Cheever somewhere by car."

"Jesus," Ludlow said. "Why'd McGuire do it?"

"The way I see it, he and Cheever had some sort of falling out and McGuire must've called his guys from the boat and told them to meet him."

"If you thought that, we sure could've used this call back then," Ludlow said. "Maybe the senator would still be alive."

"I know," Ben said, tiredly. "I thought we were watching a payoff. We never saw the gun until the moment he killed him."

"Explain that to his widow and kids."

"I will," Ben snapped. "And I'll explain how if the FBI kept their investigations open on McGuire, you'd have been there yourself."

There was silence on the end of the line.

Ben took a deep breath, and then started again. "I think McGuire was going to dump Cheever at the site itself. There was some new construction underway and he could've been buried and left to be covered with cement the next day."

"I suppose," Ludlow said. "Yeah, I guess there's not much chance they'd stick with that plan now."

"Look, the film is the evidence," Ben said. "You go look for McGuire and I'll get that ready. Meet us at *Insider*. Also, we're going to need protection on my family and on Sarah's daughter."

"Sure." Ludlow took their addresses down and Sarah's cell phone number. When he was done, he said, "I'll say this, Harris—you and Taylor got yourselves a hell of a story."

Ben thought of Cheever, sitting drunk and defiant in Ben's studio. Talking about his honor and how he still loved his wife and two boys. Ben had believed him then. Now, even with the evidence to the contrary encapsulated in the little black canister in his pocket, Ben realized he still believed the man. At least about the wife and kids.

Ben said, "Lucky us."

The main lobby of the office building was dimly lit, but the elevator to the fifth floor was not locked out. "Somebody's here," Sarah said, putting her key away.

When they reached the floor, Ben put his finger to his lips and Sarah stepped out behind him quietly.

They could hear a faint electric clatter up ahead.

Ben and Sarah continued around the elevator bank to the news offices.

They heard the sound again. The unmistakable sound of a calculator printing on a paper ribbon. Light was spilling from Kurt's office.

Ben walked quietly to the doorway. At first, Kurt didn't see him. He was staring intently at the spool, his eyes worried. A pad of yellow paper covered with figures lay in front of him on the desk. Beside him, his laptop was open, a spreadsheet glowing on the color monitor.

Ben said his name quietly.

Kurt started, obviously surprised. "Jesus," he said. And then his lips tightened when he saw who it was. "What're you doing here?"

"I was about to ask you the same." Ben pulled Sarah into the light before Kurt could answer. Saving them that awkwardness.

Kurt looked at Sarah, hesitated, and then put on his blandest smile, and said, "Just trying to make the budget work."

Ben looked at him. Considering it all. "Sarah," he said. "Are you going to start writing this up?"

"Sure am," she said.

He nodded. "Kurt, maybe you can join me while I do these prints."

"Really?" she said. She looked at Kurt unhappily and he flushed.

"Really," Ben said. "He's the editor and like Ludlow said, this is a huge story."

"What prints?" Kurt asked.

"Come on," Ben said, and after a moment, Kurt followed him.

*   *   *

Ben asked Kurt to wait outside the darkroom until he had the film loaded into the developing tank. While it was rinsing, the two of them stepped into Huey's cubicle and Ben told Kurt what had happened.

Kurt's face turned sheet white. He put his hand on the edge of the desk. "Oh my God. They *killed* him? That woman and McGuire?"

Ben looked at Kurt carefully. "And she was the same woman— at least wearing the same clothes—as the woman that Peter photographed earlier. The one whose face we couldn't see."

Kurt's hand was shaking. He reached out and grabbed Ben by the upper arm. "I didn't have anything to do with that. You've got to believe me. I've told you everything. The beginning, middle, and end of it, you know everything I did. I had no idea this woman was connected with McGuire."

Ben did believe him.

That didn't make it any easier.

Kurt sighed. "Of course, there's no way of knowing if what I did was a factor in his being killed, is there?"

"Not without an investigation," Ben said.

Kurt sagged. He covered his face briefly, and then seemed to gather himself up. "Well. This changes everything."

"I'm afraid it does."

He straightened, and adjusted his tie and sleeves. "I'll give a statement to this FBI agent when he gets here."

Ben said. "You might want to call a lawyer."

Kurt nodded. "Yeah. But Andi first. Come show me the pictures when you're done. Unless they arrest me tonight, I'll still help you get this story out." He laughed bitterly. "Biggest of my career."

Ben stopped outside of Sarah's office with the contact sheet. She was working on the story, her fingers flying on the keyboard.

"Did you get the shot?" she asked.

"It's dark, but it'll do. Come look."

They went into Kurt's office. The three of them pored over the shot. Indeed, the gun flash had provided enough light for some detail.

"Should do the job," Kurt said. His voice was wooden, but Ben could tell he was trying to stay focused. "Especially with the other shots identifying them in sequence." He gestured to the computer. "May I?"

Ben locked eyes with him. Kurt could scan the negative and they could more quickly get a feel for the various printing options than it would take Ben to burn and dodge the shot for the most detail. But letting him muck with one of his shots was a little hard to swallow, considering.

"All right," Ben said, finally. "Let's see what it looks like."

Minutes later, the shot was on the screen. Indeed the image was a bit murky, but recognizable. Following Ben's requests, Kurt lightened some sections and darkened others to bring up the detail in the faces of the three people.

"It's all there," Kurt said, saving the file. "You've got everything you need on the negative."

Ben looked at his watch. "I'm surprised Ludlow isn't here yet."

"He called me on the cell phone," Sarah said. "He's got men waiting outside my place and your family's house."

"Good," Ben said. He asked Kurt if he had talked with Andi yet.

"Not yet." Kurt avoided his eyes and said, "The trick on this is going to be holding on to the rights so that this shot doesn't come out anywhere until we release it on the cover of *Insider*. I'll push up the deadline immediately, and I'm going to get Huey in here so we can make sure we've got the best scan of every frame and that we're happy with the prints before the FBI locks the negatives away in some evidence vault. If they want to guard us while we're doing that, all the better."

Just then, they heard the sound of the elevator door opening.

Ben took the negative and contact sheet and stepped out into the hallway. "That'd be Ludlow," he said.

Sarah joined him as Kurt stayed behind, shutting down his laptop.

Ludlow came around the corner. He nodded to both of them. "Sorry it took a while."

"What'd you find?" Ben asked.

"There wasn't a body down at the site, but there was some blood. Looks like the body was dragged toward the boat dock."

"Damn it! McGuire must have spun around right after losing us."

Ludlow nodded. "Look, we've got to get down to the scene now. You need to lay out exactly what you saw so they can try to match as much physical evidence as they can. It's a frenzy like you wouldn't believe. A senator murdered? The *Globe* and the *Herald* are down there now, asking who the hell we're looking for."

"So they don't know yet?"

"Not yet. But somebody'll spill. Then all hell will break loose."

"How about McGuire?"

"Still looking for him and his boat. Coast Guard's on the job, state police, Boston Police." Ludlow looked at him intently. "So did the shot work out?"

Ben took him into the light of the hallway. "See for yourself." He showed him the contact sheet. "We can get the final print a lot clearer than that."

The agent shook his head, admiringly. "Goddamn. You've got it." He looked at his watch. "OK, let's get moving. I'll need the negative and any prints for safekeeping."

"Well, we need to discuss that," Ben said. "We can't have the shot showing up on the evening news before we release it ourselves. And I know you need to keep the negative for safekeeping, but we need some time to make more scans."

Ludlow's eyes hardened. "We've got no time for that. I've got to insist you give me everything, including any prints, right now."

Ben put his palms up. "I'm afraid I've got to insist, too."

Sarah joined them. "What's the problem?"

Ludlow ignored her. Then, he gave a short little laugh, as if to himself. "Goddamn reporters." He reached under his arm and pulled out a gun. An automatic.

"What're you doing?" Sarah cried.

Ben backed away, pushing her behind him.

"Let's try it again. Give me all the negatives, all the prints. Do it now." He snatched the envelope from Ben's hand, and looked in at it. "There's only one strip here. I want the entire roll."

"Parker's going to crucify you," she said.

"He's not working for Parker," Ben said. "Or the FBI."

"Smart boy." Ludlow drew Sarah from behind Ben and put the gun to her head. "Now give me everything or get ready to watch her bleed."

CHAPTER 42

BEN SAW KURT'S OFFICE LIGHT WAS OFF.

He purposely looked away and headed to the lab.

Up ahead, Ben caught slight movement inside Ed Liston's office—Kurt ducking down behind the desk.

Ben took a quick right, making a little jog around Huey's cubicle to get to the lab. Hoping that Kurt wouldn't try anything then with Ludlow holding the gun on Sarah's head.

Ludlow said, "Match every negative against each of these shots on this contact sheet. I want to see every one accounted for."

"And then what?" Ben asked. Speaking loudly enough so that Kurt could hear.

"And then we go have a conversation. McGuire wants to see you."

"Wants to kill us himself?"

"Maybe," Ludlow said with a small shrug. "He *is* a hands-on kind of guy. Probably just a function of youth."

Sarah balked. "So why should we move an inch if he's going to kill us anyhow?"

"The best reason of all," Ludlow said. "You get to live between now and then."

*   *   *

Ben's mind raced as he stood over the light table.

Kurt.

Ben could just as easily walk them back to the elevators past Ed Liston's door as the way they had come.

If he took them by Kurt again, what would he do?

Ludlow was bigger than Kurt, strong-looking. No doubt he was well trained physically. Kurt alone would be no match for him.

But together . . . Ben put the negatives and the contact print on the light table and matched them number for number while Ludlow watched with the gun at Sarah's head.

The agent grunted when he was finished. "All right, put them in the envelope."

Ben nodded for Sarah to go in front of him, and Ludlow let her. Ben placed his hand on her side, giving her the faintest pressure to go around the cubicle toward Liston's office. He said, "We'll be all right, honey. We'll work this out somehow."

She moved under his hand easily, certainly aware of Kurt somewhere in the office, too.

"Don't count on it." Ludlow shoved him.

Ben's breathing began to quicken. He tried not to make it obvious. It was as if everything slowed as the door came in view. He felt the rush of adrenaline.

The door had been partially closed. About halfway. Kurt would have had to come around the desk to do that.

Good.

Ben envisioned him just on the other side of the door. It would take Kurt time to open it further, get out into the hallway, and take Ludlow from behind. Ben slowed as they came parallel to Liston's open office. Ludlow crowded up behind him slightly and Ben tensed himself as they continued past the door, telling himself that he should spin to the right, toward the office. The gun touched the back of Ben's head and he prayed that Kurt had the foresight to sweep the agent's arm up.

But it seemed Kurt had more foresight than that.

He didn't make a sound.

He didn't make a move.
He didn't do anything.

Five minutes later, they were in Ludlow's car with Ben at the wheel and Sarah beside him. The agent got in the backseat, right in the middle.

"Is Parker in on this?" Ben asked. His anger at Kurt roughened his voice, swept away some of the near debilitating fear that had been surging through him.

Ludlow snorted. "Get serious."

"What's that mean?"

"It means he doesn't have the imagination that I do. Or the debts."

"So everything you said before is bullshit. No one knows about Cheever."

"That's right," Ludlow said, drawing it out. "No *Globe* and *Herald* questioning a team of FBI agents down at the construction site. No Coast Guard search for McGuire. It's just your little story and I'm afraid you're going to find it seriously edited before the night is out."

"Where are we going?"

"I'll tell you along the way," the agent said. "You'll get a kick out of it."

Ben looked into the mirror. "What do you mean?"

"You'll see. Now drive." It had begun to rain and the streets were black and slick, reflecting the lights and colors of the buildings surrounding them. They continued down Boylston Street and took a left between the Boston Common and Boston Garden. Ludlow said to take a left onto Beacon Street.

Ben looked over at Sarah. Her face was pale in the light from the dashboard. Her eyes flickered to the dashboard itself, and then she looked away.

He looked down, and saw what she'd been looking at.

And he remembered the click he had heard when they first got into the car. She had put on her seat belt. Her hand rested on the belt now, her other clasped to the door handle. She met his eyes again and looked away.

Ben reached for his shoulder harness and snapped it in.

"What kind of shit is this?" Ludlow said, sitting forward.

"What do you mean?" Ben asked, as he began the hard left onto Beacon Street. And then he let the wheel go straight and stood on the gas pedal.

Ludlow threw himself forward and tried to wrest the wheel back, but Ben held it with all his strength.

They popped over the curb of the small island and slammed head-on into a light pole.

It was one of the black ones surrounding the Garden. Heavy, ornate, and strong as stone.

The dual airbags deployed. Something that Ben felt as much as saw, a white explosion that punched him in the face and body, holding him off as his body tried everything it could to shove its way through to the windshield.

They were no longer moving.

Ben could feel that. He touched his chest.

Still alive.

The gun went off. An impossibly loud noise in the cramped space.

Sarah screamed. Ben twisted violently in his seat, banging his head against the roof as he tried to move from the sound without being fully conscious.

The gun went off again.

Ben came to, fully, and recognized the noise for what it was. But the car was so cramped, he could hardly move. The steering wheel was just inches from his chest, the deflated bag lying on his lap. There was a soft/hard weight pressing down on him to the right.

"Sarah!" he cried.

His right knee hurt like a bastard.

"Are you hit?" he said.

He couldn't see her. For some reason he couldn't see her beside him.

"No. I've got it," she said. "I've got his gun."

Ben shoved at the door, but it wouldn't open. And then he realized that the pressure to his right, that soft/hard mass, was Ludlow. And that his head was through the windshield.

"I've got his gun," Sarah repeated.

"So you're alive," Ben said, stupidly.

"You are, too."

Ben reached over and touched Ludlow's neck. Right before the rim of broken glass. Bits of safety glass stuck to Ben's knuckles, what with all the blood. "He's not."

People came running up. A young guy, most likely a college student, stood beside the window. Big, scared-looking kid. Two girls behind him.

"Is it going to blow up?" One of the girls said.

The other saw Ludlow and turned away abruptly.

"Oh Jesus, mister," the young guy said, looking at the agent, too. "Your friend."

Ben fumbled for the seat belt and released it. "Give me a hand, will you? Ask the girls to help her." His voice was not much more than a croak.

"You're not supposed to move hurt people," one of the girls said.

"Please," Ben said.

The kid shook his head. "No, mister. I really shouldn't . . ."

He backed away.

"Damn it," Ben said, straining against the door. It wouldn't budge. "Come on, help us!"

"We'll call the cops for you," the kid said, turning away.

Ben hit the wheel in frustration.

And then Kurt was there at the window. He was out of breath. "Thank God," he said. "How bad are you hurt?"

Ben was stunned. "Where were you?"

"It took me a while to get the car out. I followed down the stairs, and I just saw you driving out, and then I had to run back and get my car."

Kurt tried to open the door, and couldn't. He reached in through the window. Ben put his arm around his shoulder and he was able to pull himself out. Kurt immediately hurried around the back of the car to help Sarah.

Ben looked at Ludlow's head outside the window.

The agent's face was practically gone. Ben swayed and then abruptly knelt down and vomited. ''Jesus,'' he whispered to himself, and then got to his feet and made it around the car just as Kurt was pulling Sarah through.

Ben held her, touching her face, her arms, her body. ''Are you all right?''

Her face was bloodied and she was shaky. But she smiled wanly. ''I'm OK.''

He looked back into the car. ''I guess I better get those negatives.''

She looked back into the car and shuddered. ''I guess.''

Ben leaned in through her window, making a conscious effort to control the impulse to gag again. Ludlow's blood covered the dashboard; the car reeked of gasoline. Ben braced himself against the passenger seat, found the envelope folded inside Ludlow's inside pocket, and tugged it free.

Sirens began to wail in the distance.

Good, Ben thought. *Somebody called the cops.*

And then Ludlow's car phone began to beep.

Ben picked it up and extricated himself from the window. He said into the phone, ''Ludlow.''

''You got them?'' a voice said. It was McGuire.

''Uh-huh.''

The phone went silent.

''Who's this?''

Ben paused.

''Who the hell is this?'' McGuire repeated.

Ben identified himself.

Then it was McGuire's turn to hesitate. Finally, he said, as if asking after an irresponsible buddy who never showed up on time, ''So where's that goddamn *Ludlow?*''

''He's dead.''

''Jesus Christ,'' McGuire said. ''You can't buy good help these days. So all right, I'll deal with you directly. Bring me the negatives and you can name your price.''

''No deal. The cops are on the way.''

"Then you better get your ass out of there."

"Now why would I do that?"

"Far as I can tell, you've got four good ones." He heard McGuire moving, a car door opening and closing.

"Four reasons? And what would those be?"

"First is you're already dirty. You already tried to blackmail Cheever, so I know you've got nothing against selling your pictures for profit." McGuire's voice was cheerful. "So that's reason number one."

"Wrong guy," Ben said, his eyes on Kurt. "I never blackmailed the senator."

"Bullshit. Then who did?"

"What's my next reason?"

Ben heard a bell. What sounded like a front door bell. Familiar.

And then his stomach twisted and he stood away from the car. "You son-of-a-bitch."

"Shut up or I'll do the reason number two right here for you on the phone."

Ben heard a woman's voice. Muted in the background. And then McGuire talking, his voice smooth and courteous. Saying he had Ben on the phone and could she speak to him?

Andi's voice filled the line. "Ben? What's this all about? What're these FBI—?"

Suddenly Andi's voice was in the background, as if the phone had been ripped away from her. Ben could hear Andi's voice rise, could hear shocked questioning. "Hey! What are you doing? What are you doing?"

Ben could hear Lainnie and Jake.

"You *bastard,*" Ben said, his voice shaking. "You fucking *bastard.*"

Back on the phone, McGuire said, "Reasons three and four just joined us," McGuire said. "Now think about this, Harris. With what you've got on me right now, *I've* got exactly zero reasons for not taking them all out if I get so much as a hint of a cop following you home. So you'd better get moving. Or else you're gonna be spending all your weekends by yourself from now on. Tell Ms. Taylor I want to see her, too. Tell her, I've got two guys outside her apartment right now who'll do her daughter and nanny if both of you aren't here in fifteen minutes.''

He broke the connection.

CHAPTER 43

THE THREE OF THEM PUSHED THROUGH THE SMALL CROWD FORMING around the car and hurried off to Kurt's car. They quickly jumped in and Kurt pulled away from the curb.

"What about those people?" Kurt said. "They saw us, they could give my plate to the cops."

"They weren't the most get-involved types," Ben said. "Just drive." Ben kept hearing his kids' voices over the phone, muted behind McGuire's cheerful threats. He fumbled for ideas, for the next step, but came up blank.

Sarah was silent until they pulled onto Storrow Drive. At that point, she said, abruptly, "I can't do this. I'm going to call the cops." She took the phone from her belt and dialed 911.

Ben reached into the back seat and snatched the phone away from her. "If the cops show up at your place, then it's one call and my family is dead."

"Sarah, we've got to work together," Kurt said.

"Work together, shit." She grabbed at the phone, and Ben held her back. "Give it to me!"

"No."

She slapped him. "She's my daughter!"

"I know," he said. "But don't do that again. I'm trying to think and this doesn't help."

She slumped against the window suddenly, covering her face.

He squeezed her shoulder. "You understand the spot we're in as well as I do."

Her voice was shaky, and she wouldn't look up. "I understand, all right. We've got *nothing*. We're going to walk in there, he's going to take the negatives, and then he's going to kill us. And he's not going to leave any witnesses in your house."

"Even if that's true, he's got no reason to kill Cindy—if you show up."

She sniffed. "Logically that's true, but what does logic have to do with anything with a guy like him."

"I know this," Ben said. "If we show up with the police, we'll be standing outside the house while the gunfire starts. And then he's got reason to take revenge on you through Cindy. So let's stop and think."

Her breath shuddered in, and she turned back from the window to meet his eyes. She was visibly trembling. "I'm trying. . . . I'm just coming up empty. I keep thinking of her with those two men."

Ben thought of Burnett, the hostage negotiator at the Johansen site. Talking afterwards, wiping the sweat from his face. "Thought I had him settled in," Burnett had said. "I thought I knew what he *wanted*. I knew he wanted that media attention. That's the trick—knowing what they want. Problem was that he wanted more than what I'd bargained on. Hell of a lot more."

What did McGuire want? Beyond getting free from the murder rap, what was he afraid of? Ben asked himself. Who did he go to when he was in trouble?

Uncle Pat. The guy who'd saved McGuire's ass more than once. Sent him off to Stanford after the home invasion. Came charging in before McGuire could spill too much in front of the reporters.

The guy who promised Ben and Sarah their families would be safe.

Ben looked at his watch. At the rate they were going, they'd be at the house in ten minutes. He shifted his legs, feeling cramped and claustrophobic.

He reached down to move Kurt's briefcase and realized it was the notebook computer. "You brought this along?"

Kurt looked at it, surprised. "I guess I had it over my shoulder the whole time. I was on the way out to join you when I saw Ludlow pull the gun."

Ben held up the little computer. "You saved the image on this, right? You've got the shot of McGuire killing Cheever."

"What's this got to do with anything?" Sarah said.

Kurt looked at Ben, confused. "I guess so. Sure, I saved it."

Ben looked at Sarah's phone. Saw that it had a modem jack.

"Huh," he said.

"What?" Sarah asked.

"Do you have that little pack of business cards you're always collecting?"

She reached into her jeans and came up with the little leather card wallet. "What've you got?"

"Something," he said. "We've got something."

CHAPTER 44

KURT STOPPED THE CAR AT THE BEND BEFORE THE HOUSE.

Ben got out of the passenger side and walked around quickly to take his place behind the wheel. Kurt stood beside the car, holding the computer in its bag. His face was bloodless, and he looked flat-out scared.

Ben said, "You know what to do?"

Kurt said, "Listen, I should go in there with you."

"Forget it," Ben said. "Just do what we worked out."

"Yeah." Kurt wiped his mouth. He held up the computer. The screen was partially open and glowing. "It's all set."

"Good." Ben put his hand out and Kurt shook it. Ben said, "We're counting on you."

"I'll come through," Kurt said.

"We better go," Sarah said, looking at her watch. "We're coming up on fifteen minutes."

Without a word, Kurt took off up into the woods. Ben and Sarah continued around the corner to his former home.

Andi opened the door.

Her face was white and her lower lip trembled. But her voice remained clear. "He says to tell you there's a gun pointed at my head. If you've got any weapons on you, to hand them over now."

Ben held his arms wide. "Nothing."

Andi backed away from the door and Ben and Sarah stepped in. He took in the scene in an instant with a dreadful sense of déjà vu from walking into the barn with Johansen.

The kids were sitting on the stairway with McGuire. He sat between them with his arms around them both. His right hand held an automatic that was pointed directly at Lainnie's belly.

Both kids were trying their best to shrink away from him, but there was little room on the stairs.

Lainnie cried, "Daddy," and she started forward.

McGuire pulled her back.

"Let them go," Ben said. "They don't know anything about this."

"They do now," McGuire said.

The tall man who had been on the bow of the boat was standing beside the bannister, his gun pointed squarely at Ben. The man had black hair and was wearing a sport jacket that was too short for his long bony wrists. "Let's just do this and get out of here," he said.

"Shut up, Paulie," McGuire snapped.

Teri Wheeler was standing farther back in the hallway. Somewhere along the way she'd put on jeans and a white shirt. Her face was pale, her lips tightly compressed. She said to Ben, "You goddamn snoop. Put your nose in it, and now everybody's got to pay."

Lainnie began to struggle again and McGuire tightened his grip. "Stay here, kid. Don't you want to tell me any more about your vacation?"

"I don't want to talk to you," she said. "Stupid bastard."

This brought a hoot of laughter from McGuire. "What a mouth." He gestured to a photo on the wall of Lainnie and Ben standing before the fireplace in the cabin. He said to Teri, "Don't be so tough on the man, honey. He's got alimony to pay and a little blackmail on the side must go a long way toward keeping his kiddies in new clothes, and still have enough cash to keep a cabin in Maine."

"Please let go of my daughter," Ben said.

"Sure." McGuire casually brushed the gun against Lainnie's hair, and then aimed at Jake. "Pow."

"You son-of-a-bitch!" Andi started up the stairs.

McGuire stood and put the gun on her forehead. "Back off."

Lainnie started to cry.

Ben walked over and took Andi's hand. "Come on."

She abruptly turned her back on McGuire, her face high with color.

Jake put his arm around Lainnie, saying, "Sssh, sssh." His eyes were locked on Ben's.

"We'll be OK, guys," Ben said.

McGuire came down and stood inches away from Ben. He spoke quietly, confidentially. "I don't think so, Dad. But you tell them whatever you want."

McGuire snatched the envelope from Ben and pulled out the negatives and contact sheet. The gunman came over and patted Ben and Sarah down for weapons.

"This everything?" McGuire asked.

Ben didn't answer.

The gunman thumbed the hammer back on his revolver. "You were asked a question, shithead."

Ben drew his breath, shuddering. He could feel Sarah watching him.

He waited until McGuire looked up from the contact sheet and repeated his question.

In the library, Ben heard the phone ring. "No," he said. "No, it's not everything."

"What's this shit?" McGuire exploded against Ben, shoving him against the wall. "You call the cops?"

"Better than that," Ben said. "I called your uncle."

McGuire watched in stunned silence as the faxed photograph of him shooting Cheever slid out. Ben, Sarah, and Teri were alone with him in the library while Paulie kept his gun on Andi and the kids in the hallway.

"That's what your uncle got," Ben said. "And then I talked to him."

"Who's sending this? Who's sending this to us right now, mother-fucker?"

"The kid's stepfather, Kurt Tattinger. My ex-wife's new husband. But you can just think of him as our revenge if you harm us. I made a deal with your uncle."

"What deal?" McGuire looked at him incredulously. "I've got a gun on your kids, I've got the negatives!"

"And we've got an image on a computer file that clearly shows you killing a U.S. senator that is one keystroke from being faxed to the Associated Press, as well as to the police, the district attorney, and a good friend who I trust at the FBI in Washington. Someone I'm sure you haven't bought."

"Oh, Jesus," Teri said, passing a hand over her face. "Amateur hour."

"Shut up!" McGuire snapped.

"Now, your uncle understands families," Ben said. "The way it looks to me is he's been bailing your ass out all your life. Covering up for you, sending you away to Stanford. Killing people to cover up."

"Like we're going to kill your ass," McGuire said. "Like we're going to chew you up into pieces."

Ben nodded. "Maybe. I'd say there's a good chance, seeing as I took the shot."

"And her." McGuire waved his gun at Sarah. "The bitch was there, too."

"That's right," she said. "Ben and I are witnesses."

"But my family isn't," Ben said. "And neither is her little girl. So here's the deal." Ben stepped a little closer so the kids wouldn't hear. "Listen, I know you're planning on killing every one of us, you little punk. So I'm not negotiating whether or not we'll send that file to the papers. We are. The only question is *when*.

"At midnight—ten minutes from now—that file goes out unless you release Andi and the kids. Their stepfather can see the back and sides of the house. If he doesn't see them drive away at midnight, he pushes the button. After that, you leave—with me in tow—and he waits one hour with me calling in every fifteen minutes. If he doesn't hear from me within that time, he pushes the button. Either way, he pushes the button one hour after we leave.''

McGuire shook his head. ''Screw you. I've got you right now, I've got your kids. Tell him to get his ass down here. Or I pop your kids one at a time.''

''You do that, he pushes the button. He doesn't have a gun, but he's got that computer. If you harm these kids, it's his only recourse. And he'll damn well take it. Your life is over.''

''Let's get out of here,'' Teri said, to him. ''Come on, baby, let's find a way to break free.''

He shoved her away.

''Talk to your uncle,'' Ben said. ''I expect he's putting something together for you. A private jet, maybe. Probably send the two of you to Europe or South America. Arrange for new faces, new I.D. I don't know. You'll be alive and rich, you just won't be here.''

''Jimbo?'' Teri said. ''Your uncle could do that, right?''

''What about your contacts?'' McGuire said to her sharply. ''What about all the people you've told me about who can make things happen?''

She laughed, shortly. ''Those people would make us dead. No one's going to want to be tied to us when this comes out.''

''Seven minutes,'' Ben said.

''*If* it comes out,'' McGuire said.

To Ben, he said, ''How do I know you haven't already sent it? How do I know the place isn't crawling with cops out there?''

''Because all we care about are the children.''

''I want to hear you make the call to your guys telling them to drive away from my house,'' Sarah said. ''If I don't go out to Kurt and wave my arms, letting him know you've done that, the same thing happens. He pushes the button.''

''Maybe I'll just send Paulie up and pop old Kurt. Save me a lot of trouble right there.''

Ben shook his head. ''He can see the whole house from the woods. Paulie tries to make that hike, Kurt will see it, and run down one of about a half dozen trails to his car before Paulie even starts up.''

''So why hasn't my uncle called me if he's got this big plan together?''

''I don't know,'' Ben admitted. ''But I expect he's been busy. It sounded like he was going on the run himself.'' Ben reached in his pocket and drew out a piece of paper with Clooney's car phone number. ''He gave me this.''

The blood drained out of McGuire's face. This more than anything Ben had said seemed to convince him. The number he probably knew by heart, sitting in Ben's pocket.

''Five minutes,'' Ben said. ''Make your call fast.''

CHAPTER 45

McGuire told Ben and Sarah to leave the room while he made the call.

The two of them went into the hallway, and Andi looked up from the kids who were sitting on the last two steps. The gunman moved back slightly, letting Ben and Sarah come forward.

"What's happening?" Andi whispered.

"Daddy, I want them to go away," Lainnie said. "Please."

"Dad?" Jake said. "They'll let us go, won't they?"

Ben knelt beside Andi. "We wait. If all goes right, you and the kids will be leaving in a minute."

"What about you?" Andi said.

"We'll go with him."

Her face blanched. "What does that mean?"

"It means we get the kids free," Ben said, quietly. "Bear in mind this goes for Sarah's girl, too. No arguments."

Andi looked up at Sarah and stood.

"Strange circumstances to meet," Sarah said, wiping at her eyes.

"Your girl's in this?" Andi asked.

"There are men outside my apartment."

Andi touched Sarah on the shoulder. Then she leaned forward abruptly and the two women hugged each other.

Ben looked at his watch. Less than two minutes left.

He said to the gunman, "It's time. I've got to tell him."

"You stay here," Paulie said.

"You don't understand . . ."

"No, *you* don't." The guy raised the gun.

Ben started toward the library door, and he heard the gun cock behind him.

The library door swung open and McGuire and Teri stood there. McGuire's face was impassive and he held his gun up to Ben's face and said, "Me and Uncle Pat had a better idea."

Paulie had Ben sit on the floor, his back to the wall. Then the gunman propped the hallway door open so he could watch McGuire take Andi out on the back deck. Paulie said, "This should be good."

McGuire threw Andi against the sliding glass door as soon as they stepped out and screamed out into the darkness. "Right now, Kurt! Get down here right now!"

Ben started to move and Paulie cocked his gun. "Stay still."

"Come on!" McGuire screamed. "I'll spread her brains and then I'll do the kids."

"Boy's a nut," Paulie said. "He'll do her, too."

"Mom!" Lainnie cried.

"Shut up," Teri said. Her voice was cold and flat. "Shut your goddamn mouth."

Sarah moved up the stairs and put her arms around both kids.

"Mom!" Lainnie screamed again at the top of her lungs.

Ben saw McGuire lift the gun and put it right to Andi's ear.

Ben made it to his feet before Paulie regained control. He deflected Ben's grab for the gun with his left arm, stepped in, and cracked Ben behind the ear with the gun butt. Ben fell to his knees.

Paulie slung him back against the wall and placed his foot on Ben's chest.

"Sit still," Paulie said. "Jimbo's got a plan. You'll see."

Paulie cocked his head toward the deck, a half smile on his face. "There we go," he said, abruptly. "Your boy is down."

Paulie took his foot off Ben and leaned back against the doorjamb, laughing. "That Reynolds. Guy's the size of a frigging moose, but he's a ninja when he wants to be."

Ben looked out onto the deck.

Standing beside Kurt was the big guy with the Hawaiian shirt who had been handling security for McGuire.

"Fucking Reynolds," Paulie said. "Fucking Reynolds to the rescue. Jimbo had him waiting up there in the woods to watch out for cops before you ever showed up. Taking out old Kurt was just a phone call away."

Kurt was standing there, the notebook computer open in his hands. Reynolds gestured for him to stand beside Andi. He took the computer from Kurt, looked at it briefly, and then smashed it on the deck. He kicked it against the side of the house, and then stomped on it repeatedly, reducing it to a mass of flattened metal and splintered plastic.

"Oops," said Paulie. "There goes your picture."

Then McGuire went to work on Kurt.

He was brutally efficient, whipping Kurt across the face with the gun with steady, powerful blows. Once, twice, and a third time.

Ben saw Kurt's knees buckle.

Andi cried out, and tried to help him, but Reynolds grabbed her arm.

McGuire shoved Kurt's bloody face against the glass door with the flat of his hand and said, "I'll know the truth when I hear it. Did you push that button? Did you send that picture?"

Ben leaned forward. His own vision was clear now, and though his head ached, he was fairly certain he was all right. He stared at Kurt's face. Trying to divine the truth by looking at him.

And so when Kurt spoke, Ben slumped back against the stairway even as Paulie chuckled, even as McGuire looked over his shoulder at Reynolds and said, "All right. Well, all *right*."

"No," Kurt said. "He got to me first."

Reynolds shoved Andi into the kitchen, and then pulled Kurt away from McGuire and shoved him in, too. The big man stepped into the hallway and took in all the people watching him.

Reynolds shook his head. "Jesus Christ, Jimbo. Six people. What a goddamn mess."

"I've worked it out so far," McGuire said. "You keep doing what I tell you, we'll get off clean."

Reynolds rubbed the bridge of his nose. "Yeah? This I've got to hear." He took McGuire by the arm and gestured toward the library. "There any more people in there that I need to know about?"

"No."

"Good. Then how about we go in there and you tell me this plan. Your uncle called and said I was supposed to get you out of the shit one last time, but I'm damned if I know how I'm gonna pull it off."

CHAPTER 46

JAKE HAD TO PEE.

It was crazy, with all that was happening, but there it was. Now that his mom was back sitting beside him, he didn't want to move. He just wanted to stay with his arms around her.

But his leg was jiggling.

When the new guy they called Reynolds came out of the library, he was wearing glasses. He had something in his hand, and it looked familiar. Jake looked at it, his curiosity running parallel to the urge to run up to the bathroom and relieve himself.

It was his mom's appointment book.

Reynolds tipped down his glasses on his nose to read it. Somehow this made him look nicer, but Jake knew that wasn't true.

"I see you have a cleaning lady coming in tomorrow morning, is that right?" he said to Jake's mom.

She hesitated, then nodded.

He made a face.

"I tell you, right there," McGuire said, pointing to the picture of Lainnie standing in front of the fireplace with their dad up in Maine. "They've got a place up there. Sounds like it's private. No other cabins within a mile."

"Says who?"

"Says her," McGuire said, pointing to Lainnie. He grinned. "Back when she was saying that her dad was going to bury me up there once he showed up." McGuire looked at Jake's dad, and there was a little smile on his face. He said to Reynolds, "I tell you, it'll work."

"Huh." Reynolds looked at the photo closely. He too looked at Jake's father, and then at Lainnie and Jake. His eyes narrowed. Jake pulled back against the wall, trying to escape his gaze. It was as if the breath was sucked right out of him, being stared at by those cold gray eyes. Still, Jake's leg jiggled.

"You got to pee, son?" Reynolds said.

Jake looked at his mom.

She nodded.

"Yeah," he said.

"All right," Reynolds said, sighing. He looked at Jake's dad again. He didn't seem to be angry like before. More like he was just thinking.

"All right," he repeated. "I can see it. Paulie, take the kid upstairs, and watch him while he takes a piss. Then follow him into his room, see that he packs one bag, and takes the stuff you'd usually take on a vacation. Underwear, socks, shorts, bathing suit, toothbrush, all that shit." He jerked his chin at Teri. "You do the same with the little girl. You think you can handle her without a weapon?"

Teri said to McGuire, "Who's running this, you or him?"

McGuire said, "He's just implementing my plan. Do what he tells you. Reynolds's great at logistics."

Reynolds seemed to laugh, like it was to himself. "That's me," he said.

Jake's bladder felt like it was going to burst. He stood up. "Can I go?"

"Paulie," Reynolds said, waving his hand.

As Jake hurried up the stairs, Reynolds's voice drifted up: "Lady, show me where the keys are to your van, then go pack for you and hubby. You better hit the head too, because from what I hear, it's a long drive to your place and we're not stopping once we get started."

*   *   *

Jake filled a soft canvas bag. "You heard the man," Paulie said. "Hurry up. Vacation stuff."

Jake felt that he might puke. Now that his bladder wasn't full, that's what occupied him next. Would he blow lunch right in his room?

His mind kept seeing Kurt's face.

Jake felt like he should be doing something. Something heroic like the kids he saw in movies. Fighting the guy, or tricking him by locking the door and climbing out the window, running for help.

But then he would come back to Kurt. The way he was sitting downstairs on the hallway floor, his head down. He was a grown-up and they handled him like he was nothing.

And then Jake saw the Buck knife his dad had given him the year before last. It was sitting on top of his dresser right behind his digital camera.

Without giving himself time to think, he swept both into his bag.

"You about ready there?" Paulie said.

"Uh-huh." Jake slung the bag over his shoulder and the man followed him down the hall to the stairway. Everyone looked up at him as he came down. His mom, his dad. Kurt. Those two men. All looking at him, just a kid, not knowing that he now had a weapon.

CHAPTER 47

THE RAIN HAD STOPPED AND THE STARS WERE OUT. PAULIE HAD backed Andi's van out of the garage, and faced it outward beside McGuire's car.

"OK, you take the wife, hubby, and kiddies," McGuire said to Reynolds. "I'll take Harris and Ms. Taylor."

"You sure?" Reynolds said, as he cut lengths of clothesline with a pocket knife.

"Yeah." McGuire stood close to Ben. "Harris knows if he tries something I'll have you waste his family."

"You shouldn't be using your own car," Reynolds said.

McGuire shrugged. "Nobody's looking for us."

"Even so, we stop before we get on One-twenty-eight and pick up a couple new plates for both vehicles. And don't speed."

"Yeah, sure." McGuire snorted impatiently as Lainnie tore away from Paulie's hand and ran to Ben, hugging him about the waist. McGuire raised his voice. "Paulie, what is this? Can't you even control a little girl?"

"Get over here, kid," Paulie said, coming up behind Lainnie.

Ben hugged her back and then said, "Go on, honey. Go to Mommy."

"C'mon, C'mon," McGuire said.

But Lainnie wouldn't let go.

Jake came up alongside. "Daddy," he said, his voice breaking.

He threw himself onto Ben, standing just over Lainnie. He hugged Ben with all his might. Ben whispered in his son's ear, "I'm going to find a way. Just look after your sister."

"I will," Jake said, his voice muffled.

"I love you so much, buddy." As Ben said it, he felt his son slide something into his back pocket. He stiffened slightly and Jake held him even tighter, stopping him from reacting further. "I love you," Jake whispered.

McGuire pulled both kids away and shoved them to Paulie. "Tie their hands. I'll take care of Harris." McGuire spun Ben around and shoved him against his own car and began tying his hands behind his back.

When he was done, he let Ben turn around.

Ben looked him in the eye. "What did Reynolds mean in there, 'I can see it.' "

McGuire said, "Nothing."

Ben stared at him. And he saw that even McGuire looked a little uncomfortable, and then it came to him. Ben's voice was a hoarse whisper. "You're going to make it look like me."

McGuire looked at him and then shrugged. "Hey, it makes sense. Ludlow told us about the restraining order they were talking about slapping on you. It's in the paper all the time, some guy goes nuts. Kills his ex-wife and kids, then offs himself. Only difference is you've got your girlfriend along, and they get killed more often than wives."

Ben's knees almost buckled.

Framed for killing my own family.

The hell of it was he could see it playing. *Had* seen it, had come in behind the police to find the bodies splayed about the room like bloody rag dolls.

Divorced man. An earlier violent incident reported to the police. A restraining order considered, and then dropped. Recently fired then rehired by the new husband.

Ben saw those women in prison.

He sagged against the car door.

McGuire watched the other two men finish tying up Andi and the children. Perhaps some impact of what Ben was feeling sunk into McGuire, enough so that he lifted his shoulders slightly and said, "Hey, you didn't leave me any choice, following us like that." He turned away, not waiting for an answer.

Ben looked over at Kurt. Looking for help, somewhere. Ben's breath was rushing fast and he thought he might be sick.

But Kurt's hands were already bound, and he was looking down at them dully, blood dripping down his face onto his shirt. He looked dazed, out of it. Possibly concussed.

"Get them in the van." Reynolds pushed Andi toward the open door. "Get them in and tell them I don't want to hear a peep the whole way up."

Andi looked over at her former husband. "Damn it, Ben," she said, and then Reynolds pushed her head down, and forced her into the van.

Ben's arm swelled and he strained against the rope until it bit deeply into his wrists.

"Women," McGuire said, coming back to him. "Always bitching about something, huh?"

"I'm going to find a way." Ben stared at McGuire. "I'm going to find a way to get to you." As he said this, Ben slipped his fingers into his back pocket.

"Sure you are," McGuire said. "That'll provide some entertainment on the long drive up."

Ben could feel it then. He kept the exultation from his face, the sudden awareness that a window had opened, if only a crack.

Jack had slipped him his Buck knife.

McGuire positioned them inside the big Chrysler: Sarah at the wheel and Ben beside her. McGuire and Teri got in the back.

"OK, kids," McGuire said. "We snug up tight. Teri, put your gun behind her ear like this . . ."

He showed her on Ben, purposely scraping the sight against the back of Ben's head. Ben involuntarily pulled away and McGuire swung his arm around his neck and pulled tight. "Like this, nice and close."

He said to Sarah, "If you try driving too fast, or screwing with me, I just call the boys sitting outside your house and tell them to go visit your sitter and kid.''

Sarah took off slowly down the driveway and turned left. "You'll leave her alone after, right?" she said. "You've got no reason."

McGuire shrugged. "You don't give me one, I don't. She's just a kid, knows nothing."

Ben saw Sarah nod slightly, as if to herself. She drove carefully, following the van.

They came to the first intersection and turned right. The asphalt gleamed in the headlights, still slick from the rain before. The digital clock on the dashboard showed it to be just after midnight.

Just before the highway entrance ramp, they came upon a restaurant in a big white colonial building. They followed the van to the back of the lot, and parked near the Dumpster. Reynolds got out and quickly took plates off a black Toyota and a van. He quickly screwed them on to his and McGuire's vehicles.

McGuire slid his window down as Reynolds finished.

"You get the directions from him yet?" Reynolds said.

"Just follow me north. I'll get it out of him as we go. I may have to give you a call, prove I mean what I say if he gives me trouble."

"You want me to put one of the kids in with you now?" Reynolds reached in and chucked Ben on the back of the head. "What do you think? I gotta put one of them through that?"

"I'll tell you," Ben said. In his mind's eye, he could see the inside of the cabin. Three steps across the small living area to the master bedroom. Two big steps to the rear closet in the bedroom.

His shotgun was propped up inside. It had been on display over the mantelpiece for years. But after Jake continued to show interest in shooting it, Ben had put it away.

It wasn't loaded. Deer slugs were on the top shelf, God knows how old. But he could see the box, knew it was there.

Somehow, he'd have to get in there alone, load the shells.

He said, "Go Route Ninety-five north for about three hours. I'll show you after that."

"That's it," Reynolds said, and straightened.

"Let's go," McGuire said.

Sarah took them onto the highway. Ben tried to turn his vision off, to let the monotony of the rushing yellow stripes, of the lit green signs, quell the fear he felt for his family, for Sarah, for himself. Instead, he focused upon that bedroom and the shotgun.

Get in.

Load the gun.

Problem was it was a double-barreled shotgun. Only two shots before he had to reload. And he had three people that needed shooting. Four, if he had to do Teri Wheeler. But he was fairly certain she wasn't armed.

Ben opened his eyes. Looked at the dashboard clock.

He couldn't see an answer to the reloading problem. Or to the larger question, of whether or not he could actually kill three people, even with all that was at stake.

He closed his eyes, visualizing the cabin. He told himself that he knew every inch, every board. That he had seen a lifetime of horror and cruelty through his camera lens and surely he had learned something about violence besides despising it.

He told himself that his father would have found a way.

As they reached the New Hampshire border, McGuire nudged Ben with the gun. "Hey. Got a question for you. How much did you clip off of Cheever blackmailing him?"

"Nothing."

McGuire shoved the gun at him again. "C'mon, how much?"

"That wasn't me."

McGuire snorted. "Yeah, bullshit. Bet you didn't get a dime. Guy was a stubborn bastard, wasn't he? All the time we were in bed, he put his hands over his ass once he knew who was really putting it to him. Like it made a difference if it was me or if it was Goodhue telling him to sign Stockard up."

Ben cleared his throat and said, "Your uncle must've been proud. The hoops you made Cheever go through."

He waited until McGuire answered before he shifted around as if to hear better. Ben slipped the knife out of his pocket and clasped it in his palm. He closed his eyes and McGuire's words washed over him. In a sequence of harsh, black-and-white still frames, Ben saw how it had all played out: Jimbo McGuire and Teri Wheeler, playing the high-stake sophisticates—and making brutal mistakes along the way. Ben remembered the cop, Brace's, words as they sped through the night: *Never said they were smart.*

"Sands was working for you?" Sarah asked.

"Not me," McGuire said. To Teri, he said, "How about you? Want to tell them?"

"I want you to shut up," she said.

He laughed. "She's embarrassed," he said, as if his girlfriend had been inexplicably rude at a cocktail party. "*She* whipped up Sands. She's always telling me how connected she is—well, Sands was one of the boys you call to get something done if you're tied in with the Free America movement."

Sarah cocked the rearview mirror so she could see Teri.

"Go on," McGuire urged Teri. "The two of them are *interested.* Look at them, goddamn bloodhounds for the facts."

Teri said in a flat voice, "We knew someone was following us, we didn't know who. That reporter kept following me in your van. So I had Sands follow him back to your place."

McGuire snorted. "Hell, you didn't even send him after the right guy."

"Turned out I did," she said. There was a silence.

"And?" he said.

"And Sands called me," she said, impatiently. "He said he'd looked inside the van and apartment, figured out that Harris was the photojournalist for *Insider* who nailed Jarrod Johansen. That was enough for him to kill you right there. I freaked because I figured you had a photo making me as the link between Cheever and Jimbo. So when Sands said he wanted to wire something that night to take you out, I said do it."

"Peter figured it out," Sarah murmured.

Ben opened his eyes to see her look at him; her eyes were shining with tears. "He made the connection."

"Smart-ass reporter," Teri said. "Look what it got him. Look what it's going to get you."

"All this over the picture of you two together," Ben said, slowly. "But her face wasn't even visible."

"Tell me about it," McGuire said. "I didn't even know who Peter Gallagher was until I read in the paper the next day that he blew up. Couple days later, Teri comes crawling to me, says she made a big mistake. She thought Sands screwed up, got the wrong guy. That the picture must be someplace in your apartment. So I sent Dawson. Another frigging fiasco.''

''The cops didn't show the photos to you? Brace or Calabro?''

''Naw. I own some cops, but not those two. I didn't know you couldn't see Teri's face until you two came in and laid the photo out on my desk. You're telling me you were on vacation, that it was Gallagher who made the shot, and I'm trying not to laugh in your face. I let you think that it was Suzanne in the picture and you went for it.''

''So why'd you kill Cheever?'' Ben asked.

''He was going to spill it all,'' McGuire said. ''He got religion.''

Ben turned in time to see McGuire's grin.

''Besides, I've got a problem with authority,'' McGuire said. ''I can't stand it when people won't do what I tell them.''

CHAPTER 48

Kurt stared at his hands.

So much of his blood had dripped down onto them.

He sat beside Jake. Third seat back. Window seat. Wedged in tight with Jake in the middle, the one called Paulie beside him. The gun on Paulie's lap, finger inside the trigger guard.

Lainnie and Andi sitting in front of them.

Reynolds was driving, the map spread out on the passenger seat.

An American family, Kurt thought. *Out for a drive.*

Kurt's entire head pulsed. His left cheekbone had puffed up into his line of vision, a white blur just under his eye. He touched his cheek and winced. His eyes immediately began to water.

The cheekbone must be broken, he figured.

But his figuring was abstract, thoughts that he recognized as his own, but from far away.

Maybe the damage from that gun whipping in his face had been so severe that he truly had no choice.

The thought was comforting. *No choice.* Kurt took it for a while, hid with it, avoided Jake's questioning looks, his scared eyes.

Jake whispered, ''What are we going to do?''

Andi turned in her seat. ''Leave him alone now. He's hurt.''

Damn straight, Kurt thought. He *was* hurt. And this was no longer his problem.

He let his forehead settle against the cold window glass and watched the night stream by in miles and miles of time.

He'd done what he could, he told himself. And maybe it would be enough.

That was always a possibility.

But until it came true, he was hurt. He was keeping to himself. That's all he'd ever had, was himself. And that's all that it looked like he was going to leave with.

Maudlin, self-pitying, weak thoughts. A part of him knew that.

But still he kept his head against the glass and let the miles pass by. Looking at his hands.

To try to do anything more would be a foolish gesture.

He'd done all he could.

CHAPTER 49

BEN WAITED UNTIL THEY STOPPED TO PAY THE SECOND TOLL BEFORE opening the blade. McGuire was leaning back in his seat, keeping his face out of sight as the woman in the booth took Sarah's money.

"Going up late," the woman said.

That was when Ben did it, opened the blade with his thumb and forefinger. The faint snicking sound was hidden under Sarah's voice as she said, "We want to get a start on the weekend."

She pulled away.

"That's good," McGuire said. "Just keep that up."

"How about calling those guys off my daughter," Sarah said, looking in the mirror.

McGuire was silent for a moment, and then said, "Yeah, why not?" Ben heard McGuire tap a number into his cell phone. "It's me," he said, moments later. "Go home. You're done."

Sarah's shoulders relaxed. "Thank you," she said.

"What the hell," McGuire said. "I'm only doing what I have to do. No more."

Ben slipped the blade between his wrist and the rope. And slowly began to run the blade up and down.

*   *   *

The sky was just beginning to lighten as they pulled in the narrow dirt road leading to the cabin. Ben's shoulders and neck were stiff from the tension and effort of keeping his arms behind his back. He felt the remaining strand that held the rope together to be certain he could break it with a hard tug.

He had slipped the knife back into his pocket, the blade still open. As Sarah wheeled the car in front of the cabin, he pushed the blade a little farther down into his pocket, being careful not to catch it in the cloth.

"Nice old place," McGuire said. "I could use something like this myself." He said to Teri, "You want me to buy something like this up here, babe?"

Ben heard her sigh. "Jimbo, you're dreaming. All this stuff we're doing now, that gives us some time maybe. A few days. But we have to leave, we have to do what he was talking about before, go to Europe or South America, change our faces. How're we going to get past all this? Past *them*."

"You'll see," McGuire said.

"No," she said. "I don't want to. You do what you have to do, but I don't want to see it."

"Calm down," McGuire said. "It'll never come back to you. It's going to be on him."

Ben turned.

Teri Wheeler couldn't meet his eyes.

Reynolds stared at the cabin, then the woods around them. "Private, all right," he said. "This might work out."

"Told you," McGuire said.

Reynolds drew the revolver from his holster and said to Ben, "You come with me." He looked back at McGuire. "Send them in when I tell you."

McGuire said to Teri, "It's what my uncle's always said about Bobby. You give him a plan, he makes it happen."

Reynolds pushed Ben up to the door. "Where's the key?"

Ben nodded to the low-hanging eaves of the porch roof. Reynolds squinted, and then saw the key. He took a handkerchief from his pocket, took the key down, slid it into the lock, and opened the door.

It was dark inside, the gray light just barely penetrating. The familiar smell of the cabin came back to him, of smoke, of split firewood.

Ben felt the presence of his father and grandfather more strongly than ever before. He could feel them waiting and watching him. Looking to see how he would protect his family.

Reynolds scanned the room, his quick eyes taking it all in. He looked at the fireplace, and brief irritation flashed across his face. "Where's the shotgun? The one behind you and your daughter in that picture."

Ben's stomach dropped. "Sold it," he said.

"Bullshit," Reynolds said. He walked over to the kitchen area and flipped a light switch. Nothing happened. "Where's the circuit breaker?"

Without waiting for an answer, he looked around the room quickly and then came back to Ben. He shoved him up against the wall. "Show me the circuit breaker box. I want that shotgun, and I want it right this goddamn minute."

Ben stared at him and then said, evenly, "The police and FBI know we were looking at McGuire. My van's not even here. Who's going to believe Sarah and I came up with Andi and Kurt?"

Reynolds shrugged. "It's not perfect. But his uncle said to give him a few days to get out of the country, get free. And this'll do it. Hell, you might go a week before somebody finds you in this god-forsaken place."

"Why are you protecting that little shit?"

"Don't waste your time on that. I do what his uncle tells me. He says save the guy's ass."

"Even if it means killing my kids. Making it look like me."

Reynolds grimaced. "Jimbo told you that? Sadistic bastard. I can't explain this so it'll be right. If it was up to me, I'd shoot the prick and be done with it. Fact is, when I was up in the woods I called his uncle for permission to do just that. But the old man said no, the kid's family, that's it. And Clooney told you himself to stay away."

"He also told me he wouldn't take it out on my family."

Reynolds gave a small shrug. "Yeah, well things got complicated, didn't they? Now show me that circuit breaker."

*   *   *

Reynolds kept Ben in front of him as they went into the bedroom. It was dark, with the morning light just beginning to filter through the pine trees out back. Ben went straight for the closet door, and Reynolds said, "Hold it."

He shoved Ben to the middle of the room. "You stand right there." He slid along the wall and opened the closet door.

Ben tensed his muscles and the strand of rope broke behind him. He grasped the knife, squeezing it tight. He had to fight the urge to lick his lips, to not wipe away the sweat that was beading his forehead.

The shotgun was right there, propped up against the right wall of the closet.

Reynolds didn't see it at first, and Ben made himself wait until he did.

"Here we go," Reynolds said, reaching down.

Ben took one big stride and grabbed the man's wrist, the one holding the revolver. Reynolds pulled the trigger immediately, and Ben felt the flash alongside his thigh, but he wasn't hit. He could feel more than see the next move, that Reynolds would club him with the shotgun.

Ben knew he couldn't win a fight with Reynolds. The man was simply too strong, too experienced.

So Ben did what he had been visualizing those long hours up in the car. He hadn't known who it would be, whether it would be Paulie, or Reynolds, or McGuire. But he had known if his chance came at all it would come down to this.

Ben jabbed the point of the little blade into Reynolds's throat until he felt it grate on bone. Then he pulled the cutting edge straight back. He was covered instantly in a gout of hot blood.

The gun flashed again, and Ben's ears were ringing too much to hear what Reynolds was trying to say as he grabbed at his ruined throat, and fell to his knees.

Ben wrested away Reynolds's gun and ran out of the bedroom.

CHAPTER 50

KURT STOPPED BREATHING.

The second gunshot made a hollow booming inside the house, and McGuire looked at Paulie, surprised. "Already?"

Paulie started to the front door. "Hey, Reynolds, I . . ."

He suddenly bent down, raising his gun. But before he could get off a shot, it seemed like he was punched once by something. He staggered, and there was another gunshot, and the hair on the back of his head moved, and he fell onto the porch, one leg twisted beneath him. A small red hole streamed blood from his forehead.

Ben stepped through the doorway, and over the gunman. He was covered in blood, a shocking amount. From his chest down, he was dripping red.

Andi and Sarah turned and threw themselves onto the children. Andi onto Lainnie; Sarah onto Jake.

Kurt stood there. Not as dazed as before. The fear, bright and sharp in him now. Unable to move.

Without a word, Teri Wheeler started to run back to the cars. But McGuire backed away and swung his arm around her neck to pull her in front of him. He reached around to shoot at Ben.

Ben fired back, the two guns booming in the early morning light, shocking flashes of light.

Suddenly Teri Wheeler's white shirt was covered with red. She looked down at herself, her palms open wide, looking down at the spreading stain on her shirt. ''Jimbo,'' she said, her voice quavering. ''Jimbo, look at me.''

He reached over her shoulder and took aim at Ben.

With the sense of remoteness he had known all his life, Kurt could see how it was going to play out.

Ben hesitated.

He stood there looking at what he had done to Teri Wheeler, and the gun wavered in his hand.

McGuire shot him. The bullet threw him back against the wall.

''Dad!'' Jake screamed.

Kurt looked at him. Grief and shock and fear all welling up in an instant in the boy's face. The woman, Sarah, her face showing the same even as she tried to hold the boy back.

Kurt felt as if his head were on a swivel. Just the observer.

He looked back at McGuire as he dropped Teri's body to the ground.

Foolish gesture.

The words triggered for Kurt the image of himself, cowering behind the office door when Ludlow had abducted Sarah and Ben. Kurt had told himself the same then, that it would be a foolish gesture to attack Ludlow. That he couldn't possibly win.

Jake got free of Sarah.

Andi saw what he was doing, saw that her boy was going to attack McGuire. ''Stop, Jake!''

McGuire saw him, too, and whipped the gun around onto the boy.

Andi was scrambling herself now, trying to catch him. But she wouldn't make it.

Kurt reached out and grabbed Jake. He threw him to the ground and stepped up to McGuire. The gun moved to Kurt's midsection.

Foolish gesture, he thought.

He said, ''I sent the fax. I sent the picture.''

McGuire hesitated. His eyes widened momentarily, and then he screamed, ''You *bastard.*''

Kurt threw himself onto McGuire.

CHAPTER 51

BEN SAW A HOLE ERUPT OUT OF KURT'S BACK AND ANOTHER ON his side.

Later, Ben realized he had been moving as fast as he possibly could.

But his sense of it at the time was an agonizing slowness, as he stumbled off the porch and switched the gun from his useless right arm and fumbled it into his left. Already the grip was bloody, and the gun slipped in his hand as he raised it up. The barrel pointed at an awkward angle, like a broken finger. Ben's legs were shaking. "Move," he said. Andi and the kids were too close. "Move!" His voice sounded separate from him. He stumbled, and then regained himself.

There was another muffled shot, and then Kurt was rolling off McGuire, clutching at the gun as he went, but down on his side.

"Let go of it," McGuire said. He tugged at the gun, but still Kurt held on, and McGuire made a sound somewhere between a laugh and a cry. "Let go of the fucking gun!"

He shot Kurt again.

Kurt jerked once and then Ben was standing over McGuire. Ben put the gun on the young man's head and pulled the trigger three times.

Ben's revolver clicked twice on empty chambers. But it didn't really matter. The first round had done everything he needed.

CHAPTER 52

ANDI TURNED TO KURT. "OH MY GOD," SHE SAID. "DON'T DO THIS. Don't do this."

Kurt was curled into a ball, blood spreading beneath into the dirt.

Ben grabbed Jake and said, "Go in and call that number taped over the phone for the police and tell them people have been shot and we need an ambulance."

Ben sat down heavily in the dirt. His right shoulder was bloody and felt as if someone had just swung a baseball bat into it. "Jesus," he said as the first wave of nausea swept over him. He felt dizzy.

"Stay down," Sarah said, coming to him. "I'm going to get something to raise your legs."

He obeyed her, suddenly feeling very weak. He watched Andi as she ripped open Kurt's denim shirt. His left side was punctured with three red holes. There was the smell of burned flesh and Ben could see blisters already forming on Kurt's belly from the flash burns.

His face was white, with deep red circles around his eyes. Andi said his name, but he didn't respond.

"Kurt!" she said louder.

Nothing.

She turned to Ben, her hand going to her mouth. "Oh God."

Ben leaned over and put his hand to Kurt's neck. There was a faint pulse. "He's alive."

Kurt coughed abruptly, and then curled tighter. Blood bubbled from his mouth, and his breathing was labored.

Sarah came back with pillows, blankets, and a stack of towels. "Let's try to slow this bleeding down, and keep them warm. Raise their legs for shock."

Ben could see Andi become visibly calmer now that she had something to do. She knelt beside Kurt and Sarah helped roll him over so they could slide a compress of white towels beneath him. Then she covered him and lifted his feet onto a pillow while Sarah turned to help Ben.

"You sticking with me?" Sarah said to Ben.

"You bet," he said. Lainnie stood behind Andi, her lower lip quivering. Tears streaked down her face.

"Come over here, honey," he said. "Keep me company, will you?"

"Daddy," she said. She hurried over and knelt by his head. She touched his face. "Are you going to die?"

"Not a chance," he said.

"Did you see what Kurt did for Jake? Did you see?"

"I saw, honey."

Sarah said to Ben, "Let me look at your back." She helped him roll over, making a face when she saw the wound. "I guess that's good. Just like Kurt, the bullet went all the way through." She put towels under him and then folded one onto his chest. She sat up, dug a roll of adhesive tape out of her pocket, and tore off long strips to bind the towels to him.

"How's he doing?" Ben said quietly.

"I don't know," she said.

Just then, Jake came out with the portable phone. "They said a helicopter was already on the way back to Portland, and can reroute to us in just a few minutes. The doctor wants to talk to Mom."

Andi took the phone and quickly outlined the men's wounds. Ben could see the former reporter in her, the way she accurately recounted the facts regardless of the tears streaming down her face. She gave the phone back. "He said we're to try to keep him conscious."

Ben saw Lainnie looking at Kurt and then back to him. He reached up with his good hand and pulled her down. He kissed her, smoothed her hair, and said, "Help your mother now. Help Kurt."

"Stay with us," Andi was saying into Kurt's ear. "Damn it, you stay with us, is that clear?"

"That's right," Lainnie said, suddenly. Lainnie moved over from Ben and took Kurt's hand. "I don't want you to go!"

Jake knelt beside him and touched Kurt's knee. "Stay."

Kurt coughed. He wiped at the blood on his lips.

"Damn it, Kurt," Ben said. He forced himself to sit up. "Open your eyes."

Kurt coughed again. Then his eyelids fluttered. "Yeah," he said. "I'm here."

"Good," Ben said. "Stay here." He lay back on the ground, exhausted.

Sarah held his hand tight, and smiled down at him.

"You, too," he said.

"I'm not going anywhere," she said.

"Yeah," he said, looking over at his family.

He closed his eyes and kept them that way. He listened as Sarah talked to him quietly; he listened as Jake and Lainnie left Kurt for a time to come sit with him.

"Is he going to be all right?" Lainnie asked Sarah.

Ben heard the beat of the helicopter.

He opened his eyes. Kurt was talking with Andi still.

Ben smiled at his daughter and son. His voice sounded hoarse. "It looks like we all will."

ABOUT BILL EIDSON

Boston-area resident Bill Eidson is the author of four previous novels: *The Little Brother, Dangerous Waters, The Guardian,* and *Adrenaline*. He was born in Savannah, Georgia, and grew up in Rhode Island. A graduate of Boston University, Eidson worked in advertising until stepping away from the corporate life to pursue his career as a writer, and as ''an occasional photographer.'' Eidson is currently the New England Chapter President of the Mystery Writers of America.

Eidson, Bill.
   Frames per second

JAMES PRENDERGAST
LIBRARY ASSOCIATION
JAMESTOWN, NEW YORK
Member Of
Chautauqua-Cattaraugus Library System